Sally Stewart

A London childhood was dominated at home by the mixed pleasure of having four elder brothers. Unused to the country, I declined to stay there more than a month or two as an evacuee, and returned in good time for the Blitz. Later schooldays were spent watching doodlebugs flying overhead or ducking those that failed to fly overhead.

Working life was, first, a long connection with the *Reader's Digest*. I worked for its chairman, travelled to other *Digest* companies in Europe and America, and learned from my boss anything I know about the writing of English.

Marriage eventually meant separation from London. My husband and I moved out of the shelter of a huge concern, to try running our own small one. We missed the boom, caught the backwash, and finally failed . . . back to being employed again. This time, to broaden our experience if not our minds, we entered the groves of Academe.

Then I entered a magazine story competition and, astonishingly, won it. Now, many stories later (published by *Woman's Weekly*, *Woman & Home*, Mills & Boon, Piatkus, and Corgi) I am an addict, and reach for my pen as an alcoholic reaches for a glass.

My husband's and my retirement from Oxford University brought us to the green hills of Somerset, and the pleasurable oddities of village life. We like to roam about Europe, or contentedly apply ourselves to the other good things of life – friends, food, wine, music, and our garden.

A ROSE FOR
EVERY MONTH

Sally Stewart

St. Martin's Press
New York

For THOMAS
with whom Italy was discovered

ISBN 0-312-10498-7

First published in Great Britain by Corgi Books.

First U.S. Edition: March 1994
10 9 8 7 6 5 4 3 2 1

1

The troubled, restless spring of 1925 offered most people in London little to be optimistic about. The war was still a wounding memory, and the land fit for heroes promised by Lloyd George scarcely matched the reality of mass unemployment, industrial strife and dwindling prosperity. But for one family, at least, there *was* something to celebrate, even though the adult members summoned to attend James Rushton's dinner-party got ready for it with varying degrees of enthusiasm.

At Vine House, anticipating no pleasure at all from the evening ahead, Jane Rushton stared out of her bedroom window instead of getting dressed. The river outside was the earliest memory of her life; she knew the Thames in all its moods and changing beauties. But in a cold, wet, April dusk the prospect wasn't inviting. Darkness crept slowly across the water, first blotting out the Surrey bank and then the tuft of trees on Chiswick Eyot in midstream, directly opposite the house. She shivered in her thin dress and closed the window; it was time to go downstairs.

Charles, her only remaining brother since Johnny had been killed in the war, was ambling down from his own quarters – a converted studio on the attic floor. She smiled at the sight of him; he was her truest friend among the people who would soon be sitting round her father's dinner-table.

'We're both late,' Charlie observed with gentle satisfaction. 'Father won't be pleased.'

'True, but look on the bright side,' Jane recommended. 'We've given Laura time to exert her usual spells. Everyone will be feeling more or less in charity with one another, and Papa will be congratulating himself once again on having the perfect hostess and daughter-in-law!'

Charles grinned, hearing no bitterness in his sister's voice. It showed remarkable forbearance when Johnny's widow had supplanted her so completely in their father's house; but in his considered view Jane *was* remarkable. He loved her quite as much as he disliked Laura Rushton.

'If Aunt Alice is in charity with *anybody*, I'm a Dutchman, and if her mad-brained daughter isn't even now holding forth on the iniquity of a family wedded to the capitalist system, I'm willing to eat my Sunday hat.'

'Eliza may have discovered Beatrice Webb and Socialism but she has more sense than to hold forth here. Have faith, Charlie dear – they will all be eating out of Laura's hand.'

So it seemed to prove, he admitted to himself later on. Family dinner-parties at Vine House were never uproariously merry occasions, but this one was going more cheerfully than most, and seated at the head of the table his father looked positively benign.

James Rushton had reason to feel satisfied – everything was just as he required it to be, thanks to dear Laura. The old, fragile wine-glasses in front of him caught the glow of candlelight, the silver shone with its proper frosty sparkle, and course followed course in the elaborate meal with the decent pauses due to good food and vintage wines – Rushton wines, chosen by himself with the precision of a connoisseur.

At last, with the Vacherin Chantilly disposed of, he stood up, waiting for the rest of them to turn towards him. Only Jane refused him this compliment – she knew already how he would look . . . impressively upright and elegant for his age, unshakeably confident that he knew best at all times, for his family and for the firm of Rushton's. Instead, she chose to watch the cousin who sat opposite her – Uncle Edward's second son, William. Like the others, he had turned to face the head of the table. She could safely look

6

at him for a moment or two, just for the pleasure it gave her.

'My dears, there are no speeches this evening,' she heard her father say. 'We are simply sharing a family celebration. Let us drink to the King, God bless him, and to our absent friends as usual, but add one extra toast in honour of the occasion – to Rushton's! Long may it survive and prosper.'

They rose around the table, obediently chanted the litany and subsided again, feeling that they'd been let off lightly. Across the table William smiled at Jane.

'I've just lost a bet with myself that tonight Uncle James would yield to the temptation to put the firm before the King!'

'It gets put before most other things,' she said gravely. 'Let that be enough for it.'

Beside her, Edward Rushton – James's younger brother – cleared his throat to make himself heard. He would far rather have sat quietly, sipping golden dessert wine that tasted of nectar, but Alice would say he must exert himself. After more than thirty years of marriage he still tried, however hopelessly, to do what she expected of him.

'Does everyone realize that it was a hundred years ago this very day that Grandfather William founded Rushton's? Quite a brave gamble, when you come to think of it – he was a young man in 1825, and Europe was still recovering from the upheavals of the Napoleonic Wars.'

'Brave but long-sighted as well,' William put in. 'He judged the right moment to start, and was rewarded with sixty years of peace and prosperity that put Rushton's firmly on the map. I think we should drink a combined toast to my namesake and the Great White Queen!'

James frowned, although the laughing suggestion came from the least objectionable of his nephews. Edward's brood of children, and more especially Edward's wife, were a cross James felt obliged to bear. They were Rushtons . . . family, despite their failings; but William was the most personable of them and he had his head screwed on the right way. It was a pity he wasn't always quite serious enough . . . didn't *look* serious enough to a man born in the reign of Victoria. Even tonight he was wearing some newfangled garment he called a dinner-jacket, and James was prepared to swear there wasn't a trace of starch in his nephew's white evening shirt. But women's clothes nowadays were even worse. The delicate lace and chiffon that once veiled feminine Edwardian beauties had given way to the hard, bright shine of satin; seductive frills and ruffles had been replaced by shapeless tunics that ignored the proper curves of a woman's body.

'Laura is looking very pretty tonight,' said a voice in his ear. 'Mark my words, James – she won't be a widow much longer.'

He turned to face his neighbour, Edward's wife. Her eyes glinted with the malicious pleasure that came of knowing she'd disturbed him; he thought she watched him with the interest of a scientist dissecting a live frog. No-one else ever dared to remind him that Laura had been widowed at the age of twenty because Johnny, his golden boy, lay buried under stinking Flanders mud. He forced himself to sip peerless Château Guirard Sauternes but it might have been vinegar in his mouth. He hated Alice Rushton, who probably guessed that he prayed to God Almighty every night that no other man would come and take Laura away from him. If Laura went, David would go too – the son Johnny hadn't lived to see. All James's hopes for the future now rested on this child who slept in the nursery upstairs. Fate had been wickedly cruel to take *his* best-beloved and leave Edward with three ambitious sons. James accepted that they must be allowed a share in Rushton's, but he would make sure before he died that it was John's boy who took control of things.

'Laura can't help looking beautiful,' he said at last. 'It's a gift that isn't bestowed on many women.' He allowed his glanced to travel along the table – Alice's elder daughter, Eliza, was distressingly horsefaced, and the girl his nephew, George, had recently married was even worse. 'It wasn't given to *your* daughter-in-law, I'm afraid, but at least she looks very . . . robust!'

The gentle afterthought irritated Alice quite as much as he hoped it would, but she rallied after a moment or two.

'Harriet will give George robust children, too. You ought to be pleased about that – a new generation of Rushtons. No good leaving the future entirely to Charles.'

No good leaving *anything* to Charles, she might just as well have said, and in his heart the head of Rushton's agreed with her. His younger son, too sickly to have followed John to war, had two ambitions in life – to learn everything he could about art and as little as possible about wine.

'Time enough for more grandchildren of my own,' James insisted sharply. 'Charlie's not thirty yet.'

Alice gave a little smile. 'But so like his mother, I always think – not quite forceful enough for his own good.'

That was true, too. Cecily Rushton hadn't been forceful at all, and she'd taken so little pleasure in the physical side of marriage that her three children had been dutifully conceived and born with difficulty. The running of Vine House had mostly been left to servants while she painted watercolours, and stitched the exquisite chair-covers they now sat on in the dining-room. She'd died unresistingly in the influenza epidemic that ravaged Europe at the end of the war. James couldn't help feeling that the harridan sitting next to him wouldn't have let herself be carried off with so little complaint. His face suddenly looked sad and old, and Alice was prompted to lower her sword. There was one important matter on which they were agreed; it hadn't made much progress so far and they felt equally frustrated.

'I suppose you'd prefer Jane and William to provide the next generation? Well, so would I, but they ought to be getting on with it; Jane is thirty-one. With Laura here you'd think she'd be glad of a home of her own.'

'Two women can't run the same house; she agreed that it should be the job of Johnny's widow,' said James, scenting criticism. 'In any case when William settled down again after the war we took it for granted that he'd see the wisdom of marrying Jane quickly. She's never looked at anyone but him, so what are they waiting for? Women are unpredictable creatures, but Jane's more rational than most; William must have done something to upset her.'

Alice bit back a hasty reply; it would do no good to come to cuffs with James. Apart from the useful inheritance Cecily had left her daughter, there was the fact that marriage to Jane was bound to lead to a partnership in Rushton's for William. She was still searching for something soothing to say when Todd came into the room to put port decanters on the table. At the same moment Laura got up to lead the women upstairs. James expected the whole family to appreciate the choice burgundies and clarets that Rushton's shipped from France, but in his house the ritual of sampling port was reserved exclusively for men.

Jane smiled sympathetically at her brother as she left the table. Poor Charlie hated port, and in any gathering of Rushton males he was certain to be the odd one out. *They* would talk wine, tariff protection, and whither post-war, troubled Europe. If *he* said anything at all, he would only offend – disapproving of the way the Continent had been carved up by horse-trading politicians, and infuriating his father with the suggestion that William Morris's brand of ideal Socialism was the only salvation for England's restive, modern society. Jane would have stayed to help him if she could, but she was expected to leave the room and she had problems of her own upstairs.

The drawing-room on the first floor ran almost the whole width of the house. Long windows faced the river, and the huge stone fireplace and panelled walls remained as master-craftsmen had left them two centuries before.

Victorian excess had been quietly and gradually removed while Cecily Rushton was alive; now, freed of stuffed birds in glass cases, bobbles fringing every inch of draped material, and a thick encrustment of occasional tables, the room had regained its original serene beauty. Whenever she went in, Jane compared it in her mind with the rich tastelessness that ran riot in Aunt Alice's drawing-room a short walk away in St Peter's Square. Her gentle mother, so despised by Edward's wife, had managed a better memorial after all.

She went to stand by the hearth, staring down into the leaping flames of the fire. There had been time enough in the years since her mother had died to learn that Laura preferred to play the rôle of hostess at Vine House alone.

'You've been neglecting us,' said a voice at her side. She turned and found the youngest of her cousins, Alexandra, looking at her accusingly. 'I don't blame you; *of course* you'd rather stay here . . . it's lovely and tranquil.' A home filled with an overbearing mother and sister was *not*, she implied, and Jane didn't comment on what her own was like with a sister-in-law who saw no virtue in sharing. Instead, she made haste to rouse Alexandra from the depressing effect of a family dinner-party.

'Tranquillity from *you*, dear coz? I thought you wanted to taste life, the more fast and furious the better!'

'So I do – I want to see everything, go everywhere . . . and there isn't much time. If I don't get started soon, tasting won't do. I shall have to gulp life down.'

'Not a moment to waste at just turned twenty-one,' Jane agreed solemnly.

She watched her cousin's entrancing face break into a smile and marvelled once again that Edward and Alice Rushton could, between them, have produced such a daughter. Perhaps bright-haired, laughing William, and this beautiful changeling creature had been a reward for their other three children. George was a pompous bore who wouldn't be improved by marriage to Harriet

11

Jennings, and Eliza was Aunt Alice writ small; but Lionel was the worst of all. Jane had never forgiven him for beheading her favourite doll when she was seven years old. Whenever he guffawed now she could still hear him laughing over *that* ancient slaughter.

'George is preening himself on getting Harriet pregnant already – indecently quick, if you ask me, after four months of marriage! Eliza's even worse – behaves as if she won the vote for women over thirty single-handed. She's now been fired by the example of Lady Astor and wants to be in the House of Commons in time for our next Labour Government. Can you think of anything more dire? No wonder you hesitate to marry into my family!'

Alexandra's grin faded because her cousin, usually so quick to share amusement, wasn't smiling back at her. 'There isn't any real doubt about it, is there?' she asked uncertainly. 'Mama regularly blows the dust off her wedding-finery, and she is always the knowing one; but if you and William don't hurry up I shall be a very elderly bridesmaid.'

'And I shall be an even more elderly bride! Sorry to keep you waiting.' Jane smiled faintly but had nothing more to say on a subject that exercised the rest of the family. 'Time to be sociable, I think. Shall we remember our manners and join the others?' She was the first to move and Alexandra watched her walk away; a slight, brown-haired woman who'd been unlucky enough to miss both Cecily Rushton's delicate prettiness and James's clean-cut features. She was intelligent and humurous, but so little of a beauty that it was all the more surprising, in Alexandra's view, that William should want to marry her. Clever of Jane to pique his vanity, though; the only way to keep her brother wanting something was not to give it to him for the asking.

Laura was presiding over the coffee-tray when the men reappeared. An antique chair-back framed her red-gold hair, and against the covering of old green velvet her bare

12

arms and shoulders gleamed like mother-of-pearl. She didn't have Alexandra's loveliness of feature, but she was an elderly man's dream of womanliness – enticing and soft. What young men like William thought of her Jane also supposed she knew. Her father knew it too, and without loving him, she felt a stir of pity. His only defence against the buccaneers who might steal Laura and David away was to bribe her into being content to stay. The 'scheming immoral actress' Johnny had insisted on marrying before he sailed for France had become the indispensable provider of James's grandson.

The party disposed itself about the room as family parties usually did – while James, Edward and George continued to discuss which of their clients should be recommended to lay down what from Rushton's previous autumn shipments, the rest of them were free to entertain each other. Foreseeing a wasted evening, William selected a subject most likely to provoke an argument, then skilfully withdrew from it himself once the pros and cons of 'the Irish Question' were being tossed around the hearth. Jane made the mistake of allowing him to catch her eye, and realized that he had intended all along to separate the two of them from the general conversation.

'Darling Jane, don't pretend you were enjoying the details of Harriet's morning-sickness, and I've yet to discover that she can talk about anything else; or was Eliza holding forth on the imminent demise of capitalism?' His blue eyes glinted with mischief and the caressing warmth he couldn't help offering any woman he talked to. He was unfairly able to charm and, even knowing that he managed to beguile everyone alike, she couldn't sound severe.

'Whether I'm any happier to listen to *you* depends on what you're going to say.'

'Ah . . . a warning not to throw myself at your feet again and implore you to make up your mind to marry me?'

She had to smile because he was scarcely describing his courtship so far – it had been surprisingly persistent but not impassioned. 'Not your style at all . . . not the *Rushton* style, now that I come to think of it; our heads are supposed to remain cool. Johnny's grand passion for Laura was an exception, but no doubt you're about to point out that *she's* exceptional, too!'

She wondered whether he'd feel obliged to deny it, even though his eyes strayed so frequently in Laura's direction.

'Attractive – very; exceptional – no,' he said surprisingly. 'She's also that unlovesome thing in woman, a tease. Uncle James needn't worry; an occasional flirtation to keep her hand in, but nothing more serious than that. Laura won't be rushed into another marriage. Why choose the crude demands of a husband and the discomfort of bearing more children when she can be indulged and protected here?'

Jane thought it was likely to be true – William was experienced enough in the ways of women to know. All the same, he'd spoken with a trace of bitterness that seemed out of place between cousins by marriage.

'*She's* happy enough,' he said next, 'but what about you? Playing second fiddle to a sister-in-law younger than yourself can't be much fun. In fact I should have thought playing second fiddle to *this* one would be damnable.'

That was true, too, even though she smiled cheerfully. 'Do I look as resentful as all that? So much for imagining I wore my rue with a difference! Never mind, I shan't stay here for ever.'

He stared at her, noting the signs of strain in her thin face, while she observed that for once he looked entirely serious.

'I think Uncle James has been bullying you again. Dear Jane, grand passion is a trifle out of place between cousins who began their relationship by squabbling over toys in the nursery; we know too much about each other for that. But wouldn't a marriage built on liking and true affection be better than the life you lead here? Can't you bring yourself to believe that it would work? I promise you we'd *make* it work.'

14

He sounded sincere, as well as serious, and she could believe, easily enough, that they'd contrive the kind of partnership the world judged successful. William would share her bed from time to time, and there proximity might do instead of passion. He would treat his wife considerately, and perhaps even learn to love the children that were begot as a matter of duty. Her father had pointed out delicately that it was as much as a plain, thin woman of thirty-one had any right to expect, but for once James Rushton had been wrong, although she hadn't felt inclined to tell him so. She required passion, not courtesy; needed William to love her with some, at least, of the fire and fevered longing and infinite tenderness she felt for him. If he would only pretend to believe that even childhood squabblers might become a man and woman who needed each other, then she could marry him. But William's honesty began where most people's left off – he kept it for important things. He proposed to marry her, but made no pretence of loving her. She forced her mouth to smile, ignoring its reluctance to find humour in the situation.

'Laura reckons I was born to be a spinster aunt; I think she's probably right.'

He didn't fall into the trap of protesting too much; instead, her hands were suddenly imprisoned in his, and he felt them tremble. It was too public an act, but she didn't know how to say so. He was too liable to sense the weakness spreading through her body, and she didn't know how to deal with that, either.

'My dear girl, it doesn't matter *what* Laura thinks. It doesn't even matter that everyone is watching us now to see whether I finally manage to make you change your mind! Only you and I matter, Janey.'

Perhaps he used the name as a deliberate echo of childhood, but he was suddenly the boy who'd tipped her in the river by accident and manfully hauled her out again; he was the lad who'd remembered to go back for her when his brothers ran away leaving her a prisoner on the island

15

in midstream; he was the man who captivated her, and his face was now full of a man's rueful, irresistible tenderness. She nodded without being entirely sure what it was she agreed to, but it seemed that, without intending to, she had committed herself at last. If this was the moment to be certain that nothing would be worse than *not* marrying him, it wasn't the moment she'd have chosen for the discovery. The glare of family attention made her wince outside, but she couldn't free her hands, or deny the little confident smile that suddenly touched his mouth. She would take the joy and pain of being his wife, and if God was merciful William might even find he needed no-one else to make him happy after all.

Aunt Alice, as usual, watched, and then marched in where the rest of them weren't certain enough of themselves to tread.

'Don't tell me you've made up your minds at last?' Her bright, cool glance rested on Jane's pale face and on her son's slightly flushed one. 'Yes, I can see you have; well, it's something else to celebrate tonight. Do you hear, James?'

He was inclined to say sharply that there was nothing wrong with his hearing or his understanding; but satisfaction at having got what he'd almost given up hoping for enabled him to swallow the irritation his sister-in-law always managed to provoke.

'A glass of champagne, I think, even though it won't be properly chilled. Charlie, will you go and see Todd?'

The wine was brought and drunk, the shower of good wishes sounded well meant, and William's hand still held hers as if he liked the feel of it there. Happiness lit Jane's face with a shy, charming radiance, and Charlie breathed a sigh of relief. She was happy, after all; he'd been a fool to imagine her trapped at last in a cold-blooded arrangement that happened to suit both sides of the family.

16

2

Laura would have preferred life at Vine House without Johnny's brother or sister there, but of the two of them Charlie was the lesser evil. For one thing, he was absent most of the day. James didn't attach any importance to what his son did at Rushton's offices in the City, close by London Bridge, but he required him at least to go there. While David was still so young, anyone of his own was better than no-one at all as a counter-balance to Edward's ambitious sons. Charlie filled his working days in ways that suited him – dreaming a good deal of the time about a different kind of life, and otherwise illustrating the charming brochures and labels that had become associated with the name of Rushton. They were more appreciated by the clientele than by the family, but that didn't worry him; he was used to being valued only by Jane. At home he had chosen for himself a large, unused room on the attic floor, from whose windows he watched and painted the life of the river. Apart from his occasional appearances in the dining-room, he and Laura could forget that they shared the house at all.

She couldn't forget Jane, but the pleasure of getting rid of her now didn't make up for the loss of William. They had been careful in their intimacy; his cousinly concern for Johnny's widow had misled even Aunt Alice's all-seeing eye, and Laura had been able to enjoy a relationship that had excitement in it but no real threat to her father-in-law's affection for her. She would have minded Jane's engagement less if the only Rushton male worth bothering with had been won by a challenger she considered worthy of losing to. In front of James she had to smile as usual, but bile rose in her throat now whenever she looked at Jane.

When William sauntered into the drawing-room at Vine House one evening she was almost swamped by a wave of jealousy. The black and white severity of evening clothes suited his tall figure and fair hair to perfection; he was a handsome, sophisticated man and *she* ought to be the one going out with him, not Jane. She craved something more exciting than the safe, comfortable routine of being James's widowed and devoted daughter-in-law.

'You'll have to make do with me for a little while, my dear William,' she said brightly. Anger sparked in her eyes and gave a dangerous edge to her smile. 'Jane only came in ten minutes ago, and the poor girl needs quite a lot of time to get her warpaint on.'

William ignored the spurt of malice, aware of regret as strong as Laura's for his changed status at Vine House. 'Todd told me that she got held up, but I'm early in any case.'

'A visit to the Music Hall this evening?'

'Certainly not; Jane has it in mind to educate me. There's a new play by Shaw called *Heartbreak House* – sounds a trifle ominous to me, but it's time I started to grapple with the fact that life is real and life is earnest!'

'Time you grappled with matrimony, in fact! Poor William – what a prospect . . . this *evening*, I mean. Still, the company of an adoring fiancée will probably make up for it.' She selected her next dart and launched it with a sweet smile. 'An early wedding, I suppose . . . to please the family? You know we're all agog to see William, "the married man"!'

Jane's work of education hadn't yet gone far enough for him to catch the allusion but he knew that Laura was enjoying herself at his expense. He ought to take hold of her and shake the venom out, but, however much she deserved the shaking, it would really be an excuse to touch her. He would deny them both a pleasure by resisting

18

temptation. The perfume she used reached him across the space between them, and her hair flamed against the whiteness of her skin. She was lovely and desirable, and perhaps even angry enough to throw safety overboard at last. The pity of it was that she'd reached that point too late for both of them.

'It won't be a *very* early wedding,' he said after a moment. 'A trip to Spain and Portugal with Uncle James is suddenly on the cards. I'm acquainted with the sherry people at Jerez de la Frontera, but he thinks it's time I was introduced to the grand old English gentlemen at the Factory House in Oporto. The place is rather impressive, I'm told.'

'By the sound of it, home from home . . . just the perfect setting for the Port Wine Shippers Association – Chippendale furniture, Coalport china, and back numbers of *The Times* for the last hundred years!'

'Still rather impressive, I insist,' he replied, smiling but firm. 'Don't jeer at ancient traditions; I quite like them myself.'

Laura's face suddenly lost its sparkling malice. She moved a step nearer to William and stared at him with huge, desolate eyes. 'Rushton traditions will probably *suffocate* me in the end. I have to stay here for the sake of my son; it's what Johnny would have wanted. But if you knew how I long to escape, your heart would bleed for me, William.'

She had been an actress, he remembered, but there was enough truth in what she said for him to feel acutely sorry for her. Playing housekeeper to James Rushton was death in life for a girl of twenty-nine who had known what it was to be a wife passionately loved. The hands she held out to him pleaded for comfort, and without quite knowing how it came about, he found that he had taken hold of them. Her body was now so close that it pressed against his, insistently reminding him of its warmth and softness. He told himself that she was too young and desirable to be buried at Vine House . . . it was cruel, even criminal, to a woman who needed to be loved.

'Darling William, help me persuade James that it would do David good to go with you to Portugal. He was sickly all the winter thanks to this beastly, dank, river air we live in. A sea-trip and a change of scene would make a different child of him.'

'Am I also supposed to persuade James that *you* should come too?'

'Well, of course; I must be with David.' Her expression changed again, pleading wiped away by sparkling mischief. 'Who knows – I might even help Rushton's by captivating the old English gentlemen as well!'

'No doubt about it, sweetheart, if you were allowed inside the sacred portals, but it would be like trying to lay siege to the defenders of the Athenaeum here.'

'All right, I'll promise to stay outside; but wouldn't *you* like a change of company occasionally? Is it enough to listen to James for weeks on end, arguing the merits of Old Tawny versus Vintage Red?' She still stood deliberately close to him, and he was almost sure that he was being mutely offered what had always been withdrawn before at the last minute.

'Risky, my dear Laura,' he muttered.

She didn't pretend to misunderstand. 'But all the more enjoyable for that! Darling, we're not living in the Victorian age . . . there *are* precautions now against danger!'

The most obvious one of all was to leave her behind at Vine House, but he wasn't quite a married man yet and excitement was beginning to run like a flame through his body. It wouldn't hurt Jane, and *this* poor girl deserved a little happiness before he settled down. They both understood the rules of the game; *she* wouldn't taunt Jane with his unfaithfulness, any more than *he* would give *her* away to James. Really it was delightfully neat from every point of view.

'I'll talk to James,' he said finally, beginning to smile. 'All *you* have to do is look wistful, and worried about David.'

Her lips curved enticingly, and her body seemed to melt against his. It was too public, insanely rash in fact, but his eyes saw only the temptation of her mouth. He pulled her hard against him, and opened her lips with his own.

By the time the sound of Jane's evening sandals clattered on the polished wood of the staircase outside they had managed to drag themselves apart and were standing decorously separate. She pushed open the drawing-room door and walked into an atmosphere of such tense excitement that she feared she had interrupted a quarrel. William seemed to find some fascination in staring at the fire, and Laura examined her fingernails as if she had never seen them before. Jane advanced into the room, trying to smile normally.

'Sorry to keep you waiting, William, but at least Laura was here to talk to you.'

His hands still trembled a little but she couldn't be aware of the fact because they were hidden in the pockets of his jacket. He thought she looked composed as usual and, alongside Laura's vivid appeal, just as plain as usual. It was cruel to measure them, of course, but the alternative to being cruel was to feel guilty. She must know by now that no-one would notice her in a room that also contained Laura Rushton; surely she had no right to expect him not to want to make love to a woman so different from herself? Still, madness had got the better of him a few minutes ago; he must smile, and kiss his fiancée's cheek, and survive an evening listening to that intolerably prosy bore of an Irishman. But if the actors didn't yammer at each other too loudly, he could sit and plan his approach to Uncle James. It was perfectly clear to him now that young David must have a little sea air, and that he himself could take whatever pleasures the trip offered without feeling guilty. He deserved a little reward for going to church with Jane when they were all back in London, because he fully intended to be a most considerate husband.

It wasn't a habit of James Rushton to feel sheepish, but when he announced to Jane a week later that he'd persuaded Laura to brave the Bay of Biscay and go with them to Lisbon, he wished for a moment that he'd let William break the news to his daughter. She stared at him in silence, but something in her level gaze made him feel less comfortable than usual.

'It's for the boy's benefit,' he explained sharply. 'He's been looking very pulled down since the winter, and Laura can't be expected to take him away on her own.'

Jane despised the dishonesty of pretending that she and her sister-in-law would be glad to go away in each other's company, but there *were* alternatives she could offer.

'My cousins would have gone with her – Alexandra especially; she longs to travel and get away from St Peter's Square.'

'She may do; but I wouldn't trust *her* to help Laura with a child abroad, and I wouldn't inflict my other niece on *anybody*. Eliza's only fit to chant slogans with her long-haired revolutionaries; let her stay where she belongs.'

A smile briefly touched Jane's face, wiping away strain, and James saw the change with a twinge of remorse. She'd got even thinner than usual; when her head was down-bent he could see the hollows at temples and cheek-bones. Without being in the least like her mother, she sometimes reminded him of Cecily; it was a matter of expression, not feature. His wife had had just that same intelligent gaze, and the disconcerting gleams of amusement that lit his daughter's face had been hers also.

'All right, I retract the offer of Eliza,' Jane agreed peaceably. 'In any case, she's probably too busy – did you know that she's going into active politics?'

'Good God! A hundred years ago Edward could have had her locked up, out of harm's way.' James fidgeted with his watch-chain. 'No point in asking *you* to come with us – you've got your wedding to think about. William says he's leaving it to you to decide where you live.'

Even in the midst of her distress, Jane interpreted correctly the note of doubt in her father's voice. James couldn't bring himself to believe that a matter so important as a house should be left to the choice of a woman; on the other hand, with five children to consider, Edward couldn't do more for William than for the others, and the new house was going to be bought with Jane's inheritance. It seemed only fair, even to James, that she must have a say in what was chosen.

It was a relief to James when she finally nodded and agreed that she had too much to do to think of going away. His impression a few minutes ago that she'd been stricken by his plan to take Laura and David with him had been sheer imagination after all. She was a level-headed woman who accepted things without fuss, thank God, unlike Alice's hysterical daughters. He would ask Laura to choose a nice little gift for her in Oporto; really, she deserved *that*, now that he came to think of it.

The travellers set off at the beginning of May, and Jane kept the vow she had made to herself that she would see them off cheerfully. For the past week or two William had become very attentive, and when he said goodbye even managed to sound warmly proprietorial.

'Sweetheart, you're looking tired. I command you to rest while I'm away striving with might and main for Rushton's – a little gentle diversion with Charlie if you like, but no strenuous search for houses, and *no* running errands for my dear mother. She has two daughters of her own, and the constitution of an ox besides! Promise to miss me, and not to go near St Peter's Square.'

His voice was gentle, and his goodbye kiss unexpectedly tender. For a moment she was certain, against all probability, that he wished he wasn't leaving her behind. She

23

promised herself that she would find them a lovely house to live in while he was away. Her mouth suddenly clung to his and its sweetness roused him to frame her face in his hands and kiss her again, still more thoroughly.

Only when he released her did she become aware that Laura waited in the hall, watching them. A mountain of luggage had been brought downstairs, but some vital piece was still missing, and she suddenly turned to rend the chambermaid who'd been stupid enough to leave it in her bedroom. David rushed about, noisy and white-faced with excitement, but suddenly unsure that he wanted to go if Aunt Jane wasn't coming too. James lost patience with so much confusion and finally swept them outside, insisting that they were already late. A moment later they were gone, and the house seemed suddenly not only quiet but permanently abandoned by life. Jane climbed the stairs but didn't go into the drawing-room; she wanted to remember the tenderness of William's goodbye, but not in a room that nowadays had a constant echo of Laura's perfume hanging in the air.

A week later she was poring over brochures collected from Harrods' Estate Office when Charlie came home from the City. He rarely talked about his days at Rushton's, but this evening there was news to be passed on.

'You won't believe this, Janey, but Aunt Alice has taken to her bed. According to Uncle Edward, acute tonsilitis has developed into something called quinsies, which are reckoned to be even more unpleasant. Lionel says it's really extreme mortification she's suffering from. Eliza has now thrown in her lot with the Communist Party, having decided that her Socialist friends are losing their nerve, or verve, over a Bolshevik revolution. She is, of course, too busy to pay any attention to her mother.'

'Poor Aunt – I can't help feeling that even *she* doesn't deserve Eliza. Well, at least Alexandra's there.'

'Not so . . . she's marooned in Oxford with a badly

sprained ankle; the result of cavorting about at a Commemoration ball.'

'Which means that *I* shall have to go to St Peter's Square after all. With the best intentions in the world, Uncle Edward will fuss Aunt to death, and all she can expect from Lionel is a polite enquiry on his way out to tennis at Hurlingham.'

Charlie's shy grin appeared. It was rare for Jane to be waspish, but he rather enjoyed it when she was. '*Still* not your favourite cousin!'

'Given a choice, I'd even take Eliza,' she said after a moment's consideration. 'At least the worst of *her* is on view; Lionel smiles and hides his teeth.' She smiled suddenly as if to apologize for her vehemence . . . "Old, unhappy, far-off things and battles long ago" . . . childhood's still with me, you see! It's nothing to be proud of, but Johnny always said I had the memory of an elephant!'

Charlie glanced at the leaflets spread out in front of her. He was aware that he'd scarcely commented on her engagement to William, and that the omission must be noticeable because they were the closest of friends.

'House-hunting already? I shall miss you, Janey, and moving out will be a wrench for *you* – you've always loved this house.'

They had both loved it, and all their childhood happiness had been woven around it and the Thames just outside. Cecily Rushton had led them into Kenneth Grahame's magic river world, but that had been a long time ago. They were too old now to play Mole or Badger, and Ratty hadn't survived the slaughter on the Somme. Jane's thin hand sifted through the papers in front of her, describing houses that any woman in her sane, right mind would find desirable; houses that were adequately heated in winter and didn't have water lapping over the doorstep every time a high spring tide came flooding up-river. But, cold and wetness notwithstanding, she would have stayed where she was for the rest of her life, given the chance.

'I shall learn to love a house of my own,' she insisted in a low voice. Charlie nodded, and they left unsaid what both knew – that Vine House had now become Laura's house. They were talking of homes, not husbands, but she didn't *want* to know what Charlie thought about her marriage. She was sure he *did* know that William had always been the cousin she loved, just as Lionel had been the one she hated.

'It will work out all right in the end, Janey,' he said hopefully, 'bound to, I reckon.' New home or marriage? She still didn't know which he referred to, but it seemed better not to ask.

The next morning she walked along Chiswick Mall to her uncle's solid, double-fronted house in St Peter's Square. Its cream-coloured stucco fought a losing battle with London grime, and the lace-edged blinds Aunt Alice kept half-drawn over the large bay windows gave it a blinded look. Jane felt depressed at the sight of it every time she turned the corner of the Square, but the discovery years ago that it had the same effect on her mother had made subsequent visits bearable.

Edward met her in the hall and reported that the worst of his wife's misery was over; the doctor had just been to lance the painful abscesses in her throat, thus releasing the poison. Jane found her aunt looking drawn and pale after this ordeal, but stoically uncomplaining. Eating was impossible, but she sipped barley-water and promised to try to swallow the beef-tea Jane had brought from Mrs Todd's store-cupboard at Vine House.

Alice watched her niece move quietly about the untidy room, setting it to rights, and accepted with scarcely a murmur of protest the relief of being washed and put into a fresh nightgown.

'Kind of you, Jane,' she whispered. 'Servants mean well . . . so does Edward . . . but they always need telling what to do.'

26

'Uncle Edward didn't spend the war years as a VAD!' Jane pointed out with a smile. 'Dear aunt, sleep as much as you can; it's the best healer of all. I'll come again tomorrow and expect to find you much better.' She surprised herself by kissing Alice Rushton with something like real affection, and left the room thinking that, along with other, less acceptable characteristics, fortitude had certainly been bred in the last of the Victorians.

Downstairs Edward was getting ready to bustle off to the City now that he was sure his dear wife was more comfortable. Saturday mornings were always busy, and with James and William away there was a great deal of extra work for him to see to. He peered at the watch dangling from the gold chain across his waistcoat, looking so like the White Rabbit that she waited for him to say, 'Oh dear, oh dear, I'm late,' but he gestured instead to the door of the breakfast-room.

'Your cousins are in there, my dear. Eliza's back from wherever she chose to stay last night and Lionel's eating a late breakfast after some kind of party.'

Jane was greatly tempted to follow her uncle out of the front door, but unaccustomed anger was beginning to burn in her and she marched along the hall. Lionel, unjustifiably pleased with his appearance in a purple silk dressing-gown, sat buttering toast at one end of the table. Eliza faced him, smoking a cigarette in between sips of black coffee. Her greeting was merely a wave of the long holder, but Lionel managed to utter a few words of welcome.

'Cousin Jane, as I live. It's delightful to see you, coz, but isn't it a trifle early for social calls?'

She took a deep breath and promised herself that she would *not* shout at them.

'Not a social visit, as it happens,' she said quietly, 'and it *is* half past ten. If either of you are remotely interested, I can report that your mother is still very unwell but not in quite such acute discomfort as she has been. I dare say that quite puts your minds at rest.'

27

A little silence fell, only broken by the scratching of Lionel's knife against his toast.

'A note of censure, do I detect?' asked Eliza at last. 'Have we been remiss, brother?'

Lionel brushed crumbs from his blond moustache and smiled sweetly. '*You*, not I, dearest. Men are not required in sickrooms, although I can fairly say that I *did* look in on Mama yesterday morning.'

Jane turned to Eliza. 'Aunt Alice must have been in great pain last night and she's had an unpleasant session with the doctor this morning, but, even knowing that Alexandra was away, I suppose you were too busy saving England from itself to stay and help her.'

'You suppose right . . . I *was*. With a husband and four servants in the house she wasn't exactly abandoned and, unlike my sister's frolics at a university ball, what *I* was doing was important. *You* wouldn't understand, of course, but you and every complacent fool like you will sneer at us once too often one of these days.'

Jane stared from her cousin's intense face to Lionel, now helping himself to coffee. 'I hope you've explained to your brother in *his* fool's paradise that he'll be among the first to be swept away,' she said politely. 'No more silk dressing-gowns, and servants bringing in his breakfast, I'm afraid, even if he manages to survive the initial holocaust.'

The change of expression on his self-satisfied face made her smile, but the amusement that released her from anger had the effect of inflaming Eliza. Martyrdom for the cause was welcome, but mockery was unbearable.

'What about *your* little self-deceptions?' her cousin suddenly rasped. 'Shall we now enjoy a laugh about *them*?'

'First you'll have to tell me what they are.'

The grave statement didn't check a woman unbalanced by a night's heady talk with her fellow crusaders. A revolution that seemed entirely feasible when she was with *them* lost its bright glow in the suffocating respectability of her mother's breakfast-room; she hated Jane for making the fact clear, but there was something she could make clear in return.

'You can't seriously imagine that William *wants* to marry you.'

Jane began to feel sick. It wasn't even a question that had been flung at her, so sure was her cousin of the answer she already knew. The time had come to stop hiding from the truth and consider what she *did* truly imagine – that she had been chosen because she would make a kind, competent and loving wife; the loving was important, needed for *her* contentment as well as William's pride, because he would *want* even a plain, unexciting wife to be happy. He would also expect her to understand that he couldn't spend the next forty years never glancing to left or right. Jane had promised herself that she would understand, and not let her heart be broken.

'What William and I imagine is our own concern,' she answered finally, 'but remember that *he* asked *me*; he had no need to if he didn't want to.' Eliza suddenly looked so pleased, that Jane realized she would have done better to say nothing at all.

'Of course he needed to. My brother has expensive tastes and grand ideas. Your father's notion of a living wage is not *his*, and he can't wait for two vigorous old men to die and still not be sure of running Rushton's; you're going to be useful.'

'If I can help William, then I'm glad to be needed,' she insisted steadily. She would *not* be sick in front of them, nor show her wounds.

Lionel wiped his mouth with a napkin, leaving a sly smile behind.

'Dear coz, no need to pretend with *us*. Glad as you are, it must be even sweeter to know that William and Laura will have to behave themselves in future . . . well, after this little trip together, at least! Of course, by then my brother might not mind too much, having exhausted *all* Laura's charms, but she will have to watch you carry off *her* property. Maddening for her!'

He suddenly noticed the extreme whiteness of Jane's face and looked extravagantly contrite. 'Don't tell me you *didn't* know. Oh God, Eliza, we've been indiscreet. Shall I pretend I was joking, after all?'

'*I'd* rather you didn't say another word,' Jane answered quickly. She felt deathly cold and feverish at the same time, but if she died in attempting it she must somehow get out of this dreadful room without letting them know that she was mortally hurt.

'I told Aunt Alice I'd come back tomorrow . . .' she muttered between stiff lips.

'No need,' Eliza said brusquely. 'I'm not anyone's idea of a born nurse, but I suppose even I can see what needs doing; if not, Mama will have the pleasure of telling me.' She hesitated, now feeling uncomfortable. The conversation had got out of hand, and although she and Lionel had said only what was true, she supposed they needn't have said it at all.

Jane nodded, without saying goodbye, and forced her legs to move in the direction of the door. Somewhere a clock chimed three-quarters to eleven as she walked along the hall. She counted the chimes and didn't believe that they correctly measured the time since she'd arrived in St Peter's Square. Outside, the air felt cold against the dampness of perspiration on her face, but it revived her and she was grateful for it. Chiswick Mall looked no different from when she'd left it an eternity ago; perhaps only *she* had changed. Instead of going indoors, childhood habit still held and she took her trouble to the river.

Beyond the narrow road in front of the house their garden sloped down to the water's edge, and there sat the old wooden seat that had always been their look-out post on the world beyond the river. There was nothing in the blankness of her mind except the need to watch a seabird's aerial dance over the water. She sat without moving for a long time until a string of barges went fussily downstream, attended by creaming furrows of wash and an escort of noisy gulls; her watch said that it was long past the hour for lunch, and at last she went indoors and climbed the stairs to Charlie's studio.

'I've been river-gazing,' she said abruptly.

'I know – I could see you down there.' He stared at her white face. 'Something wrong, Janey? Aunt Alice hasn't got worse, or died, has she?'

She tried to smile but nearly wept instead. Rushton heads were supposed to rule – she had told William so – but more was lacking in Rushton hearts than she'd imagined when even her gentle brother had to struggle to sound concerned because his aunt was ill.

'Aunt's a little better, and nothing's wrong, but I've decided to go away . . . before William gets back.'

Charlie's eyes continued to examine her while he considered what to say. 'Shall I ask why, or not?'

'Better not, I think. Just tell me where you recommend. I've always imagined I should like to go to Italy.'

She stared at him out of haunted eyes that implored him not to shatter her bright, fragile self-control.

'Why not?' he agreed after a long pause. 'I seem to remember they taught you Latin in that seminary of yours – you'd be able to pick up Italian in no time, being quick at that sort of thing.'

She nodded, wondering if it was to be the extent of his help when, for once in her life, she would have been thankful to be told precisely what to do.

'Try Tuscany,' he suggested gently. 'The English have been going there for years and years. That'll be the place, Janey.'

Since it no longer mattered where she went, she accepted what he said. Tuscany, where her half-forgotten remnants of Ovid and Virgil would undoubtedly be useful, would be just the place.

3

By the end of May the summer had arrived in Florence, but still gently for the time being. Jane's guidebooks warned of the blanket of stifling heat later on that would drop from the surrounding hills, but for the moment she found the warmth a blessing after a London spring. In the clear Tuscan light the city was painted in colours that seemed extravagantly rich to English eyes – a harmonious muddle such as she had never seen of earth-brown, ochre, faded red, and rose. How Charlie would have revelled in it, and approved of the contrast provided by the dark green shafts of cypress trees, marvelled with her at a sky stained blue as the glass in cathedral windows at home.

It was a mistake to think of Charlie; she told herself she was fortunate beyond words to be sitting on a sunlit hillside, trying to sketch the rose-red cupola of the Duomo floating above the skyline of Florence. But loneliness was harder to keep at bay on Sundays when she had no Italian lessons to attend, and everyone else around her seemed to belong to a family; the hillside was scattered with them – laying out their luncheon alfresco, shouting to each other and surveying the view of their city with proper Florentine pride.

It was perilous to remember Vine House, and David perched on the bank outside, fishing for non-existent Thames dace, while Charlie frowned over a canvas that didn't quite capture the watercolour light on the river. His letters reported that the travellers were still away and that Aunt Alice continued in a state of frustrated rage about her niece's sudden disappearance. Jane thought she would have been happy to see even Alice Rushton materialize on the wind-ruffled grass in front of her. She didn't dare allow herself to think of William at all. Loneliness could be come to terms with in time, but not the bitter anguish of having been duped. Poor, plain Jane Rushton . . . poor James if he ever discovered the truth about a daughter-in-law he'd made up his mind to idolize. What fools they'd both been.

'*Mi scusi, signorina . . . mi sembra che Lei abbia perduto questo foglio.*'

The grave enquiry made her blink away the tears that pricked her eyelids. She found herself looking at a man somewhere between youth and middle age, who had politely removed his hat in order to speak to her. His clothes, like his voice, were quiet, and she had the strong impression that he was as isolated from the chattering groups around them as she was herself. The sheet of paper he held out was indeed hers, but she felt embarrassed to have to say so. Even assuming that not every present-day Florentine could draw like Leonardo, her sketch of the city's skyline left a lot to be desired. She inspected his face for signs that he thought so too, but it remained a courteously unamused blank.

'*Sì . . . è il mio; grazie, signore.*' Her daily attendance at the British Institute language classes, and much labouring over books of grammar, hadn't been in vain. It was a triumph to have understood him but, better still, she had even achieved a suitable reply. If he would now walk away without unleashing a further flood of Italian, she needn't admit to being where she didn't belong. It seemed likely that he would go, because his air of self-withdrawn containment was the loudest thing about him. He almost certainly didn't make a habit of addressing strangers, and perhaps not of talking much to women at all.

'The signorina is English, I think.'

She blushed for the humiliation of it – identified the moment she opened her mouth, after all. 'I hoped the accent might be better than the sketch,' she said honestly. 'Apparently not!'

'Both are charming, as a matter of fact.' The drawing was studied with a good deal more care than it deserved before he heroically brushed aside the rules of art. 'We needn't concern ourselves with tedious matters of draughtsmanship and perspective.'

They could scarcely do so, she thought, when the tower of the Palazzo Vecchio leaned confidingly towards the cathedral dome, and Giotto's slender campanile wavered in the opposite direction. Still, it showed real kindness on his part . . . the peculiarly Italian generosity that was offered to strangers.

Under the brim of the severe straw-boater planted squarely on her head he saw that her eyes were suddenly bright with laughter. Amusement tilted the corners of her mouth, transforming a face that had seemed primly middle-aged a moment before.

'My excuse is that I'm *not* a student of art,' she explained. 'This is for my brother at home, and he will be willing to award marks for effort rather than achievement!'

Really, for a member of a volatile, emotional race the man in front of her was scandalously inexpressive; he still stared at her without the vestige of a smile.

'The English point of view; that shows an important difference between us,' he finally replied. 'Here, unless we can be sure of achieving, we fail to try at all. It's one of the reasons for centuries of failure and humiliation.'

Jane stared in turn, surprised by the serious direction the conversation had taken, and conscious of a mixture of pity and irritation. If he was right, it seemed a remarkably feeble point of view, but his air of gentle resignation to fate might have some personal cause she didn't know about. Rather than risk offering comfort or contradiction, it seemed safer to bring the odd conversation to an end. She was about to use the obvious excuse of looking at her watch when the chapel bell of San Domenico chimed the hours of midday below them on the hillside.

'I must begin my walk back to the pensione at once, signore, or be late for luncheon.'

'A pensione in Fiesole, no doubt?'

'No, in Florence.' Amusement glimmered in her face again because his was now registering something at last – astonishment, or was it disapproval, at such unfeminine physical excess? 'Long, health-giving walks are something else the English are prone to,' she explained kindly.

Without waiting for an answering smile that probably wouldn't come, she set off briskly down the hill. For the moment her own loneliness was forgotten in thinking about the man she had just left. The failures he'd referred to had perhaps been his own, and she suspected that he knew even more about the coldness of being solitary than she knew herself.

Ottavio, elder son of the Marchese Buonaventura, stayed where he was to watch her go. He might have guessed that she would scorn the path and plunge directly down the hill through the rough, flower-starred grass. Florence had been a magnet to her countrywomen for a hundred years, and they had always behaved with the sort of independence he both admired but would have been shocked by in his own womenfolk.

He replaced his hat with a faint sigh and set off across the face of the hill, on a track leading eventually to a curving stone wall, and a wrought-iron gate set into it. He let himself into the lowest terrace of the garden and villa that belonged to his brother-in-law, Ernesto Lambertini. Above it, other terraces climbed upwards to the Villa dei Pini itself; they were laid out with mathematical precision, and even the wistaria and clematis blossom foaming over retaining walls seemed aware that it might be vigorous but not unduly rampant. The neatly pruned lemon trees in ancient terracotta pots, the trim dark edgings of box, and smoothly raked gravel paths, all spoke of their owner's thirst for perfection and also of the wealth that made it

35

possible. Ottavio compared it in his mind's eye with the garden at Castagnolo, climbing a different hillside to the south of Florence . . . no perfection there, only a green wilderness that would end one day by invading the house itself. He'd grown accustomed to the wildness . . . in fact, preferred it to Ernesto's determined attempt to subjugate nature. But there was nothing wrong with the house that his brother-in-law had bought as a ruin and gradually restored to its original eighteenth-century beauty. The amber-coloured stucco seemed to glow with the sunlight it absorbed and then released again, and shutters that were neither entirely grey nor green protected the tall graceful windows.

One of them facing on to the top terrace of all was open when he reached it. His sister, Anna, waited there, smiling as he went towards her. She looked what she was, the wife of a Roman banker who couldn't help but think her Florentine family hopelessly provincial; her elegance always made him conscious of his own shabbiness.

'Caro . . . you came to welcome us back too soon! Battistina said you'd arrived and disappeared again.'

He kissed her formally on both cheeks, and even smiled a little himself. 'I should have remembered that you would prefer to take the train with the children. It didn't matter; I went for a walk . . . it's health-giving, I'm told. You're here for the summer, I hope?'

'Yes . . . yes, I suppose so.' Unaware of having sounded forlorn, she turned away from him to pull dead petals off the mauve and white pansies massed in a stone urn.

'You're missing Ernesto, my dear. It always happens when you first leave Rome. After a week or two you'll feel at home again in Tuscany . . . *non è vero?*'

'I suppose so,' she said again. She hid her hands in the pockets of her jacket of cream linen and turned to smile at him. 'Who told you walking was good for you – not Mamma, surely? As far as I know, she has never taken an unnecessary step in her life.'

36

'Nor does she now. Nothing has changed at Castagnolo,' Ottavio confirmed. 'Father remains invisible in the tower, continuing *his* examination of the stars, while Mamma dabbles in her own strange brand of astrology. With Venus due to move into Taurus quite soon, or possibly the other way round, she is hopeful of some exciting event to relieve the tedium of her days. I'd prefer her to be wrong.' He heard the sombre note in his voice and smiled ruefully at his sister. 'In *our* chaotic affairs, excitement usually means disaster; I prefer tedium myself!'

'You still haven't answered my question,' Anna reminded him.

'If you remember our childhood you might have guessed the answer. I met a compatriot of dear Miss Addison. I retrieved a drawing for her that had blown away and in return she kindly recommended the beneficial effect of exercise, before setting off to stride all the way back to her luncheon in Florence!'

'I can picture her perfectly – indomitably English and incurably unfeminine!'

Ottavio considered this for a moment and then shook his head. 'You'd be wrong, as it happens – she was a slender, rather graceful lady. Her eyes smiled when she was amused, but they were full of tears when I first spoke to her.'

Anna stared at her brother. She was accustomed to his habit of observing other people – it was almost the only positive one he had; but where women were concerned he was usually too shy to take a close-up view.

'I expect she was feeling homesick. It's a thing one notices about the English. For all that they travel the earth so diligently, they're absurdly attached to their rainswept little island.'

He accepted this because it was well known to be true, and put away the memory of hazel eyes under an unbecoming hat-brim that Anna would certainly have despised as being unfeminine. There were more troubling subjects to be touched on quickly, so that they could be avoided afterwards.

'Fausto's still in Rome, I suppose, dancing attendance on the Duce. Do you and Ernesto see much of him?'

She wasn't misled by the politeness of the enquiry. It was Ottavio's way of dealing with the worst of their family ills. A wry joke could be wrung out of the Buonaventuras' chronic poverty, and even out of the oddities of their parents if the tragic incompatibility of their lives together could be ignored; but the quarrel between Ottavio and his brother was a sore that never ceased to bleed. There was nothing to be wrung from it but pain.

'Of course we see him,' Anna answered calmly. 'Apart from being part of the family, Fausto isn't the only Fascist we know.'

'I realize that. An influential banker like Ernesto is bound to collaborate with the people in power – they need each other. He can't fight the Fascists even if he'd prefer to.'

'He *doesn't* want to,' she insisted, pricked to sharpness. Ottavio's irony was all he would permit himself, but she knew what it concealed. One day the bitterness and anger that he kept hidden would explode, and the fragile façade of family unity would be shattered beyond her own or anyone else's ability to repair.

'Cara Anna, don't tell me Ernesto *likes* the men he has to deal with now?'

'Why not?' she suddenly flamed. 'Listen to me, Ottavio, and have the grace to admit for once that it is *you* who might be wrong. Consider the history of this country – its never-ending story of domination by foreigners because it's been incapable of ruling itself; its suffering in a war that yielded almost nothing; and the incompetence and corruption of every government that it's had since 1918. You may not like the way the Fascists have come to power, but admit that for the first time in centuries we are no longer despised by the rest of the world, and we are being governed effectively by *Italians*! Isn't that a great deal to be thankful for?'

'Yes, it is; but the price is too high, Anna. Benito Mussolini came to power by violence, stays there by *more* violence, while our constitutional freedoms are gradually taken away and we are left the slaves of an evil system.'

'You are still agonizing over the death of your friend, Matteotti, last year. It was tragic, of course, but . . .'

'. . . not his death, Anna, his *murder*,' Ottavio shouted suddenly. 'Giacomo was butchered and left to rot in a ditch because he was brave enough to denounce Fascism in the Chamber. What method of government is *that* to feel grateful for?'

She stared at him white faced, and her lips trembled, but she tried to speak calmly.

'There is always a price to pay for change; without it we should have had a revolution. Say what you like, Ottavio, the Duce has saved us from that.'

Ottavio heard in her voice the tremor of a woman who tried to convince herself as well as him. He was almost sure that she failed, because she knew the truth of what he said. But she was Ernesto's wife; her life was among the people who ran the country in Rome, and she must believe what her husband believed or be torn in two.

'My dear, forgive me,' he said in a different tone of voice. 'I came to welcome you back to Tuscany, not to quarrel over a state of affairs that, in any case, we can do nothing about.'

She accepted the peace-offering by kissing his cheek.

'*D'accordo, caro.* Now, shall I tell you how beautiful and perfect in every way *our* babies are, or would you rather I listened to you talking about *your* beautiful and perfect children?'

His faint smile reappeared, but he shook his head. 'Beautiful, perhaps; perfect, no. You'll discover no improvement in Marco, I'm afraid. He has the temper of the devil, and a fixed determination to get his own way.

Francesca is less fiery but quite as stubborn, so their relationship is stormy! The one person who seems able to restore harmony is their grandfather, but I suspect that's only because they feel sorry for someone who seems to them so immensely old and frail!'

'Not perfect, as you say, but at least they sound interesting! Tell Elena to bring them soon; better still, why don't both of you have a rest from storminess by leaving them here for a while? Marco will be bored with a baby like Emmanuele, but Francesca and Lorenza are near enough in age to make friends with each other; it's time they did.'

She didn't suggest bringing her own children to stay at Castagnolo, but Ottavio had no expectation that she would. Occasional duty visits to her mother during the summer would be as much as either of them could bear. The Marchesa Giulia disliked being reminded of past mistakes. She had been even *more* beautiful as a young woman than Anna . . . more spirited and much more entrancing; the old friends she now rarely saw still assured her that it was so. But at the age of eighteen she had been married to Giuseppe Buonaventura and condemned to a mouldering medieval castle, a neglected estate and a husband whose hands had preferred to caress his telescope instead of her. It was bad enough to look at Anna's elegance and rich contentment, unbearable to have to watch her with a successful man like Ernesto Lambertini.

'If you're serious about the childen coming here, Elena will be delighted. She's made friends with an American couple recently. They have been trying to persuade her to go with them on a Mediterranean cruise, but she hesitated about leaving the children.'

'Could you not both go?'

Ottavio's mouth twisted in something that wasn't quite a smile.

'The Harringtons wouldn't make the mistake of even inviting me – they don't see me as an entertaining addition to a party! In any case, I must stay at Castagnolo.' He collected the hat he'd deposited on the stone head of an unidentifiable Roman emperor, and kissed his sister good-bye. 'I should have said before that it's lovely to have you back. *Arrivederci, cara . . .*'

He ran down to the stables by different flights of steps from the ones he'd climbed up by, retrieved his horse from the loving care of a small boy who was the son of Anna's gardener, and rode slowly southwards towards his own home. The brief, sharp dispute about the Duce had been unpleasant, and he felt ashamed of having raised a subject that they had a tacit understanding not to discuss. But there were so many subjects it was becoming unsafe to discuss. He had very nearly given away how much he disliked the Americans his wife had made friends with. Anna might suppose that he resented them for their wealth, and hidden in his own mind was the shameful fear that she'd be right.

The horse ambled back to Castagnolo at its own pace, stopping to nibble at any greenery it fancied. Ottavio made no attempt to hurry it – useless, in any case, because it was as self-willed as his small son; but at the moment he found relief in being alone. He avoided his mother's feverish attempts to foretell the future for him, and always refused to believe that astral influences and conjunctions could make the slightest difference to their lives. All the same, some vague but persistent foreboding clung about him nowadays. It had something to do with the state of Italy, and disaster that he could do nothing to avert; but Castagnolo itself *was* his responsibility, and he couldn't shake off the knowledge that it was sliding further into ruin all the time. The memory of what he had found himself saying earlier that morning echoed in his mind: 'For fear of failing, we attempt nothing' . . . it was more true of him than of most Italians. He'd accepted failure as inevitable, something so ordained by Fate that he needn't even attempt to rescue his home, his family and his marriage to Elena. The truth, unswallowable as a live toad in his throat, was admitted at last: the Englishwoman was right – he hadn't tried hard enough.

The vestige of a wry smile touched his mouth; the signorina *inglese* might think the confession was a beginning, at least. He remembered the lop-sided sketch and her transparent disappointment at the accent that had given her away. Women, in his experience, dissembled as naturally as they breathed. This one had been different; her eyes under that monstrous hat had been direct and honest. He pictured her now in her pensione dining-room, surrounded by visitors like herself – dutifully inspecting dim, alien churches and eating alien food without enjoyment, until it was time to go home. But Anna had been wrong in supposing that the English signorina had simply been missing England. She wouldn't have wept just for homesickness. Ottavio knew almost nothing else about her but he was sure of that.

4

Marco was missing from the luncheon-table, as usual, when Ottavio finally walked into the dining-room himself. Elena, beautiful but bored, toyed with the food on her plate, scarcely pretending to listen to the Marchesa's petulant complaints about her grandchildren. It was a familiar story heard many times before, but without it they might have sat in total silence, having long since exhausted anything they had to say to one another.

'Your son should be made to eat luncheon *here*,' Donna Giulia said, turning her attack on Ottavio.

'Don't worry about him, Mamma. He's at home in every farmhouse on the estate, and I'm afraid he rates cold polenta and bread dipped in olive oil more highly than the food he would be offered here. I doubt if he'll come to much harm on what Lucia Scarelli gives him.'

Elena roused herself to join in the conversation. 'Your mother isn't concerned about Marco's health,' she pointed out sweetly. 'He might not learn to use the right knife and fork in a farmhouse kitchen.'

Probably not, Ottavio thought, but the boy would be made welcome there. He would even suffer the indignity of being hugged against Lucia's comfortable bosom, knowing that he could escape afterwards to a world of tangled woods and hills that seemed limitless to a small child. Marco knew that it was all his, because he was a Buonaventura, but he shared it gladly with the small wild creatures that also lived there. By comparison there was nothing *inside* his home to attract him except the topmost room of the tower, where his grandfather sometimes allowed him to peer through a telescope at a different magical world, and murmured to him the lovely names the stars went by.

'Time enough to learn about such things as table manners,' Ottavio suggested peaceably. 'He's only nine, after all.' As usual, trying to placate them, he had managed to irritate both women, but he tried again, offering a different topic of conversation. 'I rode over to see Anna this morning. She and the children arrived safely . . . she hopes you'll visit them soon; it's always the same when she first arrives – she hates being separated from Ernesto.'

'She could invite us to visit her in *Rome*,' the Marchesa complained. '*We* have to live in Tuscany all the time. I see no great pleasure in being able to stare at Florence from the north of the river for a change, instead of from the south.'

'Nor in being stared at pityingly by Anna,' Elena added, for once in temporary alliance with her mother-in-law. 'I suppose she was wearing clothes that came from Paris as usual?'

'My dear, how should I know! But whatever she wore, she'd look no more elegant than you always manage to do.' Ottavio's simple statement of what he regarded as a fact irritated his wife again, but she made an effort to reward him for the compliment with a brief smile. His strained face relaxed, released for a moment from the fear of never making her happy.

The Marchesa observed the shared glance, and felt confused by emotions that tugged her in different ways at once; regret and sadness and longing stirred sickeningly beneath the more familiar layers of boredom and resentment. She had wanted a lover who would look at her as Ottavio looked at Elena; she had deserved a husband who gave her the pleasures that Ernesto showered on Anna; instead, she was even deprived of the only one of her children who really understood her.

'It's time Fausto came,' she said desperately. 'He stays away because you quarrelled with him, Ottavio.' Her eyes that were still beautiful slowly filled with tears. It was the last, inevitable cruelty of her life that it should be the son she saw every day who was so entirely like his father. The sparkling gaiety and charm that belonged to *her* family, the Ruspolis, had all been given to Fausto.

'I will write today, Mamma, and beg him to come,' Ottavio promised her gently. 'Now, why not take a little stroll outside? The afternoon is beautifully warm, and I noticed that your special favourite – the *rosa damascena* – is just coming into bloom.'

His mother's tragic expression lightened immediately. Astrology helped to pass the time but roses were her passion; she loved them for their fragrance and knew their history. The only garden extravagance Ottavio allowed was the rare varieties that she discovered to be still available, and was permitted to order.

'Then of *course* I must inspect my darling . . . Pietro is sure to be neglecting it.' She redraped the floating chiffon scarves that now had to be used to conceal her plumpness, and got up from the table. On her way out to the terrace she delivered a parting shot to her daughter-in-law. 'Afterwards I shall expect Francesca in my room to be read to as usual. *Someone* has to begin her education, unless *she* is to be allowed to run wild with peasant children, too.'

Silence fell on her departure from the room, broken only by the sound of Elena's chair scraping on the marble floor as she, too, got up and walked to one of the long windows. She stood staring out over the terraced garden – neatly tended near the house, and shaded by the cypress trees that mercifully hid the wilderness it soon became. Ottavio couldn't see his wife's face but he knew how it would look – beautiful but remote, because she'd withdrawn again into some private world that she refused to allow him to share. She was filled with alluring warmth and life only when she was happy. He wanted more than anything else in life to make her happy, and he'd known from the first day and night of their marriage that he was going to fail.

He went to stand behind her and wrap his arms round her lovely body. She permitted the embrace . . . endured it, he thought with a flicker of pain.

'Tesoro . . . Anna suggested that the children should go to the villa and stay there for a while. I think it would be good for them, and it would mean that *you* could go with the Harringtons.'

He wanted her to turn round and smile at him, to say that a cruise with her American friends would be enjoyable but that he and Castagnolo were all that she really needed. For a humble man, it was a great deal to ask; he realized that, and anticipated her answer before it came.

'Perhaps I *will* go, then,' she said slowly. 'I don't think Howard and Verna mean to be away for very long but there'll be time for Anna to take the children's education and table manners in hand; that ought to make your mother a little less unhappy!'

'Dearest, she doesn't mean to sound so carping, and in any case she thinks I'm more to blame than you; just as she's convinced it's my fault, not Fausto's, that she never sees him.'

Elena's slender shoulders lifted in a shrug. 'It doesn't matter who's to blame . . . all that matters is that our lives are as they are.'

'And as *your* life is, you'll be glad to escape for a little while. Elena, my love, I'm sorry that I had to bring you here, but Castagnolo *has* to be our home, and the place where our children are brought up. There's nowhere else we could have gone to live by ourselves. Can you bear it more easily if I promise to try to make sure that you can sometimes enjoy a different life?'

She nodded, and suddenly hid her face against the thin tweed of his jacket. The pleading in his eyes hurt her, but it irritated her just as much. He was an altogether kinder, better, more gentle man than she deserved; she was well aware of that. But God and the Virgin Mary knew how much she required him to be *less* kind, less good and gentle.

She was a woman of flesh and blood and rousable desire; she wanted to be loved and used and even sometimes abused, if necessary, by a man who never made the mistake of putting her on a pedestal.

'My dear one, go with the Harringtons, but please don't stay away long; I do love you so.'

His hand under her chin forced her to look at him. She tried to smile, but her mouth trembled instead. For a moment he was almost convinced that she was about to say she wouldn't go away after all; but that wouldn't do . . . he must be strong and cheerful so that she could go and be carefree with her friends. His mouth touched hers, clung tenderly, and then released her, even though she knew by the trembling of his body against her own that he longed to make love to her. 'Dearest, you are to go; I insist on it.'

The matter was settled, and he was touched by un-expected happiness. He remembered what the English-woman had said, and he could suddenly see the power that was hidden in it. Achieving this small pleasure for Elena by insisting that she go was a new beginning. While she was away he would exert himself in other ways as well . . . and start by dragging his father away from con-templation of a distant universe for long enough to consider the decaying world of Castagnolo. His mother, the children, Fausto . . . surely they could all be dealt with if only he tried hard enough.

Jane's morning lessons were over but she remained in the library of the Institute. It was a cool, quiet retreat in which to ponder how to answer another tirade from St Peter's Square. Most of it, airing Aunt Alice's extreme displeasure with her niece, could be ignored, but not the question that it ended by asking: 'What, in Heaven's name, do you imagine you are going to do in a place almost entirely filled with noisy, excitable Italians, once the novelty of watching them has worn off?' Jane could smile at her aunt's opinion, made crystal clear, that Italy might be bearable if only it were *not* filled with Italians, but the question of what to do with herself needed answering. She couldn't hide in Florence for ever, attending language classes and visiting museums.

'Miss Rushton . . . I hoped I might find you still here.'

The pleasant, middle-aged woman she now knew as Gabriella Artom, secretary of the British Institute, had come to stand beside her. In the course of Jane's attendance there they had established a friendship, formal but pleasant, which they both enjoyed. Jane had several times been invited to the apartment which the signorina shared with her elderly mother. She was given English tea, but relished equally the old lady's vivid recollections of a time Aunt Alice would have approved of, when the villas of Fiesole and Bellosguardo had been filled with non-Italians.

'Am I interrupting an urgent piece of correspondence?' Miss Artom enquired.

'It isn't urgent.' Jane's fleeting smile suddenly routed the sadness from her face. 'In any case, I couldn't decide what to write! Why did you come to find me, signorina?'

'You spoke the other day of finding work in Florence. If you were serious, I have something to suggest to you. Would you consider teaching two small children – Italian children, not English? If so, I could arrange for you to meet their grandmother, with whom they live. I am not personally acquainted with the entire family, but the director of the Institute is. It would mean living a short distance outside Florence.'

Her shrewd eyes inspected Jane's face. 'You look doubtful, my friend. Perhaps the suggestion disappoints you. Did you hope for something more exciting, or is there a different difficulty? Perhaps your family would object?'

Jane thought of James Rushton's likely reaction to the news that his only daughter was considering the profession of governess. 'My family have probably washed their hands of me already,' she said calmly. 'I should like you to arrange the interview, please. It sounds quite exciting enough for someone who has never given a lesson in her life!'

Miss Artom was efficient; within two days of that conversation Jane found herself being driven out of Florence across the river in a south-easterly direction, along the road to Arezzo. The coachman who had come to collect her in an antiquated carriage turned round from time to time to smile encouragingly; otherwise the journey was a silent one until he flourished his whip at the skyline ahead of them. '*Montagne, signorina . . . Appennini,*' he roared with explanatory pride.

Before the road had begun to climb sharply he turned aside into a lane curving round the flank of an outlying foothill. It was marked by two stone pillars crowned with animals, worn by the weather past identifying, but the imposing gates that should have connected them were missing. The surrounding land was a tangle of scrub and woodland that grew wilder as the lane climbed. Saplings of oak and sweet-chestnut struggled through the under-growth of bramble and juniper until another crumbling wall broken by another empty gateway led into a different and more or less cultivated landscape; now, wavering lines of overgrown vines straggled across the south-facing hill-sides. Clusters of small, pale-green fruit already promised some kind of harvest, but even to Jane's ignorant eyes, the land looked neglected, weed choked, and sad.

The drive climbed up terraced levels and ended finally on a sloping ramp of gravel. Above her, walls of golden-brown stone reared up like cliffs. The castle – she could find no lesser word in her mind to describe its towered, castellated grandeur – rested on a spur of rocky hillside, held by retaining walls which she hoped were as solid as they looked. But this was by no means sure. Everything except the gardens immediately outside the iron-grilled windows bore the same dispirited air of neglect. She was glad to escape from the heat and stuffiness of the carriage,

49

but shivered because the castle tower blotted out the sun. It seemed an ominous welcome. Not the splendour of the castle's position on its spur of rock flying out over the valley, not even the distant view of Florence encircled by fold on fold of blue and purple hills, could persuade her that *this* was a place where she might live happily.

Inside the immense doorway a dim, frescoed hall felt deathly cold after the hot sunlight outside. Her heels sounded noisy on the stone floor, and she felt altogether too modern and alien for surroundings that seemed to require ladies in gold-meshed wimples and ermine-sleeved gowns. A mournful-looking manservant took her in tow, but she stopped involuntarily at the sight of a small, dark-haired child watching them from an open doorway. He was surely one of the children she was supposed to be capable of teaching, but at once she doubted the possibility of it. Studied defiance spoke from every inch of his thin body, and his expression offered her an adult mixture of hostility and derision; she thought he matched the alien spirit of the place completely. A smile that should have reassured her, but didn't, flitted across his dark face, and then he suddenly turned and disappeared – not in the puff of smoke she half-expected by now, but just as unnervingly.

It seemed craven to beg the servant in front of her to go no further, but she was almost framing the request in her mind when he knocked at a half-open door and ushered her inside. The room was lit by tall, lancet windows and seemed marginally less depressing than anything else she'd seen so far, but instead of being cheered by it her eyes were riveted on the man who got up to greet her. She had seen him before, on a sunlit hillside above Fiesole. He looked just as serious now as he had then, and he either failed to recognize her or preferred not to refer to their earlier meeting.

'Miss Rushton . . . my mother sends you her apologies;

50

unfortunately she is indisposed. My name is Ottavio Buonaventura.'

Jane found it hard to begin by announcing that there was no need for an interview at all, and said instead, 'Perhaps I should talk to the Signora Buonaventura in that case.'

'My wife is away on a brief holiday. There remains only my father for you to see as an alternative to me, but he rests during the day – the consequence of studying the heavens at night.'

For a moment she was tempted to imagine that his grave face concealed amusement; then, deciding that it didn't, reckoned that his wife deserved a holiday from a man who never smiled.

'There are the children themselves, of course,' she pointed out, 'but I must be honest at once, and apologize for wasting your time in coming here. Even if you were kind enough to approve of *me*, I'm afraid I should not be able to stay here. I have never taught children before, and I now realize that it was absurd to imagine that I should be able to start with yours.'

It was the best she could do, short of saying that Castagnolo's isolation and decaying grandeur oppressed her, and that if his other child was anything like the one she had first seen, she would do well to admit defeat immediately.

'You seem to have changed your mind very quickly, Miss Rushton.'

'I know, and I apologize for having to come here before understanding my mistake. It is my fault entirely; but it would be worse for your children if I started and then was found unsuitable.'

She hoped she sounded adequately apologetic, but firm as well; apparently so, because he gave a little sigh of acceptance.

'Very well; there is no more to be said, except that I am sorry. You were recommended very warmly by my friends at the British Institute.' He glanced at her unhappy face and looked away again. 'I'm quite often there, using the library, if you should happen to change your mind. Meanwhile, the driver shall take you back to Florence . . . unless you insist on walking again *this* time!'

'Th – thank you; I believe I'll settle for the drive,' she muttered, confused by the discovery that he had recognized her after all. His answering smile confirmed that she had misjudged his age considerably, but not his kindness; he even handed her back to the waiting servant without reminding her of the rest of their earlier conversation.

'I hope you will soon find just the person you need for your children,' she said earnestly.

'I hope so, too; goodbye, Miss Rushton.'

There was no sign now of the child who had watched her arrive; in fact no other sign of human life at all. Somewhere – in the tower, presumably – an old man sat up at night and watched the stars, but she was unable to imagine women there making any impression of grace on the starkness of the castle, or children's laughter penetrating its massive walls. She would leave thankfully on her own account, but with a stab of pity for the people who were obliged to live there.

There was the respite of Sunday before she need confront Gabriella Artom again; but when she was ready to leave for the Institute the following morning a man's tall figure detached itself from the shadows in the hallway and stood in front of her.

'Good morning, Jane . . . what a good thing I took the precaution of calling early!' said William Rushton.

She had forgotten the true golden brightness of his hair, the English fairness of his face and the grace of his upright body. Her heart missed its normal beat, then raced on again, leaving her short of breath. She couldn't stand staring at him for ever, but it was hard to take in the fact that he was there at all, harder still to stifle the hope that it might mean the end of her exile.

'I . . . I didn't expect you,' she said hoarsely at last. 'When you didn't write, I thought there was nothing to be said.'

'Of *course* there are things to be said, but not *here*. Isn't there *one* civilized room where we can talk?'

'This is a Florentine pensione, William, not the Ritz Hotel, but perhaps you'll accept the garden instead.' She turned back to the staircase, not waiting to explain that the garden would be found on the roof of the building. It would incense him still more, and she could recognize the signs of anger in his face already.

The roof garden was her favourite place in the pensione, not only for the blossom and greenery that spilled out of flowerpots and tubs of every size, but also for its bird's-eye view of Florence. She could look down on the patterns made by a myriad of pantiled roofs and watch the changing-coloured ribbon of the river threading its way through the city.

William regarded a neighbour's washing-line with distaste and then stared at Jane.

'It's time to end this nonsense, you know. I've humoured you to the extent of coming to take you home; now it's your turn. Be sensible, my dear, and settle your affairs here – we ought to be able to catch the night train to Paris easily.'

Her expression changed and he had the clear impression that she had put more distance between them than the small space allowed. There was another impression as well, that he hadn't time to analyse, but it had to do with the fact that she looked younger than he remembered . . . more attractive even. An apologetic smile wiped ill-temper from his face – he was suddenly the charming William she recognized.

'Jane, forgive me – I didn't mean to bark at you like Uncle James in his favourite rôle of head of Rushton's!

This place doesn't agree with me as much as it does you, but we can certainly wait until tomorrow, if you prefer.'

'I don't know that I shall be ready to leave then, either.'

She saw his face darken again, but he strove with himself to sound reasonable.

'Janey . . . hasn't this little show of independence lasted long enough? I was under the impression that I'd left you in London happily planning our wedding. If you were upset at being left behind, you should have said so. Will you forgive me if I promise to insist that our journeys include you in future?'

'Will they continue to include Laura?' she asked gravely.

He knew her well enough to realize that the question hadn't been asked at random. A trace of colour touched his cheekbones, but he managed a careless smile. 'She went this time because your father was concerned about David's health – you *knew* that.'

'It's what I thought I knew,' she agreed. If he said honestly that he'd been ensnared, that he'd been a fool but it was over . . . if he'd said anything but what he did say, she might have gone downstairs and got ready to leave Italy.

'My dear girl, this is absurd. I *might* find a little jealousy on your part flattering, but surely it's unkindly misplaced about Laura? You can't possibly suspect Johnny's widow . . . your own sister-in-law. Really, I'm more hurt for *her* than I am for myself.'

He protested too much; she knew it because he always had when he was in the wrong. His handsome face was flushed and she had the cold certainty that he lied – just as he would always lie to her about other women, and tell himself that a plain wife must expect to be betrayed.

'William – my letter meant what it said,' she murmured after a long pause. 'I'm sorry you've had this long journey for nothing, but I'm not going home.'

He walked towards her, still confident that resistance would crumble as soon as he touched her. He'd been a fool not to kiss her at once. His hands gripped her shoulders, warm and hard through the stuff of her jacket, but she jerked her face away from his mouth, steeling the nerves in her body not to weaken. He was suddenly angry enough to force her to surrender, but he knew her too well – she would never forgive him.

'Something happened while I was away – Lionel, or perhaps my dear sister Eliza, put a spoke in my wheel. Jane, you *can't* have been fool enough to believe them.'

The difficulty was that she *had* believed them, unfair as it was when she'd disliked them as much as she loved him.

'They merely reminded me of what I'd known all along – that our engagement was a mistake,' she explained carefully.

Their marriage was to have been very useful; but apart from losing its practical advantages he was enraged by her cool dismissal. She had no right to have recovered from the years of loving him; it was the most serious change of all, but there were others that irritated him because they seemed to separate her from the past. Her jacket and pleated skirt were a becoming pale green against skin warmly tanned by the sun; her hair was shorn of its unflattering bun and framed her thin, brown face attractively. She looked composed when she should have been distrait, and he wanted to hurt her.

'What happens if you reject a last chance of marriage? Do you plan to stay here, eking out a genteel inheritance by giving a few English lessons . . . growing old and lonely . . .'

'. . . becoming one of Trollope's "strong-minded, migratory old maids"? I think there might be worse fates,' she said unconcernedly, 'but in fact a job has been offered me. If my father is at all concerned to know, you can tell him that I'm about to become that much-prized thing here, an English governess!'

'Tell him yourself, my dear Jane, but I'll give you a word

of advice – don't go crawling back to Vine House if your new profession doesn't work out; he won't forgive you.'

She stared at his flushed face, wondering why it had ever delighted her. He was vain and greedy and unkind, and her regret at losing him had been her worst stupidity of all.

'Thank you, I'll remember,' she said finally. 'Now, perhaps you'll find your own way out. I should like to stay up here.'

She didn't watch him go, but listened to the sound of his steps on the stairs, fast and furious and gradually fading into silence. He left blankness behind. Nothing remained of the life she had known except a fragile link with Charlie. There was nothing to look forward to except the need to make good her boast to William. Ottavio Buonaventura might have changed his mind about accepting her; if not, she was going to Castagnolo after all.

5

Dottore Moroni was desolated; his best pupil, so punctual as a rule, making such excellent progress, had this morning failed to appear.

'I have been too stern with the Signorina Rushton, perhaps, but when an English lady for once possesses such a true "ear" . . .' His voice trailed sadly away, and Miss Artom attempted to cheer him. A slight indisposition on his student's part, a touch of sunstroke, or the stomach disorder to which all foreign visitors fell victim sooner or later. She was warming to this theme when the missing one walked in – pale but, God be praised, Dottore Moroni murmured, at least capable of moving.

Jane apologized to her teacher, received his earnest congratulations on her return to health and smiled at her friend when he had finally bowed himself away.

'It seemed unkind,' she told Gabriella Artom, 'to insist that nothing more dramatic than an unexpected visitor from England delayed me this morning!'

Miss Artom judged from Jane's pallor that the visit had been dramatic enough. It was a severe temptation to enquire, but she must remember that the English were reticent. 'Not bad news, I trust?' was all she allowed herself to say.

Jane shook her head, and the secretary didn't persist. 'Tell me about your visit to Castagnolo,' she suggested instead. 'Did you see the Marchesa?'

'She was unwell, but I met her son.' Jane hesitated a moment, then added, 'He mentioned that he often comes here, if I should want to get in touch with him.'

'He consults our archives of nineteenth-century

Anglo-Florentines. The subject fascinates him even more than it does my mother – I believe he is even writing a history of it. Do you *wish* to get in touch with him?'

'Yes, please.' Miss Artom's curiosity was painful to behold but Jane could only smile and promise to be punctual for her lesson in future.

For a week afterwards she lived in a vacuum that was strange but not unpleasant. The direction of her life seemed to have been taken out of her own hands, and sooner or later she would know what Fate intended for her – perhaps that grim castle on its hill, but if not, she was oddly certain of one thing; she wouldn't be going back to Vine House again.

Then, one afternoon, she left the Institute as usual and walked back home beside a river now shrunk to summer size by lack of rain. The fisherman she always saw was in his usual place, forever hopeful and forever unrewarded, as far as she knew, by even the smallest fish. The view that she stopped to look at was familiar now; in time perhaps it would obliterate completely the memory of a different river, steel-grey under rain and silver when sunlight danced on it. William would be back there by now, and the whole family would know that plain, prim Jane Rushton had taken leave of her senses for good and all.

'Good afternoon, signorina.'

She recognized the quiet voice beside her and turned to see Ottavio Buonaventura standing there. Was Fate about to show its hand at last, or was he there by chance? She didn't know.

'You are fascinated by our mighty river?' he enquired.

Her face lit with the amusement he remembered. 'Do you know what an American, Mark Twain, said about it? "They honestly think it is a river, do these dark and bloody Florentines. They even help out the delusion by building bridges over it . . . I do not see why they are too good to wade!" There's more, but I've forgotten it.'

'It's enough to demolish the Arno in summer, but

perhaps your American never saw it in November, flooded by rain from the mountains.' He frowned at the fisherman on the bank below them, then spoke again. 'Miss Artom said that I might overtake you here – you wished to see me, I believe.'

Jane stared up at the cloudless sky, wondering if she imagined the sound of the gods laughing at the lunatic choices mortals made. Mistake or not, she couldn't change her mind again now. 'I'm still not sure that I can teach your children, but I should like to try.' His face looked so blank that she felt obliged to make it easier for him to reject her. 'It's too late, I expect; you've already found someone else.'

'I've found no-one.' In the road behind them two motorcars began an argument with horns, and instead of looking blank he was now harassed and unhappy. 'This is scarcely the place . . . but I don't quite know . . .'

He sounded so like Charlie at home, that by sheer force of habit she took charge.

'It will be more peaceful in the Boboli Gardens – shall we walk there?'

He fell into step beside her, noticed the books she carried, took them away from her with a muttered, '*Permette signorina*,' but said nothing more until they were inside the gardens. Jane selected a stone seat near the entrance to the cypress walk and sat down waiting for him to find something to say. He seemed in no hurry to begin, and she stared pensively at the statue in front of her – an ample lady somewhat oddly crowned with a pile of grapes. Memory played odd tricks in what it retained and mislaid. Jane thought she would remember the lady with her festoon of grapes long after the rest of this crucial interview had been forgotten.

'Miss Rushton, I think I should begin by telling you about the Buonaventuras,' he muttered finally. 'We possess an ancient name, an ancient castle and much of the land between Florence and Arezzo. That sounds impressive, does it not? But the castle is medieval and uncomfortable, the land is comparatively worthless, and the Buonaventuras are too poor to do anything to improve either.'

He stared miserably at Jane and she realized that she was expected to say something.

'*Not* so impressive,' she agreed cautiously. 'Is that the end of the story?'

'By no means. My father has found his own escape – into the tower, to study the stars. My mother comforts herself with her own peculiar brand of astrology. My children prefer to spend *their* time in the farmhouses on the estate.' His mouth twisted in a bitter smile. 'I forgot my brother, Fausto. Unlike us, he *prospers* in Rome – but only in the depraved cause of Fascism.'

He hadn't mentioned his wife, Jane couldn't help but notice, whose own escape was presumably to take holidays that didn't include her husband. Well, it wasn't too late, even now. She would explain how clear it was that his chaotic household didn't need an alien spinster steeped in Protestant, middle-class ideas . . . she could say she was homesick for England . . . say anything but what, a moment later, she heard herself announce with lunatic clarity.

'Not being a trained governess, I'm not very expensive; I should think you could afford *me*.'

He stared at her face beneath its sensible straw boater – hazel eyes under strongly marked brows, unremarkable nose, mouth unremarkable too until she smiled, and determined chin. He knew almost nothing about her, but just as a drowning man might suddenly feel solid ground beneath his feet, he was aware of no longer being swept further and further out into a sea of misery that threatened to overwhelm him.

'I thought you wouldn't come . . . I thought I'd frightened you away,' he said finally.

Jane remembered the small boy who had watched her arrival at the castle.

'Your children frighten me,' she said after a moment. 'Perhaps we'd better agree on a trial visit.'

She said goodbye to the staff at the pensione and to her teacher at the Institute who shyly presented her with a farewell gift of three perfect yellow roses.

'For effort!' Jane explained, surprised when her employer called himself to drive her to Castagnolo and stared at the flowers she hadn't wanted to leave behind. 'Dottore Moroni realized how hard I was trying; that was more important than all the things I failed to learn. Even so, I'm afraid your English puts my Italian to shame.'

'We had what I wanted for my own children – an English governess and friend. She died just before the war, and is buried in the Protestant cemetery. Perhaps you've been there to visit the grave of Elizabeth Barrett Browning?'

'Yes . . . I talked to an old lady who told me it is covered with wild anemones in spring. She even remembers being taken to the Casa Guidi as a small child . . . it's hard to believe that Italy still wasn't completely unified when the Brownings were here.'

'Your frail poetess was a passionate supporter of the Risorgimento – it's one of the reasons why she and the other Anglo-Florentines of that time are still remembered with gratitude here.'

There were subjects they could have discussed more usefully, Jane thought, but if he preferred to hide behind his favourite hobby horse she couldn't force him to talk about his family instead.

'You mentioned Fascism the other day, not proudly, much to my surprise. In England it's believed that Signor Mussolini has achieved a great deal for Italy. Is yours the aristocratic view . . . that the son of a blacksmith isn't a fit person to govern the country?'

'Most of the aristocrats and the industrialists and the bankers here agree with the English view. Mine is the view of an Italian who longs to see the end of violence and corruption. We still have both under the Fascists, and if you're about to tell me that these are simply the growing-pains of a new system, I shall insist that violence is like the appetite your Shakespeare spoke of – it grows with what it feeds upon.'

His voice remained quiet but she heard in it the echo of his sadness.

'But your brother doesn't think so?' she commented after a moment.

'Fausto believes what the Duce proclaims – that Benito Mussolini is the incarnation of God and all the Caesars combined in one heroic man; that he has come to save Italy from itself.'

'Perhaps it's just as well your brother lives in Rome.'

'Not from my mother's point of view, I'm afraid, or from my son's; they both adore Fausto. Even knowing that he always does precisely what he wants, my mother prefers to believe that he doesn't come to Castagnolo because I keep him away.'

Ottavio glanced at his companion's thoughtful expression and almost smiled. 'Is it any comfort if I mention one *normal* member of the family? My sister, Anna, is married and also lives in Rome, but she comes back to spend the summers in Tuscany. You will meet her soon.'

Jane murmured a polite response and turned her attention to the countryside. They were already inside the Buonaventura domain, driving through the vine-scattered hillsides.

'You said the land was mostly worthless,' she remembered suddenly. 'Can't something be done about it?'

'Nothing my father is interested in doing or that we can afford. Apart from those drawbacks, there is the mezzadria system itself – traditional in Tuscany. The landowner provides the capital for livestock, seed, tools, and receives half the value of what is produced. The peasants receive the other half, but no wage, and live rent-free in the houses the landowner provides. The old men are content with the system, but the young men are not; the tradition is breaking down, and with it a whole way of life, not to mention the prosperity of all concerned.'

Jane opened her mouth to protest, and closed it again. Gentle and courteous the man beside her might be, but she had been put firmly in her place about his anti-Fascism. It was a reminder of what she was there to be – the children's governess, not their father's inquisitor. The castle loomed up in front of them and, when they went inside, felt just as chillingly vast and old as on her first visit. She would have preferred to be left to come to terms with it alone, but she was instructed to follow Buonaventura when he had spoken to a servant hovering in the hall.

'My mother is waiting upstairs; I'll take you to meet her.'

They climbed beautiful, shallow stairs to the *piano nobile* on the floor above, and Jane began to understand that no single age had made the castle; centuries of changing styles and swings in family fortunes all had contributed their alterations to the original medieval stronghold. When she was shown into the *salone*, it was like seeing an old lion decked out in circus trappings. The frescoed walls and vaulted ceilings were now the incongruous setting for the spindle-legged, gilded furniture of the French Empire. Blinds filtered the afternoon glare to a green, underwater light by which she made out not one but two women sitting there.

'Mamma, may I present Miss Rushton to you? Signorina . . . the Marchesa Buonaventura, and also my sister, Signora Lambertini.'

Jane smiled with relief at the younger woman – praise Heaven the 'normal' one was already there – but she advanced first to clasp the Marchesa's hand. She thought she understood the large and languid lady to murmur in Italian, 'Modern . . . how strange that anyone should prefer them.'

63

Anna Lambertini smiled pleasantly and gestured to the posy Jane had forgotten she still clutched.

'My mother likes old-fashioned roses, Miss Rushton. We are very glad to see you here . . . are we not, Mamma?'

'It depends,' the Marchesa said fretfully. 'When is your birthday, signorina?'

'January 17th.'

'Capricorn! How *very* unfortunate . . . not at all compatible, I'm afraid.'

It appeared to be the extent of her interest in the conversation. She rearranged several of the pieces of chiffon in which she was draped, and relapsed into silence; but from her unhappy glances at the newcomer Jane suspected that she was still brooding on the disastrous possibilities of importing into the household someone born in January.

Anna Lambertini covered the silence well enough until Ottavio asked where the children were.

'Out, as usual,' the Marchesa bestirred herself to reply.

'Mamma, I particularly asked for them to be *here*.' Ottavio sounded, for once, almost stern.

'But you forgot to particularly suggest how your son might be kept indoors when he felt inclined to go out. Was I to chain him to his bed?'

Anna hurried into the conversation. 'I'm afraid it was my fault, Ottavio. Marco couldn't be expected to play with two seven-year-olds and a baby. *They* are on the lower terrace with Nurse.' She looked at Jane's face and smiled faintly. 'Might this not be a good time to take Miss Rushton on a brief tour without them?'

It seemed to Jane the most sensible comment she had heard so far. Her heart warmed all the more to Ottavio's elegant sister when it became clear that Signora Lambertini herself intended to act as guide.

'If we don't reappear in an hour you'll know I've forgotten my way about,' she said cheerfully. 'It's a long time since I've lived here.'

'Some of us are less fortunate – we *still* live here,' her mother observed acidly. Her eyes reproached Ottavio for some miracle he had failed to provide; then, aware of having made an impression on the Englishwoman, she suddenly smiled enchantingly at Jane. 'I don't expect *you'll* like it here, either – everyone runs away in time.'

Jane abandoned the search for something to say and thankfully followed Anna Lambertini out of the room.

'Castagnolo isn't nearly as dreadful as my mother likes to pretend,' the signora said, trying to beat out whatever sparks of terror had been ignited in the bosom of the new governess. Jane Rushton *looked* sensible and she *was* of calm English stock, but there were still hurdles to come – Marco, for example.

'Well, it's on a rather larger scale than anything I'm used to,' said Jane.

'But not as large as it seems from the outside. Look . . . on this side of the corridor you can see what I mean – it's a hollow square. Not an ideal arrangement nowadays, but think how convenient when your enemies were laying waste the countryside. Everyone took shelter here, and their livestock were simply herded inside the courtyard as well!'

'What could have been more cosy?' Jane agreed faintly. Then they both smiled at the ridiculous word, and liking was born between them.

A quarter of an hour later they had reached the arcaded top of the castle, roofed over in the Tuscan way, but not completely enclosed. By making a circuit of the covered walk, they could survey the entire countryside – Florence lying in the river valley and, beyond it, the Apuan Alps white with marble instead of snow. To the north and south softer hills faded into blue distances, while eastwards the castle tower looked out on the wooded foothills of the main Apennine range. All around them near at hand lay the lovely Tuscan landscape of olive and vine, still worked by hand because the steep slopes defied machinery.

'It's very beautiful,' Jane said eventually. 'Even the farmhouses look as if they had grown there, along with the olive trees and the cypresses.' She turned to glance at her companion's thoughtful expression and selected from the questions that puzzled her the one that seemed least likely to give offence. 'Your brother spoke about Buonaventura land . . . he called it worthless, but it looks so richly fertile. If the system doesn't work now, can't it be changed?'

'The land isn't worthless if it's properly worked. Ernesto, my husband, would tell you that all it needs is a *padrone* interested enough to supervise what his tenant-farmers are doing, and forceful enough to support a *fattore* – agent, I think you would call him – whose socialist-minded peasants want to strike instead of work.'

'The Marchese is *not* interested, I gather.'

'Not in the least and, with no encouragement from anyone else, nor is my brother. Marco *does* show signs of being passionately fond of his inheritance, but by the time it's his, it will probably be too late.'

Jane thought of the child who had watched her with such adult composure. Given the family he lived among, it was scarcely fair to expect him to be like any other child of nine years old. 'I get the impression,' she said cautiously, 'that he's accustomed to doing as he pleases.'

'We *all* are! It's our problem in a nutshell, Miss Rushton. If you realize that, you will understand why my poor family is in such a muddle.'

Jane thought of the two Buonaventuras who didn't seem to be talked about. She could think of no acceptable way of enquiring about the woman who seemed to be content to leave husband and children to muddle along without her while she cruised the Mediterranean; but surely it was permissible to ask about the other child she was supposed to teach?

'Is Francesca like her brother – as independent and . . . wild?'

'Not wild at all.' Anna Lambertini smiled at the relief on Jane's face, and regretfully dispelled it. 'But I'm bound to say that she's not quite what you might expect! You'll discover that for yourself before long. Now, shall we retrace our steps and go downstairs?'

'Yes, as long as you don't tell me that I must be longing to meet my charges.'

Anna's vivid face broke into a smile. 'Don't give up without a struggle.'

'I can't. Your mother would say that's the trouble with Capricornians – they haven't the sense to know when they are beaten!'

6

'Francesca . . . come and look. Old Margherita's spell didn't work on a foreigner. The Englishwoman is here, walking on the terrace.'

Francesca looked, as instructed. 'She is not beautiful like Mamma.'

'No-one is beautiful like Mamma,' Marco insisted fiercely. It was true, but why did their mother not understand that nowhere else could be as perfect as Castagnolo and come home? She had been away before, but never for as long as this. The worry couldn't be shared – Francesca was too young, and his father always seemed to be too busy with his books and papers to be disturbed. Marco often wondered about the books and papers; they seemed to have nothing to do with Castagnolo, whereas the things that he knew *were* important, because the *fattore* told him so, were not attended to. He knew that too, because Gino Scarelli always looked worried nowadays.

Now, on top of everything else, there was this new *governante* come to disturb them still more. Others had arrived, and left again soon enough, but they hadn't been English. He remembered what Zio Fausto had said about the *Inglesi* – obstinate, arrogant people who despised everyone else, but especially the Italians, because they had no empire.

'I shall go down and speak to her,' Marco said definitely. 'You stay here, but when you meet her remember *not* to smile or say the English words Papa has taught you.'

'Why not? She'll think we are stupid.'

'Then she'll get tired of us and go away all the sooner. But I shall frighten her as well, to make sure.'

He smiled at the idea and ran out of the room, leaving his sister to station herself by the window. She had perfect faith in *him*, though none in old Margherita, whose spells were for the *contadini* to believe in. It would be no surprise to see the *signorina inglese* run away, as a German Fraülein had done when Marco offered his hand and released into hers a shiny black beetle with antennae longer than itself.

But nothing so pleasantly dramatic was happening this time, and the tall, thin woman who wasn't beautiful seemed more interested in Nonna's roses than in the boy who had appeared beside her on the terrace.

Marco launched his campaign with deceptive affability and a bow that would have done credit to a Spanish grandee.

'*Buon giorno, signorina. Io sono Marco Buonaventura. Il mio nonno è padrone di tutto che Lei puo vedere.*' His arm swept the horizon, indicating ownership as far as the eye could see. '*Il nostro castello è bellissimo, non è vero?*'

Jane turned to stare at the massive pile which overshadowed them, having to take on trust the early-morning sun that must be rising somewhere behind it. It was grim, grand and starkly impressive, but *not* in her view remotely *bellissimo*. She looked at the child, aware that his bright dark eyes watched her intently; he would be offended whether she lied or spoke the truth, and she decided on the lesser evil.

'Castagnolo is your home; it's beautiful to *you*. I am not accustomed to living in castles.'

Marco's black brows drew together in a frown. The Englishwoman understood and spoke Italian, and he was aware that it put him at a disadvantage. There was nothing to be gained by speaking *her* barbaric language less well than she seemed able to speak his. While he considered what to say next Jane seized the chance to grasp another nettle.

'I saw you when I came here once before, but not to speak to . . . I expect you were too busy to say hello.'

His eyes gleamed with something she couldn't identify; this one wasn't like the others at all, and it made the battle more enjoyable.

'I am always busy,' he said deliberately, 'too busy catching scorpions and snakes on the hillsides to sit in the schoolroom listening to English lessons. We have many of these dangerous creatures, and spiders also, of course, that bite!'

His hand crept out, then swept downwards on the stone wall, imprisoning something. Smiling with pleasure, he held it out and, not knowing what to expect – bite, sting or sudden death – she was obliged to accept it on her own hand. There was a moment in which to see the pulse beating in the lizard's throat and recognize it as being more frightened than she was herself before she replaced it on the wall again and it disappeared in a flash of brilliant green. If he next introduced her to some small charming viper caught on the hillsides he was so proud of, she had no idea what she would do. He would clearly want her to faint or go into hysterics, and she must do her best to disappoint him, but compared with David at home, she found him an unpleasant child – arrogant and unkind.

'Do you not want to learn *English*, or not want to learn anything at all?' she enquired at last. 'Perhaps you prefer to remain ignorant like the children of the *contadini* who, poor things, have no choice in the matter.'

'I am *not* ignorant – I can read and write and know many things already. I can learn *anything* if I decide I want to.' He flung the words at her as one who delivered a clincher.

She smiled faintly, realizing that her only hope was his Buonaventura pride; it might force him to prove to her how capable of all things he was. 'But in case you fail with English, you prefer not to try. Very well; perhaps your small sister will feel more brave.'

His dark face was now flushed with rage, and the unhappy certainty that his uncle had been right. The

English were far from being as other people were. He would discover in time how to deal with this one, but if he didn't appear in the schoolroom she would call him a coward.

Jane watched his hands clench into tight fists at his sides, and suddenly felt her dislike melt into pity. He was a child still, and his muddled upbringing had left him so far with too much knowledge, and too little of the security that came with discipline. He almost certainly knew that his inheritance was crumbling to pieces and that a bitter gulf divided his father from the uncle he adored.

'Marco . . . there are things I can teach *you*, and many things that you can teach *me* – about Castagnolo and all this lovely land of Tuscany. Shall we . . .' she struggled to remember the words in Italian, '. . . strike a bargain and agree to help each other?'

The angry colour had faded from his sun-browned skin but he stared at her inimically. 'The English are not to be trusted – my uncle says so.' Then, without waiting to hear what she might say, he leapt down the stone steps to the lower terrace level and disappeared.

Jane bent down to smell the scent of a glorious crimson rose just unfurling in front of her – one of the Marchesa's preferred old-fashioned varieties, no doubt. It was humiliating to discover that her hands were trembling, perhaps with rage at her own stupidity in being trapped at Castagnolo. Her first instinct to escape had been right, but she was there because of her own face-saving boast to William that she had a job to go to.

'Miss Rushton . . . you are up early.' Anna Lambertini had come to one of the open windows to smile at her. 'The children are given their breakfast upstairs. Shall we join them?'

She glanced at Jane's face as they began to climb the stairs together. 'I doubt if you slept well. It is usually so the first night, when you wake and cannot even remember where you are.'

71

The night had seemed endless in a cavernous, gloomy room in which she would probably freeze to death if she was still there when winter came; but the evening that preceded it had been worse. The Buonaventuras might be poor, but their meals were long and elaborately served by white-gloved servants. The children were absent, being given supper in their own quarters, but a frail, silver-haired man had joined them and been introduced to Jane as the Marchese. His stately courtesy had embalmed them all in his own formality, and only Anna had persisted with a conversation that kept threatening to die. When she returned to her own home presumably the family would sit in silence.

'I met Marco this morning,' Jane said abruptly to her now. 'Does he *not* eat breakfast, or do *anything* that a normal child might do?'

'He and Francesca used to visit their mother for breakfast, I believe. It started as a game and became a habit.' Anna Lambertini hesitated, then went on. 'Would it help to remember that Marco misses her all the more because he longs for her to love him and is never quite sure that she does?'

They reached the wide corridor leading to the nursery wing in silence, and she turned to smile encouragingly again at her companion. 'Castagnolo stairs are punishing, but you'll get used to them.'

'I wasn't silent for lack of breath,' Jane confessed finally. It was too soon to admit the truth – that it would be easy to hate a woman who left her children so bereft. Instead she said, 'Now let me discover Francesca's opinion of the English – I already know what Marco and Zio Fausto think of them!'

The nursery where the two small girls sat eating breakfast was unexpectedly cheerful. Morning sunlight slanted through the open windows, and Lorenza – a small edition of her elegant, black-haired mother – was chuckling over something her cousin had just said.

She held out her arms lovingly at the sight of her mother and saw no reason not to smile as well at the other woman who came in. Beside her sat a child with long, straight, brown hair and remarkable eyes – Francesca Buonaventura, who had stopped smiling and now frowned at the plate in front of her. Her brother's instructions had been clear and in general she obeyed him. Zia Anna looked displeased with her but she sat where she was, briefly hating Lorenza for getting down from her chair to go and welcome the newcomer.

Lorenza didn't know why her cousin was refusing to play this pleasant game of making grown-ups happy; it was nicer to have them smile approvingly than not, but if Francesca wouldn't join in, she didn't mind performing alone.

Jane sipped the coffee the nursery maid had brought, and pretended to swallow a roll that tasted of ashes in her mouth, while Francesca silently struggled with a problem of her own. Marco had failed to explain what she should do if the new *governante* spoke to her in Italian. Even at the age of seven, she resented seeming dumb and stupid while Lorenza chattered happily beside her.

Jane watched her sullen little face and finally plunged with the courage born of desperation.

'I don't know my way about the gardens yet, Francesca. Will you show me?'

'I can't – I have to go with my grandmother to church.' In her relief at remembering it was Sunday, she almost smiled, then scowled instead – the picture of a child so determinedly unresponsive as to break the heart of even the most dedicated governess.

'Perhaps *after* mass, then,' Jane suggested quietly, and wondered what to do with the piece of bread in her mouth that now refused to be swallowed at all. When breakfast was over she hid in her own room until pride, and dislike of its cold gloominess, drove her downstairs and out on to the terrace again. She had no idea which members of the household had gone to pray for the good of their everlasting souls but even if every other human being on the estate had disappeared she couldn't have felt more desperately alone. The roses twining themselves over the balustrade in front of her were the very scent of a summer's day at home, but she was in an alien place whose people rejected her. She closed her eyes to shut out a view that would be beautiful but not the one she needed to see; she wanted clouds and soft rain, not the hard blue monotony of an Italian sky. Loneliness was a physical pain that left her disinclined to do anything but weep.

'You were so deep in unhappy thoughts of your own that you didn't here me come,' said Ottavio Buonaventura, suddenly beside her. 'Shall I tactfully walk away, or remind you that I saw your eyes full of tears once before – the first time we met?'

'You make it sound like a habit,' she said resentfully. 'It must be the deplorable effect Italy has on Anglo-Saxons.'

He smiled because she scrubbed at her cheeks like a small boy ashamed to have been caught weeping, but spoke with his usual gravity. 'As long as it's not the effect my home and family have on you . . . please don't make up your mind already that you can't be happy here.'

Her mouth trembled in its attempt to smile. 'Tactful, signore, but shouldn't we face the fact that it scarcely matters *how* I feel? Marco has made it clear that he isn't going to accept me, and Francesca is equally determined to copy him.' Real amusement briefly lit her eyes at the memory of the Marchesa. 'That doesn't take into account your poor mother who finds my starsign incompatible!'

'Nor my father, who has almost forgotten that normal human beings focus on one another occasionally, instead of on distant planets. At least admit that you have seen enough by now to know that we need help, Miss Rushton.'

His brown eyes pleaded for her to agree and his gentle mouth beneath its neatly clipped moustache drooped with the certainty that she was going to say she knew but didn't care.

'Even so, I can't drag Marco into the schoolroom and lasso him to his desk, any more than I can teach Francesca something *she* refuses to hear. You would have done better to find anyone but me – why are your children so determined not to like the English?'

'They don't *know* the English,' he pointed out, 'but if you stay they will have the chance to know *you*.'

It was, she realized with another twinge of wry amusement, much the same tactic she had used on Marco – only cowards ran away. She stared resolutely at the view and remembered something else. 'Your son is very proud of Castagnolo.'

'And you think that I am not . . . that I spend my time in Florence delving into history while Castagnolo slowly falls to pieces here? I'm afraid you don't understand our hopeless, Italian way of life.'

Pleading had suddenly disappeared; the note of faintly outraged hauteur in his voice could have sounded louder, but not more clear. Jane objected to it less than the feeble frame of mind that *accepted* everything, even hopelessness. She was irritated enough to forget that what happened to this impossible family was nothing to do with her.

'I remember what you said about the system, but it surely needn't be clung to until ruin closes over your heads? I'm also capable of understanding what I've *seen* – that even the steepest, stoniest hillsides here are made beautiful and productive by the man who loves them enough to work them properly.' Her hand lifted in a gesture that took in the weed-choked vines and unpruned olive trees below them. 'If Marco is anything to go by, the Buonaventuras have their fair share of pride in what they own . . . but to someone like me, who doesn't understand the Italian way, it seems that they haven't loved it enough.'

She heard the words fall into a silence complete except for the tolling of a church bell, invisible but unexpectedly close at hand. It was late to remember what she was supposed to be – the newly imported governess to a family that had built the castle when Cosimo de Medici was first ruling Florence. She waited for him to remind her of the fact, but either even that effort was too much or he couldn't bring himself to punish her with the snub she deserved.

'You could point out that I'm not here to concern myself with your inheritance, but with your children,' she suggested hopefully.

A faint, reluctant grin tugged at his mouth. 'You aren't required to do that on Sundays, surely . . . your day of rest? In any case they are attending mass with their grandmother and my sister.' Invincible courtesy would ignore her lapse, apparently, and she, too, was expected to pretend that what they were enjoying was a trivial conversation.

'Our chapel also acts as the parish church,' he explained politely. 'You can't see it, or the village of Castagnolo, from here – both are tucked into the other side of the hill – but when you feel the need to escape from my family, there *are* other people not far away. She blushed faintly to have her thoughts read so accurately, and acknowledged to herself that *his* way of putting her in her place was the most effective he could have chosen after all.

'Marco is disinclined to welcome discipline, Miss Rushton, but like the rest of us he must learn to endure what he cannot change. Would you prefer *me* to make that clear to him?'

The note of irony in his voice stung like iodine on an open wound, and she made a private vow not to underrate him in future.

'I would rather you left it to me,' she answered slowly. 'If I can't manage the children on my own, the sooner you find someone else who can, the better.'

He gave a little bow and walked away, leaving her to recollect that cutting off her nose to spite her face was fast becoming a habit with her.

76

Lunch, at which for once everyone but the Marchese appeared, passed off more or less normally. Jane was conscious of Marco's measuring stare whenever she glanced in his direction, and depressed by the knowledge that if he had chosen silence as his weapon against her, it would be the most difficult one to counter.

Even the children, it seemed, were accustomed to rest during the afternoon heat of midsummer. Jane obeyed the Marchesa's instruction and went to her room, but it offered no welcome and its shadowy gloom oppressed her. After a fruitless half-hour spent considering whether the furniture could be arranged more comfortably, she picked up her straw hat and crept downstairs again.

The unshaded flagstones of the terrace burned through her shoes, and the view she hadn't wanted to see earlier in the day was now lost in a shimmering white haze. The cypresses at the far end of the terrace were not living trees at all, but dark-green shapes pasted on the livid-blue stuff of the sky. Nothing moved in a world that seemed wrapped in incandescent heat.

Below the Marchesa's rosebeds another flight of crumbling steps led down to a still-lower level of the hillside. Its wildly neglected tangle of trees and shrubs offered a sanctuary from the burning glare outside and she picked her way thankfully under the tunnel of greenness. Overgrown paths still outlined what had once been a formal garden and led her finally to its heart.

Trailing shoots of ivy and bramble climbed over the stone curb of the pool, but she could see that it had once been beautiful. There was only a stagnant layer of weed left now, but in the centre remained something magical – the small bronze figure of a boy astride a dolphin. The long-ago artist had made of them friends and playmates, and the child was laughing; but what he laughed at was no longer there.– the silver drops of water that should have fallen from the creature's mouth into the pool.

At last she roused herself from a daydream of what the

secret garden had once been like, went slowly back up the steps again and braced herself for the onslaught of the sun on the open terraces above. Walking willingly for the first time into the cool dimness of the hall, she realized that there was something to be said, after all, for the thickness of the castle walls and the smallness of its windows. While the rest of the long afternoon dragged past, she sat in her room considering what she would do if the children appeared in the schoolroom the following morning . . . wondering still more what she would do if they did not. At last, with her mind made up, she stripped off her clothes, poured water from the ewer into her washstand bowl and finally dressed again in fresh clothes. She had thought of somewhere to go until it was time to endure the pre-dinner wait in the *salone* – worse tonight because Anna Lambertini would have returned to Fiesole by now.

High up on the ramparts of the castle a breeze brought coolness and the scents of juniper and wild herbs gathered from the hot countryside during the day. Now, she could see what she had missed before – the real life of Castagnolo that was lived outside its overpowering stronghold. Old stone farmhouses were scattered over the hillsides, each with its sentinel clump of cypresses or ilex trees. On the north side of the arcade she walked round she could look down on the tiled dome of the church and the village clustered just below it. Normal life existed there, and normal people, like the servants she could see sitting in the inner courtyard of the castle, laughing and talking together. There was nothing wrong with Castagnolo after all, only with the people to whom it had belonged for too many hopeless centuries.

Pat with the thought came the unexpected squeak of a door opening just behind her. It led from the top storey of the tower, and the Marchese himself now appeared with the uncanny timing of the Demon King in pantomime.

'Good evening, Miss Rushton. You came in search of a breeze, I expect.'

'Yes, but I hope I didn't trespass in coming?'

'My dear signorina, of course not.' The gesture of his thin hands seemed to disclaim the idea, but she felt sure that this airy, rooftop level of his home was one he expected to enjoy alone. He was altogether the most solitary man she had ever met, but if *he* didn't need the rest of the human race, his wife surely did. Jane thought of the poor, plump, dissatisfied woman downstairs and decided that his evening appearance at the Marchesa's dinner-table wasn't a sufficient contribution to matrimonial life.

'You find our heat trying, no doubt, after England,' he said politely. 'It is a question of accustoming oneself.'

'Not only to the climate, Signor Marchese, but to much else that is strange in another country.'

'Of course. Why else come to Italy if it should turn out to be a replica of England? But *that*, you are about to assure me, it is *not*! So small but confident is England . . . so powerful and so rich; not like Italy at all.'

They ran true, the Buonaventuras. The hostility might be courteously veiled in the Marchese's case, but it had been handed on intact to Fausto and, by him, to Marco. It must have been Ottavio's one small rebellion in life to ignore the prejudices of his family and bring her here. She could walk away and leave the *padrone* unchallenged on his lonely rampart, or round off an unpleasant day by wading into battle again. Charles Rushton would have said, knowing his sister, that there wasn't any doubt about what her choice would be.

'I've heard it said here that *we* dragged Italy into the war, signore. We are also blamed because the cost turned out to be unexpectedly terrible and the rewards not very high. Well, the price to us was terrible too, but we paid it in order to honour commitments that seemed inescapable. *Your* politicians took Italy into a war its people didn't want, it seems to me, for nothing more than the advantages they could squeeze out of it.'

If she'd expected to rouse him to anger, he disappointed her and offered a sad smile instead. 'I know how it seems, Miss Rushton, and I know all about our politicians in Rome . . . corrupt, incompetent men who kept each other in power for years in a travesty of parliamentary government. They have been displaced now, and we narrowly avoided instead the revolution that Ottavio's Communist friends longed to involve us in; but the price for *that* escape is that our last state is likely to become worse than our first. I am a Tuscan . . . too old to become one of Il Duce's new Italians. I prefer to stay up here gazing at a world too far away for us to spoil.'

'You are fortunate to have the choice,' she pointed out drily. 'Not many people can.'

'One of the few rewards of rank,' he agreed. 'Perhaps your own father enjoys them in England, where I believe such things are not quite unknown?'

Whatever effect he'd anticipated in his turn, it wasn't the luminous smile that suddenly transformed Jane's face. 'Dear sir, my father's only connection with our aristocracy is to sell them fine French wine! He despises *them* for their decadence, and the working-class for *their* stupidity. He's confident that the middle-class to which he proudly belongs is England's greatest asset!'

Someone down below in the courtyard looked up as the rare and extraordinary sound of the Marchese's laughter floated on the evening air.

'I shall hope to make his acquaintance one day. Most definitely you must invite him here, Miss Rushton.'

'Perhaps, sir, when we know whether I am to stay myself! The arrangement with your son is not confirmed.'

Sober again, the Marchese stared at her intently. 'Let me tell you something. When Ottavio told me that he had invited an Englishwoman here I told him that she would leave again even more quickly than her predecessors. Now, I see a chance that he was right after all – I am inclined to think that the contest with my grandchildren is at least equal.'

Not certain whether she was cast for the rôle of lion or gladiator, Jane could only hope that he was right. 'You don't offer, as your son did, to give me a little help?'

'Certainly not . . . that would be unfair!' He consulted his watch and gave a little sigh of regret. 'Time to descend, I fear . . . what a pity when it is so agreeable up here. I've no help to give you, Miss Rushton, but I wish you well tomorrow.'

She smiled and walked back the way she had come, leaving him to descend in his own way . . . perhaps by broomstick, since nothing about the castle and its inmates would now surprise her.

Nevertheless she *was* surprised the following morning. Walking into the schoolroom after breakfast, outwardly calm but with a heart thumping in her breast and the certainty of failure almost accepted, she found her pupils already there. They looked anything but friendly or eager for a lesson but, thanks be to God and all the saints, at least they were *there*.

7

Charlie sat at his attic window and stared out at a grey, wet world – sky, river and the persistent drizzle joining the two together seemed to consist of a single watery element. Somewhere there might be warmth and sunlight – in Tuscany, for sure – but not in the Thames Valley at the tag-end of this inglorious summer. The prospect inside his home was no more cheerful. He was certain that Laura felt confident enough, now, to announce her intention of marrying William. James had done his best to keep her from wanting to remarry at all, but she wanted William. Charlie could imagine her explaining sweetly that a Rushton son-in-law would mean the minimum of disturbance to the family circle. William would simply exchange St Peter's Square for Chiswick Mall, and David would remain where James wanted him to be – under his own eye.

It seemed to Charlie that no-one but himself now thought about Jane. As long as their own lives were neatly rearranged, it didn't matter that *she* might need something from them . . . might long to be persuaded back into the shelter of her home. But with Laura married to William, she would never come back and he himself would probably be forced to quit Vine House. He was thinking how loth he would be to leave it, when the attic door was pushed open and his nephew walked into the room.

'Can I come in, Nunk?' David asked the question with the politeness his grandfather insisted upon, but with the courtesy went a certainty inherited from his mother that no-one would refuse him anything.

'Bored with the holidays?' Charlie enquired. 'Wondering how to pass the endless weeks until term starts again?'

David's thin face broke into a grin. He had Laura's white skin and auburn hair, but in feature and long, slender build he was – to James's great contentment – entirely Rushton. 'Nothing wrong with the holidays, only the weather. I hate boring, beastly rain.' He glanced idly at a loose sheet of paper on his uncle's table, then looked at it again.

'Those aren't yours, are they? What weird-looking animals.'

'Not weird at all; in fact in Italy they're rather famous.'

'Did the pictures come from Aunt Jane?'

'Yes, although she didn't draw them. They were produced by a friend of hers I've yet to meet. Let me introduce you to the white oxen of Tuscany, as seen by Miss Francesca Buonaventura! For a lady of going on seven, the drawings are really rather good.'

'I still don't see why you've got them here.'

'Well, that was your aunt's idea – an exchange of artistic effort! I'm bound to say Francesca's rendering of Castagnolo was more interesting than anything I could produce for her of Vine House, but she does have the advantage of living in a castle.'

David still frowned over the oxen. 'Whoever saw animals with tassels on their noses?'

'It's not everyday wear. These splendid creatures are dressed for an occasion – bringing in the grape harvest.'

'Haven't the Italians heard of tractors? No wonder Grandpa says they're stupid people who don't know how to make decent wine. Cousin William doesn't think much of them, either – apparently they're rotten at soldiering as well.'

That disposed of the Italians. Charlie was still fond of his nephew, but there were times when he wondered for how much longer that would be true. Humility, tolerance and artistic appreciation were virtues a boy was unlikely to learn from the Rushton family.

'Before you damn all Italians, remember this,' Charlie suggested gently. 'They've produced *most* of the world's sublime artists – painters, sculptors, architects, musicians; and even if they're not natural fighters, they did get the hang of soldiering sufficiently to best the Austrians in the end.' Seeing the look of mulish obstinacy on David's face, he decided to drive the lesson home. 'Tractors are all very well, but machinery, however efficient, tends to roll down very steep hillsides; oxen don't.'

After a thoughtful silence David tried another tack. 'I wish Aunt Jane would come home. Castles are all very well, but do you suppose she really wants to stay in Italy?'

A charming smile suddenly lit his uncle's face. 'I don't know, but thank you for making me realize that it's time I went and found out!'

Later in the day, when his decision had been aired downstairs, he ignored his father's comment that he didn't do enough work to need a holiday, and sat down to write to Jane. Her prompt reply sent him to St Peter's Square in search of help. Alexandra stared in astonishment at the list he showed her.

'I thought it was supposed to be *Italy* she'd gone to – the land of sunshine and blue skies and improbably handsome young men serenading their ladies all night long with passionate love songs.'

'Neapolitans, you're thinking of,' Charlie said firmly. 'Janey's castle is in the foothills of the Apennines, dear heart, and when it was constructed five hundred years ago they built for security, not comfort. It's lovely at the moment, but she'll freeze to death in winter.'

'Nonsense, she survived a childhood in Vine House; Italy can't be worse.'

Charlie's smile conceded the point. 'All right, but will you come and find the things Jane wants? I can manage the books, but the clothes she asks for defeat me.'

Alexandra nodded and rubbed the tip of her beautiful straight nose – a sign, Eliza would have said, that she was engaged in thought. 'Better still, as well as hunt out the clothes I'll help you deliver them!' She saw the look of horror on his face in case she might be serious, and in the same moment the notion that had only just crossed her mind became the one thing in the world that could offer her salvation.

'Charlie dear, *don't* say no . . . you wouldn't if you knew how I *pine* to escape from this house. Between Mama's good works and Eliza's ghastly causes I shall suffocate to death or marry some well-born nincompoop in sheer desperation.'

Her face was suddenly full of such urgent pleading that he couldn't laugh at her or pretend to believe she wasn't serious. *He* would be serious himself about wanting to escape from Eliza Rushton and his aunt's monument of bad taste in St Peter's Square. All the same, sweet reason must be tried.

'Alex *dear*, we're not still living under Victoria and Albert the Good. Women aren't obliged to sit at home any more, sewing nightshirts for the poor and waiting for some eligible man to marry them.'

Her huge blue eyes reproached him for failing to understand. If she began to weep he would be lost and, since there was no justice in things, Aunt Alice would certainly blame *him*.

'Charlie, I could be a shopgirl or factory hand if I wasn't Alex Rushton; I could be a nurse or teacher if I didn't faint at the sight of blood and dislike runny-nosed children; I could be almost anything in this emancipated age if I had a modicum of brain, but the truth is that I'm *fatally* stupid! It's the only thing my brothers agree about, so that rather proves it, don't you think?'

With her eyes drenched in tears she put both her hands on Charlie's chest in a gesture of desperate pleading.

'Let me go with you. Mama won't make a fuss if I'm with you, and at least I shall have seen *something* before I have to come back here.'

Charlie accepted defeat, but made the best terms he could. 'All right, but I'm going to check up on Jane, and to get some painting done; *you* can look at things worth seeing if you like, provided you promise to stay out of mischief. No scrapes and no adventures, Alex.'

She smiled ravishingly at him and kissed his cheek. 'Not a single one, darling; cross my heart!'

Florence, which they reached a fortnight later, basked in the gentle heat of early September; Charlie had felt sure it would be beautiful, but the wash of golden light enriching every colour took his breath away. The palette he used at home wouldn't do for Tuscany, not by any means.

At breakfast, the morning after their arrival, Alexandra smiled kindly at him. 'Try as you will not to gaze out of the window, you're dying to make a start! Why don't you? I can amuse myself looking at the jewellers' shops along the Ponte Vecchio.'

'*Exactly* what your father would most dislike to hear! I'm sure it's my duty to keep you away from temptation, but it seems hardly fair when I have the feeling that this is going to be a sinful place for both of us.' He was still surprised by the discovery that his beautiful cousin wasn't nearly the nuisance he had feared – in fact he was rather enjoying the company of a girl he had tended to avoid at home.

'In any case, there won't be time this morning for anything but a stroll to the Duomo and back. We've come to see Jane, and her note said that she'd be here at lunchtime.'

They waited for her an hour or two later, both expecting to see the girl who had left London three months earlier; both, for different reasons, were taken unawares when she walked into the lobby of their hotel, smiling with the pleasure of seeing them.

'You've had your hair cut short,' Alexandra observed, pouncing on the most obvious change. 'I never thought you would.'

'I never thought I'd spend the summer in Tuscany –

it gets very hot here,' Jane explained apologetically.

'It suits you, and you've got alluringly tanned, coz! Thank God someone's persuaded you to stop wearing beige at last. You're looking different altogether.'

'Credit where credit is due – thank Francesca. She demanded to know one morning why I always looked so *"triste"*. We established eventually that it was the colour of my dresses she objected to; so now I'm obliged to be quite gaudy!'

Charlie watched his sister's expressive, brown face and registered different changes.

'You're not obliged to be *enjoying* a governess's life, but something tells me you now are! What happened, Janey? Your first letters sounded so depressed that I expected you to throw the job in straight away, or throw yourself in the Arno.'

'I think pride must have come to our rescue – mine, and Marco's. We both refused to give in and let the other win. He's too intelligent not to enjoy learning, so for as long as I can hold his interest, learn he does, instead of running away to roam the countryside.'

Alexandra looked appalled. 'It sounds like a battle-ground, not a schoolroom.'

'Well, yes . . . but I was warned about that!' Jane smiled at the memory of her first long conversation with the Marchese, and it suddenly occurred to Charlie that the word his cousin had applied to her was no longer out of place. She would never have Alexandra's faultless beauty, and her charm had been too elusive to be noticed at Vine House, where Laura spun a web of sensual appeal to trap men in. But Italy had changed her, and he had a sudden sad certainty that he would never persuade her to go back to England.

'The castle sounded frightful, too,' Alexandra put in, 'just the place to find headless ghosts flitting about the battlements; no wonder the Buonaventuras all sound mad or melancholic.'

'Not *all* of them,' Jane objected, 'but I'm hoping you'll want to come and see them for yourself.' She delved into her handbag and produced a crested envelope addressed to her cousin. 'It's an invitation from the Marchesa – she got quite animated when she discovered that you shared her birth-sign. Did you know it's a particularly dangerous time for Librans at the moment? Venus is opposing Pluto!'

Alexandra read the brief message couched in the Marchesa's rather stately English and turned to Charlie a face sparkling with excitement. 'I and the esteemed brother of the Signorina Jane are invited for a long weekend. Of course we want to come – I can't wait to meet the Marchesa.'

When lunch was over Alexandra disappeared to compose a letter of acceptance. Charlie, left alone with his sister, smiled shyly at her.

'It's lovely to see you, Janey. I expect you're wondering how I came to be travelling with Alex?'

'I can guess – she implored you to help her escape from St Peter's Square! I don't suppose anything has changed there, or at Vine House.'

He toyed with the empty coffee cup in front of him, choosing words with care.

'Things *are* about to change, and if you don't come back soon, it will be too late, because Laura will marry William. I don't know how you feel about *him* now, but you will lose your rightful place at home as well.'

'I've been losing it for years,' she pointed out quietly. 'Laura doesn't share, she takes.'

'Pride didn't come to your rescue with *her*?'

Jane's brows drew together in a frown of anger against herself. 'I'm ashamed to say I got demoralized, slowly but surely. I was even craven enough in the end to accept William, although I *knew* in my heart what he was going to marry me for – Rushton's and my inheritance from Mama. I can't imagine, now, how I became so spineless! It wasn't until he came here that I saw him clearly for the first time – exposed in this merciless Italian light. For years I'd loved a man who didn't exist at all.'

Charlie grinned at the disgust in her voice, but refused to be side-tracked. 'You're happy at Castagnolo because you feel needed there. What happens in a few years' time – another family to help, even though you might find them less appealing than the Buonaventuras?'

'Perhaps, although my long-term plan is to entice *you* out here to live with me. Think of it, Charlie – we could rent a floor of some old palazzo for next to nothing, and enjoy a happily eccentric old age together; no Rushton dinner-parties, no need to make useful friendships and unnecessary amounts of money!'

'Sounds all right,' he conceded, 'in fact, it sounds like the kingdom of Heaven to me – something to cling to this winter in my foggy cubby-hole next to London Bridge. I got the books you wanted, by the way, and I've been glancing through them . . . why the sudden concern with how wine is made? I thought you weren't interested in Rushton's.'

'I wasn't, but I am now.' His puzzled expression made her smile. 'Wait till you come to Castagnolo – then you'll see for yourself. There's a lot I don't understand yet, but I mean to understand it before I'm done; otherwise Marco will be left with nothing but a derelict inheritance.'

Charlie recognized signs familiar since childhood – Janey on the warpath.

'God help the Buonaventuras,' he murmured piously. 'The poor deluded creatures must have seen you at a weak moment and thought they were taking in a timid spinster thankful to be given houseroom and a pittance.'

'I shan't do them any harm,' she protested, trying not to laugh. 'In fact, *all* my intentions are good.'

'Then I should certainly warn them!' He grinned at the thought, but suddenly grew sober again. 'Perhaps I should warn *you*. Isn't it an occupational hazard to be guarded against – getting too involved with your charges?'

'I *am* involved already, because they're all so muddled and unhappy. It isn't just the estate, Charlie, although that's heartbreaking enough; it's the people themselves. By the traditions of this country, they ought to be loving and close-knit. Instead of that they all swim about in isolated pools of misery. We have to *try* to do something about them.'

'*We?*' he enquired nervously, and was rewarded by his sister's luminous smile.

'I think I may need your help,' she said serenely, as Alexandra reappeared with her note for the Marchesa.

They were driven to Castagnolo three days later and Charlie's whimpers of protest at being dragged away from Florence died as they approached the golden-brown hulk of the castle, left stranded on its hilltop by the receding tides of history.

'Janey forgot to mention that it's gloriously beautiful,' he muttered.

'Now, *yes*; but think of it in midwinter with night falling and a howling wind blowing off the Apennines.' Alexandra shivered at the vision her imagination had conjured up. 'Do you suppose there's a bathroom or lavatory hidden in this pile of masonry, or do we tip-toe out into the night when necessary?'

She tried to smile when he looked at her, but her mouth quivered, and he was astonished to see that her eyes were full of fear.

'Dear girl, we've come for a long weekend, not eternity; and although they *do* live in a medieval fortress, the Marchese and his family are civilized, twentieth-century Italians who even have the grace to speak English! There's nothing to be nervous about.'

Alexandra nodded, but her next remark seemed to have strangely little to do with the rest of the conversation. 'I remember telling Jane ages ago that I was in a hurry to taste life – funny that *she* should be responsible for bringing me here.'

There was no time to enquire what she meant. Jane and a solemn, brown-haired child were waiting for them on the steps leading up to the huge door. Charlie advanced smilingly to meet his fellow-artist, and Alex followed, explaining to herself that the first sight of the castle had made her fanciful. He was right to laugh at her. She would leave after a few days and soon forget that she had ever been to Castagnolo at all.

By mid-afternoon she had relaxed sufficiently to enjoy herself. The children disconcerted her with their measuring stare, but they transferred their attention to Charlie – who didn't seem to mind them at all – and she could keep her end up easily with gentle Ottavio and his charming, plumply indolent mother who seemed delighted to welcome a fellow-Libran.

After luncheon, when Charlie accepted Marco's invitation to *'andare via per le colline'*, Ottavio surprised his son by suggesting that they should all go together. Only the Marchesa had an objection; the complexion of the signorina was too fair and delicate for such long exposure to the sun; she would be safer left to make a gentle inspection of the roses, now in their last flush of glory.

Alexandra perambulated up and down at the stately pace set by the Marchesa, but smilingly declined the siesta which her hostess next recommended.

'So beneficial, my dear, to health and beauty,' the Marchesa assured her earnestly. 'Besides, what else is one to do until it is time to dress for dinner?'

'I should like to explore a little, Donna Giulia. My home is in London in a street crammed with large, ugly houses as like each other as peas in a pod.' Her hand gestured to her surroundings – 'Oleanders and lemon trees in the shade of a castle tower! I must enjoy them while I can.'

'*Poverina*,' said the Marchesa unexpectedly. 'Beauty and a free spirit are the gifts we Librans are cursed with. I should not have been trapped here, and you should not

91

be forced to live in an ugly house in London. Life arranges itself very wrongly.'

She spoke with such sad regret that Alexandra wanted to agree with her, but a Protestant conscience couldn't accept quite so sweeping a denial of all responsibility.

'Perhaps it is *we* who get things in a muddle, Marchesa, by making the wrong choices,' she suggested gently.

Donna Giulia's plump shoulders lifted in a shrug. 'No, my dear – it is the pattern woven for us . . . we can do nothing about that.' She sighed heavily, waved one of the floating scarves in a little gesture of farewell and went to her beneficial siesta.

Alex watched her go, half-convinced in spite of herself that there was something in what her hostess had said. She wondered whether the woman who absented herself from Ottavio was another free spirit, with a less resigned attitude to the pattern laid down for her than most wives allowed themselves.

It was pleasant and peaceful wandering about the terraces built into the hillside, but everywhere she could see signs of neglect in gardens that had once been beautiful. She found her way back to the upper level again and recognized the long open windows of the *salone* by which the Marchesa had led her outside. Deep in the un-accustomed business of thought, she didn't notice the man who stood at one of the windows, watching her cross the terrace. He saw a slender girl in a dress of cornflower-blue linen that matched the colour of her eyes; her bright cap of hair gleamed in the sunlight and her face was beautiful. He thought she was the most unlikely governess he would ever see in his life.

'*La governante dei bambini, mi sembra – la signorina Rushton, non è vero? Io sono Fausto Buonaventura.*'

Alexandra halted some distance away from him, blaming the many steps she had just climbed for the fact that her heart was thumping uncomfortably. She distinguished no single feature in that first, dazzled glance – only the rich soft colour of his voice and the quality he possessed of being vibrantly alive.

'Miss Rushton,' she murmured breathlessly, 'but not my cousin Jane, who understands Italian, as I must rely on *you* to understand English. *She* is the children's governess. Her brother Charles and I brought the clothes and books she needed from England, and the Marchesa was kind enough to invite us here.'

'So . . . Miss Rushton proposes to make a long stay, and the English are here in strength – had I known that . . .'

The sentence faded away but his meaning was clear and Alex finished it for him. '. . . you would have postponed your visit; presumably *not* – ' her eyes wandered over the massive pile behind him – 'for fear that there wouldn't be room for you.' She was recovering now, determined not to be intimidated by his hostility.

He found *her* altogether too confident, beauty adding its gloss to the infuriating certainty of knowing herself English and therefore immune to the idiocies of other people. He was tempted to say that he hadn't expected his mother to fill her home with the relatives of the governess; but the words, though true, struck him just in time as being offensive to someone who was there as an invited guest.

'I came to see my brother, but chose the wrong moment if he is occupied with visitors,' Fausto explained with stiff courtesy. 'I hope Castagnolo pleases you, signorina.'

'It overpowers me, as a matter of fact. Jane says that its proportions aren't favourable to people, and now I know what she means – we are made to feel insignificant.'

'Proportions in this case are related to past function,' he said coolly. 'Perhaps neither of you is intimately acquainted with living in an ancient building like this one.'

'There is that,' she conceded. 'We haven't needed strongholds in London for quite a long time.'

His dark eyes searched her face for signs that she was privately amused; her mouth was suspiciously demure, and his glance couldn't help but linger on it . . . such a beautiful mouth in such a lovely face – but she was English and, damn her, she *was* laughing at him.

'My mother is still resting, no doubt, but why are you alone?'

'Your nephew is leading the others on an expedition through the vineyards; the Marchesa and I inspected the roses and then she retired.' Alex hesitated, reluctant to make concessions to a man who seemed determined to be hostile. 'She is a very kind and charming lady.'

'Who doesn't normally exert herself with visitors,' he said, surprised into honesty. 'She's more likely just to go to sleep!'

'Perhaps I'm privileged because I share her sign. We have a free spirit in common,' Alex explained gravely.

'So confidences were exchanged over the roses. You learned that my mother is bored and lonely, that my father neglects her as well as the estate, and that my brother and I normally avoid each other like the plague. We are, in effect, one happy family.'

The bitter words, made worse by the conversational tone in which they were delivered, fell into the silence of the golden afternoon. It was the strangest conversation she had ever shared with someone just met for the first time, but to her own surprise she wasn't angered by the bitterness he seemed to want to direct at herself. Without knowing why her usual stupidity was not a bar to understanding in his case, she was certain that Fausto Buonaventura was not by nature a harsh, embittered man.

'I didn't learn any of *those* things from the Marchesa,' she said with a little air of dignity, 'but I *can* now tell the difference between a *rosa gallica* and *rosa polyantha*, and I even know what *that* is called in Italian.' She pointed to the wild rose that foamed over the balustrade in a cloud of pink blossom. 'The "rosa di ogni mese" may not be as showy as its cultivated cousins, but I find it even more appealing, and its name is beautiful – a "rose for every month". It's a sort of promise that there will always be loveliness if we know where to look for it.'

She blushed for the unwise confession to a man who would probably think her mad or boringly naïve, and waited for him to find an excuse to walk away from her. Instead he put out his hand in a sudden imperative gesture and she found herself putting her own into it.

'May we begin again, and forget that I have said things for which I should apologize?'

For the first time she saw him smiling – his eyes were bright with shamefaced laughter, and his mouth had lost its sneer and become gentle instead; but she was only dimly aware of these things. Her hand was still held in his and it seemed so certain of belonging there that she had to pull it away sharply and hide it in the pocket of her skirt so that he shouldn't see it trembling.

'Signorina, allow me to present to you Fausto Buona-ventura. He has always been known for his readiness to dislike the English, but he is now reluctantly about to admit that he may *sometimes* be in error!'

'I'm Alex . . . Alexandra Rushton,' she said breathlessly, 'who is *happy* to admit that she's wholeheartedly in love with Italy.'

His smile faded and he stared at her intently instead, as if seeking the answer to a question he hadn't put into words.

'*Zio Fausto . . . caro zio, eccoci.*' Marco, leading his expedition home, had caught sight of them from the terrace below, and his joyous shout broke the tension that held them locked in stillness. Alexandra silently commanded her legs to move from the spot on which they seemed rooted, and turned to see Ottavio, Jane and Charlie climbing the steps towards her. It seemed a long while since she had parted company with them, and a long journey she had made into some strange country on her own.

At any other time Jane might have noticed the strange expression on her cousin's face, but she was occupied in watching Ottavio. She realized that she'd been hoping for a little miracle; but the times were out of joint for miracles. Il Duce might have done a great deal for Italy, but he was also responsible for what she saw now – two men, who should only have remembered they were brothers, staring at each other like enemies.

8

The Marchesa looked happier that evening than Jane had ever seen her. Dressed in silver-grey satin and slung about with several ropes of remarkable pearls, she smiled at her guests and, especially, at Fausto. It was easy to see in her now the beautiful young woman Giuseppe Buonaventura had brought to Castagnolo thirty-five years earlier. The Marchese's pleasure in the company wasn't made so obvious; he'd lost the habit of frivolous conversation with a young woman, but he looked appreciatively at Alexandra and enjoyed engaging his other guest in a discussion on seventeenth-century metaphysical poetry. Jane had no opportunity to see how Charlie was faring in this contest; she was occupied herself in parrying Ernesto Lambertini's sly assault on the English political system. Anna's husband had arrived in Tuscany for a holiday and then to shepherd his family back to Rome now that the summer heat was over. To Jane's interested eye he looked intelligent but difficult to please. She liked Anna enough to wish for her a less demanding, kinder man.

Ernesto remembered at last that he was also required to talk to Donna Giulia, and Jane was free to observe her cousin, sitting next to Ottavio. Alex was dressed in black chiffon, scattered with tiny diamanté stars that glimmered in the candlelight. The sophistication of her dress was something new to Jane, and so was the gravity that seemed to enhance her dazzlingly fair beauty this evening. It was probably due to the elaborate formality of the Marchesa's dinner-table and the grandeur of the room they sat in; at least, so Jane thought until Alexandra stared in an unguarded moment at Fausto. Jane realized then that her cousin would have no recollection afterwards of a single thing Ottavio said. The rest of them might not have been there for all the impression they made on her.

With Ottavio and Anna equally determined to keep the after-dinner conversation in safe channels, all went peacefully in the *salone* until Ernesto idly asked about the prospects for the vintage.

'You've driven up here – need you enquire?' Fausto answered for his brother. 'The prospects are as they *always* are – a miserable harvest of grapes from which we shall make a quantity – small, thank God – of almost undrinkable wine.'

'We had a late spring frost,' Ottavio said defensively, 'and no rain when we needed it to swell the fruit.' He ignored his brother's derisive smile and tried not to dislike Ernesto for leading them into danger. It was a pity that even very intelligent bankers like his brother-in-law understood nothing but money.

'You city-dwellers don't need to notice the seasons and the weather,' he pointed out more calmly than he felt. '*We* are at the mercy of whatever Almighty God sends us, and it doesn't always seem to be what we need.'

Now was the moment to steer the conversation back to safety. Jane flogged her brain for something harmless to say, but Fausto was too quick for her.

'My dear brother chooses not to mention that we're at the mercy of other things as well – a system that hasn't changed for half a millenium, and a workforce that *has*. The system might have done well enough in the past, but it's unworkable now with peasants drunk on the heady brew of socialism today and revolution tomorrow!'

'Fascist ranting,' Ottavio said fiercely. 'You know as well as I do that revolution is something hawked by anarchists in cities; countrymen have got more sense. All the same, they deserve what they *do* ask for – a wage they can count on and fair labour contracts.'

'They have nothing to complain of here,' Fausto flung

98

back at him. 'What is the result? An estate running steadily downhill into complete ruin.'

In the silence that fell on the room Jane stared steadily at the Marchese. She required him to exert himself for once as the head of his divided family; he must take charge now and save them from disaster, and her eye upon him told him so.

'Landowners live always on the edge of ruin,' he explained to Ernesto calmly, ignoring Ottavio's pale face and Fausto's flushed one, 'that is *one* fact of life. Another is that Italians are unchangeable. Monarchists, socialists, Fascists, can try to apply whatever political theories they like; in the end we remain what we have always been – ungovernable!'

He smiled faintly at Jane, but walked over to his troubled wife.

'Cara . . . the sky is especially beautiful tonight. Take a stroll on the terrace with me and I can show you Arcturus *and* the Pleiades shining brilliantly.'

The skirmish was over and no blood had actually been shed this time. Jane let out the breath that she seemed to have been holding, but it was an evening for anxieties to spawn like mushrooms. If one died, another appeared. She had to watch Fausto offer his arm to Alexandra and lead her out of the room in search of stars. He was too experienced not to know his effect on a young impressionable girl. Jane decided that she disliked him, and relieved her feelings unfairly by glowerng at his brother.

On Sunday mornings she had formed the habit of attending mass with the Marchesa and the children. The priest had gradually got over his distrust of a Protestant heretic in the congregation, and she enjoyed meeting the wives and daughters of the men who worked on the estate; as a result, when she walked down to the village now, she was among friends.

The morning after the Marchesa's dinner-party

sleeplessness drove her out of bed even earlier than usual; it was much too soon for breakfast with the children or for going to church. She let herself out into the misty coolness of dawn, and a world that was silent except for the whistling of swifts and house-martins tumbling in the air around the tower. She walked with no direction in mind, but arrived at the place she now thought of as hers amid the huge extent of Buonaventura land – the lily-pool garden and the laughing boy on his dolphin. The creature still didn't spout his silver cascade, but there was water in the pool once more instead of weed, and the paths were clear of brambles.

She sat on the stone curb and trailed her fingers in the water, wondering why Fate should have brought Fausto home at the exact moment of Alexandra's visit. The Marchesa would have insisted that it was part of a pattern, prearranged and inevitable; Jane was more inclined to blame the temptations with which daily life was strewn so regularly in order to trip them up.

'*Buon giorno, signorina*,' said a voice behind her. She had conjured up the man himself by thinking about him. He walked towards her with the springy stride of an athlete. She knew that he had won a high reputation during the war; he still held himself with a soldier's uprightness and a grace that was all his own. There was a family likeness to Ottavio, but his colouring was darker and his features more handsomely defined.

'I see changes since I was last here,' he remarked, glancing round the garden. 'I used to imagine this as the impenetrable thicket in which I might one day fight my way to Sleeping Beauty.'

'I would rather be able to see *him*,' said Jane, pointing to her friend in the middle of the pool, 'and so would the children. We've been clearing up the garden between us.'

'English pragmatism, signorina! Is *that* what you're teaching them? You have a saying for it, I think. "The bird

100

in the hand is worth two in the bush." It is not the Italian way.'

'Left to the Italian way, Sleeping Beauty might never have been woken up,' Jane said tartly. She had promised herself she wouldn't let him provoke her, but his dig had been deliberate. 'I don't think I'm teaching them anything specifically English except our language, and that won't do them any harm.'

'I'm surprised that Marco has allowed *you* to teach him at all.'

Again the barb was intended to get under her skin and this time she made no attempt to ignore it.

'You're surprised, and also a little disappointed, I think. It isn't that you don't want Marco to learn; you don't want him to learn from *me*. Why do you dislike us so much?'

'Ah, the knife of candour slipped in under the ribs – gentle but sharp! That isn't usually a woman's trick; they fight more deviously as a rule.'

'You haven't answered the question,' Jane pointed out.

'I will now. I'm an Italian, Miss Rushton; I know what my countrymen are capable of, and it does not entitle *yours* to despise them as they do. Only our politicians have been despicable in the past, but now even that is no longer true. Il Duce is the saviour of Italy, and under his marvellous, strong arm we shall discover our greatness again.'

The words were not what an Englishman would have dreamed of using, but Jane had to recognize their fervour and Fausto's total belief in the man that Ottavio hated. How many other Italian families were riven in this way – brother facing brother across a gulf that affection couldn't bridge?

Fausto saw the sadness in her face and spoke again in a different tone of voice. 'Signorina . . . for *you* England matters, for *us* Italy; for the Buonaventuras that means Castagnolo. You can see for yourself the state it is in. It needs money as well as effort put into it to reverse its decline. We have no money, but Ottavio could receive grants to improve the land, replace outworn vines and olive orchards and rebuild derelict farmhouses. He refuses because the money would come from the government and he is anti-Fascist. In short, my brother is mad, but it is Marco who will have to pay for his madness.' Fausto's face suddenly relaxed in a charming smile. 'Perhaps English pragmatism might persuade him.'

'I doubt it, even if an English governess didn't happen to share his views.'

Her eyes held his in a glance that was like sword-blades meeting – they tested each other's strength, and then disengaged; opponents, recognized as such.

'The children will be expecting me to breakfast,' she murmured finally. He gave a little nod and she walked past him up the steps in silence.

On her way back through the gardens she thought of a curious omission from their conversation. Ordinary civility might have required him to say that he'd enjoyed meeting her brother and cousin; but perhaps none of the ordinary standards of behaviour applied to Fausto Buonaventura.

As the day wore on, something else became even more noticeable, and more worrying: Alexandra made no reference to *him*, even when she returned alone with him from an afternoon walk they had all started out on together.

'Francesca insisted on an inspection of all the white oxen we could find, for Charlie's benefit,' Jane remarked casually afterwards. 'After that we lost you – much to Marco's regret; he regards Zio Fausto as *his* property whenever he gets the chance.'

Alexandra emerged from the remoteness in which she seemed to be wrapped. 'Marco must learn, like the rest of us, that he can't always have what he wants.' She heard the sharpness in her voice, and looked shamefaced. 'Sorry, Jane – I didn't mean to snap. Perhaps this visit was a mistake; much more of castle life and I should be ruined for going back home!'

102

It was a brave attempt to conceal the real cause of her bewitchment. She was already well aware that it wouldn't be the lack of castle life that ailed her when she got back to St Peter's Square.

Dinner was peaceful that night, no subject touched on more controversial than the Tuscan villas and gardens a visitor ought to see before returning home.

'Two of the most famous ones are still owned by your countrymen,' the Marchese pointed out. 'The Actons are at La Pietra, and those very strange Sitwells at Montegufoni – sufficient in themselves to preserve your country's reputation for rich eccentricity!'

Charlie grinned, finding his host's brand of humour much to his taste. 'Well, I should hate to be one of Sir George's sons, but my heart warms to a man who asks anyone entering his house never to contradict him – on the grounds that it interferes with his gastric juices and his ability to sleep at night!'

The Marchese's laughter floated up into the high, echoing spaces of the room, and even Ottavio and Fausto exchanged smiles. For a moment it seemed possible that Buonaventura family life wasn't beyond the reach of normality after all. Jane clutched at the hope that brother did not hate brother in the year of Our Lord 1925; no tragedy menaced Castagnolo itself nor the beautiful Tuscan hills outside. She had allowed herself to be morbidly affected by the atmosphere of the castle; its walls held the memory of past violence, and she was losing her English common sense.

Even Alexandra's pale face when she said goodbye the following morning could be kept in proportion. She'd been falling in and out of love since the age of fifteen, and Fausto couldn't have made an impression in two days that would survive much beyond the journey back to London.

Marco's goodbye to the visitors was distinctly offhand because the English lady had monopolized his uncle, but Francesca seemed reluctant to part with her new friend, to whose name she now insisted on applying her own pronunciation.

'Carlie . . . more pictures from London, please; not houses – I want *animali inglesi* . . . *come si dice*, Marco? . . . lions and tigers and giraffes.'

Carlie gravely promised to do his best with these home-bred animals, then turned to kiss Jane goodbye.

'Father will expect to be told when you're coming home; do I have to say that this *is* your home now?'

She nodded, surprised by her own certainty. 'For the time being . . . in fact, for as long as I'm needed, I think.' Her face was suddenly lit by a rueful smile. 'He may huff and puff a little, but you know as well as I do he won't really mind, as long as he has Laura and David.'

'I shall mind,' Charlie said sadly. 'Still, there's our old palazzo to look forward to. I'll sketch something you might fancy before we leave.'

She was made sad by his sadness, and suddenly desolate by the knowledge that her affection for him was as real as her infatuation with William had been unreal.

'I don't insist on a palazzo,' she said unsteadily. 'A villa up at Fiesole would do, with a little terrace to look down on Florence from, and an olive tree or two.'

'Sounds almost too good to be true, but we'll find it one of these days, Janey.' He smiled at her, then touched her cheek gently with his fingers. 'We won't see you again before we leave . . . I hate goodbyes, don't you?'

She watched him being driven away with Alexandra until they were out of sight. Castagnolo was her home now, but loneliness almost drowned her in a suffocating wave. She was saved by something totally unexpected – the touch of a small warm hand being tucked into her own. Francesca's face was solemn as usual – she was a child who wasn't generous with smiles – but now she offered something that Jane recognized as comfort.

'Carlie is . . . is *molto gentile*,' Francesca said, defeated by the task of finding the words in English. 'Will he come back, Yane?'

Instinctively, she had chosen this moment to abandon the formal 'signorina' for the first time. After finally making up her mind, she was letting the *governante* know that she had been accepted.

'Yes, he'll come back . . . he promised.'

Francesca did smile then, and so did Jane. They walked back into the shadowy hall and climbed the staircase to the schoolroom together, content in each other's company.

When Alexandra's prompt and proper note of thanks to the Marchesa arrived it was accompanied by a letter to Jane. Unexpectedly, it came from the Villa dei Pini at Fiesole.

'You'll be as surprised to know that I am here as *I* am,' Alexandra wrote truthfully.

I'll tell you how it came about: Anna called at our hotel in Florence and found me alone because Charlie was out sketching. We agreed that it would be cruel to tear *him* away from a place that offers something paintable at every street corner but I accepted Anna's invitation for myself and, I think, pleased us all. Ernesto is not here – his holiday had to be cut short and he is back in Rome. Anna feels incomplete without him, and since I feel incomplete myself at the moment, we seem to be good for one another.

The days are beautifully peaceful here – we play with the children (angels, if you'll forgive me for saying so, compared with your frightful pair), and talk together so freely that I keep forgetting what very new friends we are.

Charlie will hate going back to London, and so shall I, but at least we shall have had these weeks in Italy. Dear Jane, what a blessing *you* came, or we shouldn't have come either. Missed opportunities are missed for ever, I now realize. My only pleasure in going home will be to report to William what a beautifying effect this country is having on you. Better still, I shall be able to tell dear Laura that you fit into Castagnolo as to the castle born!

Write to me sometimes, please.

Jane reread a letter that was both typical of her cousin and, in its sad restraint, not typical at all. Alexandra would pick up her London life again, but any other man who wanted to be loved would have to be measured and not found wanting against a taut and dangerously charming Italian. His dark good looks and athlete's body made their own appeal, but Jane realized what his real attraction for Alexandra had been – he lived life twice as intensely as the average placid Englishman.

Fausto was unexpectedly patient with his mother, explaining again and again why it was necessary for him soon to hurry back to Rome. Liking him at least for his kindness to the Marchesa, Jane tried not to think that he had set out to enslave Alexandra, just to prove to himself that English women were made of no sterner stuff than any other. It was perfectly clear, for example, that his combination of maleness and charm drew visitors to the castle who didn't bother to call on the Marchesa when Fausto wasn't there.

Jane watched Francesca watching *them*, interested to observe that in this one matter of devotion to Fausto the little girl refused to follow Marco's lead. She had a streak of cool, sweet common sense that rejected her brother's violent swings of mood. Neither of them spoke about their mother, and Jane was careful not to refer to Elena Buonaventura herself. She suspected they'd agreed to pretend that she was there; if they pretended hard enough, one day she suddenly *would* be there.

Once Fausto had left, the regular routine of every day was resumed: morning lessons in the schoolroom and weekly visits to Florence, where Francesca reluctantly endured Miss Flint's dancing classes and Marco was given his first introduction to the mysteries of Greek and Latin by a Jesuit priest. None of this did he now seem to mind, nor the midday meal eaten under his grandmother's eye, with due regard for the baffling array of knives and forks she insisted upon.

There was the pleasure of the afternoon to come, always spent out of doors. He no longer regretted the days before the arrival of their English *governante*. He had half-enjoyed the long hours spent roaming by himself; did they not prove that he was the bold *padronino* – the '*ragazzo veramente cattivo*' that he knew the servants called him? On the other hand, there had been times when the world seemed frighteningly empty except for him, and his heart had ached with loneliness.

Now, if he wanted to, he could run fast and outstrip Jane and Francesca; but when he did, it left no-one to talk to. His new English friend knew much, but not how to imitate the black-cap's song that, in turn, imitated the nightingale; she couldn't copy the *contadino*'s cry of 'heu-yah' when he wanted to get his team of oxen moving again, and she still had to learn what *he* knew about the magic world they lived in – that it would rain all day if the wild marigolds hadn't opened by seven, that on St Anthony's day the farmers must take an armful of hay to be blessed so that their beasts wouldn't lack fodder. Francesca's Yane had still to be taught that lessons stopped for the *vendemmia*, because *everyone* picked grapes, and that the olives must be gathered carefully when December came, so as not to damage the delicate twigs.

It was strange that a lady could grow to be as old as their *governante* was without knowing these things, but Zio Fausto had said that the ways of the English were strange. Only, he *hadn't* said other things: that she would go with them into the farmhouses of their friends and enjoy the milk and crusty, unsalted bread that the *massaia* offered them. He *hadn't* said that she would laugh and sing with them and look happy when she did. Marco trusted Zio Fausto to know all there was to know about almost everything, but it began to seem as if he didn't know quite all there was to know about these strange people called the *Inglesi.*

9

Charlie's month of freedom was almost over; it was time to turn his back on happiness and return to his Rushton cubby-hole. Jane pictured him getting ready to leave with Alexandra, and charted in her mind the progress of a silent couple on the long train journey home, both of them wishing themselves back in Italy. By the time Anna Lambertini came to say goodbye to her parents before *she* left Tuscany as well, Jane reckoned them almost within sight of London. It was the moment to discover that, far from nearing home, Alexandra was climbing out of Anna's motorcar instead.

'Was Charlie absent-minded enough to leave you behind?' Jane enquired coolly.

'No . . . I'm going to Rome with Anna, just while Ernesto has to go abroad.' Alexandra played with the scarlet petals of a geranium in one of the courtyard urns, and was careful not to catch her cousin's eye. 'Dear Jane, I can feel waves of disapproval from here! I promise you that I've written to Mama – she'll know that Charlie did his best to persuade me to go home.'

'She must know already that she has a very headstrong piece for a daughter; short of tying you to the luggage, I don't suppose there was anything more he could do.'

Alexandra abandoned the geranium and stared directly at Jane. 'You're angry with me, though . . . aren't you?'

'My dear, not angry – anxious . . . and not for Charlie's fate at the hands of Aunt Alice; he will smile sweetly and agree with everything she says. I'm anxious for *you*.'

'Because you think I'm running after Fausto, and don't realize that he will have forgotten me already? I *do* realize

109

it, only too well. He enjoyed my company for a little while – that isn't boasting, Janey; I *know* he did. But his real life is given to working for Il Duce, and for Italy; women are simply pleasant, frivolous interludes, not to be taken seriously.'

'Then, Alex dear, why hurt yourself still more by seeing him again?' Jane asked gently.

'I probably shan't see him at all; most of his time is spent visiting Fascist groups in other cities. I'm going to Rome because it helps Anna to have someone with her while Ernesto is away. It's quite a new rôle for me – being useful! I never am at home.'

Jane smiled at the note of pride in her cousin's voice but wasn't to be side-tracked. 'Granted that Anna misses her husband, she must surely have friends in Rome?'

Alexandra's face looked unexpectedly sad and serious. 'I don't think they're of much help at the moment. She adores Ernesto, but she's deeply anxious as well. It's all right when he's there to convince her that there's nothing to worry about; when he isn't, she gets into a state of anguish about the future. Loyalty makes her argue fiercely with Ottavio about the Fascists, but all the time her fear is growing that Ernesto and his friends may be proved wrong in the end. If I'm there, she forgets politics. We play with the children, and laugh, and enjoy the sunlight – the simple things life ought to be made up of.'

The morning was warm, but Alexandra shivered suddenly, as if the breeze had touched her with a dread too vague and distant to be identified. She looked beautiful but vulnerable. The future no longer seemed predictable, and the problems that beset other people had somehow become *her* problems. Jane found herself wishing desperately that Charlie had found a way of persuading her to return with him to England.

'I was going to give you an excellent piece of advice about not taking sides,' she murmured ruefully, 'but . . .'

'. . . you've remembered just in time that you've already

110

taken a side yourself.' Alexandra didn't smile as she said it. 'I hope we never find ourselves on *different* sides, Janey.' She was aware of sounding mournful and made an effort to prove that she was nothing of the kind. 'No need to worry. I shall keep Anna so busy showing me the sights of Rome that she'll have no time to dwell on the future before Ernesto comes home. Then she will be happy again and I can go back to safe, well-ordered, unemotional London – with memories to last a lifetime, but no permanent harm done!'

'I shan't worry if you tell me not to,' Jane agreed soberly, and then amusement lit her face, chasing away care. 'And I've remembered some good advice for both of us after all: women and politics don't mix – only think of Eliza!'

Alexandra gave a sudden chuckle but shook her head. 'Not until I have to! Time enough to remember *all* my nearest and dearest when I'm back in St Peter's Square.'

Still smiling they walked back into the hall again, so that Jane could say goodbye to Anna.

Later that morning Marco danced into the dining-room, big with news. He was pleased to find that for once, instead of being in Florence, his father was there to eat luncheon with them.

'Papa . . . Gino wants to see you – he says the grapes are almost ready; not tomorrow, but the day after that we can start picking.' Marco turned his attention next to Jane. 'No lessons then, you know . . . I must help drive the carts to the *cantina*.'

'Perhaps we can all help,' she suggested.

'You can help, but not with the carts,' he said firmly. 'Women pick grapes – *men* drive the oxen.'

'Of course . . . how silly of me not to realize that picking would be *our* job.' She smiled at Francesca and, watching them, Ottavio saw a child he thought of as sullen smile enchantingly back. 'We strive always to please and we shall be glad to do *exactly* as we're told while you amble up and down with the oxen.'

Marco grinned and nodded at this satisfactory state of affairs, then kindly invited his grandmother to ride with him on 'his' cart. She didn't refuse, Ottavio noticed with a slight sense of shock; but there were other changes that had gone unobserved while he'd found reasons to stay loitering in Florence. The family luncheon-table had somehow become something that didn't need avoiding – his mother now smiled cheerfully at the children, and they seemed to be present from choice, not coercion; strangest of all, his father was there as well, and since no-one else looked surprised, it seemed certain that they now took it for granted that he lunched with them.

Ottavio's glance moved on to the woman he had first met on the hill at Fiesole – a sad, middle-aged lady homesick for England. How could she have become *this* serenely smiling girl without him noticing it? She had lived in his home for months and he still knew no more why she had been sad then than that she should look happy now. It was something to realize that for once he'd been right; the afternoon they'd sat talking in the Boboli Gardens had been the beginning of his family's salvation, and even Elena, when she tired of her rich American friends, would find Castagnolo a more cheerful place to live than when she went away. But he found himself unexpectedly glad to know that Jane Rushton was happy, too – that she sat among them as if she belonged there.

Marco wound spaghetti neatly round his fork, but his mind was still on more important matters. 'Papa . . . should we not go to see Father Francesco? Otherwise he may forget to ring the church bells for the start of the *vendemmia*.'

'We'll go this afternoon,' Ottavio agreed. 'We'll see him together and arrange everything.'

'What about the *chianini*, Papa?' Francesca put in anxiously. 'They must wear their red tassels, you know – will you arrange for that, also?'

'Everything, my dear – I promise.'

Jane looked at their contented faces and couldn't decide whether to laugh or weep. It was beautifully, maddeningly, Italian – this insistence on the rituals that must be observed because, without them, some virtue would be lost. It scarcely mattered that the harvest would be poor, as long as the church bells rang it in as they had always done. The hillsides looked beautiful now, garlanded with swags of golden vines that were turning to crimson, but Fausto's prediction was almost certainly right: there would be too few grapes, and the wine they made would be too thin and sour to sell. When the olives were gathered in December there would be the same inadequate harvest, and it would be disguised by just this same careful attention to familiar ceremony.

In bed that night she lay awake, depressed but determined to wrestle with the future. There was nothing to be done about this year's vintage except persuade Ottavio to sell it young, while it was still drinkable. Charlie had confirmed what her books said – mediocre wine grew worse, not better, with age. They must sell what they could, and begin to plan, as soon as the *vendemmia* was over, for a better harvest next year. Tired but sleepless, she thought about the problems and Ottavio's fatalistic reluctance to grapple with them. He had told the children that 'everything would be arranged'; somehow she must make him see it as a kind of undertaking given for the future.

The small night noises she'd grown used to in an ancient house settling down to slumber were just as usual; she was almost lulled by them over the edge of sleep when a sound that was *not* as usual brought her wide awake again – a persistent, gentle tapping at her door.

She was startled but not seriously afraid. Ghosts, of which Castagnolo must surely have its share, didn't knock politely, and nor did thieves or violent men. She was about to climb down from her enormous bed and find out who was at the door when it opened carefully and a man's figure appeared behind the glow of the candle in his hand.

She recognized Ottavio, and knew in the same moment that she was very frightened indeed. His wife had been long away, perhaps he was tired of being left to sleep alone, and thought the governess would make a better bedmate than no-one at all. The long corridor outside her room stretched to eternity in her mind's eye. She could scream herself hoarse and be heard by no-one, except the children sleeping on the far side of the schoolroom; but it was impossible to think of rousing them.

Then, over the frantic speeding of her heartbeats, she heard him say, 'Signorina . . . forgive me for this intrusion. I didn't dare go on knocking at your door.'

Surely no man bent on rape ever sounded so apologetic, or looked so drawn with anxiety as this one did? She took a grip on sanity and managed to speak despite the dryness in her throat.

'Something is wrong . . . one of the children . . . the Marchesa?'

'No-one here inside the castle, but I remembered what you said about nursing injured soldiers during the war. Will you come with me to the house of the *fattore* – help is needed there.'

The clock on her bedside-table showed it to be almost three – an extraordinary hour to go visiting, and the lowest one of the twenty-four for human beings who were intended to sleep through the dark time of the night. Courage and hope were at a low ebb then, and although she didn't know about Ottavio's courage, she had never seen a man look more drained of hope.

'I'll be ready in five minutes,' she murmured. 'I was never a midwife, though, if *that* . . .'

'The trouble is not of that kind.' He interrupted her. 'Thank you . . . I will wait for you in the corridor.'

She pulled on clothes by the light of the candle he had thoughtfully lit from his own, and found the box of bandages and disinfectants she kept ready for the children. Ottavio led her down the staircase but said nothing more until they were in the corridor leading to the kitchen quarters.

'Gino Scarelli's wife is away visiting a sick daughter, otherwise I wouldn't have disturbed you.' He opened a door she hadn't noticed before and suddenly they were out in the soft darkness of a starlit night. The courtyard they were now in connected the castle directly with the estate buildings – the *cantina* where the grapes were fermented and left to mature into wine, the granary, the *frantoio*, where the olives were pressed, and the farmhouse of the *fattore*, Gino Scarelli. She was familiar with these places by day, but washed by the silver light of a three-quarters moon that was now sailing clear of the tower, they looked mysteriously beautiful and strange. The cypress trees were black arrow-shapes against the paler sky, and from the rooftop of an outbuilding near by, an owl floated its mournful cry.

Ottavio's hand on her arm tightened painfull, bringing her to a stop. He stared at her pale, moonlit face, seeing for the first time that it was not ordinary at all.

'I shouldn't have involved you in all this,' he said suddenly. 'Go back to your room and forget that I was stupid enough to wake you.'

'Forget that someone needs help? How can I . . . now that I know? If I look nervous, it's because I'm afraid of not being competent enough, not for any other reason.'

He nearly smiled, so determined was she to sound calm and matter-of-fact . . . so resolutely, endearingly English in the face of Italian weakness for melodrama and mayhem.

'Very well, then. God knows we can't afford to turn away help.'

She followed him up the stone staircase that, in the usual pattern of the countryside, climbed the outer wall of the farmhouse. A central archway led to the yard behind, livestock used the stalls on each side of the entrance at ground level, and the living quarters for the *fattore* and his family were up above. She had been there before and knew the man who opened the door to Ottavio's knock – Gino Scarelli, a thin, taut-featured man whose Tuscan ancestry could be traced in a hundred canvases on the walls of the Uffizzi.

'I've brought the signorina, Gino – she will help Mario if she can.'

Jane followed the *fattore* up an inner wooden staircase, concealed behind a door. It led to a room whose ceiling was the rafters of the house itself; no doubt bitterly cold in winter, she could imagine Scarelli's children choosing it when they were young as their own private hideaway. It still kept a secret, undiscovered air, and she suspected that it explained why the young man stretched out on a narrow bed was *there*, and not somewhere more comfortable. She recognized him as Gino's eldest son, but only just. His face was lividly pale, except for a trickle of blood that oozed from some wound hidden by his mop of thick, dark hair. Much more blood had soaked through the right sleeve and front of his jacket, where the material was torn as if it had been slashed. He looked white and motionless enough to be dead, but when Jane found the pulse in his wrist it was still faintly beating.

'I need clean water, warm water,' she said, as calmly as she could, 'and a soft blanket to put over him.' There was no need to fear that the blanket would not be clean; Lucia Scarelli would have seen to that.

'The water is ready, signorina. I did not dare touch him myself,' Gino murmured, 'but I can help now if you will tell me what to do.'

'I need you to hold the lamp for me, please,' Jane said, and then steeled herself to set about the task of cutting away Mario's blood-stained clothes. Once she'd begun to work, her trembling hands steadied themselves and the self-control learnt during the war reasserted itself. She didn't falter even when she saw the stab wounds that scored Mario's arm and chest.

'He should be seen by a doctor,' she muttered. 'These need stitching, and he's lost a great deal of blood . . .' Her voice trembled in spite of herself. The strangeness of their leaping shadows thrown by the lamplight on the white-washed walls was unnerving enough, but worse was the smell of fear that permeated the silent room.

'There is no chance of a doctor tonight,' Ottavio said quietly. 'Perhaps tomorrow it can be arranged, but for the moment we can only rely on *you*.'

She wanted to weep, to implore him to find someone more competent than herself, because otherwise Gino's son would probably die; but the expression on Ottavio's face confirmed that he had spoken the bare truth. They had to manage alone, because whatever had happened tonight was more complicated and dreadful even than it seemed.

She cleaned the terrible wounds, covered them with pads of antiseptic dressings and then, while Ottavio and Gino lifted the boy, bound them in place with strips of linen torn from one of Lucia's snowy-white sheets. The cut on his head was messy but not serious and she took a little heart from the thought that his face looked marginally less grey than before.

'It's all I can do,' she said tiredly at last. 'You'll have to pray to God above that it's enough until we can find a doctor.'

Tomorrow might be too late, but they knew that as well as she did. Gino's face seemed to have lost whatever vestige of spare flesh it had ever possessed, and his eyes were sunk back in their deep sockets; but they didn't move from his son, as if by sheer looking he might keep the boy alive.

'I shall stay with him,' he said softly. 'If he should try to move, signorina, I shall hold him still, like a tiny baby.'

Jane nodded and took the hand he held out to her. It was hardened to the consistency of tanned leather, but she had seen its gentleness when he touched his son.

'I shall come back in an hour or two,' said Ottavio. 'You must sleep then, Gino; I can watch the boy as well as you.'

117

'You can, but we shall watch together, Signor Padrone! Signorina Jane . . . *tante grazie.*'

On an impulse that took them both by surprise, she kissed Gino's cheek and then followed Ottavio down the stairs to a world that now hovered on the edge of dawn. Stars were still bright in the darkness of the western sky, but a thin line of light rimmed the hills to the east. A different faint glow in the topmost windows of the tower reminded Jane of the man who sat up there, contentedly watching the heavens.

Ottavio glanced up, too. 'How strange that for my father the night is normal.'

'Are you going to tell me why it *isn't* normal, or am I supposed to pretend that Mario suddenly slashed himself with a dagger because he couldn't think of anything better to do?'

She stumbled over the words because tiredness and shock and the early-morning cold had suddenly combined to set her whole body shaking. The bedroom she had still to reach seemed immeasurably far away, and faintness was gaining on her. She ducked her head, but felt herself pulled against the warmth of Ottavio's body. His arms held her with the tenderness he would have offered to a frightened child, and she accepted his comfort because to rest against him seemed for the moment the most natural thing in the world.

He didn't seem to mind how long they stood there, but she lifted her head when she was sure of being able to speak without stammering. 'I'm all right now . . . thank you.' It sounded so absurdly prim that she smiled, and he realized that he would never be able to look at her again and think her plain.

'A small glass of brandy to make certain,' he murmured, 'otherwise you will start shivering again.'

She was led to the room that had been her first introduction to the castle, four months ago. Then she had insisted that she would be unable to take the job he offered her. Now, she was part of Castagnolo. The windows of the study faced east and she was careful to look at the line of light growing brighter along the hills while she waited for Ottavio to pour the brandy. He put an old, paper-thin glass into her hand and then went to lean against the wall between the windows. The withdrawal was deliberate, she thought, in case she had misunderstood his kindness out in the courtyard.

'Shall I tell you what happened?' he asked quietly. 'Mario was in Florence this – no, yesterday evening, attending a meeting of the local Peasants' League. It is a dangerous thing to do nowadays, but young socialists like him aren't easily cowed and they take care not to advertise their meetings. All the same, he was set upon as he came out – probably not killed outright only because he is known to come from my brother's home estate. A comrade managed to bring him back here.'

Jane stared at the golden liquid in her glass, remembering her advice to Alexandra – but perhaps *men* and politics were even more terribly self-destructive.

'Why couldn't we get Mario to a doctor or a hospital?' she asked at last. 'He needs professional care.'

'Because it would have meant taking him back to Florence, and the Fascists have it under siege at the moment.'

It sounded medieval, unbelievable – her expression told him so, but he went on calmly with a story that scarcely belonged to the twentieth century.

'They'd set out to teach a group of their opponents a lesson – it was to be the turn of the freemasons; but the plan misfired and a Fascist leader was killed instead. Vengeance required the whole of the city to be terrorized. Mario is just one of dozens who have been killed or "punished". Cafés and offices have been set on fire and examples made of anyone suspected of being anti-Fascist.'

'It's *worse* than medieval,' she muttered, 'it's the Dark Ages come alive again.'

'My dear, it's Italy! We've forgotten nothing, learned nothing – we never shall.'

It was what, apart from his gentleness, she would always associate with him – acceptance of the way things were. Acceptance was a less shaming word than despair, but she must make him see that it came to the same thing.

'I wasn't asleep when you knocked at my door,' she said abruptly. 'I was lying awake wondering how we should set about saving Castagnolo for Marco.'

The stupified expression on his face would have made her smile at any other time; now, she was too intent on what she must say.

'*We* set about saving it?' Even if it had been the outraged aristocratic slap she might have expected, it wouldn't have stopped her now. She was launched, and he would have to hear the rest of it.

'*We* can't save Italy, but it's survived even worse things in the past than Fascism. Our only responsibility is to save what we can – *this* bit of it that belongs to you.' She broke off in mid-flight. 'Are you steeling yourself to annihilate me by pointing out that what happens to Castagnolo is nothing to do with me?'

The last thing she expected – a smile of pure amusement – touched his mouth. 'My dear, you're Britannia personified . . . I shouldn't dare! I was about to remind you instead of something Fausto said – our system hasn't changed for five hundred years, but our peasants – especially Mario Scarelli's generation – have.'

'Then we must *change* the system a little here, persuade the peasants a little there; before next year's harvest we must find *some* way of making Castagnolo fruitful again, instead of wringing our hands and saying it can't be done.' She smiled ruefully herself, remembering something else Fausto had said. '*Your* brother would probably sneer at English pragmatism; *mine* would call it Rushton obstinacy that doesn't know when it's beaten!'

She put down her glass and stood up, hoping that

120

extreme fatigue and brandy wouldn't defeat her intention of walking in a reasonably straight line to the door. Ottavio got there before her, and stood blocking her way.

'We shall have to continue this conversation another time because *you're* worn out and *I* must go back to Gino, but it reminds me of the first morning we met. You told me then that effort matters more than achievement; it's an article of faith for you, I think.'

'Yes . . . but there's nothing wrong with achievement now and then, as well! Will you tell Gino, please, that I'll come over to see Mario before breakfast?'

He nodded, still without moving away. His arms didn't enfold her, as they had done in the courtyard for a moment or two, but she felt just as close to him. She was too tired now to consider why it didn't feel strange, only natural.

'Go and sleep now, my dear Yane.' He smiled because he'd borrowed the name Francesca used, and gently touched her cheek with his fingers. Then at last he opened the door and she was free to go.

10

The Lambertinis' home was a tall, seventeenth-century building in the Piazza Navona in Rome. Anna explained this to Alex as their train travelled southwards.

'It's quite small by Roman standards, but we all manage to fit in – apart from ourselves, that means Ernesto's widowed mother and the small army of servants required to run an inconvenient house and to keep *her* more or less happy.'

'I think I detect a note as of patience tried!' Alexandra commented with a faint smile. 'Is Mama-in-law not much of a friend?'

'In her own view she remains what she was – the Contessa Andriani! Lambertini money was married and permitted to prevent the family palazzo from falling down, but Ernesto's father, who was a kind and charming man, always had to remember that they were living in *her* home, as we have to now. I'm afraid I hated her to begin with. In the years since then I've learned to feel sorry for her, but *that* has to be concealed as well – a Florentine provincial like me doesn't pity a Roman aristocrat!'

'Couldn't you and Ernesto have left the palazzo to her and lived somewhere else?'

'It's not the Italian way, I'm afraid. Whatever else we don't accept, we're bound to accept allegiance to our families. We can find ways of getting round most laws, but that one we all obey.'

Alexandra thought about Italian families – Ottavio and Fausto trying to overcome a gulf that not even Buonaventura loyalty could do anything to bridge, and Anna herself torn to breaking-point between what she *felt* and what as Ernesto's wife she was obliged to believe.

'Does the Contessa approve of the Fascist system? As a Roman aristocrat left over from a previous régime, I suppose *not*.'

'Then you suppose wrong! An Andriani wouldn't normally even acknowledge the existence of a blacksmith's son who was an unwashed firebrand revolutionary in his younger days; but like thousands of other women, she's enthralled by *this* one now – a man who tells the Italians that he'll make them great again, with or without their help. You'd have to hear him speak to understand the hypnotic power he possesses. He is not slow to liken himself to Caesar, but there are plenty of people ready to call him a god.'

She lifted Emmanuele out of the arms of his sleeping nurse, and sat holding him, for the reassurance, Alex thought, that his small, warm body gave her. Then she turned and smiled at her guest.

'You've heard a lot about *our* problems; what about yours – or don't England and the Rushtons have any?'

'Our problems are much like yours, I suppose,' Alex contributed thoughtfully. 'The war that was to have changed the world turns out not to have changed very much at all. There are still the same old injustices – a few people with too many advantages, and a great majority with not enough; there's unrest, unemployment and unhappiness in England as well as here. I suppose the *difference* is that although we're rather pleased with dear King George, we're *not* inclined to think any of our leaders godlike!'

'That disposes of England – what about the Rushton family?'

'Ground between the millstones of Jane's father – the head of both family and firm – and my mother, who thinks she has an even better idea than he has of what we should all do and be.'

'Is that why Jane came to Italy – to escape from Papa?'

'No, I'm afraid she came to escape from my brother, William, and from her own home.'

'She disliked them both?'

'She loved them both; but after her elder brother was killed in the war, there wasn't room at home for *her* and Johnny's beautiful harpy of a widow. Even being mistress of Vine House wasn't enough for Laura; she wanted William as well. He was to be allowed to make a nice convenient marriage as long as he went on being in love with *her*. Jane must have realized it just before it was too late.'

'It sounds as if this Laura is the millstone, not Jane's father at all.'

'Well, Uncle James is infatuated with her, too, up to a point, but it won't make any difference to what happens in the end. Laura can get William to marry her in place of Jane, and beget half a dozen more sons – Uncle James will still see to it that Rushton's is kept for Johnny's son, David.'

Anna's strained expression was wiped away suddenly by amusement. 'Now why, I wonder, did I think *our* affairs were complicated! I'm not sure how Jane described her father, but in such a way that mine is longing to meet him.'

Alex looked doubtful. 'If the Marchese imagines a gentle soul like Charlie, dreaming of the masterpiece he knows he'll never paint, then he'll be in for a shock. My dear uncle would march round the estate and return confident that he knew exactly what ought to be done with it. Offered the slightest encouragement, he'd probably give some *more* advice as well – replace King Victor Emmanuel, His Holiness the Pope, and Benito Mussolini with Englishmen and Italy would *then* be on the road to salvation!'

Anna's peal of laughter woke her son who, seeing his mother happy, laughed too.

'Papa would *love* to hear him. Dear Alex, I hope he comes, but I'm not sure his advice will be needed. Ottavio knows perfectly well what should be done; it's just that someone has to keep him from . . . from – oh, I forget the English word.'

'Backsliding? Well, in that case the sooner his wife returns to Castagnolo, the better.'

Anna shook her head. 'Elena is no help in that way; she has no interest in the estate and only wants him to pay attention to *her*. It isn't hopeless, though, because you've forgotten someone else. I have the feeling that James Rushton's daughter might do quite as well as her father!' She smiled again at the astonishment on Alexandra's face and then started collecting the various bags and packages strewn about the compartment. 'I must wake Lorenza and Caterina. We shall arrive in ten minutes.' There was time for one more confession, which she made ruefully. 'I can never make up my mind whether Rome is the place I love most or hate most in the world.'

The palazzo that was 'small by Roman standards' looked sufficiently grand to Alexandra as they drove towards it, but she was much more enchanted by its setting. The Piazza Navona wasn't, properly speaking, a square at all, but a long rectangle that clearly showed its original purpose. It was studded with three marvellously ornate fountains, and her first impression of it remained her most lasting – the magical sound of falling water.

'The experts like to refer to this as Baroque Rome because the square was laid out in the seventeenth century,' Anna explained, 'but it was built over a much older part of the city. In the cellars of the houses, ours included, you can see the foundations of the seats that lined Domitian's Stadium, and the church of Sant' Agnese over there covers the ancient Roman brothel where the poor girl was martyred. Why do you smile – it is a very affecting story!'

'I wasn't laughing about St Agnes, only about the extraordinary way you all have here of living with history and times past. Domitian's chariot races weren't exactly run within living memory, but they still seem as real to you as that street market over there, and Agnes's fate might have overtaken her yesterday.'

125

'Perhaps that's our trouble,' Anna said sombrely. 'The past is so long ago, but still so visible, that it blinds us to what is going on now.'

They were back at her own private agony, Alexandra realized, but she forced herself to sound cheerful. 'Well, at *this* moment I'm thinking about the present ordeal of meeting your mother-in-law. I shall do my best for England, but I'm bound to say she sounds terrifying.'

'Smile, look quietly sure of yourself – nervousness earns her scorn! – and leave the rest to Lorenza. My daughter is the only creature I know who can humanize her grandmother.'

Confronted by a tall, thin, elegant woman who kissed Anna on both cheeks before staring at her guest, Alexandra was aware of being raked by a comprehensive glance. It took in her face, the quality of her blue linen jacket and pleated skirt, and the immaculate neatness in which she always contrived to arrive after a journey. Only then did the Contessa offer a thin hand weighed down with antique rings, and a frosty smile that had to be taken on trust as welcoming.

'Good day, Miss Rushton. What a pity that you have no Italian conversation. *We* shall be obliged to speak English, which is such a barbaric mixture of German and French, I always think.'

Alexandra admitted regretfully to herself that the English she was listening to was faultless. It gave the Roman dragon an unfair advantage, but she smiled, as instructed, and kissed nervousness goodbye. Anna's mother-in-law was a blue-blooded bully who would seize on the slightest sign of weakness. It was quite like being at home again with her own mother. 'We prefer to think we combine the best of German and French,' she said firmly.

The Contessa changed tack. 'This is your first visit, I believe. Be more original than most of your compatriots, I implore you, signorina. Allow Anna to show you a little more of Rome than Miss Babington's English Tea

Rooms and the house where your poet Keats expired.'

'Oh, I intend to keep her so busy that she will finally regret inviting me.'

'I doubt if she's explained that you've come at a very important time – my daughter-in-law doesn't entirely realize how fortunate we are to be seeing the beginning of a miracle in Italy. If you can help her to see *that*, your visit will have been very worthwhile.' Otherwise not, her cool voice clearly implied. She examined an exquisite fob-watch pinned to the front of her dress. 'Anna, I shall have to see the children when I return – I'm already late for an appointment.'

She swept out leaving silence behind and a faint breath of perfume lingering on the air.

'God Almighty,' Alexandra muttered after a moment or two. 'If I'd been Ernesto's father I'd have let the Palazzo Andriani fall down.' She caught Anna's eye, began to smile, and suddenly the two of them were helpless with laughter.

'I've never been able to find it funny before,' Anna admitted, finally wiping her eyes. 'You're a treasure, my dear friend, even if I *do* have to speak this barbaric language with you! Now, let me show you how to find your way around and then I'll leave you alone – you'd probably prefer to unpack yourself rather than have a maid do it for you.'

An hour later Alexandra left her bedroom at the back of the Palazzo; it looked out over an interesting tangle of pantiled rooftops and small green oases of gardens hidden away among the jumble of stone and stucco, but she wanted to find her way back to the *salone* on the first floor. Its long, balconied windows overlooked the square, offering a perfect vantage- point. From there she could look down on Bernini's statues, glistening under their falling cascades, so instinct with life that she half-expected them to clamber down from their carved rocks and mingle with the people who talked and gestured around them.

'A century ago Miladi's coach would have driven through deep water down there,' someone behind her explained quietly. 'The square was regularly flooded during the heat of summer "to refresh the air"!'

The soft, beautiful voice belonged to the man she had assured Jane she wouldn't see in Rome. He was staring at her as intently as the Contessa had done, and surely with as little welcome. Perhaps he'd forgotten for a little while at Castagnolo that she belonged to England, but was now remembering it again. It was cruelly unfair of him not to want her there when the sight of *him* gave her such joy that her heart seemed to stop beating.

'You were going back home with your cousin,' he said sharply. 'Why are you *not* in London . . . or am I dreaming that you're here?'

She put out her hands in an unconscious gesture that invited him to touch her and prove that she was real. He'd forgotten that spontaneity – with her, to think a thing was to do or speak it – just as he'd remembered not nearly adequately enough her astonishing beauty. Even in England she must surely stand out, but among his black-haired, sallow-skinned countrywomen she seemed to attract light itself, and it reflected itself back in her dazzling skin and hair. He had expected her to be safely out of reach in London by now; he didn't want her here in Rome, complicating still more their complicated lives.

He ignored her hands and for something to do with them she pushed them into the pockets of her jacket instead. Time and space had become unreliable. The past few minutes seemed as long as all eternity, and the space between them, the mere width of the Contessa's old Persian rug, was a desolate waste she didn't know how to cross in order to reach him.

'I'm here because Anna invited me to keep her company while Ernesto is away,' she explained briefly. 'Before *you* give me good advice as well, let me tell you I *insist* on seeing the house where John Keats died . . . I shall go there every day, probably.'

There was no glimmer of the quick amusement she half-expected, and she knew for certain that he'd become a stranger. *This* unfamiliar Fausto offered instead a frown of displeasure that drew his brows together in a dark, emphatic line.

'I take it that you've met the Contessa,' he said after a moment or two. 'Don't be put off by my sister – Anna finds her mother-in-law formidable because she has the ancient Roman virtues of courage and a bold heart.'

'Never one to be daunted, I'm sure,' Alexandra agreed cordially, spurred by loyalty to her friend and anger at his attitude. 'But nor is Anna either, which is just as well in my opinion.'

She was recovering from the shock of seeing him. The pain of knowing that he didn't want her there was something that would have to be felt later; for the moment she kept Roman virtue in mind and sounded carelessly bright and brave. 'We didn't dream of finding you here at all, much less the moment we arrived. Anna said you were scarcely ever in Rome.' In order to underline the message that it didn't matter whether he was there or not she didn't wait for him to reply, and walked on to one of the small balconies overlooking the square. When he followed her every nerve and fibre of her body told her so. He came to stand behind her and she could smell the faint, fresh scent of his skin and of the soap he used. Weakness invaded her, but the balcony railing was there in front of her; she could cling to it without him knowing how much she needed its support.

'I ought to be in Naples, not here, but there are times when one's own family seems more important than any-thing else.'

His voice had changed; in place of hostility she heard such sadness and regret that she could turn round and face him.

'I know – it's the law you all obey – Anna told me.'

'And you'd like to tell *me* that it's the only reason she stays here, sharing a home with Ernesto's mother!' A faint, rueful gleam of amusement shone for a moment, then faded again. 'I promised him that I'd try to be here when Anna got back, but something happened last night that obliged me to come.'

He shook his head at the question her face asked even before she put it into words. 'Nothing to do with Ernesto . . . but there was some trouble in Florence that got out of hand. It's under control again now, but when men are frightened they lose their heads and behave like mindless fools.'

'What sort of trouble?'

'One of our men was killed in a . . . a necessary operation; it provoked his comrades, of course, and violence bred *more* violence, as it always does.'

'Florence, you said . . . has something happened at the castle as well?'

'The uproar spread through the province, I'm afraid, but Castagnolo is all right; only the *fattore*'s son got hurt. He was in the city, stupidly attending the sort of meeting with his socialist friends that always leads to trouble. Everything will be responsibly reported in the press, of course, but I didn't want Anna to read about it alone. Without Ernesto here to help her she doesn't always understand *important* things . . . the things that sometimes have to be put first.'

'Pity her – she can't help seeing Ottavio's point of view, as well as yours and Ernesto's.'

'I know; that's why I came.' He stared at the beautiful face of the girl in front of him. She belonged to a country that knew nothing of Italy's long agony; how could she even try to understand the sacrifices that had to be made?

'You didn't know this country in the years just after the war,' he said slowly. 'How can you possibly imagine what it was like – the bitterness over a terrible war we shouldn't have fought, and its legacy of still more muddle, corruption

130

and despair than before? We've never known anything else. But this time, instead of accepting it, we were travelling down a road that led only to revolution and civil war. Benito Mussolini saved us from that, and it's enough in itself, God knows, to justify the excesses that sometimes happen now because men make mistakes. But the Duce will do much *more* than that – he'll rescue us from every want and weakness and shame if we're prepared to live and die for him. *That* is what Anna forgets whenever a little unpleasantness comes to upset her.'

His face that had so enchanted her when it was laughing now seemed even more beautiful when it was grave. She understood . . . how could anyone *not* understand and share his burning faith? But what she *loved* him for was not his faith in Italy's saviour, not even his masculine strength and charm, but the sweetness of heart that had brought him to make sure that Anna, who didn't understand important things, would be all right without her husband. Alexandra heard the word 'loved' that she had spoken in her mind – it was there and couldn't be rejected.

'I can't support her as Ernesto does, but I can help a little by staying until he gets back,' she said after a moment or two. 'In fact, it's why I came.'

Fausto's hand touched her cheek, signalling another change. His work for his Fascist dream was all that absorbed his life, but for *this* small space of time she knew he was aware that she was there. 'I'm sorry I snarled at you, Alexandra,' he said gently.

She wanted to weep but tried to smile instead. 'I shouldn't be here because I'm one of the hated, arrogant English . . . is that it?'

He shook his dark head. 'No, my dear. You should be in London because life is safe and neatly ordered there, and *I* should be learning to forget a girl who walked towards me on the terrace at Castagnolo one afternoon.' His hands clamped themselves to her shoulders and now there was no gentleness in them; she could feel his strength

131

through the thin stuff of her jacket, and the passionate conviction in his own body that must pass into hers. '*Tesoro*, listen to me . . . there's no time for us . . . do you understand? With so much to be done, and some of it bound to be harsh . . .'

'At home I'm accounted the fool of the family, but I do understand,' she said simply.

He stood staring at her for a long time, apparently unaware that his hands still held her prisoner in full view of everyone in the square below. Then he let out his breath in a long sigh.

'Yes, I really believe you do.' His smile was so full of tenderness that it was like being kissed.

It needed courage to speak calmly, but perhaps she'd have made a good Roman after all. 'I'll leave you to tell Anna about . . . about what happened in Florence, but when it's time for you to leave I think I shall be able to keep her reassured. We seem to be friends who have known each other for years.'

Fausto's hands suddenly cupped her face so that she was forced to look at him.

'Alessandra . . . perhaps it doesn't matter because you won't be here for very long, but *think* before you choose a side. Your cousin Jane *has* chosen – a different side from the one that I have to be on.'

It would have been a simple matter to say that choice didn't come into it because she must choose whatever he had chosen, but the warning had been given again – *he* had much to do for Italy, and *she* wouldn't be there very long. Somehow she must stop herself from saying that she would stay for ever if he asked her to.

'All right, I'll go away now and . . . and have a little think,' she promised instead. He half-smiled at the gravity in her voice and finally released her.

When she reappeared in the *salone* Anna was there with Lorenza.

'Alex dear . . . look who's here to welcome us home.'

132

Anna sounded pleased but added with a little touch of nervousness, 'There was a disturbance in Florence last night, Fausto says, but it's all over now; you are not to feel the slightest anxiety about Jane.'

Alexandra selected her most cheerful smile. 'No need to tell me that – I've never seen my cousin look so well and happy as she does here. The Duce's Italy suits her down to the ground, if that odd expression doesn't try your English too far!' She said it confidently, ignoring a small protesting voice inside. It wasn't a lie, after all, to say that Jane was happy.

She was careful not to look at Fausto, but heard the soft approval in his voice when he spoke to Anna. 'Cara, I *have* to leave for Naples tonight, but even if I'm held up there, I shan't worry. I can safely leave you in Alexandra's hands.'

He remained away from Rome for three days, then walked in on them one morning when the Contessa was giving Anna her instructions for the day – there was an elderly cousin of Ernesto's, affronted by being left alone all the summer, to be visited and pacified.

'*Signora Contessa . . . che piacere di vederla.*' Fausto kissed her hand with irresistible grace and even managed to sound sincere. Alexandra watched with fascination as the Contessa's answering smile melted into something approaching warmth. 'Shall I let you all enjoy a family visit without your English guest, by looking after Miss Rushton for you?' he asked helpfully.

It was a hope of happiness so great that she held her breath waiting for the Contessa to guess and deprive her of it.

'Perhaps that would be as well; the signorina *still* speaks no Italian,' said Anna's mother-in-law contemptuously.

The signorina received the jeer with a dazzling smile that defeated even the Contessa – how was one to deal with a girl who didn't even understand when she was meant to look crushed? She gave a little shrug and hustled Anna and the children towards the door.

When they had disappeared Fausto smiled at Alex. 'What shall we do, poor little English-speaking one? The day is ours . . . Rome is ours.'

'I leave it entirely to you . . . anything . . . I love it all.'

It was a declaration that covered much more than the day in front of them, but she thought Fausto need never know that. The day would end, her visit would end and then there would be only emptiness to look forward to, but he wouldn't know that either.

They did the things that visitors do – bought flowers from a stall at the foot of the Spanish Steps, walked, watched fountains playing, climbed the Capitoline Hill to admire Marcus Aurelius's prancing bronze horse and came at sunset to the vantage-point in the Borghese Gardens where St Peter's could be seen outlined against the dying splendour of the sky.

'Was the day well left to me?' Fausto asked out of the silence that had fallen between them.

'You don't need to ask . . . you must *know* how happy I've been,' she answered truthfully.

His hands cupped her face as they had done once before. 'I *did* know, but I wanted to hear you say it.'

Her lips still parted easily in a smile, even though the day was nearly over and only unhappiness lay ahead. 'I shall never forget it – but I think you know that, too.'

He intended to release her . . . felt so certain it was what he was going to do, that he didn't know how his mouth suddenly came to be touching hers. Her lips opened under his as naturally as a flower opens to the sun and she was pulled so hard against him that the heartbeats she could feel were his, not hers. Her hands buried themselves in his hair and there was no-one left in the twilight world except the two of them, locked together.

'Alexandra . . . this is madness,' he murmured against

134

her cheek, when it finally became necessary to breathe. 'My dearest girl . . . we are insane.'

She pulled herself away from him a fraction and tried to smile. 'We're happy, I *think* . . . is that insane?'

His hands were suddenly hard and hurtful. 'Dear God, I keep telling you there isn't *time* for happiness, and even if there were, you don't belong here. *Amore* . . . you can't stop being English just because you've fallen in love with what you've seen of Italy. There's a lot you haven't seen and, until we've won the war we're fighting now, some of it is certain to be violent and cruel. Even then you *still* won't belong here; go home and forget you ever came.'

A strange little smile touched her mouth, then faded again. 'It's what the Contessa also keeps telling me. I've only myself to blame for wishing that I weren't so . . . so unacceptable!'

The passion that had leapt between them like a flame a moment ago still hovered, waiting to be released again, but his trembling fingers traced the outline of her mouth with gentleness now, not desire.

'Not unacceptable, my little love – just out of reach.'

'I told you I understand, and I do,' she said steadily. 'I shall go home, when the time comes and Anna no longer needs me – and, being English, I shall have to go without fuss, I promise you! Until then, I'm free to go on loving – Italy.' She even smiled to convince him that he needn't worry about her; God above knew that she was Livia, Calpurnia, Theodora – every bold-hearted Roman lady there had ever been rolled into one.

He nodded, and kissed her hand, not trusting himself to touch her mouth again. It was time to turn their backs on happiness and St Peter's and go home.

11

Before Lucia Scarelli returned home from welcoming a new grandchild into the world they knew that her son was not going to cancel out that birth by dying. It was sufficient blessing to be going on with, even though Mario's future, once he was completely healed, had still to be thought of.

The doctor whom Ottavio had fetched from Arezzo examined the injuries with an expressionless face and was careful not to enquire what had happened. He said instead that, although the wounds needed stitching, they were free of infection thanks to whoever had taken care of him. When the job was done he showed no inclination to linger, and even seemed reluctant to go with Ottavio to the castle to be paid for his services.

'You are the nurse, no doubt,' he said, looking at Jane. 'There is no need for *me* to come again; you are perfectly capable of changing the dressings.'

Gino stared after him as he hurried away.

'I spit on that one, signorina; but you see what the Fascists have done to us – we are either murdering bullies now or cowards. What a prospect, eh, for Italy?'

'Not as bad as that, Gino,' she said comfortingly. 'There are enough people like you and Lucia to make sure that Italy survives.'

'I thank the Mother of God she wasn't here; she'd say that this was my fault – I should have stopped Mario meddling with politics. Can you tell me how you stop a young man doing *anything* he has a mind for? We all have to make our own mistakes.'

'Is it a mistake to want to change a world he finds

unjust? Didn't you want to change things when *you* were young?'

'Not I, signorina . . . there was no need at Castagnolo. There's *still* no need to change the system, as long as the *padrone* and his people trust each other.'

Jane hesitated, then grasped the nettle in both hands. 'But *something*'s wrong, Gino – the estate doesn't prosper. I know reasons can always be found – a frost, a lack of rain, a moon that waned instead of waxed when seed was planted – but they aren't the true reasons, are they?'

'No, signorina, the true reason is *this*,' Gino answered slowly. 'Men get fooled too easily; they can be talked into believing in miracles. "Organize yourselves into a league," Mario's friends tell them, "then you can demand anything you want and strike if you're not given it." But while they are so busy demanding and striking, the vines go unpruned and a carpet of weeds soaks up the moisture the olives need. They call that progress! Anyone who understands the land calls it madness.'

The weather-scored lines on his face suddenly re-arranged themselves and she realized that Gino was trying to offer her a rueful smile.

'You could say that I, also, talk to much, signorina, while there is much work waiting to be done. We are short-handed without my son, and tomorrow the harvest must begin.'

Jane accepted that it was all he was going to say for the moment. No changes could be achieved without his help, but she knew that a Tuscan's confidence could only be won slowly. She walked back across the courtyard to the castle. In the daytime it looked familiar and ordinary; except for Mario still lying in his cot under the rafters of the farmhouse she could have imagined those few moments when she'd stood in a mysterious moonlit place, held in the shelter of Ottavio's arms.

* * *

137

Lucia returned home the following day and, by the chance that contrives such coincidences, someone else was driven from the railway station in Florence up the tree-lined drive to the castle.

The huge entrance doors were folded back as usual, and Elena Buonaventura stepped suddenly from golden sunlight into the dimness of the hall. Nothing had changed in the months that she had been away – it was as dark and dismal and menacing as it had always been. She found her husband in his study, and *he* looked unchanged as well – vaguely untidy, vaguely unsure of whatever it was he was doing there. But something *was* different this time. He didn't drop the book he held and come running towards her to cover her face and hands with kisses. For a moment she even had the astonishing impression that she wasn't to be welcomed at all. Four months was a long time to stay away, but she would have sworn that Ottavio would always forgive anything she chose to do.

She stopped in front of his desk, disconcerted by the strangeness of not being in control of a difficult interview.

Ottavio stared at her, privately registering the fact that a cruise in the Mediterranean had suited her. She looked beautiful – the product of wealth and luxurious indulgence, from the shining cap of dark hair to the white buckskin shoes she wore. Her perfectly shaped body was held in a way that obliged men to notice it. Once he'd been too enthralled by it to realize that the lure was deliberate; now, he did realize, and felt ashamed of his stupidity.

'Say *something*, please – even if it's only "*buon giorno*"!' she said lightly. It was inconceivable that she couldn't disarm him in the end, but he wasn't going to make it easy for her.

'I shall say welcome home, my dear Elena. Forgive me for being so slow . . . but your last letter said nothing about getting back soon; I'm overcome by surprise.'

'Overcome, but not overjoyed! Did I stay away too long this time to be forgiven?'

Ottavio recognized, with his newfound clarity of mind, a tactic that she had used successfully in the past – whatever she did he must forgive; otherwise the fault became *his*. He always *had* forgiven her, rather than fail in love or understanding.

'It doesn't matter about me, but you might need forgiveness from the children – Marco, especially. He hasn't been able to understand why you took so long to come home. He looked for you every day to begin with.'

'And then forgot to look, no doubt, because without me he could run still more wild than usual.'

'Not at all,' Ottavio said politely. 'I found the children a new governess while you were away – an English lady. They attend lessons, and even the meal-table, so regularly now that I conclude they quite like *not* running wild.' He played with the ivory paper-knife on his desk, staring at its carved handle as if life depended on memorizing its intricate pattern. 'Have the Harringtons gone home?'

She'd anticipated the question, but not the bluntness with which this different, forthright Ottavio asked it.

'Not yet – their ship sails from Genoa in two days' time.'

Elena walked over to the window and stood staring out at the landscape – fold upon fold of hills, darkening with distance from blue to the soft grape-purple colour of the fruit hanging on the vines closer at hand. She had never seen any beauty in it; it was a prison she had hated.

'Ottavio . . . I'm not back to stay,' she said abruptly. 'I'm going to America with Howard.'

The words dropped into a well of silence – she could hear them echoing in the stillness of the room, returning to her in little waves of sound.

'You . . . you mean you're going on a visit there, with Harrington and his sister?'

'No . . . dear God, please *listen* to what I say. I'm going to stay there, with Howard. Do you understand *now*, Ottavio? I shall go on doing what I've been doing for some time – I shall live and sleep with a man who understands what I need – love and laughter and life, instead of being caged in this decaying museum.'

He could have said that she'd been given more love, at least, than she deserved. Instead he murmured after a long time, 'Then you'll be living in mortal sin. Does *that* not worry you?' He saw her shake her head. 'Well, perhaps *this* should worry you – what happens when Harrington gets tired of living with a woman who cannot be his wife unless I'm dead? My dear Elena, even to help *you*, I don't intend to die until I have to.'

She was aware again of the change in him – the shattered creature who would implore her to stay on whatever terms would make him and Castagnolo bearable had been a figment of her imagination; instead she was faced with this pale but ironical and self-controlled stranger.

'Howard doesn't concern himself with outworn conventions any more than I do,' she said contemptuously. 'We shall be living in New York, *not* among some stifling European bourgeoisie. He has a son already to carry on his name, so wedlock no longer matters.'

'You won't mind, of course, if *our* children stay with me?' Ottavio suggested politely.

Her mask of expensive sophistication faltered for the first time. They had reached the heart of the matter and she was no longer certain of winning.

'I thought we . . . we might share,' she said after a moment or two. 'Marco must stay here, of course – to await his rich inheritance!' The jibe was a revenge for his insulting suggestion that any man might tire of her. It made her feel better, and she spoke more confidently. 'I want to take Francesca with me; she is too young to be left without her mother.'

He had removed the horn-rimmed spectacles he wore indoors and she saw a flame leap in his dark eyes. If he had ever been angry with her he had never shown it before. She waited with a strange, perverse pleasure, wondering whether he was sufficiently changed to lay rough hands on her. Perhaps he would even choose this moment to shake out of her into the light of day a truth that had never been acknowledged between them.

'Francesca is too old not to make her own choice. I suggest that we go and ask her.'

Elena stared at his set face, wondering whether she had ever known him at all. 'You're mad,' she cried. 'The child is scarcely seven years old; how can she be expected to know what is best for her?'

Ottavio's mask-like face almost smiled. 'I think you'll find she *does* know. Shall we go?'

'Bring Francesca *here*, where I can talk to her, for God's sake.'

'I'm afraid you must talk to her in the schoolroom – it's where she feels most at home.'

He opened the door with a courteous inclination of the head, and stood waiting. She could see a servant outside in the corridor, watching with avid curiosity in her face. There was nothing to be done except climb the stairs with him towards her children.

The schoolroom door stood open to the sun slanting through the corridor window – Elena saw a shaft of golden light pointing along the floor to the slender figure of her son, who stood tip-toe at a blackboard, writing down words in English. He was smiling at what he wrote until a sound from the doorway made him spin round.

'M . . . Mamma . . .' The chalk fell to the ground and broke with a little sharp snap. Only then did he move. 'Mamma . . . *sei venuta*.' He hurled himself the length of the room, forgetting in the sudden rush of joy that his mother had never seemed to want the love he offered her. He'd almost given up believing she would come, but finally she was there.

She bent down so that his arms could fasten round her neck, but quickly released herself and stood up. A tall woman uncoiled herself from the desk that was normally Marco's – the English lady, no doubt – but she was of no

141

interest to Elena. Instead, there was Francesca, grown more tall and slender in the last four months, but certainly not less plain; her brown hair was pulled back and tied with a ribbon to match the green pinafore she wore, and the severe style accentuated her lack of prettiness. Her features were at odds with each other, and a gap where a missing tooth hadn't replaced itself didn't improve matters when she finally smiled at her mother.

'*Tesoro . . . eccomi,*' Elena said gently. '*Sono tanto, tanto felice di rivederti, bambina.*'

'*Di rivederci tutti,*' Francesca corrected, '*Babbo, Marco, la Nonna . . .*'

The list would include everyone his literal-minded daughter could think of but Ottavio chose to interrupt her. 'Elena . . . let me present Miss Rushton, who manages to be our friend, as well as teaching the children.'

Elena nodded, without offering her hand. '*Buon giorno, signorina.*' She looked from the tall slender Englishwoman to the children, and then her husband's impassive face.

'We interrupt the lesson, my dear; why not say what you came to say?' he suggested.

She felt a flash of rage, mixed with new respect for a man she had previously despised. But rage was the stronger of the two. This unnecessary interview, conducted in the presence of a stranger, was intolerable, and not at all what she had anticipated. She had been going to explain kindly but firmly that no woman in her right mind could endure life at Castagnolo. Made to see that the blame was his, Ottavio would let her leave with the child he wouldn't care about losing, and an emotional scene with Marco could be avoided altogether.

'There are presents for you downstairs,' she began, trying to smile at the children. Then she looked at Jane. 'Perhaps you'd be good enough to leave us, signorina?'

'No,' said Ottavio definitely. 'Miss Rushton stays.'

Elena threw him a glance of pure hatred and began again.

142

'Well, I really came to . . . to say goodbye . . . for the time being, at least. I am going to travel in a big ship to a place called America, where many Italian people choose to live.' Her son's face had turned lividly pale beneath its surface brown, but she looked away from it and smiled at Francesca instead. 'Marco must stay with Papa, of course, but I thought it would be nice, darling, if *you* came on the ship with *me*.'

Jane waited for the terrible moment when Marco would reject his father and cry that he, too, would go to America. The moment didn't come; instead he said nothing at all, and seemed locked inside such complete and frozen stillness that he might have decided never to move again.

Francesca was silent as well, and Elena was forced to repeat her question.

'Would you like to come, *tesoro*? We shall have a lovely time crossing a huge ocean, and then . . .'

'Come without Marco and Papa, you mean?' Francesca interrupted her. 'Without Yane and Zia Anna and . . .' This time she cut the list short herself because Elena was already nodding her head.

'*They* have to stay here . . . to take care of Nonna and Nonno.'

Francesca took a step sideways that brought her close beside her brother.

'I, also, take care of them, Mamma. I shall stay here with Marco and Papa and . . .' she turned to look at the white-faced woman who hadn't spoken at all, '. . . with Yane.'

Ottavio stared at his wife, consumed with a mixture of pity and terrible fear. She had a weapon in her hand if she chose to use it. He had been cruel – so could she be if she wanted to.

They were *all* under a spell of stillness now, that lasted until Elena finally accepted defeat. She opened her lips to speak, but changed her mind and gave a small, eloquent shrug instead. Then, with a certain brave dignity of her own, she walked out of the room.

Ottavio stared over the children's heads at Jane, then followed his wife out into the corridor. It was the signal for Marco's rigid self-control to crumble. He suddenly flung himself across the room at Jane, and her arms opened to enfold him. His small dark head butted against her like an animal with no words to express its pain, and his body was racked by great shuddering sobs. Francesca watched while Jane held him, and gave him little pats from time to time – the only form of comfort she could think of offering.

When he finally grew quiet enough to make sense of anything that was said, Jane spoke as if the emotional storm had never taken place. There would be a time for making him understand about his mother, but the time for trying wasn't now.

'What do you say to having our lunch up here today?' she suggested calmly. 'The *vendemmia* begins tomorrow and there's still a lot that you haven't explained.' Marco's tear-sodden eyes stared at her, unable to focus on anything but his own grief. She remembered another drama that had been driven from her mind.

'Gino Scarelli's son, Mario, has been in an accident. There will be a great deal of extra work to do. Can you really manage an ox-team on your own?'

'Of . . . c-course,' Marco insisted between sniffs.

'A silly question – forgive me!' she agreed quickly.

She was rewarded with a tremulous, sweet smile. 'I don't suppose I really could *quite* manage, but the *chianini* don't need telling what to do, Jane – they know!'

'You'll have to help *me*, though; this is my first *vendemmia*, remember.'

Marco nodded and a kind of normality had been restored, sufficient to get them through that first, difficult day. Neither of the children mentioned their mother again, nor did they ask to see the presents she had brought them. They would slowly come to terms with the fact that she had now left them for good, but Jane had no such comforting certainty about Ottavio – she was haunted by

144

the suffering on his face as he'd stood looking at her in the schoolroom.

At dinner that evening the Marchesa exerted herself and talked with such sublime triviality about everything but the subject that filled their minds that Jane came close to disgracing herself. An insane desire to burst into laughter was becoming impossible to resist when she was saved by the Marchese, who deliberately chose to drag them back to reality.

'My dear, you are doing nobly,' he said with a charming smile for his wife, 'but shall we agree not to pretend any longer? Yesterday and today have been very painful, in their different ways; but young Scarelli is mending and Elena will eventually grow tired of her American friends. Wounds heal and meanwhile life goes on.'

Ottavio lifted his glass but, instead of drinking from it, stared at the amber-coloured wine glowing richly in the lamplight.

'You're right, my dears, except in one thing: Elena will not come back this time – she has gone for good. We must not pretend about *that* because the children have to learn to do without her.'

He didn't say that, first of all, he must learn himself, Jane thought compassionately. His own loss wouldn't be mentioned because he was an intensely private man whose pain belonged only to himself. She had begun by thinking him weak and was coming to realize by slow degrees that a thread of steel lay at the heart of his gentleness.

The Marchese nodded, accepting his son's correction, and Donna Giulia got up suddenly to kiss Ottavio's cheek in a rare display of affection. Thinking that the three of them might prefer to talk among themselves, Jane murmured that it was time she inspected Mario's dressings, and removed herself from the room. On her way back half an hour later, she didn't immediately go indoors; the night air was soft and a full, orange moon hung like a paper lantern in the sky between the cypress trees.

' "Every prospect pleases and only man is vile." ' She muttered the words out loud, then nearly jumped out of her skin because someone unseen answered her.

'As bad as that, Jane?' Ottavio materialized as a dark shadow on the terrace directly above her. She climbed the steps to the upper level to find him leaning over the balustrade: the tip of his small cigar glowed in the darkness like the fireflies that haunted the night-time garden in the summer.

She went to stand beside him, and it didn't occur to her that he'd been waiting in the hope that she would come back this way.

'I didn't expect to be overheard sounding so glum,' she answered, suddenly remembering his question. 'All the same, human beings certainly do their best to spoil a world that's entirely beautiful left to itself. Charlie would remind me that people also create wondrous things of their own, so there's *that* to be remembered as well.'

'And something else besides – some human beings offer each other a sweetness and generosity of heart that makes life bearable.'

'Like Francesca this morning,' Jane agreed, bravely returning to a subject that held endless possibilities of pain.

'It wasn't she I had in mind but, yes . . . Francesca this morning. I, on the other hand, was needlessly cruel. I told myself the children must know from Elena herself that she was never coming back – otherwise they would keep looking for her. The truth is that they needn't have known she came at all. I call myself a civilized man, but I made them all suffer.'

She knew better than to say that pain bred cruelty; his own was not to be touched on. 'It was better the way it happened,' she insisted instead. 'Muddled up in Marco's grief was anger with himself for loving someone who hadn't loved him in return. He wept *that* out of his heart after you'd gone.'

'I might have lost him if Elena had offered to take *him* with her,' Ottavio said quietly.

Jane turned to look at him, able to see his face clearly now that the moon had swung clear of the cypresses. 'He wouldn't have gone – he would never have left you and Castagnolo, however much he loved her. But you might have lost your daughter.'

'She's not my daughter.'

Somewhere below them on the hillside the church bell chimed the hour of ten. Jane found herself counting its slow, deliberate strokes, wondering whether she would have found something to say by the time it got to the end of them. She hadn't, and it was Ottavio who finally spoke again.

'My wife made rather a habit of escaping from Castagnolo. The year before Francesca was born she spent a lot of time in Florence with some English friends, and went with them on a holiday to Austria. I knew from the beginning that it wasn't my child that was going to be born, but the man had nothing to offer Elena, and she and her daughter needed me. He was killed soon afterwards in a skiing accident, but I met him in Florence once before that happened. He stared at me with just the same clear grey eyes that Francesca has inherited. Elena hasn't been happy since; perhaps she will be now with Harrington. She was generous this morning – I was afraid she would tell Francesca the truth.'

'Would you really have minded losing a child who wasn't yours?' Jane asked gently.

Ottavio threw away his cigar. It had gone out because he'd forgotten to smoke it. 'She belongs here. Francesca herself has understood that all along, but I didn't fully realize it until this morning.'

Jane listened to the quiet confession, thinking that it made clear much that had puzzled her before.

'You are shocked into silence, I see . . . our Italian melodramas are too extravagant for the calm, cool sanity of the English. Is that it, Jane?'

'No it is *not*,' she said with a sudden flash of anger. 'And I'm tired of being told that we don't have feelings like everybody else. Whenever you compliment us on being rational and more or less in control of ourselves, it's always in a complacent tone of voice that says, "Thank God we're warm-blooded, chaotic, but utterly endearing *Italians*!" '

In the profound quietness of the night she could hear nothing except the thumping of her own heartbeat; then a cough beside her was stifled, repeated, broke into a chuckle, and finally exploded in a shout of laughter that woke a sleeping bird in the ilex tree below them.

She hadn't heard Ottavio laugh before, had almost supposed that he didn't know how; the discovery *now* that he did only made her still more angry.

'There's nothing *funny* about it . . . I'm *serious*.' She had to shout the words above the noise he was making, and suddenly the situation she was in became absurd. She began to smile herself, to choke with laughter, and the next minute they were *both* caught in a helpless gust of merriment.

When it was spent and they'd grown sober again, he stared at her moonlit face.

'Jane . . . dear Jane, I thank God you are *exactly* as you are, and not like us at all. That doesn't mean I doubt your ability to *feel* – apart from the fact that you already love my children, it's always seemed to me that you came to Italy to escape some unhappiness in England. Am I right?'

'Well, yes,' she agreed with a faint smile. 'But I got over William so quickly that I'm probably not cut out for furious, lasting passions!' She said it so regretfully that he wanted to burst out laughing again. It was so long since he had felt like doing anything of the kind, but the idea of wanting to do it today of all days suddenly sobered him.

'I thought that without Elena *we* should fall to pieces –

that's why I always forgave her when she came back. Now I know that we shall be all right as long as you are here.'

Before she understood his intention he leaned towards her and kissed her mouth. His lips were warm and had a pleasant male taste of cigar tobacco; there was nothing demanding in them – only the sweetness of affection.

She knew a sudden frantic longing to ask whether he would ever get over *his* passion for Elena. The unforgivable words were almost in her mouth when she was saved by the recollection of the errand that had brought her outside.

'I f-forgot to report my news – Lucia is back, thanking the Queen of Heaven for another beautiful grandson; Mario's wounds are healing well; and Gino's best home-made wine is more potent than I realized.'

'If he offered you *that* you have indeed been taken to the hearts of the Scarellis.'

'Well, Lucia did kiss me three times!' The thoughtless reference to being kissed made her stumble quickly on. 'I w-wouldn't have wanted Mario hurt, b-but perhaps it will turn out to be a blessing in disguise. Gino doesn't know it yet, but we've got to have *his* help in getting Castagnolo on its feet again.'

'You think we are going to do that?'

'Of course! My father would say that it's a matter of examining the problems dispassionately one by one, and then applying the remedies.'

Ottavio bowed, still aware that it was difficult to remain serious. 'Very well, my dear, dispassionate friend; as soon as the harvest is over we shall give your father's English method a try, and see what it makes of hidebound Tuscan tenacity! And now for God's sake go to bed – the children will be expecting you to pick grapes in a few hours' time.'

She was free to move and finally managed to command her legs to carry her away. Ottavio lingered outside, thinking about a day that had ended even more astonishingly than it had begun. It should have seen him shattered by the grief of losing Elena, but his strongest regret about

149

the events of the morning was sadness for the children's unhappiness. He should have hated Howard Harrington, but found himself hoping instead that the American would make Elena happy. For the first time in years he'd laughed until he wept and ended up by kissing a woman who shouted at him. He wondered what Jane would say to a paradox he found intriguing. Was she not, *poco a poco*, becoming more Italian at the same time as he grew more rationally, sanely English? It seemed such an odd but desirable state of affairs that he went indoors at last still smiling.

12

Father Francesco remembered to ring the church bell, and the oxen's broad white noses were suitably tasselled; even so, it seemed to Jane, the *vendemmia* began in a subdued spirit. Men and women gathered from all over the estate but stood in silent clusters while they waited to be set to work. The children caught their parents' watchfulness and made less noise than usual. Mario's injuries were common knowledge now, and a general feeling of uneasiness was as palpable as the early-morning mist that filled the river valley below them. Florence was blotted out, but not the awareness of what had happened there.

The children forgot apprehension first. They were out of doors instead of being cooped up in the village school-room, and soon the familiar game was on to fill their baskets and race with them to the carts for emptying. Golden October sunlight melted the mist and with it gaiety crept back over the hillsides. The times were un-certain, but the mounds of glistening purple and green grew higher in the *bigonce*, and God had blessed them with another harvest – things might have been much worse, after all.

Somewhere a woman began to sing, and Jane stopped to listen and to ease an aching back at the same time. The Tuscan method of growing vines looped to tall poles was something to be thankful for, but even so she thought wistfully of the sound of the *fattore*'s bell signalling the midday break. When Ottavio came to replace her nearly full basket with an empty one she was reluctant to see it go.

'You mean to be helpful, I'm sure,' she said ruefully,

'but now I have to start again. If everyone else is filling two baskets to my one, I hope you won't find it necessary to tell me so!'

'I shall only tell you that you don't have to wear yourself out competing with women who have been doing this work all their lives.'

Jane shook her head. 'All the *more* reason, I'm afraid. Marco's keeping me in view, waiting for the moment when I have to admit to less staying-power than his friends! If I die in the attempt I must disappoint him!'

Ottavio's sudden frown made her realize that he'd taken her seriously. She gave a little inward sigh, telling herself to remember in future that he was a serious-minded man who took words literally. If Ottavio Buonaventura had ever possessed the knack of taking important things lightly, it hadn't survived the troubles of his life.

'I hope you're mistaken about my son,' he said with the stiffness that still occasionally surfaced. 'It seems to me that he has great respect for his "Signorina Jane".'

'We respect each other,' she pointed out gently, 'it's the reason we manage to get on rather better together than I ever imagined we would. And now it's time I went back to work. Francesca's picking along the bottom of this row and she's getting far ahead of me.'

Ottavio looked at her sunburnt face, trying to remember a time when their lives at Castagnolo had not included her. 'All right, but try not to kill yourself for the honour and glory of England.'

Her straw hat had worked its way to the back of her head and he solemnly readjusted it to tilt over her nose. 'The hat is supposed to be worn well forward – it's a protection against the earwigs that fall out of the vines, as well as sunstroke!' A rare sweet smile lit his face for a moment and then he left her to walk along the row towards Francesca. She was squatting on her haunches tugging at a cluster of grapes and singing a song of her own she'd just invented. Jane watched him talking to the child and knew it no longer mattered that her eyes reminded him of a man who was dead.

The long, hot, golden hours slipped past, leaving in Jane's memory a gallery of pictures that she carefully stored away against a time when she was no longer needed at Castagnolo – Francesca looking like a Bacchus cherub with a ribbon of vine-leaves dangling from her hat, Marco laughing as he drove his grandmother to the *cantina*, the Marchesa sitting beside him in a dress that would have graced a garden party, and a wide-brimmed hat anchored down with a chiffon scarf. She was as incongruous as an orchid in a field of poppies but Jane thought the other women were pleased, rather than not, to see her there. Charlie would have said she added a touch of class to the proceedings.

Even the Marchese was included in Jane's store of vivid memories, because he unexpectedly appeared in the *cantina* to take a turn at pulping the grapes. The fruit had been trodden underfoot once upon a time so that the juice could be released and fermentation begin; now it was roughly mashed with poles in large, open vats. From then on, Ottavio explained, Gino Scarelli would see that the crust of stems and skins and pips that kept forming over the seething liquid was broken regularly to allow carbon dioxide to escape; otherwise the fermented wine that went into the huge oak barrels to mature would become diseased.

For as long as the glorious days of the *vendemmia* could be made to last she knew that the children were too occupied to feel unhappy. Even at night they gave no sign of missing their mother, being sleepy enough to tumble straight into bath and bed. The harvest would soon come to an end, though, and in the quietness of their ordinary life they would remember the woman who had always come back to them before after being away.

Since they didn't mention her, Jane wasn't even sure they realized that their loss was permanent. She was tempted to ask Ottavio to make it clear until one day Marco made her realize that she underestimated their clear-sighted observation of the adults they lived among. She was sitting with him on the terrace after lunch, waiting for Gino's signal to return to work, and dealing with an acacia thorn that had lodged itself in his finger.

While she bent over his hand Marco watched her face, remembering that he hadn't wanted her at Castagnolo. Her features were familiar now; he no longer judged them beautiful or not and barely even thought that she belonged to the people his uncle disliked. She was just Jane . . . there because they needed her. He'd taken the precaution of instructing old Margherita to cancel her spell, in case it had some delayed effectiveness that brought disaster; even so, fear suddenly took hold of him, clamping itself about his heart. It made his voice so high and cold that he didn't recognize it as his.

'When are *you* going away . . . in a ship back to England?'

Jane went on dabbing antiseptic ointment on his finger and made herself sound casual when she answered him. 'I don't know. Why . . . do you want me to go?'

A blue butterfly hovered above a late crimson rose. Marco stared at it. The poor thing didn't know the summer was over . . . didn't know that nothing lasted, neither roses nor mothers nor people who were needed.

'Nonna said you wouldn't stay – I once heard her tell Papa so. She said no . . . no *donna ragionevole* could be expected to . . . you'd go away, like Mamma, because you didn't like Castagnolo.'

His voice trembled in spite of himself and it seemed a long time before he got an answer.

'Your grandmother was talking about ladies in general,' Jane said calmly at last. 'Ladies are different from men, you understand . . . they might find the castle lonely and rather frightening. I did myself, to begin with, which is probably why Donna Giulia thought I wouldn't stay.

154

Now, I find it beautiful, just as you said it was, the first time we met.'

'Mamma didn't think so . . . she never liked it here.' Marco muttered the words as a statement of fact – puzzling but indisputable. 'Do you know *why* she didn't, Jane?'

He might, she thought, have asked an even harder question – why had Elena not loved her husband and children enough to accept what life had offered her, Castagnolo included?

'I don't know the reason,' she said simply. 'All I can tell you is this – people are different, one from another. A thing is beautiful to one person, ugly to another; a place is interesting to one person, dull to another.' She watched him struggling with the strange idea that anyone could see Castagnolo with eyes different from his own; it was probably too difficult for him, but at least it was better than drowning in the pain of knowing himself abandoned by his mother. Jane hesitated for a moment, then ventured on to other dangerous ground. 'People even have different ideas of right and wrong – that's why your father doesn't agree with Uncle Fausto about the *Fascisti*. Growing up means making your *own* choices about what is good, right, beautiful . . . '

Marco nodded; *that* made sense, he could see.

Jane remembered how the conversation had begun. 'Does Francesca understand that . . . that Mamma is not just taking another little holiday?'

He nodded again, afraid to trust his voice and put into words a second time a question on which their entire lives now seemed to hang. Jane saw the desperate appeal in his eyes and answered that instead.

'I hope she also understands that your grandmother was talking about *ragionevole* ladies in general, not about me. I like being here and I shall stay for as long as you both want me.'

Marco swallowed an obstruction in his throat and tried

to look unconcerned. 'She may be too little to understand
. . . but I shall tell her.'

He was the young *padronino* again, proud to belong to
a line of Buonaventuras stretching back through the mists
of time. Then his strained face broke into a smile remi-
niscent of his father's. 'Jane, I think p'raps I'll go and tell
her *now!*'

There was more than enough to think about at Castagnolo,
but anxiety about the outside world kept breaking in. She
was relieved to get a light-hearted bulletin from Alexandra
in Rome. It made a brief, cool mention of Fausto, who
had been kind enough to call on his sister, gave a spirited
account of battles lost and won against Anna's mother-in-
law, and described – graphically by Alex's usual standards
of letter-writing – their various pilgrimages around Rome.
Jane concluded – rightly – that the visit was more momentous than anything else that had happened to her cousin,
and assumed – wrongly – that her pleasure in it had
nothing to do with Fausto Buonaventura. The weeks in
Italy had been a time of discovery for Alexandra; she
would go home subtly changed from the charmingly
feckless creature who'd lived from one party to the next
and imagined that books and museums and picture
galleries were for those in whom the spark of life was dead.

Jane explained this proudly to the Marchese over dinner.
'I can't take any credit – except for bringing my cousin to
Italy at all; it's Anna who's been so good at showing her
things she wouldn't have thought of looking at before.'

'The change is lasting, would you say?' the Marchese
asked slyly. 'The beautiful Alexandra returns to England
a student of the antique, permanently attached to ruins
and masterpieces obscured by darkness and dirt?'

Jane grinned but stuck to her guns. 'I don't suppose
she'll entirely forswear balls and picnics on the river and
fancy-dress parties, but she won't forget Italy.'

Jane didn't hear from Alexandra again and only knew

from a note Anna sent a fortnight later that Ernesto was back in Rome and her guest on the way home to England.

'I miss her,' Anna wrote sadly, 'and Lorenza keeps asking what has happened to her *carina* English friend.' She was careful *not* to write about her quarrel with Fausto that followed Alexandra's departure.

'I hope you realize how badly you behaved,' she said as soon as she found herself alone with her brother.

'I don't understand you,' he answered shortly, 'and I don't think I've got time to enquire what you're agonizing about now.'

'Then *find* time, Fausto, because I insist on telling you,' Anna said sharply. 'Alexandra went home smiling brightly, but she was hurt and unhappy inside – thanks to you. I suppose it amused you to make her fall in love with you . . . to play the rôle of charming escort day after day, sparing precious time for her simply out of kindness and affection. I *hate* shams of any kind, but that was crueller than most.'

'It *wasn't* a sham. How could any normal man *not* want to be with her, given the chance?'

'How indeed? But I hope no normal man behaves as if he's found the companion of his heart and then blithely waves her away as soon as it suits him.'

'It *didn't* suit me,' Fausto shouted. 'It broke my heart to see her go.'

Anna stared at his tormented face and knew better than to doubt him. His unhappiness was as clear to see as Alexandra's had been. 'Then you were mad not to ask her to stay. She *would* have done. Does it really matter *that* much if the Duce dislikes the English?'

'No, it does *not*. Think, for God's sake, Anna . . . think of a girl who understands six words of Italian, who knows no-one here but you, who would be left constantly alone while I rushed about Italy and found myself one of these days with a communist's knife in my back. Does *that* strike you as being something to ask her to stay for?' He buried his head in his hands then lifted it again to stare at his sister's white face.

'Remember something else, too. Alexandra seemed to understand that I'm committed for life to what I have to do; she even seemed to realize that changing Italy as we must means unavoidable violence and harshness at times. But *you* find the reality of these things hard to accept, and Alexandra was bred to a softer, more temperate country. I *had* to let her go.'

'Yes, I see,' Anna murmured after a while. 'I'm sorry, Fausto . . . sorry for you both.'

It ended the conversation, and when he returned to Rome after a visit to Milan neither of them referred to Alexandra again.

At Castagnolo the first heavy shower of rain and touch of coldness in the air were followed by the *tramontana* beginning to blow steadily from the north; in the foothills of the Apennines the winter was already closer at hand than it was lower down in the valley. They made the annual pilgrimage to the churchyard on All Souls' Day, each of them carrying two bunches of flowers – one, Marco explained, for the resting-place of a long-gone Buonaventura, the other for any grave that had no visitors.

With the first days of December came the last harvest of the dying year – the olives that were hurried to the *frantoio* before they could ferment, to be pressed between two huge and ancient millstones.

Only one more festival remained – Christmas itself, for which ambitious plans were afoot to produce a *presepio* more beautiful than any achieved before. Francesca, assisted by her grandmother and Jane, was to be responsible for the small, dressed figures of the Holy Family, shepherds and wise men. Marco, helped by Ottavio, laboured with bits of wood, straw and greenery to construct the setting of stall and crib. All seemed to be going well until Francesca let out a wail of horror one morning.

158

'The *animali*, Yane . . . *non abbiamo animali*.' A *presepio* without kneeling oxen and donkeys . . . the idea wasn't to be thought of. Her huge reproachful eyes said that they were all to blame, but then she saw Jane smile.

'It's all right, *tesoro* . . . Charlie's making them; he's going to send them in a box from England.'

Francesca looked happy again. If Charlie was concerned, nothing but good would come of it and *this* crib would probably be visited by lions and tigers as well.

The quiet, busy days sped past, not much disturbed by the news from Rome that an unsuccessful attempt to assassinate Signor Mussolini had been made on the balcony of the Palazzo Chigi. There was silence from St James's Square in London, but Jane knew there was no need to feel anxious – her brother's weekly letter reported Alexandra to be in perfect health and spirits, scarcely glimpsed during a hectic social life.

'She's got some mindless sprig of the nobility in thrall now,' Charlie wrote unexcitedly. 'I've been in disgrace with Aunt Alice for abandoning Alex "among a race known to be immoral, primitive and unsound" (I quote verbatim), but the prospect of being able to claim a viscount as a son-in-law has set the milk of human forgiveness flowing freely in her veins – she's actually smiling at me now. Laura is less pleased with Alex's scoop, but her own wedding to William will be as grand as she can persuade Father to make it.'

Jane smiled over Charlie's accounts of a family he observed with such quiet relish, but regretted that the Marchese had been proved right after all – Alexandra had brushed off memories of Italy as lightly as a wedding-guest shook confetti out of her hair. The novelty of getting attached to people and doing more than skim like a butterfly over the surface of life had soon worn off. Jane considered this distinctly governessy thought for a moment and then blushed for it – it was rich coming from a woman who'd run away from her own fiancé and now read calmly of his engagement to someone else. When she tried to recollect William's face all she could remember was its mixture of guilt and wounded vanity the morning he'd arrived at the pensione. She was still the woman who had been infatuated with *him* and humiliated by Laura – but all that unnecessary pain now seemed to have belonged to someone else.

Charlie's animals arrived safely – beautifully carved and painted – to add a finishing touch of perfection to their Nativity scene. It was a *presipio* such as there had never been, and all the children of Castagnolo were invited to come and marvel at it. It was also a Christmas unlike any Jane had experienced before – shot through with a strange mixture of joy and sadness. No-one mentioned Elena Buonaventura, and if the children remembered past festivals when she had been there, they didn't refer to them. They were growing perceptive enough, and loving enough Jane thought, not to remind their father of a time when things had been different. There was nothing *she* could do for him except keep his children happy.

There was nothing at all that she could do for Alexandra, whose half-incoherent letter arrived on the morning of Christmas Eve. By then Jane already knew from Charlie that her cousin's brief engagement to the viscount was at an end. Alexandra had committed one indiscretion too many even for her bedazzled fiancé, and several too many for his dowager mother.

'She *wanted* to get out of it,' had written Charlie, 'and who shall blame her, poor little mutt; if you could have seen him, Janey – worse, heard him talk! But the fat's in the fire and Alex's in deep disgrace. What a jolly Christmas! – hope yours is better, love.'

Jane read her cousin's letter again and realized that the Marchese had been wrong – Italy had left its mark on Alexandra after all.

13

Giuseppe Buonaventura was accustomed to reversing night and day. He hadn't ever got as far as suggesting that his family might change to sleeping and waking when he did, but in recent years it had begun to seem unreasonable of them to expect him to eat dinner when he'd only just got up. Being a kindly man, he accepted a settled but imperfect state of affairs that seemed unlikely to change. The change came soon after the arrival in his household of Jane Rushton. He was still pondering the way in which it had been achieved.

An Italian woman with a point to make used words – a torrent of them, delivered *fortissimo* if she was angry, or with tears if she was hurt. It wasn't Jane's method at all. He could still recall with pleasure her look of pained surprise when he'd refused an invitation to attend his grand-daughter's first performance as a budding ballerina. He knew in his bones that he'd be present at Francesca's *next* public appearance, as surely as he now as a matter of course joined his wife's luncheon-table. Long before then Jane's clear gaze would no doubt have convinced him of many other omissions to be made good as well.

He imagined himself to be the only sinner until Ottavio climbed the tower staircase one cold January morning to ask for a consultation with his father.

'Going to Florence as usual?' the Marchese asked hopefully. 'I thought you had work to do there.'

'It seems that I have work to do *here*. It won't matter in the least if I never begin, much less finish, a history of nineteenth-century Anglo-Florentines; someone else can write it if it needs writing at all. It *will* matter if I let Marco inherit a derelict estate when the time comes, because I haven't done enough to hold it together.'

The Marchese looked wistfully at a table strewn with enticing charts – he *could* be thinking of an exciting night ahead, with Jupiter shining near a gibbous moon, and even elusive Mercury faintly visible for once – but his son's grave expression confirmed that this was not the moment for thinking about matters astronomical.

'Shall we first admit, my dear Ottavio, that I have done nothing at all for Marco's inheritance?' he suggested at last. The question didn't need answering, but his next question did. 'Even supposing that we *can* do anything now, is there a future at all for people like us and places like Castagnolo in Fascist Italy? I don't find myself convinced by Fausto's fervour, I'm afraid.'

Ottavio smiled faintly, 'Nor I, but there's another point of view. I have it on good authority that it's our duty to survive Benito Mussolini's régime and to put our *own* house in order while we wait for evil days to pass.'

'Ah . . . now I understand! But I shall be disappointed in Signorina Jane if she was forced to point this out to you in words! Wasn't her usual weapon enough – a slightly lifted eyebrow, or a small, disbelieving stare?'

'Not quite – words came into it; in fact, we were roundly accused of pride of ownership that we've done nothing to deserve.'

'Dear me!' It sounded inadequate, even to the Marchese. He began to smile, caught his son's eye and the next moment amusement welled up between them, exploding in a sudden gust of laughter. Wiping his eyes a moment or two later, Ottavio wondered how long it had been since he and his father laughed together. It was unexpected and pleasant, but it wasn't what he'd come for.

'Jane is right, Papa. We can't change the course of events in Rome, can't restore the freedoms that are being taken away from us every day; but we *might* be able to grow more olives, make better wine, keep our people content if we *tried* harder, instead of pretending to be wrapped up in other things.'

There was another failure he might have mentioned, which Jane mercifully had not. He abandoned it now as being too painful, but the Marchese chose not to let either of them off. If honesty was to be the order of the day they might as well now stare at the truth together.

'We should have tried harder at something else,' he murmured quietly. 'I have not made your mother happy; if she'd belonged to a different generation she might have left *me* as your wife left you. Can you do anything to get Elena back?'

Ottavio's face was expressionless. 'I don't know; I'm not sure that I should even try, but if she *is* to come back it must be for good this time. The children cannot be torn between hope and despair again.'

'*They* seem to me to be happy as things are,' the Marchese observed calmly; 'I was thinking of you – you're not a monk, or a priest; you *need* a wife.'

'What I need is . . . is not what I came to talk about.' His own future seemed to be as arid as a desert plain, but he must stop short of confessing that, even to a man who would probably understand. His Church entitled him to one woman, but she seemed to find it easier to live with everyone but him. Elena might grow tired enough of luxury and New York and Harrington to come home, but she wouldn't come with any more love in her heart for Ottavio Buonaventura. He thought life would be *more* bearable, not less, if he could be sure of never seeing her again. It was a truth he was ashamed of. He couldn't admit to that, nor to the fear that he might have to allow her to come back some day because she still needed him.

'We were discussing Castagnolo,' he said with sudden harshness. 'The choice is simple: we struggle on by ourselves in the hope of stopping a slide into complete ruin, or we accept government money to restock and rebuild, and government interference in everything we do – the

163

peasants forced into a Fascist agrarian league they don't want, their young men taught the arrogant violence of the blackshirt militia, and even their small children fed on the Duce's slogans and marched up and down with imitation rifles for the glory of the new Fatherland. God in Heaven, what an outlook for people who were once civilized – to be told that they must now learn to be warriors!'

The Marchese stared at his son, seeing the realities of their life written on Ottavio's despairing face. No amount of watching the remote, untouched heavens would remove from the retina of his mind after this the image of too many failures permitted or accepted.

'There *is* no choice, is there?' he asked quietly. 'Castagnolo would survive with Fascist help, and Fausto might one day point that out to Marco, but *you* would die of shame.'

'Castagnolo still belongs to you . . . the choice is yours, not mine.' Ottavio waited, unsure even now what his father would feel obliged to say.

The Marchese gave a little smile. 'Then I *shall* choose, my son. I'm too old and too stubborn to be anything but what I was born – a Tuscan! Win or lose, let us *not* call on Rome.'

With time for reflection afterwards, Ottavio decided that it was much more likely to be 'lose'. Apart from the chronic lack of money and clash of political views, there was another problem just as serious to be faced. Gino Scarelli reported that young men were steadily leaving the land. The factories of Milan and Turin that had expanded hugely during the war years offered an easier way of earning a living than trudging up and down hillsides with a heavy tank of copper sulphate strapped to their backs for spraying the vines, or rising at dawn to pick fruit and vegetables in time for the street markets in Florence. If the young men didn't stay they would take the young women with them and in time the whole fabric of country life would be destroyed. Some places could survive with fewer men and more machines, but not Tuscany – the landscape there had been shaped by the hands of men in partnership with nature, must continue to be worked in that way or die.

He worried alone over problems that grew worse the longer he stared at them. Lack of sleep combined with lack of hope made him irritable, and it was only a small relief to secretly blame Jane – but for her he could have gone on hiding in Florence among the archives of the British Institute.

She felt his withdrawal from the rest of them and supposed that any man who hungered for a missing wife was bound to look as haunted as Ottavio did. Her sympathies were entirely with *him* until he snapped unreasonably at Francesca at the luncheon-table one day. Pride kept the little girl from weeping, but she stared at her plate, incapable of eating the food that stuck in her throat.

Jane lingered behind when the others had left the room, wondering how to point out that luncheon had been more cheerful in the past without him; but before she could frame the words Ottavio picked a quarrel first, pointing to the book she was taking back to her own room.

'Are you going to be kind enough to tell me – or, better still, Gino Scarelli who has only been running this estate for thirty years – how to make wine that we can not only drink ourselves, but sell as well?'

The attack took her by surprise, revealing the extent of his unhappiness.

'Not if you know already, as I dare say you do,' she said as calmly as she could over heartbeats that seemed to be racing at twice their normal speed. 'I find myself here surrounded by vines, and the Rushton cellars in London are lined with racks of wine – it seems silly not to discover how one leads to the other.'

Ottavio's pale face glared at her with a hostility that

seemed out of all proportion to the crime of reading a book about the making of wine.

'Your father's cellars aren't lined with Chianti, I suspect. His rich clientele wouldn't be seen dead drinking anything but fine French burgundies and clarets.'

'At the moment, probably not,' she agreed coolly. 'But Rushton's might offer them fine Chianti for a change if it were possible to buy any. They couldn't buy it from here, according to your brother.'

'Fausto knows nothing about it,' he shouted, stung to fury, 'and nor do you.'

'It's precisely why I'm reading the book,' she pointed out, doing her best not to shout back. 'The children expect me to know *more* than they do – I can't be ignorant of something that happens on their own doorstep. I'm supposed to be a *governess*, remember.' She was angry with *him*, but angrier with herself for being disappointed in him. He should have understood that she wanted to help, *not* humiliate him, and there was something else to resent as well. 'You shouted at Francesca at the lunch-table – she'd done nothing to deserve that.'

Her own voice had climbed higher, died into an aweful quietness in the room ... had *she* ...? Alas, yes; his expression told her that she'd been shouting in her turn.

'Thank you for reminding me who you are – we haven't had a governess quite like you before.' He spoke with commendable restraint but, however hard she tried, she couldn't think he meant it as a compliment.

'I'm sorry – Charlie would tell you that I'm well known at home for leaping in, boots and all!'

The beginnings of a smile twitched the corners of Ottavio's mouth, but she returned with some nervousness to the delicate subject of wine.

'I should like to think that my father might come here one day and *want* to buy Castagnolo wine – is it really such a ridiculous idea?'

Ottavio gave a little shrug. 'Baron Ricasoli's bible on

Chianti tells us the vines we must grow, the method we must use. Unfortunately it *doesn't* say how we find the money to replace worn-out stock; it doesn't mention, because the Baron never knew, the problem of dealing with strife among the men we must rely on to produce the harvest.'

'Gino explained it to me,' Jane murmured. 'The young labourers want payment in cash now . . . a proper wage they can be sure of, even if it means that they have to pay some of it back in rent. It doesn't seem unreasonable.'

'Of *course* it isn't – the *mezzadria* system is medieval. They deserve a proper wage, a fair contract . . . but despair makes them fight illegally for these things, and then they attract the violence of the Fascists, who see them as dangerous revolutionaries. Older men, like Gino, see them that way too, in their heart of hearts . . . and so father is set against son, brother against brother.'

'You're going to tell me that it's Italy's most recent tragedy, and so it is. But if you dare to say once more that there's nothing to be done about it, I shall aim the Baron's book at you!'

In the midst of anger that made her voice shake, she waited for him to remind her in more brutal terms than before that a governess didn't normally offer her employer threats of violence. His usual expression of resigned despair was certainly wiped away by a mixture of astonishment and affront, but he said nothing at all. Agitation led her into completing professional suicide with another rush of words. 'We have to try . . . don't you see that, Ottavio?'

She had never used his name before, was scarcely aware that she had done so now, but the result was unnerving. He closed the gap between them in a couple of strides and propelled her to the nearest window with hands that dug painfully into her shoulders.

'Look out there, Jane! Tell me *how* we try, without going

167

cap in hand to the murderers in Rome who control our lives. I can't do that, even for Castagnolo, and nor can my father.'

She looked out, as instructed, at a desolate winter landscape raked by the bitter wind that blew off the mountains. The villages higher and deeper into the range were already under snow. If they were lucky they would escape it at Castagnolo, but it was hard to recall the breathless, burning heat of midsummer. She hadn't begun to realize until she came to live in Italy that it was a land of fierce extremes, seared equally by heat and cold, that bred extremes of behaviour in its people – gaiety alternating with suicidal despair, and frequent cruelty redeemed by tenderness.

'I have a sort of plan,' she muttered at last. 'You and Gino would have to decide whether it has any chance of working.'

He swung her round to face him and let his hands slip down her arms until they found her hands; but she jerked herself free and walked away from him because she needed to think clearly. It was hard to be the dispassionate analyser of their problems when her body remembered being held comfortingly against his own. She desperately called to mind a picture of Ottavio's stricken face as he'd stared at his wife in the schoolroom the morning before the *vendemmia* had started. Love within marriage brought problems enough, desire outside it was a certain route to hell.

She stared with horror at the thoughts taking shape in her mind, pushed them away as the fancies of a disordered brain and strove with all her might to concentrate on Castagnolo.

'One th-thing at a t-time,' she stammered, '. . . the men, f-first.' She saw eagerness die out of his face but knew that he was now listening. If he stayed away from her she could remember what she wanted to say and manage to sound rational. 'If the men are not content, we shall achieve nothing. Why not call them together and make an offer, a fresh beginning – a change of system if the *majority* of them want it; a contract of employment instead of a feudal obligation to serve, a wage instead of bartering at the *fattoria* for what they want to buy; in return, a commitment to work hard because without that the estate and they can't prosper. These things can be agreed between you – show them there's no need of a peasants' socialist league that will simply attract more punishment from the Blackshirts.'

Ottavio stared at her across the space she'd put between them. She sounded cool and rational and English. What she said made sense and he must listen carefully. He hadn't a grain of an excuse for being distracted by the faint sweet perfume she used, and the flush of colour in her thin cheeks that made her eyes so bright. She was the complete opposite of Elena – everything about her reticent or understated, except for her forthright independence of mind. But attraction didn't reside for long in calculated sexual allure, and charm had nothing to do with it at all. Any man not blind or stupid would find Jane Rushton desirable, but if he ever found the courage to tell her so, she would be genuinely astonished and probably horrified.

He dragged his mind back to the matter in hand, and because the effort was great, sounded more curt than he intended to. 'All very well – we offer wages to the men. But if they accept, we have to start paying them. A slight problem, my dear. Our income for years past has just about kept everything balanced on a knife-edge of survival; if a farm roof blew off in a winter storm, Enrico's wife in the kitchen had to go without a new cooking-stove. If a bridge fell down and had to be rebuilt, we didn't replant a hillside with new olive trees. We've been robbing Peter to pay Paul ever since I was old enough to understand what was happening.'

It was a depressing enough tale, God knew, to quench even Jane's enthusiasm for trying, but he couldn't see that she looked noticeably crushed. Instead, she dragged him in a new direction.

'Gino explained that no matter whether the season's good or bad, the wine from any one summer's harvest is left to mature for at least three years. All the books I've read, and the experts I've got Charlie to consult, agree that long ageing makes reasonable wine out of a reasonable vintage, but thin, acid wine out of a poor one. The longer it's kept, the worse it gets. Gino admits that the last three harvests have been disappointing, so why don't we sell *everything* while it's still drinkable? That would give us money in hand to pay the men and buy new vines to improve future quality.'

She smiled with pleasure at the neatness of the solution, even while Ottavio walked towards her and took hold of her again. Her smile faded but she didn't move away from him this time.

'Why not, my dear Jane, if we can just beg, browbeat, or bludgeon a Tuscan like Gino into doing something differently from the way it's been done for the past five hundred years? There's just one *other* small problem: we should have almost nothing to sell next year, and the year after that while we waited for our beautiful new vines to grow. How do we pay the men then, and keep buildings intact, and feed my family?'

She heard the desperation behind his heroic effort to sound cheerful, and had to resist the longing to cover his hands with her own, offering the physical comfort she had wanted to take from him a moment ago.

'While we're waiting we borrow the inheritance my mother left me when she died, instead of letting it sit idle in a bank. It isn't huge, but it will tide us over for as long as we need it to. I was keeping it to share with Charlie – one floor of a palazzo in Florence in our old age, we thought! – but he wouldn't hesitate to agree that it should be loaned to Castagnolo . . .'

Her voice dwindled and died in the face of the effect she

was *now* having on Ottavio. She could feel his hands trembling and even at a second attempt to speak, his normally soft voice sounded hoarse and unfamiliar.

'You're mad, my dear girl . . . entirely bereft of the smallest particle of common sense. I hope Charlie would agree with *that*; if not, your father would certainly prevent you from doing anything so lunatic.'

'He can't actually stop me,' Jane pointed out with pleasure. 'The money is mine, and at the advanced old age of thirty-one I can use it as I choose. I should think of it as an investment.'

'And I should think of it as an intolerable anxiety,' Ottavio shouted. 'Whatever else we do, it won't be *that*, and it's my last word on the subject, so don't waste your breath in useless blandishments.'

A small regretful smile lit her eyes. 'If I thought I was equipped for blandishments, I'd certainly give them a try.'

'Wrong again, my dear Jane!' It was his turn to surprise *her*, but the sudden longing to kiss disbelief from her face had to be denied. She was the governess of his children, though much else besides, and he was a man with a wife, who had no shadow of a right to touch another woman.

'The Buonaventuras' chronic lack of money need have nothing to do with you,' he said roughly. 'All the same, there's no harm in talking to Gino Scarelli first. If he agrees, we can tackle the farmers and labourers next. It's better than doing nothing at all.'

'I dare say you intended doing that all along,' she said quietly. 'There was no need for me to shout at you and pretend to tell you what to do. I'm sorry.'

His mouth twisted in a grin that was suddenly rueful and tender. 'Don't stop shouting at me, please, and expect to be called on to help me convince Gino. He would allow his English lady to persuade him that the sun moves round the moon if she wanted him to.'

Jane pulled her feet away from the spot on which they seemed to be anchored to the floor, and walked towards the door. The conversation hadn't lasted very long but it left her feeling that she must get back to the safety of the children and her proper place with them in the schoolroom upstairs. She had caught a glimpse of the pain that lay in wait if she strayed out of it again. If she remembered that Ottavio was her employer, married to an absent wife, she could survive the years at Castagnolo until Marco and Francesca no longer needed her.

She slowly climbed the stairs, forcing her mind to concentrate on money. If her inheritance was refused, along with government help . . . halfway up the staircase she stopped in her tracks and the beginnings of a smile lit her face. It didn't matter that Ottavio had rejected her inheritance – she now had another idea, and it grew better and better the more she thought about it.

14

In London, in the early spring of 1926, Laura took the name of Rushton for the second time. Her wedding to William was celebrated, as Charlie had predicted, with as much extravagant display as she could coax James into agreeing to. For the ceremony she chose a dress of silver-grey chiffon. Charlie conceded in his report to Jane that it was a graceful farewell to young widowhood. He didn't like Laura any better as William's bride than he had when she was Johnny's widow, but his eye was impartial when it came to beauty. Flanked by small attendants who looked like dryads in daffodil-yellow and carried posies of jonquils and pussy-willow, Laura could have been the model for a modern version of Botticelli's 'Spirit of Spring'. *She* was radiant, William looked proud and eleven-year-old David seemed not to mind a new father in place of the dead one he'd never known.

'Now let us thank the Lord our God,' Alexandra muttered to Charlie, sitting beside her in the pew. ' "All's for the best in the best of all possible worlds," or some such thing.'

Charlie looked doubtful. 'Can't say I agree, coz. We're hovering on the verge of a ruinous general strike, and there's much more wrong than that besides.'

'We're *always* hovering on the verge of some kind of strike,' Alexandra observed truthfully. 'In any case, I was talking about the Rushtons. Uncle James is now sure of being able to keep Laura at Vine House for life, and my dear mother can relax – she's got a roving son safely shackled to a wife who will keep him in order. She'd have had something to worry about if William had married Jane as originally planned – that wouldn't have worked at all.'

She smiled sweetly at George's wife, who turned round from the pew in front to fix her with a reproving eye.

'Dear Harriet thinks I talk too much,' Alex explained for Charlie's benefit. 'Did you know she's pregnant *again*, by the way? Uncle James can't say she and George aren't doing their best for Rushton's!'

Charlie mumbled an awkward congratulation to Mrs George Rushton; for different reasons he didn't like her any more than he liked Laura, but in this case she was right. Alex did talk too much nowadays, and if the wedding-party didn't soon emerge from signing registers in the vestry, there was no telling *what* embarrassment she would take pleasure in plunging them in. He couldn't blame his aunt for wanting to see this most headstrong of her children safely shackled as well, to a man who would keep her out of trouble. He devoutly prayed that someone suitable would appear soon; if not, the terrifying idea sometimes occurred to him that Aunt Alice's desperate fancy might alight on *him*. He was attached to Alexandra, and profoundly sorry for her, but he was quite certain he didn't want to marry her. He didn't want to marry anyone – he was looking forward to a peaceful old age with Jane in Italy.

'Haven't seen you for ages,' he said cautiously. 'I suppose you've been racketing about at parties and posh weekend visits.'

'Wrong, Charlie dear. I'm considered much too fast for the country pleasures of dinner with the vicar and the occasional excitement of a hunt ball; outer darkness still covers me socially for ditching Reggie Cullompton! Not that I care – I've been busy learning Italian. Drop me down *now* in the middle of the Piazza Navona and see me pass the time of day with all and sundry. Anna's witch of a mother-in-law could sneer in vain.'

'Is that what you'd really like,' Charlie asked quietly, '. . . to go back?'

174

Alexandra gave a little nod. 'I was happier there than I've ever been in my whole life. The trouble is that I can't see the faintest chance of going again. No-one would employ me in Italy, and Father wouldn't fund me – I'm still in too much disgrace.'

Her voice had lost its brittle edge and Charlie fancied that he even heard it tremble. His unpredictable cousin was always surprising him, but before he could say so, the wedding-party reappeared. The organist crashed into the opening bars of the Wedding March from *Lohengrin*, and the interlude was over. He didn't think of it again until the subject of Italy suddenly cropped up again in a conversation with his father.

At dinner the following evening James Rushton sat frowning at the wine in his glass. He was missing Laura, Charlie supposed, and not looking forward to a month of dinners with only his son for company while she and William wandered about the south of France. Charlie found the prospect daunting too, so it was a relief when James suddenly announced that he thought of going away as well.

'Had it in mind for some time,' he said curtly. 'David's old enough now to see where our great battles were fought during the war. We can do it while his mother's away – good time with his Easter holiday just starting.'

'Excellent time,' Charlie agreed sincerely. The chance to have the house to himself had never come his way before and the prospect was delightful, but he appreciated his father's true purpose in visiting the battlefields. David could be on friendly terms with his mother's new husband but he wasn't going to be allowed to forget, at least while his grandfather was alive, that he was the son of Captain John Rushton, MC, killed in the murderous Somme slaughter for the sake of the rest of them . . . 'At the going down of the sun and in the morning we shall remember them . . .' James did just that, Charlie realized, and he found his father's loyalty moving and admirable.

'So, it's to be northern France and Flanders, sir, is it?' he asked gently.

James fidgeted with his glass. 'Not entirely. While we're over there, we may as well go down to Italy and see this extraordinary place Jane's got herself involved in.'

Taken by surprise, Charlie coughed over an incautious gulp of wine. 'Italy? . . . I thought you didn't care for it.'

'I don't – it's a chaotic, hopeless sort of place if you ask me. Too much talk and not enough action. Still, I'm bound to say this new man, Mussolini, seems to be getting a grip on things. I suppose he *might* be able to make something of them.'

Charlie tried not to smile at the note of doubt in his father's voice. 'Mussolini does quite a lot of talking, too,' he felt obliged to point out.

'I dare say – foreigners mostly do, I find.'

'Castagnolo, you said; not Rome. You're just going to see Jane?'

'Not entirely,' James muttered again. After a moment's hesitation he pulled a sheet of paper out of his pocket and handed it across the table. 'You'd better read her letter. She's got some crack-brained idea that Rushton's ought to be interested in Italian wine. With a surviving grain of common sense my daughter admits that most of what's being produced now wouldn't even be worth bringing to London, much less offering to *our* clientele; but what *might* be produced in the future is a different matter.'

'You mean we should be the *first* to offer anything worthwhile, before someone else does,' Charlie suggested helpfully.

'Of course – that goes without saying. The question is whether Castagnolo itself is worth bothering with, although it sounds unlikely to me. Investment is badly needed, which Jane thinks Rushton's might like to supply, but from what I've heard of the people in charge, we should simply be throwing good money after bad. They don't know about her scheme, by the way, and might be too proud to agree to it, anyway.'

Charlie watched his father's preoccupied face and understood his dilemma – money thrown away on a hopeless cause was unthinkable, but suppose it wasn't hopeless and someone else seized an opportunity he hadn't had the foresight to take himself?

'It doesn't sound like something *we* want to get into,' Charlie said craftily. 'Much too risky.'

James gave a little sigh over a son who'd escaped every vestige of the family's entrepreneurial spark. 'That's what your great-grandfather might have thought when he started the firm, but fortunately it didn't stop him. Haven't you learned *anything* about the principles of running a successful business? God help Rushton's if it ever has to rely on you.'

Charlie apologized, feeling pleased with himself. If his father had been hesitating before, it was now certain that he would go to Castagnolo. Once there, he would examine the possibilities with a shrewd and open mind, and it would be up to Jane and Ottavio to convince him that Rushton investment would be justified.

Charlie reckoned he'd done the best he could for *them*, but there was one more good deed worth trying, if he could find the right approach.

'I *suppose* David's old enough to look after himself, but he'll get his clothes in a mess and probably go down with the usual continental tummy. If you're thinking of taking someone to help, I'm sure that Alex would like to be useful.'

'*That* flibbertigibbet? I'd as soon take the other one – Eliza. No, I wouldn't,' he corrected himself a moment later. 'Nothing on this earth would compel me to travel across Europe with *her*. But her sister isn't much better.'

'Alexandra is better in every way,' Charles pointed out with unusual firmness. 'You'd find her a kind, cheerful companion for David, and she'd be useful as well – she's been learning Italian.'

James's answering grunt was non-committal, but two days later David climbed the stairs to his uncle's studio to announce with stammering excitement that he, Gramps and Cousin Alex were off to visit battlefields and Aunt Jane. Charlie's main regret about not going with them was that he would miss the moment when the Marchese Giuseppe Buonaventura encountered James Rushton for the first time.

Castagnolo was looking beautiful. By the time what Fausto would have described as another English invasion was crossing the Channel, a mild, wet March had sent the first signs of spring running over the hillsides. Now, with April sunlight, vines that had looked dead were springing into brilliant green leaf. Pear and plum and cherry blossom flung up fountains of white foam and – since precious land could never be wasted – strips of newly sewn wheat and maize were beginning to paint alleyways of green through the blossoming trees.

That spell of springtime beauty, Jane allowed, was worked by nature; but Gino, the tenant-farmers and their labourers had started to achieve small miracles of their own as well. Widespread neglect was slowly retreating like a wave going home; they cleared ditches, pruned mis-shapen olive trees, tied in the new shoots of vines and waged an overdue war on the jungle of weeds that threatened to choke the life out of every other growing thing.

Pleasure and pride in work were taking hold again at Castagnolo, born of Ottavio's at first stumbling efforts to explain that the success or failure of the estate and of the people who lived on it went hand in hand. If they would only trust one another, he had said, they could manage without outside help, outside interference and outside political madness. He did not find it necessary to say that, short of a miracle, Castagnolo *couldn't* survive in the end without outside help. It had become necessary – although he didn't ask himself why – to make a fight of it . . . to

178

prove Fausto wrong, perhaps, or to help people whose lives had always depended on his family, or to try to hand on to Marco an inheritance of which he needn't be ashamed.

Jane's simple, practical suggestion of consulting the men themselves had begun to work. He told her so when they were driving back from Greve, where the Marchese had sent them to buy wine for James Rushton's visit. They drank their own estate wine every day, but Don Giuseppe had insisted that the *best* Chianti must be found for James.

'What's been done so far is only a beginning, of course,' Ottavio explained as they drove home, 'and we haven't suggested anything that runs counter to the ingrained customs of old men who see no reason to change. When it comes to tampering with the way our wine is *made*, that may be a different matter!'

'True, but we shall convince the young men first and let *them* persuade their elders,' Jane said calmly.

'Simple . . . we don't need to worry about it again!' he said with a faint smile. It was her especial gift to make problems seem soluble, and her especial grace to pretend that, without her, he would have solved the problems anyway. There was a very good chance that they would *have* to do without her when there was no more money left and ruin finally closed over their heads, but for the moment he was becoming skilled at living as children did, one day at a time.

Jane, sitting beside him, was thinking much the same thought, except that on the margin of *her* mind the fact to be faced when she was feeling brave was that the Buonaventuras wouldn't need her for ever. She hadn't repeated, because she knew it would be useless, her offer to lend money to Castagnolo, but it was becoming borne in on her that Ottavio would have to know why she'd suggested her father's visit. It was a pity that Shakespeare was so often proved right. Too many brilliant ideas, simple when first conceived, got 'sicklied o'er with the pale cast of thought'. The more she considered it, the more certain it became that Ottavio and his father would be affronted by the suggestion that Rushton's might invest in Castagnolo as a commercial venture. She'd been mad to entertain the idea, but it must be mentioned now; if Ottavio refused to consider it she must pray that her father would remember he wasn't intended to discuss it unless his host did. Alexandra's presence would help, and David's education would have to serve as an excuse for their coming to Florence at all.

'I'm glad your family are coming,' Ottavio said suddenly, 'partly because it will be a pleasure for you, of course, but also because my mother is enjoying the preparations so much. She used to love entertaining, but the more of a recluse my father became, the less hope she had of inviting guests who didn't bore him so much that he simply never appeared.'

'House-guests *and* the *"pulizia di Pasqua"* to contend with! Enrico's wife explained to me that it has to be done before the priest comes to give his annual blessing to the house. We have the tradition of spring-cleaning at home, but it seems a nicer idea to link it directly to Easter – a fresh beginning because Christ is risen.'

' "At home", you said just now – I suppose that's how you think of it, of course,' Ottavio murmured.

Jane hesitated, then plumped for honesty. 'If it weren't for Charlie, I should scarcely think of it at all. Time enough to do so when Francesca has outgrown a governess and you politely dispense with my services.'

Ottavio suddenly braked the car and pulled off the road, the better to say what filled his mind and heart.

'It makes me angry to hear you call yourself a mere governess – you teach the children, I grant you, but you must know as well as I do that our only reason for striving to do more than we thought we could is so as not to disappoint *you*, and we smile to find life so much happier than we realized it was simply because *you're* at

Castagnolo. I can't imagine a time when we shall no longer need you.'

His earnest voice faded into silence. Jane listened to the triple notes of a hoopoe hidden in a clump of ilex trees bordering the road and marvelled that moments of extreme happiness came unlooked for and without the slightest warning. Even when she was an old, old lady she would remember this stretch of road, the hoopoe's song and the sight of Ottavio's thin, brown hands resting on the steering-wheel.

Happiness was the richer for its inevitable undercurrent of pain. He couldn't imagine a time when she wouldn't be needed at Castagnolo, but *she* could imagine it only too well. If Elena got tired of being separated from her family, or Howard Harrington tired of living with a woman he wasn't allowed to marry, she would come home. Jane knew as clearly as she knew anything on earth that Ottavio wouldn't refuse to take his wife back again. That, when it happened, would be the moment for a governess to remember that she had loved England once and must learn to love it again.

She put the thought aside because there was something else that had to be said.

'Is there any reason why *we* shouldn't produce Chianti Classico just as good as the wine you've bought, and put the mark of the Consorzio's black cock on our bottles – not now, but in a few years' time?'

She sensed Ottavio's amusement even before she saw the smile that lifted the corners of his mouth.

'I'm afraid there are several good reasons, the first of them being the unarguable one of geography! The limits of the Classico region are strictly defined and the Colli Fiorentini are outside them.'

'All right, no black cock – Charlie will design a beautiful label for us instead that's all our own. But we can still produce wine that is just as good.'

'We *could* . . . with perfect growing conditions, with

181

money to invest in new stock and with stubborn men like Gino convinced of the need to make changes. They still equate success with quantity – a good year is judged by how many gallons of wine we produce, irrespective of whether or not it's barely drinkable. Quality doesn't come into it at all.' He turned to face her and suddenly took hold of her hands. His face looked so sad that she couldn't be irritated by his acceptance of situations that seemed inevitable.

'My dear girl, don't expect too much of us. The truth is that however hard we try, we shall probably fail in the end. Don't break *your* heart over Castagnolo, please.'

The advice was good, but it came too late; whatever happened to the Buonaventuras happened to her now, as well. She couldn't say so, but she must say something else instead.

'My father isn't coming by chance – I *asked* him. If you won't accept a loan from me, I thought we might encourage a business proposition from *him* . . . Rushton investment in an Italian vineyard, to the ultimate advantage of both!'

Ottavio's hands released hers as if he'd been stung; his mouth set in the lines of mulish obstinacy she occasionally clashed with in Marco, and his normally gentle brown eyes frowned.

'Impertinent interference?' she asked quickly before he could say anything. 'Don't be angry . . . it was the only practical idea I could think of.'

'How *can* I be angry when you mean so well?' he asked after a moment's struggle with himself. 'But we cannot accept charity, my dearest Jane. However kind Mr Rushton intends to be, I shall have to refuse his offer.'

Her tension suddenly evaporated into a smile of pure amusement. 'How *can* I have given such a strange impression of my father? In matters of business he is well known in London to have the courage of a lion and the cunning of a fox, but I doubt if it would occur to *anyone* to call him kind or charitable! He will offer to invest

182

in Castagnolo if Rushton's can benefit from it, not otherwise.'

'Then we shall forget that aspect of his visit,' Ottavio
said firmly, putting the car in motion again, 'and merely
enjoy his company.'

That seemed more doubtful than anything else, but Jane
held her tongue about saying so. Her last letter to Charlie
had implored him to explain the political bitterness divid-
ing the family James was coming to. But even if he managed
to avoid that fraught subject, there were others nearly as
inflammable. If Ottavio was right and her father saw
nothing to interest him at Castagnolo, she would have
inflicted a great deal of anxiety on herself for nothing.

What she hadn't bargained for was enjoyment – but it was
there, heart warming and unmistakable from the moment
her father climbed out of the car that had brought them
from the station in Florence. She hadn't seen him for a
year and there was pleasure in discovering that time hadn't
dared touch his upright, elegant figure. If he was impressed
by the grandeur of the castle on its flying spur of rock,
he didn't show it, and that was as she remembered him,
too.

'Papa, welcome to Castagnolo,' she said, and meant it.

His cool grey eyes inspected her, noting changes that he
was bound to approve – she was thin, but no longer
painfully angular; her hair was well cut, and her jacket
and skirt of jade-green wool positively becoming. More
than that, he was pleased to see that she wore an air of
ease and contentment. However forbidding this extraordinary place looked, and however odd its Italian owners
were certain to be, his daughter hadn't been intimidated;
he needn't have worried about her being a governess, after
all. He smiled affably on Ottavio, who had followed her
outside with the children to welcome him.

They remembered Alexandra from her previous visit,
but Jane was aware of them watching David – only a year

183

older than Marco, but marked out by English colouring and height. They recognized other differences without being able to account for them. Jane *could* account for them and felt sad. David was stiff because he was afraid of seeming foolish; they could understand *him*, and, although it shouldn't have mattered that he couldn't understand them, it seemed to put him at an unfair disadvantage. He hoped they realized that the English didn't have to learn other people's languages – that was what Grandpa said, and he always knew everything.

'Come and watch the men spraying the vines,' Marco suggested. 'Everything gets painted blue . . . it's good fun to try.'

David smiled and nodded – he had no idea why vines should be sprayed blue but at least it *sounded* fun after long hours of being cooped up in trains.

'Is *she* coming, too?' he looked doubtfully at Francesca, who stared back at him with her usual measuring glance.

'Of course – if she wants to.'

David felt sure it wasn't what an English girl of eight would want to do. 'I thought you liked drawing,' he said loftily, rummaging in his memory. 'I saw the pictures you sent my uncle – animals with tassels on them.'

'I suppose you thought they looked silly,' Francesca said, in clear, unaccented English.

'Pretty silly,' he agreed, angry because she'd guessed correctly.

She went with them, but she hated him from that moment on. When Yane had said the English boy would be different, she must have been trying to warn them.

With the children gone, the rest of the party moved indoors to be greeted by the Marchesa. She was splendidly dressed for the occasion, beautifully made up and happy to welcome back her dear fellow-Libran, Alexandra. Then she smiled on her other guest who, to his daughter's considerable astonishment, bowed over the Marchesa's hand with all the aplomb in the world. Excusing this lapse into effusive behaviour afterwards to Jane, he explained that a brisk handshake would have been quite inappropriate to the occasion.

'You didn't tell me,' he also pointed out, 'that the Marchesa is a remarkably good-looking woman.'

Jane apologized, belatedly realizing how certain Donna Giulia was to have appealed to her father when his ideal of womanhood was the ripe, rich femininity of an Edwardian beauty. 'Perhaps I also forgot to mention that she's kind and gentle, and radiantly happy when she's with anyone she finds congenial.'

'Well, of course,' said James confidently. He thanked God that he'd kept his figure and that his tailor cut the best evening clothes in London. He was looking forward to dining with his hostess – she would be certain to wear pearls. Nothing became a woman better, but she would be bound to know that.

The Marchesa didn't disappoint him and nor, in a different way, did his host, who appeared in the *salone* before dinner, apologizing for an earlier absence.

Jane watched them being presented to each other – her father the taller and more upright and, although they were the same age, the more youthful looking of the two. She thought he was pleasantly aware of this, just as the Marchese was aware that in the eyes of his guest he was a privileged but unsuccessful man. Giuseppe Buonaventura's aristocratic strength lay in the fact that he didn't care. Jane thought them well-matched adversaries, but she would have liked them to be friends.

'You would be welcome anyway, of course, Mr Rushton,' the Marchese was murmuring gently, 'but as the father of our dear Jane . . .' his beautiful thin hands sketched a gesture that completed the sentence. Now it was James's turn.

'You're very kind, Signor Marchese.' It sounded rum, but Alexandra had promised him that this was the correct mode of address. 'Jane's letters didn't do justice to

Castagnolo, nor to Tuscany. I now understand why we haven't been able to entice her home.'

No-one, as far as she could recall, had tried, but she accepted the speech in the spirit in which it was offered; honours so far were roughly even.

'You're interested above all in Tuscan wine, of course. What we have to offer will seem pitiable to a connoisseur of the great French domaines.' Secure in the knowledge of what Ottavio had brought back from Greve, the Marchese could afford to be modest. 'You have come to poor, backward Italy, remember!'

'Where wine has been made for the past two thousand years – time enough, I'm sure, to have mastered the art,' James said smoothly.

'We've mastered many things, but forgotten them again – it's our besetting sin, my dear sir.' He smiled at his wife, who was being informed by Enrico in the doorway that dinner was served. She took the arm James offered, the Marchese escorted Alexandra, and Ottavio and Jane, exchanging small smiles, fell into step behind them. For better or worse the Rushton visit was under way.

15

Marco and David, host and guest, remembered for a day or two what was expected of them. Outward politeness concealed Marco's scorn of someone who seemed to know nothing of country matters, and David's pity for a boy who couldn't row a boat, play cricket or seem to understand the importance of the Royal Navy. Tolerance showed signs of wearing thin and broke altogether under the strain of an argument that flared up about the war. David tactlessly forgot that Italy had taken part in it at all, and, with his sister listening, Marco had not only to remind him but also to overstate his case a little.

'Not take part?' he shouted. '*Stupido* . . . we *won* it for you. Ask my uncle . . . he was *there*; he was a hero.'

David was still awed by what he'd seen of a military cemetery, and impressed by the memory of his father's grave. It made him more contemptuous than he might otherwise have been. 'I'm talking about *real* fighting. Your uncle was never in the trenches. What does he know about the battles of the Somme and Verdun and Passchendaele?'

'Your soldiers sat in holes in the ground and waited while we climbed terrible mountains to reach the enemy. Zio Fausto swam across freezing rivers with a dagger in his teeth, to slit the throats of the Austrians on the other side.'

It was much, but David knew he could outmatch it. 'My father got a medal from the King. He *died* for England.'

'We shall fight *you* next time, and destroy your Empire.'

'Italian soldiers beat *ours*? You silly chump, they couldn't do it if we were only fighting with one hand!'

It was one insult too many; Marco flung himself on the enemy, and the next moment they were rolling in the dirt and straw of Gino's stock-yard. Francesca stared at them for a moment and then walked away. She hoped Marco would win, but not only because he belonged to her; the tall boy with chestnut-coloured hair who sat on the edge of the chair when they visited the Scarellis' kitchen despised *them* as well. Francesca knew it and hoped that Marco would succeed in making David's fine English clothes *very* dirty. But she sensed something else as well that saddened her; fighting each other was almost a necessary part of becoming friends for boys. After this, for as long as Jane's nephew was there, she would be excluded from their activities and expected to sit in the *salone*, listening to the visiting ladies' silly conversation.

It was a resentment Jane sympathized with. Much as her father revelled in the Marchesa's company each evening, he made his philosophy clear: during the day women should be left to the harmless domestic affairs that concerned them. He did *not* expect them to trail along while the Marchese demonstrated the working of his tower telescope, or Ottavio took him on long, conducted tours of the estate.

Alexandra commented on it with rueful amusement when they were sitting together in splendid feminine isolation one afternoon. 'It's like being back in Victorian England, travelling with Uncle James. We're required to look decorative and to keep ourselves more or less usefully occupied, until such time as our tired and jaded menfolk feel like being entertained!'

'It's oriental, and Mr Rushton is no different from most men,' the Marchesa pointed out unexpectedly. 'We can count on being cherished and provided for as long as we do not also ask for freedom of choice.'

She smiled at the expression on the faces of the two younger women. 'You don't like that, my dears? Nor did I, until I understood that women like my daughter-in-law cheat by accepting only one side of the bargain. Look at the unhappiness that causes.'

Then, with nothing else to do, she went away placidly to enjoy a little afternoon siesta, recommending them to do likewise.

'So that we may twinkle all the more brightly this evening,' Jane said with relish when she'd left the room. 'She's a funny one, but I've grown to love her dearly. Elena's restlessness used to affect *her*, but she seems to have learned contentment in the past few months; it makes *everybody* happier in a strange sort of way.'

Alexandra stared at her cousin's face, wondering what lay behind its composure and apparent serenity. 'I think you've made *all* the Buonaventuras happy, but what about *you*, Jane?' she asked suddenly. 'Does it content you to look after children who aren't yours, to spend your youth propping up charming, feckless people who ought to be able to run their own lives?'

'Apart from a keen anxiety to know what my father is making of Castagnolo, I'm very content,' Jane insisted. Alexandra didn't look convinced, and she felt obliged to try again. 'I think my youth, as you call it, somehow got swallowed up in the war. Now, I'd much rather be here, where I'm useful, than be eating my heart out in London watching William fail to stay faithful to a plain wife he hadn't married for love.'

'If he could see you now, I doubt if staying faithful would be much of a problem.'

Jane gave a little bow to acknowledge a comment that took her by surprise. '*Merci du compliment!* What about you, Alex dear? You're looking thin and, when you think no-one's watching, rather sad. Charlie was a bit scathing about the viscount, but you must have liked him to consider marrying at all.'

'Reggie? I think I felt sorry for him – he has a mother who could leave the Countess Andriani standing in the damning-with-faint-praise stakes. In the end it didn't seem enough to marry on, though, so I backed out.'

She couldn't bring herself to mention the name of Fausto, and nor could Jane, who led the conversation in a different direction.

'Anna is expecting another child – did you know? Her letters to the Marchesa are brief and cheerful, her occasional letters to me are not. I find the difference very worrying, but her husband is a busy, successful man – we mustn't expect *him* to notice.'

Alexandra smiled in spite of herself at the acid note sounding so clearly. Jane when laying about her on behalf of someone she valued had never been inclined to give any quarter. She probably didn't like Ernesto's political views either, but she wouldn't make Anna's life any more difficult than it already was by openly attacking the Fascism Signora Lambertini was obliged to believe in.

In doubting Ernesto's concern for his wife, though, Jane had to admit herself wrong a day or two later. A note to Alexandra from Anna was accompanied by one from him to his mother-in-law. He wasn't in the habit of writing to the Marchesa, and she took seriously the task entrusted to her of persuading Alexandra not to go straight home.

'It's kind of Anna to invite me, but I'm afraid it's out of the question,' Alex said heroically. 'I'm here to keep an eye on David for Uncle James. I can't possibly go waltzing off to Rome while they travel back to London alone.'

While Donna Giulia pondered the confusing idea of waltzing and Rome, Jane took note of the desperation in her cousin's voice. It was hard to refuse an invitation gracefully when the real reason for refusing couldn't be given.

'Explain for me, Janey,' Alex begged. 'Say that I *can't* go to Rome, even for Anna.'

Jane did her best, reverting to Italian for an unblushing description of Aunt Alice as an enfeebled lady stricken in years who needed her daughter home again. It was a well-meant lie that received the punishment it deserved when the Marchesa later condoled with James on the extreme frailty of his sister-in-law.

'Alice?' James asked incredulously. 'Dear lady, you're mistaken. There's nothing wrong with my sister-in-law,' thereby only convincing Lady Giulia that even the nicest of men failed to understand a woman's problems.

'If your daughter is unwell Alice would be the first to insist that Alexandra should go and make herself useful,' James went on, supposing that he was saying what they all wanted to hear. 'David and I can make our own way home. Of course, Alex can go to Rome.'

'There you are, my dear,' the Marchesa smiled happily. 'You can be spared for a little while, at least.'

Alex caught Jane's anxious eye, gave a little shrug and accepted the fact that Fate had taken control of her life. 'I shall be glad to see Anna again,' she said quietly.

It was settled then and there that when James and David set off for London, she would take the train south for Rome.

The normal routine of morning lessons and afternoon walks and play was suspended while the visitors were at Castagnolo. Jane rather regretted her idleness, much as she enjoyed Alexandra's company. Even the glorious celebration of Easter couldn't quite distract her from the fruitless exercise of trying to guess her father's reaction to what he was being shown so painstakingly.

Ottavio insisted that James and David must see more of Tuscany than belonged to the Buonaventuras. Siena's rose-red Campo had certainly to be visited, and the medieval towers of San Gimignano. On Easter Day the entire household also went into Florence for the ceremony of the *Scoppio del Carro* in the Cathedral. Watched by the gorgeously dressed dignitaries of the Church and a huge congregation, the mechanical dove flew along its appointed line from the High Altar to the decorated *carro* outside in the piazza, and duly ignited the fireworks with which it was filled. Marco and David enjoyed the noise and excitement of the explosions, but Francesca inevitably preferred the oxen that had drawn the cart – their horns and hoofs gilded for the occasion. Jane's private moment of joy was when all the bells of Florence, silent since Maundy Thursday, suddenly began to ring out over the city again – Christ was risen, light had triumphed over darkness again, and goodness over evil.

'Popish tricks,' James muttered to her as they made their way through the crowded piazza afterwards. 'I suppose Italians like this sort of thing – extraordinary people.'

She didn't argue; on certain subjects her father's mind was not open to change, and one of them was the dubious practices of the Catholic Church.

'The ceremony of the bird is important here,' she explained instead. 'If it flies straight back to the altar, as a good dove should, everyone knows that it will be a year of good harvest.'

'Pagan superstition – even worse!'

All the same, she suspected that he'd rather enjoyed the fireworks and hadn't even minded the service very much.

The moment of his departure for London was getting very close, and still she had no idea what impression Castagnolo had made on him. She was resigned to *not* knowing, aware that asking questions he wasn't prepared to answer would produce only irritation.

It was all the more unexpected, therefore, to have him suggest a walk together when luncheon was over. She chose a gentle climb up the wooded slopes to the east of the castle – a perfect viewpoint from which to enjoy the hill-encircled beauty of the river valley, and the domed and towered skyline of the city.

'I dare say you've got used to all this,' James murmured after a long silence. 'It doesn't look like home to me, but I'll grant you that it's fine enough in its way.'

She had sworn to herself that she would be patient . . . would wait until he was ready to say whatever he had to

192

tell her; but now she found that she couldn't bear to wait a moment longer.

'Is it fine enough to persuade you to . . . to take an interest in it?'

His reply came slowly, with what sounded like genuine regret. 'No, it doesn't persuade me of that.'

She had known it all along, she tried to tell herself – there had never been more than a remote chance that he would fall sufficiently under the spell of Tuscany to forget natural prudence, much less his prejudice against all things Italian. All the same she had *hoped*, and the setback in store for Ottavio was a pain that made it difficult to speak.

'I'm . . . sorry,' she muttered, 'but it's no good badgering you if your mind is made up. We shall have to find some other means of surviving until the estate can pay its way again.'

'I doubt if it ever will,' James said bluntly. 'Buona-ventura is a nice man, Jane – too nice to do what is required; that means bullying people here into changing the methods and habits ingrained in them. Without those changes Castagnolo hasn't any chance at all.'

He stared at his daughter's pale, strained face and knew the sharpness of her disappointment. 'It's not *your* problem, my dear,' he said with unaccustomed gentleness.

'It feels as if it were,' she said bleakly.

Another silence fell which neither of them seemed able to break, until James coughed and cleared his throat. 'Haven't said this before . . . perhaps I should have done. I suggested letting Laura run things at Vine House to keep her happy there, but I never meant you to feel that it wasn't still *your* home.'

'Laura wasn't the only reason I left,' Jane pointed out.

'I know, and that's another thing that troubles me – it didn't seem quite my affair, so I never enquired, but I always had the feeling William had . . . had behaved badly; you wouldn't have disappeared otherwise.'

'It doesn't matter now,' she said quietly. 'What matters

is that *you're* all happy at Vine House, and that *we* fight our way out of our problems here.'

James thrust his hands in the pockets of his jacket, then took them out again and stared at them. 'Got one more thing to say. My estate will be split between you when I die – David will have Johnny's share, of course; you and Charles will divide the rest. I can't recommend *Rushton's* investing a penny in this place, but if you want to use *your* inheritance to prop up Castagnolo, it's up to you; I'll advance you annual instalments as long as you understand you'll receive nothing more when I die.'

He didn't know whether to expect her to look overjoyed or appalled, but when he stared at her again she looked merely thoughtful.

'Not quite so much *your* problem as you imagined, after all?' he suggested drily.

Jane shook her head, smiling a little because he couldn't help being wrong even though he meant well.

'I was only wondering how we could persuade Ottavio to accept. He *won't* accept if he thinks the money he's being offered has anything to do with me. Can it be made to *seem* like a Rushton investment?'

'It can be made to seem whatever we want it to,' James barked, 'but I hope you'll give a grain of rational thought to the future before you make up your mind.'

'Remember, in other words, that I'm thirty-one and past whatever chance I ever had of finding a husband?' she asked with rueful amusement. 'I do realize that. The only difference between us is that *you* think I shall be throwing my inheritance away; *I* believe that by the time it's used up we shall have wine to sell that even Rushton's will be glad to buy.'

James winced at the memory of the wine Scarelli had offered him in the *cantina*. The hopelessness of his daughter's ambitions prompted him to a rare piece of kindness.

'If Rushton's are to seem to be involved, Ottavio will

194

expect us to be monitoring progress. God knows Charlie's as ignorant of making wine as you are, but I'll send him out here from time to time; it might even teach him to take an interest in Rushton's!'

Jane's face was lit with sudden happiness. 'That would make it perfect, but I hope *you'll* come again as well, at least for the Marchese's benefit! He's still hoping to persuade you that it was a mistake to make Italy into one kingdom.'

'He still believes it was a mistake to behead Charles I! If I come, it will be to enjoy the *Marchesa's* company.'

'That as well,' Jane allowed, prompted by gratitude to kiss her father's cheek and so end an extraordinary conversation.

He and David set off on the journey home two days later, leaving Alexandra to watch them go, torn between the delight and despair of not travelling with them. She wanted to go back to Rome more than she wanted anything on earth, dreaded fainting with delight if she should happen to see Fausto again, felt sick and weak and lightheadedly happy all at the same time.

Jane sensed her confused state of mind, and was tempted to persuade her not to go. 'You bewildered the Marchese at lunch,' she pointed out smilingly, later that afternoon. 'Twice when he expected you to answer no, you said yes, and when he announced that a rare partial eclipse of the sun *might* be seen, you murmured, "Oh, really . . . *again?*" We do *not* have them all the time, dear Alex.'

Alexandra's white face was suddenly flushed with colour that faded leaving it even paler than before. 'Janey – I don't know what I'm saying more than half the time. I'm hot with excitement, cold with fear.'

'You don't have to go if it's so painful . . . why not explain to Anna that you have to return to England?'

'Because knowing the muddle I'd be in, she must be

desperate to have asked me at all. It seems cowardly to run home . . . I don't want to be a coward, along with everything else.' She tried to smile at her cousin's concerned face. 'Fortunately the Marchese expects me to sound half-witted! Don't worry about me – I shall be as cool as a cucumber when I have to be, for Anna's benefit.'

Jane nodded and abandoned Alexandra's problems for pressing ones of her own. It was too late to realize that she should have insisted on knowing in what terms her father planned to talk to Ottavio. She prayed that the subject might be shelved until there was time to consult Charlie, but Ottavio had the opposite intention. When he followed her out on to the terrace before breakfast the next morning, she could only remember Alexandra's philosophy – it didn't do to be cowardly.

'You didn't warn me that your father was an *expert* on Italian wines,' Ottavio began promptly. 'I should have been more nervous if I'd realized that.'

'I didn't realize it, either. His advantage in any business matter is a commanding manner that always makes him *sound* like an expert! I hope he didn't mortally insult Gino by laying down the law about the only way to make a decent Chianti?'

'Well, certain things were made clear! Your father will only introduce the *best* Chianti to his clientele; that means rejuvenating the vineyards with new vines, reducing the proportion of white grapes to red, that at the moment only increase the quantity of wine at the expense of its quality, and adjusting the length of time it matures in the barrels before being bottled. With these small matters put right, your father thinks we might not need to be ashamed of a Castagnolo vintage!'

She examined Ottavio's grave face, looking for signs that he, as well as Gino, had taken offence. The Rushton tendency to know best about everything was irritating enough in London; out here, on the strength of one brief visit, it had probably seemed insufferable.

'If you think my father is wrong, you don't have to do what he says,' she murmured.

'We *do* have to, because he's quite right,' Ottavio said calmly. 'It would have been useless for me to say it – Gino is convinced that the *padrone* knows less than *he* does; but when a *gran'signore* whose cellars are stacked with great French wines arrives all the way from London only to see what *we* can offer, then even a stubborn Tuscan knows that it is time to listen.'

Her anxious face made Ottavio suddenly relent. He took her hands in his warm ones and smiled with all the sweetness in his heart.

'It's all *right*, my dearest Jane. I can't swear to you that disease and frost and not enough sun and too much rain won't come to ruin us; these are hazards we can only pray about. But with the investment your father insists on making and with our own hard work, we might have some wine in five years' time that even Rushton's customers feel able to drink.'

A smile wiped the strain from her face, so transfiguring it with joy that he forgot everything but gratitude for the fact that she was there. A year ago she had been a chance-met stranger on a hillside above Fiesole; he'd watched her walk away, amused enough by her prim, plain, decided Englishness to forget for a moment the failures of his life and the unhappiness of his home. Now he knew that she wasn't prim, had never been anything but beautiful, and that for as long as she was with them there was no harm they need fear.

'My father's customers are going to feel privileged to drink our wine in five years' time – word of a Rushton!' she insisted bravely. It was hard to sound calm when, for all her sensible thirty-one years, the heart in her breast was behaving like a wild thing. It was quite impossible not to be aware of Ottavio standing close to her and smiling so tenderly that she didn't know whether she wanted to weep or laugh for joy.

'Charlie is going to be given the task of keeping an eye on us,' he said, certain of giving pleasure. 'Won't that make you happy, Jane?'

'Yes . . . but I'm happy already; just being here makes me happy.'

He lifted her hand to his mouth in a gesture that was both formal and oddly intimate.

'It must be breakfast-time,' she said unsteadily, when he let her go. 'I don't know why Marco isn't down here already; he usually is by now.' On her way back to the terrace door, she halted suddenly. 'You'll explain to *him*, won't you, what you're going to do here? He's old enough to understand, and everything about Castagnolo matters intensely to him.'

Ottavio nodded, aware that she was right and that it wouldn't have occurred to *him* to include a ten-year-old boy in discussions about the future running of the estate. The main doors leading from the hall to the outer court-yard were wide open when they got inside, and the reason for Marco's non-appearance was clear – he was already outside, jumping up and down in the excitement of inspecting a brand-new motorcar. Beside it, smiling at his nephew's stream of questions, stood Fausto, bare headed, casually but elegantly dressed as usual. He bowed to Jane as she and Ottavio walked into the courtyard towards him.

'You're just in time for breakfast,' Ottavio said, deter-minedly playing the rôle of welcoming brother and host. 'Mamma will be disappointed if you haven't come to stay. A day earlier and you could have met Jane's father and nephew, but unfortunately they left yesterday.'

'I know – Anna told me. There was a meeting I had to attend in Florence last night, so I was given her instructions to come here to collect Signorina Alexandra. Anna seemed to think she might change her mind about a visit to Rome if not personally escorted.'

His handsome face was smiling and confident of its ability to please. Jane thought that she could easily have hated him instead – either for the deliberate use of a charm he was conscious of possessing, or for *not* knowing that what he possessed was dangerous. Whichever it was, the result was the same. Alexandra would fall in love with him all over again, and whether he realized and regretted it, or didn't know and didn't care, she would have a burden of fresh unhappiness to struggle with.

'My cousin promised Anna that she would go; she had every intention of taking the train to Rome,' Jane said coolly.

'But she will find the journey more interesting with me,' Fausto pointed out with a certainty that was maddening.

Jane would have denied it if she could, but it was a statement of fact and she knew it as well as he did.

'Kind of you to spare the time from urgent errands for Il Duce,' was the best she could do.

Fausto smiled and bowed again. 'He would be the first to say that a lady must be attended to.'

Conscious of having been worsted, Jane nodded and walked back into the hall. She had something more urgent to do than stay bandying words with Fausto – Alex must be found and warned that he was there.

16

By the time they reached Rome Alexandra was in that strangely heightened state of awareness – of body and mind – in which everything that happened seemed to be happening to *her*. She was the raindrop sparkling on the petals of a rose, the child laughing at its mother in a garden, and the small, dead bird lying by the roadside. Everybody's joy and pain was hers; she was alive again because she was with this man who turned his head to smile at her from time to time. Nothing was forgotten afterwards of their journey back to Rome, but it ended in the most memorable moments of all.

'I think we shall just be in time,' Fausto murmured, consulting his watch. 'There's something I want you to see before I deliver you to Anna.'

He stopped the car and led her on foot through a maze of small streets. They walked in the same direction as many other people, all drawn towards a faint, distant hum of voices that grew louder the nearer they got to it. It brought them finally to the Piazza Colonna and a crowd of rapturously excited men and women, jammed into the space in front of the Palazzo Chigi. There was a sudden roar of adulation as a figure appeared on the balcony above them. The shaven-headed man stood there, judging the exact moment at which he would command them to fall silent and listen. His piercing gaze and out-thrust jaw were just as usual. All that was different today was the strip of bandage covering a bullet-graze on his nose. But for the grace of God – women knelt in the roadway at the thought of it – Il Duce might be dead by now, killed by a half-crazed Irishwoman called Violet Gibson.

Benito Mussolini was anything but dead. His resonant voice reassured them. Once again he launched on the measured, lucid rhetoric of which he was a master.

'If I advance, follow me; if I retreat, kill me; if I die, avenge me . . .'

These people would do just that. Looking round the sea of faces, Alexandra felt sure of it. They were entirely possessed by a man who was going to do what no-one else had been able to do before – change Italy. No more hopelessness, or failure, or foreign domination; instead, the glorious future he promised them under Fascism.

'Well, what did you make of that, my dear English friend?' Fausto asked as they inched their way out of the square towards the car again. 'Was it too unseemly, that public display of emotion? . . . Too Latin for a little Anglo-Saxon to approve of?'

His voice was lightly teasing, but she knew the question had a serious intention.

'It wasn't too *anything*, except perhaps exhausting,' she said truthfully. 'I feel as if I'd been out walking in a high wind, in the thin air of a mountain-top!'

'It's only exhausting if you fight against it, as Anna does. Go *with* it and it's the most exhilarating thing on earth.'

He pulled her to a stop suddenly, gripping her shoulders so that she had to face him. 'Alexandra, couldn't you *feel* the fervour of those people – the devotion they offer Mussolini?'

'Yes . . . I even shared it,' she confessed. 'I understood as well as they did that if a half-mad woman had succeeded in killing Il Duce, it would have been an unutterable tragedy for Italy.'

Fausto let out his held breath on a long, thankful sigh. 'You *do* understand . . . what a *good* little Anglo-Saxon it is!'

His smile was as much a caress as if he'd kissed her. Until that moment she hadn't been sure that he was glad she was there. The memory of an earlier day spent together in Rome hadn't been touched on, and she might only have imagined its ending in a passionate embrace in the darkness of the Borghese Gardens. Now, and not only for his sister's sake, he accepted that it was right for her to be back in Italy.

A street market filled the roadway round the Piazza Navona; it was all noise, bustle, colour and the music of the fountains, just as she remembered it; it felt like home, and Anna was standing on the steps of the palazzo even before Fausto had opened the car door.

'Dearest friend, welcome back . . . I was so afraid you wouldn't come . . . I made Fausto *promise* he'd bring you . . .' Anna caught herself up on a laugh that became a sob. Alexandra hugged her, feeling suddenly the older of the two.

Anna's body was swollen with the child she carried, but her face was thin to the point of gauntness and her eyes looked huge and feverishly bright.

'Of course I intended to come – why do you suppose I've been learning Italian all the winter if not to take the wind out of your dear mother-in-law's sails?'

She saw amusement ease the strain in her friend's face for a moment, then fade again.

'Can you stay, Alex – for ages and ages?'

'For as long as you want me to,' she promised gently. The longer she stayed, the harder it would be to leave when the time came, but that was no-one's problem but her own, and Anna needed her.

Fausto was allowed to go back to his own urgent affairs, on condition that he returned to dine with them. Alex followed Anna into the palazzo, to be kissed rapturously by Lorenza and, with a frigid, formal peck on both cheeks, by Ernesto's mother.

'You are looking well, Miss Rushton,' said Leonora Lambertini reluctantly. 'I'm afraid you won't be able to say the same for Anna. Some women are supposed to be made beautiful by pregnancy . . .'

It wasn't so in her daughter-in-law's case, the unfinished sentence implied, but what could be expected of a provincial from the wilds of Tuscany, whose indolent mother had taught her nothing and whose father was downright eccentric? Leonora still remembered, with no pleasure at all, her only meeting with the Marchese on the occasion of Ernesto's marriage to Anna. She remembered the castle too, and had been careful to refuse all Giulia Buonaventura's subsequent invitations.

'Anna looks beautiful enough to me,' Alex said in slow, careful Italian. 'A little tired, perhaps, but I shall make her rest now.'

She smiled sweetly at the look of surprise on the Countess's face. 'If the accent is *very* bad perhaps you would prefer my barbaric English?'

She was astonished to see the Countess's mouth twitch.

'The accent is supportable, signorina, but we shall work on it together.'

'She *likes* you,' Anna remarked in tones of wonderment when her mother-in-law had departed to put the fear of God into some hapless good works committee. 'She'll never forgive me for marrying Ernesto, but she *likes* you.'

'If you're right, Fausto would say that I should feel flattered. He's full of admiration for her.' Alex didn't think her voice changed when she spoke his name, but Anna heard its revealing softness.

'Cara – I'll say it just once. Did you mind very much coming back here? I wanted to see you so badly that I persuaded myself it wouldn't be painful for you. Now, I'm afraid I was being too selfish.' She saw Alexandra smile and shake her head.

'I *longed* so much to be in Italy that I fell over myself to accept my uncle's invitation. It's true I thought I didn't want to come *here*, but now I'm happy that I did. Whatever happens, it's worth it.' She hesitated over whether or not

203

to mention the detour they had made to the Piazza Colonna, and decided to leave it for the time being. There would be other opportunities to discover how Anna's private struggle to live with her husband's faith was going.

'How was the dear *governante*?' Anna asked smilingly. 'My mother's letters from Castagnolo sound so cheerful nowadays that I'm inclined to think Jane is a witch in disguise – she's the *befana* who visits us on Twelfth Night, bringing happiness to those who deserve it!'

'She seems content,' Alexandra said thoughtfully. 'Whether that's the same thing as being happy, I'm not sure. I can't imagine her *wanting* to leave Castagnolo now, but I suppose that one day she'll have to. I wish I thought she remembered the fact: even if she does, she still loves those children as if they belonged to her for ever.' Alexandra's lovely mouth drooped sadly, then lifted in a rueful smile. 'We pay a high price for love, poor silly mutts that we are!'

'Mutts?'

'My cousin Charlie's word – in England it means fools who can't help themselves!'

'I remember him,' Anna said slowly. 'He had the kindest smile I've ever seen on the face of a man. I hope he visits Jane again.'

'He will – they're friends, as well as brother and sister; apart from that, Francesca has told him that he must be at Castagnolo for the grape harvest this year. His *own* idea of heaven would be to be left in peace to paint different bits of Florence every day!'

'It's a modest dream of heaven – I shall pray that he's granted it. Now, cara, I'll leave you to rest after the journey. Lorenza has been sworn to leave you in peace until the "five o'clock tea"; if she appears before then, deposit her outside the door.'

Alexandra smiled and agreed, and forebore to say that, far from needing to rest, her body seemed to be on fire with energy – she could run a race round Domitian's stadium in the square outside and win it, could charm the Countess into being kind to Anna . . . could stay here for ever if only Fausto would ask her to.

He didn't ask her to, of course. That evening at dinner, when he was about to announce something quite different, Ernesto guessed what he was going to say.

'I heard a rumour! You're going with Il Duce to Tripolitania . . . am I right?'

Fausto nodded, almost unable to speak for the excitement that consumed him. His dark eyes flamed with a happiness that Alex realized desolately had nothing to do with her. If she wasn't to be destroyed by useless longing she must learn once and for all that his joy would *never* depend on her.

'It was quite unexpected – I only heard the news when I got back this afternoon. We sail on the warship *Cavour* in two days' time – imagine it, seeing Africa for the first time as part of Il Duce's entourage!'

He turned to look at Alexandra. 'It's not just a ceremonial visit, though that comes into it, of course.'

'With all the ceremony in the world,' Anna interrupted him quietly, 'we shall lay claim to territory that doesn't belong to us, in order to find space and land for our hungry, overcrowded population.'

She met her husband's fierce gaze across the table and smiled challengingly. 'Or isn't that how *you* would describe it, Ernesto?'

'It's a small part of the truth,' he agreed in a cold, precise voice. 'You might do us the justice of admitting the rest of it, however. The claims that we make are nothing to those that have enabled England and France to carve out colonial empires for themselves.' He bowed across the table at his guest. 'Excuse me, Alexandra, but it is the truth! Apart from that, we shan't go empty handed to North Africa. We shall send skilled, civilized settlers capable of improving for *everyone* the life they find there.'

'Let us hope the native people look forward to being

"improved"; if not we shall have to rely on Il Duce's powers of persuasion,' Anna agreed tonelessly. 'He has great talents in that direction.'

'I know,' Alexandra broke in, because it seemed necessary to draw Ernesto's fire away from his wife. 'Fausto and I stopped on the way here this afternoon to hear him speak.'

Four pairs of eyes were fastened on her, making her realize how exposed and dangerous was her position. She chose to speak directly to Anna.

'Cara, I know there are things about Fascism that trouble you, but wouldn't we all say that, if we were honest, about the system of government we live under? About Mussolini himself I don't think you need be troubled. He will correct the system's wrongs in time, and govern wisely for Italy.'

She didn't know whether what she said made any difference to Anna, but in looking at his guest with surprised approval at least Ernesto had forgotten to frown at his wife.

'Well said, Miss Rushton. Your own government is going to have to act with the firmness Anna so much dislikes; no country can afford to let the habit of strike upon strike slide into general anarchy. Thank God it's been halted here.'

There was a small, awkward silence into which the Countess stepped with impeccable social flair to enquire about Alexandra's visit to Castagnolo. By the time the Easter Day celebrations in the Cathedral had been described, and James Rushton's reaction to them, even Anna was laughing, and Ernesto was smiling at his wife.

They didn't see Fausto again before his warship sailed, but Alexandra told herself that she hadn't expected to. It was clear that his ranking in the Party was much higher than she'd supposed. What little free time it left him with could be spent more excitingly than making duty calls at the

Palazzo Andriani. Anna's conversations about him didn't conceal the names of friends, many of them women, who had a share in his life. Not wanting to be just one more name added to the list, Alex knew that she asked too much and accepted that anyone who did was bound to get nothing at all.

Even so, it was necessary to remind herself day after day that she was in Rome to help Anna, not to sicken and die of a longing of her own. Swinging between extremes of feverish gaiety and dark despair that were both unnatural to a woman who had been well balanced and sweetly sane, Anna *needed* help. Alexandra's worst anxiety was that they no longer talked about what kept her friend sleepless at night and left her hollow eyed and exhausted each morning.

Ernesto seemed relieved to leave his wife in the care of her English friend, and more often than not didn't even come home in time to dine with them. In a colourless voice Anna would make the excuse of yet another official function, and they would hastily talk of something else. Alexandra grew steadily more angry with him, but waited for the moment when sheer rage would make her forget the undoubted fact that she was in awe of him.

It came on the morning of Lorenza's eighth birthday – a Sunday, when the children breakfasted downstairs instead of in the nursery. They were excited and more noisy than usual, Anna looked more tired than ever, and Ernesto preoccupied. Alexandra thought it an unhappy meal even before the children began to wrangle about the birthday treat that would follow family attendance at Mass in Sant'Agnese. The difference of opinion was sharp and tempers rose quickly.

'I'm the *man* – *I* choose,' Emmanuele shouted with all the conviction of a five-year-old Italian male.

'It's *my* birthday – Mamma, it's for *me* to say . . . I choose Punch and Judy in the Borghese Gardens.'

'That's stupid . . . Papa, it's for stupid girls . . .'

'Be quiet, both of you.' Ernesto's cold voice cut across the quarrel like a sword, leaving them staring at him. 'You will go where your mother and Alexandra take you.' Then he turned to Anna. 'You'll have to excuse me, I'm afraid. There's work that I *must* do here this morning.'

'It's Lorenza's birthday,' she reminded him, white lipped.

'I know . . . I'm sorry, but there *are* more important things.'

'Not to her, *now*. You won't even come with us to Mass?' She saw Ernesto shake his head, and a small, contemptuous smile spoiled the sweetness of her mouth. 'Il Duce is a thousand miles away – he won't know if you attend church and worship God for once, instead of a mere man.'

'Mussolini's views about religion have changed – you know that as well as I do, Anna. In any case, I don't live my entire life to please him. If I felt the need to confess my sins to that fool of a priest at Sant'Agnese, I should do so.' He had the small saving grace to say it in English, so that the children wouldn't understand, but Anna dragged herself to her feet and held out trembling hands to them.

'Come, both of you. We'll decide what to do upstairs. Your father is too busy to listen to any more chatter.'

Alexandra waited until the door closed behind them. 'But not too busy to listen to a home truth or two, I hope. And if you dare to walk away, I shall follow you all over the house screaming at you what I've got to say.'

She waited to be confronted by a roar of anger, forgetting that Ernesto was not a typical Italian; his emotions were deeply hidden and only his intellectual passions were ever allowed to be visible. After a moment's struggle with himself he managed to speak even more quietly than usual.

'Forgive me if I fail to see what my family difficulties have to do with you.'

'*You* asked Anna's mother to persuade me to come, and you've left her to me ever since I arrived. Much more than

208

that, she concerns me because she's a dear friend. Don't try to tell me that I'm not supposed to care if she's on the verge of a breakdown.'

Ernesto stared at a girl who'd been welcome enough in his home because she amused his wife and was accepted by his mother. She was decorative, too, and had always seemed to understand until now that men must be left to get on with the real business of running the world. He didn't recognize her in this cool, self-possessed stranger who judged him and found him wanting.

'Anna's condition is making her overwrought,' he said sullenly. 'When the child is born, she'll be herself again.'

'The child is the *trouble*, Ernesto. Can't you understand? For Anna life seems to be a terrifyingly uncertain business – she's so afraid of the future that she's almost convinced herself it's a mortal sin to bring another helpless creature into a world full of violence and unhappiness.'

'She's infected by Ottavio's madness. Even *you* understand what is happening here – why can't she?'

Alexandra heard the ragged edge of pain in his voice and realized that in one important respect, at least, she had misjudged him. Ernesto did care about his wife.

'It's easier for me,' she said at last. 'I don't belong . . . don't know the people involved, as Anna does. Some of them were childhood friends – they've been exiled or punished in some other way for not accepting the new regime.'

'I know . . . I *know*; but it is for the long-term good of Italy, Alexandra. If only she could *see* that. We can't afford enemies and the luxury of a legal opposition – this is *Italy*, not secure, well-ordered England.'

'We're not as secure as all that – strikes and unemployment and social injustices produce violence and bitterness there as well as here.'

'All right – but you have an established system to deal with them; we have Fascism, and it's our only hope.'

'I understand that – so will she if you are patient with

her and keep loving her. At the moment she feels that she and the children have lost you to a cause she fears.'

Ernesto buried his face in his hands and Alexandra was astonished to find that she felt sorry for *him*, as well as for Anna.

'It's the most difficult time of all,' he murmured finally, raising his head to stare at her. 'There's an immense amount of work to be done – a whole system of industrial corporativism to be devised and codified if we are to move out of chaos into prosperity. I'm involved in that . . . I have to be.'

'Then I suggest that you let me take Anna back to Fiesole – it's quiet and peaceful there and the children will be happy. Jane won't be far away, and there's no-one in the world like *her* for being a very present help in time of trouble.'

'The Anglo-Florentines to the rescue!' Ernesto said with a faint, rueful smile. 'But I thought *you* preferred Rome.'

'No, I shall be glad to go back to Tuscany,' Alexandra said deliberately, 'having something to escape from, too.' She walked towards the door, but turned round to deliver a parting shot. 'Come yourself sometimes – it's your child Anna's bearing; forget Italy once in a while and remember that the Lambertinis have a claim on you, too.'

Ernesto smiled whole-heartedly for once, and she glimpsed the man Anna had fallen in love with.

'Do you know you sounded *just* like Jane Rushton then!'

Anna's second son was born four months later, after a night of exhausting labour. By the dawn of a cloudless August morning, Vittorio Lambertini was safely delivered into the world that his mother was so greatly troubled by, but the doctor insisted that he must be her last child. She had been brought through this confinement by the grace of God and his own considerable skill; another one might tax them both too much and kill her.

'Do you mind very much?' Alexandra asked gently,

when he'd bustled away and she was left alone with Anna. 'Can you make do with three beautiful babies, cara? Lorenza and Emmanuele were beautiful, I'm sure, and this one certainly is.'

'He's a boy – I'd rather have had another daughter,' Anna said listlessly. She saw the expression on Alexandra's face and a tinge of colour touched her own pale cheeks.

'Say it . . . say I'm a selfish, self-pitying bitch who doesn't deserve her family and friends like you and Jane. The pair of you have carried me through this summer.'

'With the dear Marchesa's help, and . . .'

'. . . and Papa's, and the visits of Ottavio and the children . . .' Anna agreed, '. . . everyone's help, in fact, except my husband's. What a good thing I didn't have to rely on that!'

'Dearest, be fair . . . just a little bit fair. *He* knew that you were lapped in loving care, and *you* knew that these past few months have been terrible for him – torn between you and the work he feels compelled to do.'

Anna's dark eyes met hers and didn't look away. 'Yes, I did know and I do understand; but to answer the question you asked, I don't mind not having more children. Alex, I don't *want* another baby.'

'All right, don't shout! I'm supposed to be lulling you to rest, not inciting you to fury. Jane would say I'm the world's worst nurse.'

'Just for once she'd be wrong!' At last Anna smiled with her old sweetness. 'To prove it, I'll even agree to go to sleep and wake up properly pleased with my son!'

Alexandra kissed her and left her to rest. It was still too early to dress and start the day, but instead of returning to the bed she'd scarcely slept in, she let herself out of the house into the sweet-scented stillness of early morning. Swallows chattered and whistled above her head, busy about their aerial exercises, but otherwise the world was wrapped in silence. From her high vantage-point on the terrace the landscape looked much the same as she supposed it had looked for centuries – emerald-green and silver-green slopes of vine and olive near at hand, clusters of faded terracotta roofs, sentinel cypress trees and a backdrop of fold upon fold of violet-coloured hills against a blue Tuscan sky.

How beautiful it was . . . and how passionately she longed to be somewhere else! Life was for living, not watching one season die slowly into the next one. If she couldn't be in Rome, it would be better to be back in England, unable even to guess what Fausto might be doing. The visit to North Africa had been a great tactical success – he was probably established now as a man never to be far from Il Duce's side. No room *there* for a woman, especially one of the English whom Mussolini was known to dislike.

She had managed to hide her sadness from Anna, but Jane had guessed. Jane had a secret of her own that Alexandra had guessed – it wasn't hard for women in the same unhappy boat to understand one another. Neither of them would ever quite recover from coming to Italy, and in the end what a waste it would prove to have been!

She stared at the tightly furled buds of the wild rose that draped the balustrade in front of her. They reminded her of the tiny, pink fists of Anna's baby, but suddenly she couldn't see them for the tears that brimmed over her eyelids and poured down her face. She would never have a child to love and agonize over. As soon as Anna was strong enough to return to Rome, *she* would go back to England. For as long as she lived, she would be bright and busy there, and quite dead inside.

'Battistina says the child has been born safely and Anna is all right. Why are you weeping?' asked a voice behind her.

She was going mad and conjuring him out of the longing in her mind.

'Why, Alexandra?'

Dear Mary, Mother of God, he *was* there. Fate meant

her to say a final goodbye to him in *this* tear-stained state of weakness.

'I weep when I'm cross,' someone answered whom she supposed must be herself. She smeared her wet cheeks and then hid her hands in the pockets of her robe.

'Why are you cross?' He sounded dutifully interested at the most, like an adult bored at having to deal with a fractious child. Suddenly she was angry enough to shout at him.

'Why isn't Ernesto here? Did he send *you* because he couldn't spare the time from drafting some new little financial law? Does he even care that his wife might have died last night?'

Fausto stared at her, trying to concentrate on the crisis at hand while his thoughts wanted to linger on a problem of his own. He'd spent the last few months convincing himself that it would be madness to love Alexandra Rushton. She was beautiful, but so were other women; there was nothing she possessed that he couldn't find in a dozen more suitable companions. Now, tired, dishevelled and angry, she was not only unfairly desirable but also unfairly dear, and like no-one else at all. He wanted to kiss her into silence, not argue with her.

'Ernesto cares about his wife, but there are moments when life doesn't arrange itself very well. He *couldn't* leave Rome yesterday. I promised him I'd get here last night from Milan, but that went awry too.'

There was no sign of forgiveness in her face, for once she wasn't disposed to understand, and he remembered what Ernesto had said about her – 'fragile as porcelain to look at, but beware, my friend; underneath she's just as stubborn as her cousin at Castagnolo.' Obstinacy in a woman usually irritated Fausto, but Alexandra's arose from love of Anna; he found he could forgive her for it quite easily.

'There's something else you must remember, my dear,' he said gently. 'We are like soldiers . . . committed beyond everything else we hold dear, and required to remain faithful at any cost. *You* don't have to understand that, but Anna does.'

'She married a private individual; it takes time to realize that he's become something else – a public man who must put duty before his wife.'

'Of course, but if you are a true friend you'll *help* her to understand, not . . .'

'. . . not encourage her in my thoughtless English way to feel neglected and hurt! You'll have to trust me, as Ernesto does.'

He frowned at the irony in her voice, retaliated as best he could. 'Not for much longer, surely? I assume you'll return to England as soon as Anna goes back to Rome.'

'High time,' Alexandra agreed brightly. 'I came for three weeks, but that was three months ago. My dear mother would say – *does* say in every letter – that I should get on with my own life, marry one of my nice English suitors and settle down.' She smiled brilliantly as she walked past Fausto. 'Such a *bore*, though, having to choose!'

She didn't get as far as the terrace door before she was caught and held by hands that bit into the softness of her skin. Fausto dragged her close to him, aware of the faint perfume that clung to her and the warmth of her body through the thin robe she wore.

'God above knows I can't allow you to choose,' he shouted. 'You can't marry any English lover even though *he* need never neglect or hurt you because he has nothing else to do but take care of you.' A smile trembled on her mouth, but he misunderstood it. His hands tightened unkindly, almost shaking her. 'Alexandra, *listen* to me. I won't let you go away. Say you'll stay . . . you've *got* to stay, whether you say it or not.'

She struggled to free her hand and laid it across his lips. 'You're making a lot of noise, and you'll wake Anna.' More happiness than she'd supposed the world possessed shimmered like the Holy Grail in front of her, but there

214

was still the fear that she'd misunderstood him. Somehow she must stay calm a moment longer in order to make sure. 'Why shouldn't I go home?'

'Because you belong here, with me. Dear heart, say you *want* to stay and marry me.' His eyes implored her, and for once the tenderness and desire in his face were overlaid with agonized uncertainty. 'Say *something*, Alexandra.'

'Of c – course, I want to s – stay, and b – be a soldier's wife, and wait for you, and understand instead of w – worrying when you don't come home! Oh, Fausto, of *course* I do . . .'

His mouth silenced the rest of what she was going to say. The beautiful morning world swung out into space – there was nothing left but passion leaping between them like a flame; blazing need, and total surrender.

Fausto lifted his head at last, to look down at her, and her heart seemed to turn over at the love she saw in his face.

'Is this how you drive lovers in England to madness, shameless one?' he murmured unsteadily. 'If I'm not to make love to you here and now, you must go indoors at once and put some clothes on.'

She blushed as he gently rearranged the thin cotton material his mouth and hands had pushed aside. 'I *never* behave like this in England,' she said primly, 'but Italy is known to have a demoralizing effect upon us!' Then she smiled so radiantly that he caught his breath; she was beautiful beyond words, and full of brave hope, but *he* was suddenly touched by fear.

'*Tesoro* – do you promise to understand what Anna *doesn't* understand? Will you promise to believe in what we have to do . . . in *whatever* we might have to do?' he asked urgently.

Alexandra reached up to kiss his mouth.

'I shall believe and understand, and I'll help Anna to believe as well. Shall we go and tell her that she hasn't seen the last of me after all?'

215

17

Charlie's second visit to Castagnolo, arranged to coincide with the *vendemmia* as Francesca insisted, had to be hastily rearranged. James pointed out that he could make himself useful for once by shepherding his aunt and uncle to Florence for their daughter's wedding. Charlie enjoyed train journeys, and regretted that some of the pleasure of this one would now be dimmed; still, it might have been worse. For a day or two a more hideous possibility had seemed that Eliza might decide to go as well, but William took pity on his cousin. A reminder that she would be betraying her Communist principles by hobnobbing with a prominent Fascist persuaded her to stay at home and let Alexandra get married without her.

Edward Rushton set off on the journey in a state of pleasant excitement mixed with relief; it was something that *one* of his daughters seemed ready to settle down. Alice was more torn: the younger son of a marchese was a feather in her cap among the ladies of St Peter's Square, but she had grave suspicions about a foreign son-in-law.

'It's all Jane's fault, of course,' she told her husband as the train steamed out of Paris and they got ready for a night in their sleeping-compartment. 'If she hadn't started this Italian nonsense Alexandra would never even have discovered where Tuscany was – she paid less heed to geography than any other lesson.'

'Well, perhaps it was time she found out,' Edward suggested mildly. 'My dear, if you're worried about her, I don't think there's any need to be. Charlie says they're very civilized people.'

'I'm not expecting them to eat with their fingers,

Edward. Civilized is one thing, different is another. They're bound to be different from *us*.'

That much was true. He was tempted to say that Italians, being unavoidably different, might possess a few virtues not given to the English, but it was doubtful that Alice would accept this point of view. 'James liked them,' he said instead.

'I know, but I shall make up my own mind.'

When had she ever done anything else? He switched off the light before smiling in the safety of the darkness, and hoped that Alexandra had described her family to Fausto and his relatives. Fausto Buonaventura – it was an outlandish name for the son-in-law of a conventional Englishman. If he ever had to introduce Fausto to his cronies at the Club, he'd probably make a hash of it . . . he fell asleep to the rattle of the train wheels, still practising how it needed to be said.

They pulled into the station at Florence twelve hours later to find Alexandra on the platform waiting for them. She wore a rose-red suit and a white hat – looked changed already in some way Edward couldn't define; but she was beautiful as the morning and radiantly happy. He'd been right to tell Alice not to worry, even though the man beside her on the platform looked older than he'd expected.

'Different from us, would you say?' Edward murmured to his wife.

'Better dressed than Charlie, though that wouldn't be difficult. I'm bound to say he *looks* all right.'

It wasn't only a matter of looks, Alice eventually conceded; Fausto seemed kind as well. He bowed over her hand with unstudied grace and welcomed her as if the most important thing in life was to become acquainted with her. She didn't capitulate immediately, but had mellowed into affability by the time Fausto broke the news at dinner that the wedding would be a civil ceremony in Florence.

'Alexandra's fault for not being a Catholic?' Edward suggested hastily.

'Not at all – the fault of the continuing rupture between our Church and the State in Italy! The Pope still regards himself as a prisoner in the Vatican, and the State does not recognize a wedding solely solemnized in Church.'

'Extraordinary,' Alice commented with remarkable restraint. She saw Edward's pleading eye upon her and merely smiled at Fausto with the condescension of a duchess. 'We must expect things to be different here, I suppose.'

The ceremony took place two days later, but they returned afterwards to Castagnolo to be blessed by the priest who had known Fausto since he was a child. The bride and groom, surrounded by members of their families and most of the men, women and children belonging to the estate, walked up the hill to a feast set out on the terrace of the castle.

In Francesca's view the celebration fell a long way short of the *vendemmia*, but at least her friend Carlie was there. She despised the silly hat her grandmother insisted must be worn and explained that it was still on her head only by *force majeure*.

'Pity not to wear it,' he suggested diplomatically. 'I was just thinking I'd like to paint a picture of you . . . I'd call it "Francesca with straw bonnet"!'

She blushed with surprised pleasure and walked away, but the hat stayed on. He was still smiling when Jane wandered over to join him.

'You look happy to be back at Castagnolo,' she observed, looking at him.

'Seventh heaven – it's been a miserable year at home. The General Strike didn't last long, but it left a lot of misery behind and the poor wretched miners are still hanging on.' He waved a hand at the scene in front of them. 'It looks as if the whole of Castagnolo is here.'

'Not quite – a few of them, people like the Scarellis, can't forget Fausto's connection with people they have reason to hate. They have tactfully stayed away.'

'It's a turn-up for the book, this marriage of Alexandra's,' Charlie said thoughtfully. 'She looks alight with happiness, but do you suppose she realizes what she's getting into?'

Jane nodded without hesitating. 'I'm certain it's what she prayed for and feared would never happen.'

'She'll be on the other side of the fence from Ottavio, and from *you* as well, Janey . . . isn't that going to be difficult?'

'Probably, but Ottavio and Fausto have had to learn to live with the situation; Alex and I must do the same. It'll be easier for us – women cling to *people* more than to political theories!'

Charlie's gaze wandered to Anna Lambertini, apparently enjoying a conversation with Alice Rushton. There, unless he was mistaken, was a woman *torn* between people and theories.

'Anna's case is different,' Jane said quickly. 'Fascism didn't exist when she married Ernesto; now it seems to dominate their life. Alex has only known Fausto as an important member of the Party.'

'Poor girl,' Charlie murmured, and she realized that he was still thinking of Anna.

'All well at Vine House?' she asked next.

'I suppose so – we've got very social at least! Laura enjoys entertaining and William persuades James that it's good for business. I stay out of it, and David seems glad to keep me company in the studio. He's growing tall, and just like Johnny.'

Charlie observed his sister's face, under its charming wedding-hat of ivory straw, now trimmed with crimson vine-leaves. Her luminous smile shone for a moment. 'Francesca's idea – the decoration!'

'I like the entire rig, as it happens. Janey, Father told me how Castagnolo's being funded at the moment – I'm sorry he refused to risk Rushton money, but I suppose he had to think of Uncle Edward's teeming family.'

'I'm just making an investment,' she said tranquilly. 'In five years' time we shall be sending you fine wines, and I shall be getting my money back.'

'In five years' time Marco will be at the Ginnasio, or the Liceo – what happens to the governess then?'

'Francesca will only be thirteen – still needing someone besides her grandmother to keep her company.'

She saw the hesitation in Charlie's face and answered the question he didn't like to ask. 'You're thinking that her mother might have decided by then to remember that she has a daughter?'

He nodded, not daring to say that Elena Buonaventura might remember that she had a husband as well.

'If Elena comes back I shan't be needed, of course. I remind myself of that every night, in case I should be tempted to imagine that I belong here.' Her mouth twisted in a rueful little smile. 'It doesn't do the slightest bit of good, and my heart will break in two when the time comes to leave.'

'Never mind, love . . . unless Laura's persuaded Father to cut me out by then, we'll use *my* share of the inheritance to buy our old palazzo. Will that do?'

'Handsomely! But having settled the future, perhaps we'd better return to what's happening now. The Marchese's been trapped by Anna's fearsome mother-in-law, and Ernesto looks as if he needs rescuing from Aunt Alice!'

'Let *him* suffer,' said Charlie, then blushed because Jane stared at him.

'Never liked bankers – ' he explained after a moment's search – 'they aren't human!'

Charlie had always assumed that it would be his lifelong misfortune not to be interested in wine. Its kinds and qualities, the buying and selling of it, even its properly respectful consumption as taught by James – these were the things that were meant to fascinate a Rushton. He'd done his best, at least to feel a little pride in the serried ranks of *blancs* and *rouges* that filled the cellars at London Bridge; but his family's obsessive interest in the stuff had seemed hopelessly beyond him. He only wanted to paint pictures of which he needn't feel ashamed.

His ambition hadn't changed after his first glimpse of the gold and crimson hillsides of Tuscany – they simply satisfied his longing to look at something beautiful. Now he was there again, commanded by Francesca to attend the *vendemmia* this time. He arrived not knowing that he was about to be converted to wine.

Instructed and watched over by the children, he toiled in the golden sunlight with the rest of them, sang when they did, and smiled because he was happy.

Francesca observed him from under the brim of her straw hat, content to have him there. She didn't, like her cousin Lorenza, want to offer her heart to everybody, but the people she loved had to be made happy if she could see any way of doing it. Marco's inner grief, only partly hidden by spurts of gaiety, defeated her. She knew it had to do with their mother, because the only time he'd completely lost his temper with her was when she'd said they didn't need anyone but Jane.

'Stupid!' he'd shouted at her. 'She doesn't belong here. Don't you understand that *she'll* go away too, one day?'

'She *does* belong – *you're* the stupid one.' This time he had to be wrong. Without Jane their life would fall apart, as surely as the wind scattered the puff-balls of the dandelions. But Marco had shaken her until her teeth rattled.

'She's not here because she wants to be – Papa *pays* her to look after us.'

Francesca hadn't been able to go on with the quarrel. Jane loved them – she was sure about that – but it was very true that the governesses of other families they knew were paid, and *they* seemed to come and go.

The seed of fear Marco had left in her mind remained

there, hidden but dangerous. She thought of it again in the middle of the harvesting when Charlie came to squat beside her for a breather. He pushed back his panama hat and smiled, reminding her of Jane.

'Do *you* want to go back to England, Carlie?' she enquired suddenly.

His ear caught the faint stress she placed on the word '*you*', and he guessed that her question really concerned someone else who might go away and leave them.

'No-one in their right mind would choose to leave Castagnolo,' he said with matter-of-fact firmness. 'If I had the chance I'd stay here for ever – just as Janey wants to.'

He was rewarded with a brilliant smile that lit Francesca's small brown face. It was too angular for prettiness, but it was noticeable now and would become more so. Her long-lashed grey eyes were already beautiful. She was so little like Ottavio that Charlie realized she must resemble her mother entirely. He still didn't want to marry anybody, but he knew he would regret never having had a daughter like Francesca.

'You have no wife, Carlie,' she commented next, echoing his own thoughts uncannily.

He agreed that this was so.

'Never mind. When you are old you can live here with us. I shall take care of you, and Yane.'

Instead of making the mistake of laughing at her, he lifted her hand to his mouth – for all the world, she thought, as if she were grown up already. 'It sounds lovely, sweetheart, but until Jane and I get *very* old, perhaps we can all take care of each other.'

Joy opened inside her like a flower. He hadn't said that Jane would go back to England, and he was bound to know, being her brother. She would choose her moment for telling Marco so.

Afterwards, Charlie wished that the conversation hadn't taken place, or at least that he hadn't been quite so definite to a child looking for assurances. He doubted very much that Ottavio's wife would ever come back to Castagnolo, but in the end it made no difference whether she did or not. Ottavio remained married to her, and no man – not even the rich and powerful Howard Harrington – could put them asunder.

By the time the harvest was over Charlie had almost convinced himself that he was wrong about Jane. She was still the serene, contented woman who'd discovered the real purpose of her life at Castagnolo. The children, the Marchese and his wife, the people of the estate, were all she needed for happiness. It didn't matter that Ottavio seemed to be avoiding her. There was no real need for her to take part in the long discussions in Gino Scarelli's kitchen about what new vines to plant and which olive trees to be marked for grubbing-out once the fruit had been picked. Her inheritance was making the work possible – *that* was her sufficient contribution.

Ottavio seemed to spend every available moment out of doors, supervising men who already knew what they were doing. In Charlie's view he was the 'mildest-mannered man who ever scuttled ship or slit a throat' . . . or discouraged other people from guessing the secrets he intended to keep hidden. When the time came to catch the train for Paris, Charlie was almost certain that there was nothing to guess, beyond the fact that Ottavio still painfully remembered his missing wife.

To that extent he was right. Elena absent was more damnably, intrusively *there* than even a woman in the flesh could possibly have been. Every time Ottavio looked at Jane the image of his wife inserted itself between them, mocking and indestructible. She was a phantom, ever-present reminder that he had nothing to offer. Even the work of salvaging the estate couldn't be shared with Jane because it would have meant *more*, not less, time spent in her company. Instead, as the busy days and sleep-less nights crept towards Christmas, he avoided her as much as he could and prayed that no-one else felt the tension building up between them like a charge of electricity.

Jane was miserably aware of it and certain that she knew its cause. A shy, proud man had been hurt by his wife and humiliated to have to accept help to save his inheritance. She couldn't soften the longing for his wife, and he was obliged to feel grateful for Rushton money. Jane accepted his withdrawal from herself, but not his indifference to the children. Flashpoint came without warning one day when she deliberately tracked him to his study and was greeted with the frown that nowadays was meant to warn her away.

'I realize I'm interrupting some important task,' she said quietly, 'but this is important, too. We need to talk about Marco.'

'He looks perfectly well and happy to me . . .'

'Because you see him for an hour a day at lunch-time. It isn't enough to judge, in my opinion.'

'In *your* opinion,' asked the cool-voiced stranger Ottavio had become, 'what is wrong with him?'

'He needs to go to school,' Jane said bluntly. 'In case it has slipped your mind, he will be eleven soon after Christmas – it's time he was enrolled at the Ginnasio. He needs the companionship of other boys and the stimulus of having to compete with them.'

'At the Ginnasio he will be enrolled in something else – the Avanguardia! An education of sorts will be given, but what he'll really be taught, my dear Jane, is blind obedience to the Duce. He'll learn to chant the mindless Fascist anthem, "Giovinezza", and believe a little more day by day the infamous creed that says might is right and violence its own reward. I would rather my son learned nothing at all than *that* travesty of the truth.'

'Travesty it may be, but it's not an infectious disease that you can isolate him from. Sooner or later Marco will have to come to terms with the system that governs him. *He* can accept or reject Fascism; you can't do it for him.'

'While I can do it, I will. He stays here, Jane.'

Ottavio spoke with the mulish obstinacy of a man who knew his only hope was not to concede even the possibility that he *might* be wrong. He glanced at her for long enough to see the strain and sadness in her face, then looked away again. It was hard to argue with her, unbearable to have to exclude her from his heart and mind with the last ounce of strength he possessed. If she stayed there much longer, looking at him with that anxious mixture of disappointment and regret, he would have to admit that she was right. But she wouldn't give in and go away unless he hurt her intolerably.

'Between you, you and the priest and my father *ought* to be able to teach a ten-year-old child; if not, perhaps I should find someone who can.'

It was offence beyond forgiveness; *now* surely she would leave before he gave way to the terrible longing to put his arms around her and never let her go.

'I expect we shall manage if we have to,' she said after a long silence. 'There's one other thing to mention while I'm here. Marco is well, but he's not happy . . . no child *is* who is feverishly high spirited one moment and morbidly depressed the next.'

'Have you an opinion about this, too?' Ottavio enquired, careful not to look at her.

'Yes, I have. I suppose Francesca still misses her mother, but Marco's grief is worse; he's lost the chance for ever of making her love *him* as he thinks she loved his sister.'

'Perhaps that's something else he has to come to terms with.'

'He *can't* without knowing the truth.' Jane stared at Ottavio's withdrawn face and took a deep breath for what must come next. 'I think you should tell him that Elena treated him differently because she loved Francesca's father.'

There had been times – Jane remembered them clearly

– when she'd thought Ottavio's face impassive and disappointingly unItalian. She had succeeded now, at least, in shattering the mask he hid behind. He looked hurt, astounded and, most of all, furiously angry.

'You're mad to suggest such a thing – shall I tell a child of ten to keep a secret about his sister . . . shall I break the news to Francesca as well that she doesn't belong here and that the man who fathered her is dead . . . shall I try to make the children understand that their beautiful, worthless mother lived only for what *her* body, *her* needs, *her* whims demanded?'

White lipped, Jane persisted, even at the terrible cost of hurting him still more. 'I think you should tell your son *now*, and Francesca when she is old enough to accept the truth. It will help Marco to understand what at present he *cannot* understand, and it won't hurt him to know that he's been entrusted with a secret.'

'I disagree with you entirely,' Ottavio said in a voice she didn't recognize. He had to stare at her because she didn't answer, and the expression on her face goaded him into shouting at her. 'I mean it, Jane – they are not to be told now, and probably ever.'

She gave a little shrug of resignation mixed with what looked like despair at his stupidity. It provoked him into striding towards her to grab hold of her shoulders. The mistake was fatal. He realized it in the very moment of touching her, even though she stood still under his hands. It was too late now to remember anything except one overmastering fact . . . he wanted her and loved her past bearing. She was dragged hard against him as he found her mouth with his own.

For Jane there was a moment of sheer, stupefying happiness – the loneliness of weeks of exclusion from him suddenly forgotten; she was transported back to a moonlit courtyard on the night Mario Scarelli had needed help. No . . . it wasn't like that at all. There had been tenderness then, and the healing exchange of comfort. There was no tenderness now, only the hard, hurtful assault of Ottavio's mouth, and his hands trying to force her body to merge with his own.

She struggled against his strength and her own weak longing to give in, knowing in some dim corner of her mind that if she surrendered at all, the surrender would be total. Dear God . . . did it matter? *He* knew how much she wanted Ottavio to love her. She murmured something, fought no more as Ottavio's hands dealt with the buttons on her blouse.

'*S – signore . . . sc – scusi tanto . . . non sapevo . . .*'

It wasn't the sound of the door opening, or Enrico's stammered apologies at finding the room occupied after all as he backed out again. It was the sight of his face, glimpsed over Ottavio's shoulder. Like water poured over fire, the servant's reaction to what he saw killed passion dead. She pulled herself free and turned towards the window, automatically putting her disordered clothes to rights again. Instead of being feverishly warm, she felt deathly cold, and lonely, and humiliated.

It seemed a long time before the door closed again behind Enrico, but the worst thing of all was to be left there alone with Ottavio. At that moment she would have preferred never to have to face him again.

'Jane, my dear . . . I'm sorry; forgive me.'

The muttered apology scarcely reached her. His face in the fleeting glance she allowed herself showed nothing but the shame of being discovered by one servant in the act of seducing another. She couldn't know what he was thinking – that sheer passion had managed to blot out the image of Elena for a moment or two; but it was back again now, silently jeering at him.

Jane dragged together her remaining tattered remnants of pride. 'Let's forget it happened, shall we? I dare say Enrico is accustomed to seeing the governess being kissed by the *padrone*. Unless she's old or *very* plain, it's an occupational hazard, I believe!'

Ottavio took a step towards her, but she retreated at once with her hands held out to ward him off.

'No, not again, dear sir. To misquote Wilde's Lady Bracknell, once might be a misfortune, twice would look like carelessness!'

She offered him a brilliant, unamused smile and commanded her legs to carry her past him out of the room. Ottavio made no attempt to stop her and she was free to escape to her own room. He sat down at his desk and held his hands over his ears – to drown the sound of Elena's laughter.

18

Christmas loomed like a mockery of the joyous festival it was supposed to be. Jane pretended to share the children's excitement and hated herself for the pretence. Fretted by too many sleepless nights, her mind insisted that everyone knew how her quarrel with Ottavio had ended. She felt certain that they all, from the Marchesa down to the little maid who polished the schoolroom floor, waited for the next brawl between the *governante* and the signore. They could scarcely fail to notice the new formality with which he treated her. She had no idea how else he could have behaved, but his coolness surely confirmed the household view of her as a desperate spinster who had offered herself and been rejected.

She was saved by a diversion that came unexpectedly from Rome. The Marchesa reported that the Lambertini children were to spend Christmas at Castagnolo while Ernesto took his wife on a brief cruise in the Eastern Mediterranean. Anna brought the children herself, and Jane saw why Ernesto had noticed that she needed a little of his attention; she was much too thin and her eyes looked feverishly bright in the gauntness of her face.

'Aren't I lucky?' she gabbled, the moment she and Jane were left alone together. 'Instead of talking myself into getting well again after the struggle to produce Vittorio, I'm to be lapped in comfort and given the especial treat of a Christmas Day visit to Jerusalem. I've always wanted to see the Holy Sepulchre . . . haven't you, Jane?'

'Yes . . . it sounds a lovely thing to do.' Jane waited a moment, then decided not to pretend that she had missed the desperation in Anna's face. 'Are you anxious about leaving the children? There's no need to be. They'll have a lovely time here with Marco and Francesca.'

'I know – and I'd much rather stay here *with* them,' Anna burst out suddenly. 'Jane, don't tell Ernesto, but I *hate* cruises, and I don't really mind if I never see Jerusalem!'

Her hands were gripped together so tightly in her lap that her fingers were white, and the whole of her thin body was tense with some almost unbearable strain.

'Couldn't you tell Ernesto if there's something you'd rather do? It's *your* well-being he's considering,' Jane suggested gently.

'He tries – pretends to sound enthusiastic about going away; but all he really wants is to be left in peace at home. Then, while I play with the children as any good wife should, he can spend the time devising some cunning new piece of legislation for his friends.'

'Why cunning? Men in power need statutes and decrees devised for them – it's how the business of government is carried on.'

'Cunning, because in this country nothing is what it seems,' Anna insisted feverishly. 'Each "gift" from the Duce to his adoring people conceals the fact that a little more of their liberty has been removed. Apparently, we are to be "saved" from disorderly parliaments, industrial strife and a subversive press. The reality is different – a Chamber full of obedient deputies selected by the Fascist Grand Council, both sides of industry forced to do only what they are told, and every anti-Fascist newspaper forcibly shut down. Jane . . . we're fed nothing but lies, and Ernesto actually *helps* in this disgusting process. Ten years ago he would have had nothing to do with it.'

Jane took Anna's cold hands in her own warm ones and spoke with as much firmness as she could manage.

'Ten years ago he didn't see any alternative to the way Italy was being ruined. Now, he tells himself that industry is no longer crippled by constant strikes; badly-needed public works are actually put in hand; and venal politicians no longer keep each other in power. Dearest Anna, don't hate your husband because *he* believes that these things are worth the loss of some individual freedom.'

Anna's pale mouth twisted in a grimace of wry self-derision. 'In other words, why am I making such a fuss? All I need to realize is that I'm the pampered, privileged wife of an important man, with a lot to be thankful for!'

'That isn't quite what I was trying to point out,' Jane said quietly. 'You have a right to your own opinions, but Ernesto has as much right to his. If you can't accept *that*, you'll destroy your own health and happiness, and end by destroying your family as well.'

There was long silence in the room and Jane feared that, in common with most well-intentioned people, she had merely succeeded in making bad worse. But Anna suddenly leaned forward and kissed her.

'You're very good for me, Jane. Alexandra is a dear friend too, and I should be lost without her now, but she's bound to see things through Fausto's eyes. I can't unsettle *her* just to make myself feel better. You don't agree with them any more than Ottavio does, but you're blessedly calm and fair about it – blessedly English, I suppose I mean!'

'Oh, we're well known for not letting our emotions get the better of us,' Jane agreed with a crooked smile. 'Rushtons are especially good at this, and Alexandra is our only shameful exception!'

Anna relaxed sufficiently to laugh at the recollection of her friend. 'Can you believe that she has my mother-in-law eating out of her hand? Leonora's only fear is that the Duce will notice how beautiful she is! He's something of a connoisseur of women, and those chosen to receive his favour are not expected to decline.'

'It's Fausto's problem,' Jane said firmly. '*He* will have to decide whether or not to lock up his wife in an ivory tower; I refuse to worry about it.'

While Anna still looked cheerful, she quickly asked about the routine her children were accustomed to follow, and decided when the time came for Anna to leave that at least she went in a calmer frame of mind.

Lorenza was inclined to be tearful at first, but forgot that she'd been abandoned when Jane set the children to making paper-chains to decorate the schoolroom. Christmas with her cousins seemed more fun than it might have been at home, and to Jane the prospect of it suddenly became bearable. Now there were four children to be kept busy and happy while the nursemaid took care of Vittorio; they ought to be enough to keep her out of Ottavio's way completely, and that had become the summit of her ambition.

When Ernesto collected the children after Christmas, he looked more relaxed than usual; the cruise had been a success and Anna's health had improved. He also reported that Fausto's career was now to take a different direction. As a newly-elected member of the Chamber of Deputies, he would spend most of his time in Rome in future. It meant that Anna would see more of Alexandra, and so everyone was happy. Donna Giulia looked impressed, and if the Marchese disapproved of his son's new rôle, he was careful not to say so.

The Feast of the Epiphany was duly marked by a visit from the *befana*, bringing small gifts instead of the shaming lump of coal Francesca half-expected; there had been certain small misdemeanours which she feared the Witch Who Saw Everything might not have overlooked. Afterwards there was no more excitement to look forward to – only the onset of a winter harsher than most, with a bitter wind blowing steadily from the north, bringing snow well down the foothills of the mountains. Huge fires provided points of refuge inside the castle, but it was still so cold in the schoolroom that Jane and the children each had their own little *scaldino* to work by – an earthenware basket of glowing charcoal at which to warm their hands.

There was little work to be done out of doors, but Ottavio found reasons for spending his time anywhere around the estate rather than inside the castle. The scholarly gentleman poring over tomes of history had become someone Jane scarcely recognized – a countryman as impervious to the weather as Gino Scarelli. The two of them daily inspected the nursery plantations as if by simply being there they could persuade the new young vines to survive the bitterness of the winter.

Having never worried about anyone but Fausto before, the Marchesa eventually protested.

'Dearest, I *do* understand about the new plantings, but what is achieved by you and Scarelli shaking your heads over some dead-looking twig and getting chilled to the bone in the process?'

'If the vines can stand the temperature, Mamma, so can we,' Ottavio explained patiently. 'I don't suppose we achieve anything at all, but the nursery plantations are so crucial that we have to be concerned about them.' He shot a brief glance at Jane and looked away again. 'They represent Rushton's investment in Castagnolo.'

'I dare say, but I'm sure dear Mr Rushton didn't intend you to spend your days peering at his investment to make sure it was still there.'

She smiled at them and drifted out of the room, leaving awkwardness behind. Instead of escaping, too, Jane deliberately plunged into her first real conversation with Ottavio since Enrico had interrupted them in the study.

'Your mother is right – there's nothing you or Gino can do to protect Rushton's investment. It's in the nature of such things to be chancey – this one especially so.'

'Because the incompetent and unfortunate Buonaventuras are involved?' He saw a spark of fire in her eyes and quickly apologized. 'I'm sorry! What a stupid thing to say when our success or failure depends much more on Gino than it does on me.'

'It doesn't even depend on *him*. He can't stop frost or

snow ruining the new plantings, any more than you can. If that happens, will you feel obliged to blame yourself? Will you feel *less* guilty if you've managed to catch pneumonia by then?' It was a relief to be angry when she faced him, but she couldn't manage a permanent state of irritation; some other alternative was needed to cope with the embarrassment that now crippled her whenever she was left alone with him.

'You're being inconsistent – as women usually are,' he pointed out. 'You used to take me to task for not caring *enough* about what happened here.'

'Well, there was no need to fly to the opposite extreme.' She was made still more irritable by his reasonableness and by the suspicion that, for some reason she couldn't fathom, he was suddenly laughing at her. It made matters worse, and she wanted to shout at him. 'It's because you feel under some ridiculous obligation to m – my family.' In her agitation she nearly gave herself away. If he ever guessed who the real gambler was in his chancey investment he'd beggar himself to return the money sent so far from London, and probably tear out all the new vines as well.

'Humour me,' Ottavio said gravely. 'Allow me to wear my hair-shirt of obligation, even though I ought to realize that I'm doing your father a favour by allowing him to risk his money!'

Suspicion was a certainty now. He found her indignation funny and even the memory of that scene in the study didn't trouble him because he proceeded to remind her of it.

'You were right about Marco – he does need to go to school, and I consulted his priest in Florence. There's a place run by the Jesuits where he'll get what *you* want him to have without being fed an added diet of Fascism – the Fathers hate it as much as I do. Will you be happy if he starts there after Easter?'

'Yes . . . if . . . if *he's* going to be happy. We shall have

234

to wait to find that out, I suppose.' She was touched by Ottavio's willingness to accept her point of view, at least in the matter of the school, but still anxious.

'You realize, don't you, that Marco makes a hero of his uncle? Even if you manage to filter out of his life now everything you hate about the régime, he might still decide to accept it for himself later on.'

Ottavio gave a little shrug. 'He might, but on the other hand the next attempt at assassinating Mussolini might, untypically for us, actually succeed! By the time Marco is old enough to take an interest in politics, we might have a democratic government again, and by then perhaps he'll be more interested in Castagnolo than anything else.'

Jane nodded, considering for a moment the consequences of reverting to their other quarrel. In the end she decided to hold her tongue, and walked out of the room, not knowing why Ottavio smiled.

He had watched the conflicting emotions in her face and correctly interpreted them, but it wasn't her heroic self-restraint that made him smile. The simple truth was that he was happy, having discovered for almost the only time in his life that there was something he was certain of. He loved Jane Rushton, and would go on loving her until the day he died. It changed nothing, because his situation wasn't changeable, but there was happiness to be got just from accepting the truth. Self-discipline was needed to keep his secret from everyone else, but he was used to that. There would be times when his body might almost burst with its own needs but he must learn to deal with that. She would stay for the children's sake as long as he buried love and longing so deep in his heart that she was never troubled by them. Even *that* he could manage, because he must.

The Marchesa's excuse for doing very little was the time she saved in which to observe a great deal. She had never told Ottavio – he wouldn't have believed her – that she hàd foretold quite accurately the moment when boredom and frustration would finally drive Elena away for good. There had been much to observe since then – the change in the children, her husband's surprisingly frequent descents from the tower and Ottavio's even more startling conversion from absent scholar to keenly involved *padrone*. The woman at the centre of all this had been harder to observe, but the Marchesa had at least been certain of Jane Rushton's happiness. Now prophecy was foundering, confused by the fact that Jane herself didn't know whether she longed to leave Castagnolo more than she wanted to stay.

Donna Giulia came to the conclusion that something must be done. If she wanted a private discussion with her husband it meant climbing the tower stairs, but one morning she was moved to undertake even this exertion. He looked surprised but not displeased to see her.

'My dear . . . how nice! Stay until it gets dark and I shall be able to show you something beautiful – Venus shining brilliantly, and the whole wonderful constellation of Orion clear to the south.'

The Marchesa smiled faintly, but shook her head. 'Thank you, Giuseppe, but that isn't what brought me up here.'

'Your own astral affairs *not* going well, cara?' he ventured.

'I was wrong about Capricornians,' she admitted woefully. 'They are supposed to be so unemotional and calm that I foresaw no problem.' She fidgeted with the fringe of her topmost scarf and then peered at her husband. 'Would you agree that dear, clever Ottavio is not clever at all when it comes to dealing with women?'

The Marchese had never considered the question; he realized that he must consider it now, but some vital link eluded him. 'Is there a connection between Capricornians and our son, who I seem to remember was born in June?'

She gave a little sigh and abandoned finesse. 'The connection is Jane. I'm afraid that she might leave us,

236

Giuseppe, and I do *not* see how we can manage without her. Ottavio can manage least of all, but *he* is the trouble. She will go in the end because of him.'

'You mean Ottavio is . . . is unkind . . . beats her when we're not looking?' He saw the anxiety in his wife's face, as well as exasperation, and hastily apologized. 'Dearest, I'm sorry I didn't quite realize that we were being serious . . . well now, tell me what you want *me* to do.'

The Marchesa hesitated, but only for a moment or two. 'I want you to tell Ottavio to forget that he is a married man with no chance of taking another wife; tell him *we* shan't mind if he offers Jane what he can – himself! I think she might then stay.'

Giuseppe stared at his wife's determined face, uncertain whether to shout with laughter or to question what other surprise she was about to spring on him. 'It's a . . . a little unconventional, my love! Even if *we* are able to take it in our stride, I am not sure that Jane can; and I'm even less certain about Ottavio.'

'He doesn't *see* anyone else but her; he has to walk out of the room not to give himself away. He's a normal man of thirty-seven – he should be allowed to live like one. Jane may *not* agree to share his life. If she refuses and goes away, at least she will go knowing that Ottavio loves her.'

The Marchese blinked at this new light on a woman he had lived with for forty years. He hadn't properly appreciated her, and it was clear that Ottavio's stupidity with women was inherited. He went over to kiss his wife in a rare gesture of affection.

'My dearest, you are full of kindness and common sense. I'm not quite sure how a father is supposed to lecture his son on such a matter, but I shall do the best I can.'

Donna Giulia smiled and went away – forgetting Venus and Orion entirely, he realized with a touch of regret. The more he considered the task she had given him, the more delicate it looked, but he couldn't convince himself that she was wrong. Jane's thin, disciplined face looked sad when she forgot to smile, and he hadn't abandoned normal life so completely himself that he was unaware of the unnatural strain Ottavio was under.

The following evening he was still considering how and when to raise the subject with his son. Ottavio seemed disinclined to talk about anything at all, and no-one else at the dinner-table was very conversational. Given the arctic temperature in the room, the Marchese thought it understandable. There were times when even he was aware of the discomfort attached to living in a medieval castle. A fire of logs blazed on the huge hearth but its warmth scarcely reached them at the table; summer sunlight and heat were memories recollected with difficulty.

Ottavio suddenly made up his mind to speak after all, putting into words the dread that was consuming him. 'Gino is predicting that this weather will continue. If so, we shall be lucky to have a single olive next December; worse, the established vines may survive, but the young ones won't.' He looked across the table and spoke to Jane. 'In all the years I've known Gino he's never been wrong about the weather.'

She saw in his drawn face the final acceptance of failure – not just for this year but for all the years that might come after. Whatever he struggled to do would be cancelled out in the end because the jealous gods were determined to deny him even the happiness of achieving something for Castagnolo. He got up from the table, leaving the three of them to regroup themselves round the fire in the *salone*. Jane waited for the Marchese to distract his wife with a game of bezique, and then slipped out of the room herself.

She expected to find Ottavio in his study, but the room was empty, lit only by the glow of a dying fire. The dimness showed up a single lamplit window outside, shining in the darkness of the *cantina* across the outer courtyard. A few minutes later she found him there, sitting on an upturned wicker grape basket with his face buried in his hands. He was unaware of the bitter cold and of the fact that she was there until she spoke to him.

'This is a fine place to freeze to death in.'

She sounded cross, and he knew how she would look, with her brows pulled together in a little frown. He kept his head down, and only her feet were in his line of vision . . . thin, sodden shoes coated with icy slush from the courtyard. The sight of them hurt him more than anything else, seeming to sum up the whole of his failure.

'What are you doing here, Ottavio?'

This time he had to answer and had to look at her. She *was* frowning; but in the midst of his misery it still seemed to him that she was beautiful. Inside the dark cloth of a hooded cape her face was silvery-pale, like the delicate crescent of a new moon. She would go away soon and his heart would shrivel and die.

'It doesn't matter what I'm doing . . . I don't want you out here. Go back to the house, Jane.'

She moved away from him, but only to find a wicker-basket of her own to sit on.

'I said go away,' he shouted. 'I *meant* it.'

'I'll go when you do,' she said calmly. She wrapped the folds of the cape around her and sat surveying her wet shoes.

Ottavio glared at her, torn by more emotions than he knew how to deal with – mostly regret and despair, but there was frustration at her stubbornness and, suddenly, an insane desire to laugh. Their brave new beginning at Castagnolo was going to end in fiasco, of course . . . heartbreaking and humiliating. God alone knew why just at *this* moment it had become wildly, ridiculously funny as well. If he thought about the sight they must present sitting on their upturned baskets, he would begin to shout with laughter and she would decide he'd finally gone mad.

'We are both leaving,' he said sharply. 'Go before I turn out the lamp; otherwise the darkness will blind you.'

She heard the door of the *cantina* shut behind him, then

he was beside her, fumbling for her hand. The slush under their feet, beginning to freeze over again, crunched as they walked on it. Above them, immensely far away, stars pricked the clear February sky with countless points of light. It was so cruelly cold that her nose hurt with the air she breathed in; so cruelly beautiful that she wanted to weep.

The castle itself felt relatively warm after the temperature outside, but Jane suddenly found herself shivering. She tried to release her hand from Ottavio's, but he simply towed her along the bottom corridor to his own room.

'Sit down and be quiet and, for once, don't argue,' he insisted unfairly.

She was aware of having no wish to argue. Without quite knowing why, she realized that this moment was important, that all the past led up to it, and the future would be fixed by what happened now. She watched him place logs on the hearth and coax them into flame with a pair of bellows. Then, in the strengthening firelight, he knelt and removed her wet shoes, and chafed her feet with his hands.

'You're a troublesome woman, Jane,' he said quietly. She feared that he meant more than her frozen toes. Without her hornet's sting to jab him, he would scarcely have noticed Castagnolo sinking into ruin; the decay would have been very gradual and he could have been left in peace. She didn't think he hated her, but she couldn't have blamed him if he did. When he put a glass of brandy into her hand she sipped it, still quiet as he had told her to be.

'I went to the *cantina* to face the ruin of all our plans,' he said simply. 'But there is still some wine maturing from a good summer three years ago. It can be bottled and sold in the spring. If it makes enough to pay off what I've borrowed from your father so far, that's all that matters.'

'It would leave you nothing in hand . . . nothing to work with in future,' she objected quickly.

'My dear, there *is* no future.' He stared at the glass in his hand, not at her. 'Castagnolo has no future and nor do I.'

'Because you prefer to remember the past?'

His mouth twisted at the strangeness of the idea. 'I shall only remember the past when *you're* no longer here.'

'I planned to stay . . . or did you hope to get rid of me when Marco starts at the Jesuit school?'

'Yes . . . yes, that's what I want you to do – go home, Jane, and forget about a place called Castagnolo.' He was careful not to look at her so that she shouldn't know he lied.

She forced herself to think about Castagnolo, not about his wish for her to go. 'You *can't* give up just because of one appalling winter that couldn't possibly have been foreseen. Ottavio, it isn't *your* failure . . . every vine-grower in Tuscany must be in the same sad state this year; but there will be other years and they won't all be a disaster.'

'Other growers can afford an occasional disaster – I *can't*, on money borrowed from your father. That *is* my failure . . . the result of years of neglect when I preferred to think I was an historian, not a landowner.' His shrug accepted blame and despair equally. 'The only important thing now is to repay your father. What happens afterwards . . . well, *non importa!*'

'You're wrong – wrong about a lot of things,' she said steadily. 'Castagnolo *does* matter and it does have a future – *must* have, for Marco's sake and the sake of dozens of people whose lives depend on it. You're wrong about me as well. Even if you refuse to keep me here, I shall persuade Don Giuseppe to go on making use of the money that arrives from London – it's mine; so *he* and I can choose.'

'Your . . . *what*?'

She winced, not at the shout, but at the understanding that dawned in his face; with it went humiliation tinged with anger.

'You weren't supposed to know,' Jane murmured. 'My

241

father decided that it would be unfair to Uncle Edward and *his* family to risk Rushton money, but he offered to advance me instalments of what I shall inherit when he dies. The instalments will continue with or without your approval. If the new vines die Gino will be told to plant them again and again until they make up their minds to live. I won't *allow* you to give up now . . . even if you send me away.'

In the ashen greyness of his face only his eyes seemed to be alive. He covered them with his hands, but not before she had read the truth. He was in despair, and he was humiliated by what she had told him, but he lied when he said he wanted her to go away. It wasn't a great deal to go on, but it showed her the one way open to her now to restore his courage and his confidence in himself. The risk was terrible and she had no idea what she would do if she failed.

'I had a price in mind for helping you,' she said hoarsely. 'I'm thirty-two, and the only plain member of a handsome family. Even if I have to die an old maid, I should hate not to know what it means to be loved . . . I thought perhaps *you* might love me a little, Ottavio.'

She'd sounded even more brazen than she meant to – dreadfully so, because his face was rigid with shock and something she took to be disgust.

'You're mad . . .' he managed to grind out at last, '. . . totally insane to imagine that I'd . . . I'd ever dream of agreeing.'

So much for effort! She had nearly destroyed herself, and achieved nothing in the way of helping him. 'So mad that you doubt whether I should be in charge of your children?' she suggested unsteadily. Her mind and body seemed to be a bleeding mass of humiliation, but all that mattered now was to get away from him into some dark place where she could hide her pain. She started to walk towards the door, discovered her shoes were not on her feet but still drying by the fire, and crammed her toes into

242

the stiff leather. He made no attempt to stop her – she was free to stumble away.

Minutes or hours later – she'd lost count of time now – she stood staring out of her window at the starlit sky. The room was deathly cold and so was she, despite the heavy cape she'd forgotten to remove. Nothing impinged on the blankness in her mind except the distinctive sound, when it came, of the latch of her door being lifted. A moment later Ottavio walked into the moonlit room.

She had imagined her humiliation was complete, but she'd been wrong – now it *was*, when he'd thought better of rejecting the offer of a woman to sleep with after all.

'I changed my mind,' she said with bitter clarity. 'All I require of you is just to go away.'

'When I've said what I came to say.'

'*Now* . . . I won't listen.'

'You must. After that I'll go away.' His face was a vague blur, but she could hear the sadness in his voice. 'Can you imagine what it feels like for a man to be offered the only thing in life he truly needs and to know that he must refuse it?'

'Why must he refuse?' Her lips felt stiff but she forced them to form the words.

'Because it was offered for the wrong reason. I want to be allowed to love you more than anything in the world – but never in this life just because you feel sorry for me.'

The road to hell and utter damnation *was* paved with good intentions – she was living, desperate proof that it was so. She could implore him to hear the truth, but the damage she'd done couldn't be undone now.

'I . . . I didn't know . . . thought you still remembered Elena . . .'

'Oh, I do – I never forget my wife,' he agreed with bitter emphasis. 'How can I when I'm tied to her for life? That's what *our* Church says, Jane. No matter how terrible the mistake I made with her, no matter how much I love you . . . those are the things I came to say; I should have said them downstairs, but I was trying to convince myself that I had the right to ignore them. Now, I'll go away.'

'Will you still go if I ask you to stay?' A bar of moonlight slanted through the window, showing him the tears shining on her face. 'Will you stay if I say that a hundred wives blessed by the Church of Rome couldn't stop me loving you? Oh, Ottavio . . .'

It was as far as she got before he reached her. His arms enfolded her, relaxed their grip for a moment while his hands dealt with her heavy cape and then gathered her against him as if he would never let her go again.

'I wasn't serious . . .' she murmured against his coat, '. . . about the price of helping . . . I couldn't get it out in any other way!'

His arms held her a little away from him so that he could see her face.

'You mean you don't want to be loved after all? Blood of my heart, is that *really* what you mean?'

'I'm afraid of disappointing you,' she said simply. 'Ottavio – I'm rather plain and such a dreadfully virginal thirty-two!'

The mad longing to laugh that had troubled him in the *cantina* didn't need resisting now – he could shout with laughter and make her laugh too, because they were together and nothing else mattered in life. When they were both sober again his mouth found hers – gently at first, then demanding a desire of hers to leap and match his own. She was trembling when he lifted his head, but smiling faintly.

'Now are you afraid?' he murmured. 'You couldn't disappoint me if you tried, and if *you're* not beautiful I don't know what beauty is.'

The recollection of her last confession made him want to laugh again, but he dealt gravely with it. 'For unwanted virginity there is a simple remedy, my very dear Miss Rushton . . . shall we go to bed?'

*   *   *

244

The Marchese braved the snowy courtyard the following morning because he'd caught sight of Ottavio disappearing into the *cantina*. He thought he was as ready as he would ever be to lecture his son on the virtues of immorality. By the end of the first awkward sentence Ottavio looked surprised, by the end of the second, he was beginning to smile . . . by the end of the third Don Giuseppe interrupted himself with a touch of sharpness. 'Your mother was *anxious*.' The interview had seemed difficult in any case, but it became ludicrous when his son was now helpless with laughter.

'I'm . . . I'm very g – grateful to her,' Ottavio finally managed to gasp. 'Tell her not to worry . . . I promise you both there's no need, *now*.'

The Marchese stared at his son and saw that it was so.

Happiness shone in Ottavio's face, giving him back the vigour and confidence of youth.

'Well, what about the vines, my dear boy? Have they been killed by the frost?'

'I think so, but it doesn't matter,' said this new Ottavio. 'We shall plant new ones, that's all.'

Donna Giulia acknowledged the fact that her grand-children's governess was now sleeping with her son by inviting Jane into her own room one evening and handing her a small box.

'You are meant to open it,' she pointed out calmly when Jane stared at her.

The treasure inside was an antique ring of great beauty – a cluster of moonstones and aquamarines in a setting of old, chased silver.

'It was my mother's, her mother's before that,' said the Marchesa. 'I could never bring myself to offer it to Elena – she would have despised it for being old-fashioned in any case. I want *you* to have it, my dear, because I look on you as Ottavio's true wife.'

'You know . . . and you don't mind?' Jane murmured.

'I don't mind anything at all, except going back to

the way we were before you came. Promise you'll stay, *tesoro*.'

Jane blinked away the tears that blurred her eyes and smiled. 'Just try sending me away! I shall treasure the ring, and eventually give it to Francesca. *She* will think it as beautiful as I do.'

19

To Jane, even the difficult years after that seemed shot through with beauty – each spring more full of promise, each harvest more rich and golden. If the Marchese and his wife accepted that she belonged to Ottavio, it didn't trouble her that the Church and State did not; if Marco and Francesca found it natural for her to be at the heart of their lives, she asked nothing more – not even the children of her own she might have had; they *were* her children.

Anna and Alexandra guessed the change in her life without having to be told, and hugged her and each other for the satisfaction of knowing that she was within the circle of the family for good. On Charlie's next visit to Castagnolo Jane told *him*, and saw him grin with so much shy pleasure that she was moved to remonstrate.

'I thought *one* of you might protest at my life of sin, but everyone seems to think it's exactly what I was cut out for!'

'We're glad to see you and Ottavio happy,' he said simply. 'What's more you don't have to fret about *me*, Janey – my future's all fixed up. Francesca's going to take care of me!'

He came to visit them every summer after that, more often than not bringing his nephew with him to spend the long school holiday at Castagnolo. No two boys were ever less alike than David Rushton and Marco, but a friendship gradually grew up between them that simply ignored their differences.

As the strenuous years went by there were times when it seemed to Ottavio that Heaven and earth conspired to defeat them. Each small success was too often wiped out by some fresh misfortune – drought when they prayed for rain, summer storms when calm sunshine was needed. The hours of work were long, and always behind them hung the fear that the estate wouldn't be self-supporting again before Jane's inheritance ran out. But they battled on and gradually dared to believe that they were winning – good wine, worthy of being left to mature, was being made, the farms were paying their way and a feeling of optimism was in the air.

Only two things clouded Ottavio's happiness. However wicked it was to wish Elena dead, he couldn't help doing so. Above everything else in life he wanted to be able to marry Jane before he died himself. His other sadness was of a different kind, now that they'd endured ten years since the blackshirts' so-called 'March on Rome' in 1922. Since then the country had been so completely Fascisticized that he could no longer believe in an end to the régime; it controlled every aspect of their lives and now would always do so. His hatred of it was well known to the Prefect in charge of Florence but – probably thanks to Fausto's influence in Rome – he was left unpunished at Castagnolo. The only penalty for independence of mind was isolation from more prudent neighbours. This didn't trouble Ottavio for himself, but increasingly it worried him for the rest of his family.

Anxiety was brought to a head by the approach of Francesca's fourteenth birthday. They could plan a party for her, but who would feel brave enough to come?

'Am I wrong?' he asked Jane in despair one morning. 'I make you all lead unnatural lives because *I* won't accept something I can do nothing to change.'

'*You* can't change it, but outside events might,' she reminded him. 'Remember what Professor Salvemini wrote: ". . . the weak point of the Fascist system is its foreign policy; it is there that disaster will strike." If Mussolini means even a fraction of his bloodthirsty ranting, sooner or later he will plunge Italy into a hopeless war.'

'It *is* only ranting, my dearest, and meanwhile the professor has to live in exile in America! I pity him for that, but at least he doesn't have to watch his children being shunned by the people who should be their friends. Apart from the estate-workers' children, how many others will feel bold enough to come and wish Francesca joy on her birthday?'

'Probably none; but she won't greatly mind. The people she loves will be here – including her friend, Carlie!'

For once, Ottavio couldn't allow himself to be comforted. 'It's not right . . . not fair; I'm blighting their lives,' he insisted desperately. 'Not only theirs. My mother, who loves company, has none, and *you* are deprived of friends. Jane, my darling one, above everything else in life I want *you* to be happy.'

She took his troubled face in her hands and kissed him lovingly. '*Amore* . . . I *am* happy; more happy than any one woman has a right to be. Your mother enjoys company but she doesn't crave it any longer. She's never bored or lonely now and she understands why her neighbours don't call. Marco has friends enough at school, and Francesca doesn't need them. She loves Castagnolo even more than he does, and her happiness is simply in being *here*, with us. When Marco goes back to London with David offer her the chance to go, too. I'm almost certain she'll refuse.'

Ottavio's worried frown slowly faded because nothing seemed unbearable for very long if Jane was close to him. He knew her more intimately now than it had ever seemed possible for one human being to know another, loved her *more* dearly even than when they'd begun living together. He reached out his arms to her now because the pleasure of holding her was something he still hadn't got used to. He never stopped marvelling at the joy they shared – he in possessing her, she in offering herself to him. It seemed intolerable that she shouldn't be allowed to be his wife.

249

'Dear heart, I'd change things if I could,' he murmured against her hair, 'for Francesca, for everyone . . . but especially for you.'

She freed herself so that she could look at him, the better to convince him. 'Nothing needs to be changed – Francesca is content and I couldn't feel more married to you than I do now even if His Holiness the Pope gave us a dispensation! Promise me you'll stop worrying.'

Ottavio nodded and kissed her mouth, then smiled because he'd remembered something. 'You conveniently forgot another reason why Francesca might refuse to go to London – she *still* hasn't made friends with David.'

'I know.' Jane frowned over a problem that she hadn't been able to solve. 'I'm afraid it's because he can't rid himself of the ideas my father has taught him – he must never forget where he belongs, and to enjoy Tuscany too much would be a kind of disloyalty to England.'

'It's admirable in its way, that kind of loyalty,' Ottavio said thoughtfully.

'Yes, but it also leads countries to fight ruinous wars – not admirable at all! But the difficulty isn't only on David's side. Francesca is Marco's chosen friend and companion when they're here together, but only until David arrives. Your mother would say that a female must accept being put on one side occasionally, but Francesca belongs to a less long-suffering generation!'

'Well, she will have Lorenza's company at least – Anna will soon be up at Fiesole, as usual.'

'Not a *great* deal of help,' Jane pointed out with reluctance. 'David forgets England enough to be pleased with Lorenza, and that excludes Francesca still more. Her cousin is all the things she refuses to be at the moment – pliable and pretty and sweetly lovable!'

Ottavio changed his mind about thanking Heaven it was her mother that Lorenza took after, not Ernesto Lambertini. The subject of parentage was a fraught one that they still tried to avoid. Unless a conversation like this one reminded him, he managed to forget that Francesca was not his daughter. She was the product of two very different races – how could the mixed blood in her veins *not* make the business of growing up more stormy and difficult than usual?

'Anna will be glad to get here,' Jane observed quietly, aware of the direction Ottavio's thoughts had taken. 'Each summer she escapes from Rome a little more thankfully, but especially this time with Alex away in Switzerland.'

'Charlie will be good for her . . . have you noticed how peaceful and happy she is in his company?'

Jane nodded, not inclined to share her brother's secret, even with Ottavio. She had hesitated to suggest another summer visit this year simply because Anna was certain to be at Fiesole, but Charlie himself had insisted on coming. It was hopeless, but he knew that. Anna would never abandon her children or mortify Ernesto by leaving him, but Jane was certain that she knew Charlie loved her. *She* drew comfort from the fact and *he* had schooled himself to accept a situation he couldn't change. For a few weeks each year he could help Anna; it had to be enough for a brave and simple man who didn't rate his own needs very highly.

He and David arrived at the beginning of the school holiday, as usual, in time for Francesca's birthday. There was all the bustle of welcoming them at Castagnolo, and Anna and the children's arrival at the villa. Mixed with the excitement this time was the heartbreaking news that Fausto sent from Geneva. Even the eminent Swiss gynaecologist entrusted with Alexandra's confinement after two previous miscarriages had failed to deliver her baby alive. It had been a choice of Alex's life or the child's and there could be no more pregnancies.

Jane knew what it meant to them both, but especially to Alexandra. She expected to see her cousin heartbroken when they called at Castagnolo on their way back to Rome, and privately applauded the self-control that years of being Fausto's wife had taught her.

'I feel a fraud,' Alex said as they drove away. 'Jane was weeping inside for *my* sadness, when she might have wept for the children she doesn't have herself. If I thought Elena knew about her and Ottavio, I'd swear she'd come back just to ruin their life together.'

'You aren't a fraud, sweetheart – your sadness is real,' Fausto said gently.

'I know, but *nothing* could be as bad as not being your wife. Jane doesn't have *that* comfort with Ottavio.'

He turned to smile at her and lifted the hand nearest to him to kiss, then turned his attention to the road again.

Jane's distress for them remained with her, blinding her to something she otherwise wouldn't have missed on the morning of Francesca's birthday.

Among the birthday gifts there was a small one that Francesca chose not to open with the others. Its foreign stamp told her who it came from, and in the clearest moment of premonition in her life she was aware that it could only be examined when she was alone.

She emerged from her bedroom afterwards just as David walked along the top corridor towards her – for the first time that she could remember she was grateful to see him.

'Tell Jane I'm going out for a walk – I'm not hungry.'

He'd meant to try to be friendly today, but she'd spoken even more curtly than usual – as if he was one of the servants who had to put up with her tempers. She was impossible altogether – a plain, prickly girl who didn't understand that he was seventeen and almost grown up – a senior who rowed stroke for St Paul's and who secretly expected to earn a Blue when he went up to Oxford. *That* was more important at the moment than the firm, but beneath the immediate pleasures of life lay the secure knowledge that Rushton's was waiting for him.

'You can't ignore everyone else today, you silly chump – it's your birthday,' he pointed out crossly.

Pallor overlaid the usual creamy colour of her skin, but he scarcely noticed that fact in his irritation with her, or the feverish brightness of her huge, grey eyes.

'I can do anything I like on my birthday – tell them *that*, if you'd rather.'

She took to her heels suddenly and ran along the corridor away from him. He went down the staircase more slowly and delivered her message with the accurate and resentful feeling that Aunt Jane blamed *him* for Francesca's disappearance. Poor Marco to have such a creature for a sister! He thanked Heaven that his half-brother and -sister at home were too small for him to have to bother with.

After lunch, eaten without Francesca, Charlie set out for the walk he always took when he first arrived at Castagnolo. It was fixed by habit now, a small private ceremony that took him to all the vantage-points he cherished most. It didn't occur to him to remember that, since she knew of them, his friend might be waiting for him somewhere – she *was*, sitting high up on the hillside, on the fallen trunk of an old oak tree brought down in a winter storm.

He looked at her ravaged face and knew that some great trouble had befallen her; but he must wait for *her* to choose whether to confide in him or not.

'Not hungry? Well, you ought to be,' he remarked gently. 'I was always ravenous at the important age of fourteen.'

'It's certainly important,' she agreed, '. . . I haven't had a birthday like this one before.'

The thought crossed his mind that instead of sounding like fourteen, she had the self-possession of someone much older; but then her face crumpled and she buried it in her lap to try to hide a sudden, terrible storm of weeping.

Charlie waited, wishing passionately that Jane was there instead of himself; then, instinct alone operating in what was clearly a moment of crisis, he lifted Francesca's thin body into his arms and sat holding her until she grew quiet.

At last, she lifted her head and deliberately opened the fingers of her clenched fist to show him what was hidden there – a man's signet ring with the initials N.B. traced in gold on the dark-red stone of a cornelian.

'My mother hasn't written to me for years,' Francesca said in a voice still thick with tears. 'I didn't care if she'd forgotten us, although M – Marco did. He still remembers that she . . . didn't ask *him* to go with her to America.'

There was so long a pause that Charlie had to prompt her.

'Your mother sent the ring . . . ?'

Francesca's mouth quivered, but she answered him. 'As a birthday present – it belonged to my *father*, she said . . . an Englishman called Nicholas Brereton. He was killed in a skiing accident.'

There was another silence that he was incapable of breaking. It didn't occur to him to doubt Elena Buonaventura, because things that had puzzled him were now clear, but all he could notice for the moment was the astonishing fact that Francesca hadn't doubted her mother either.

'Carlie . . . why didn't they tell me before?' she asked at last in a small voice. He knew that she meant Ottavio and Jane, not Elena.

'I don't know, sweetheart . . . yes, I do,' he suddenly corrected himself. 'You belonged here, *that's* why; you must have known it yourself, because you chose not to go with your mother. What happened years and years ago isn't important now – it's an old, sad story, over and done with. It doesn't change anything, because your life is here with Ottavio and Jane and Marco. That's why they didn't tell you.'

She didn't answer; just sat quite still, staring at the ring in her hand. How much could she, should she, be expected to understand? Charlie had no idea; his only clear thought in an ordeal worse than any he had had to deal with was to lessen the damage Elena had done.

'It's a great temptation to judge people, Fran – what they do is right or wrong, we think, and if it isn't what *we'd* do, then it's clearly wrong. But people behave as it seems to them they must *at the time*, and we can't judge the rightness or wrongness of that. Some time in the future perhaps you'll decide you want to know more about your English father. *Now* just remember that you have an Italian father, too, and an English mother in Jane, and they love you dearly, as we all do.'

She nodded, without speaking. Her pale profile turned away from him was etched with the delicate, pure precision of a head on an antique coin, and he realized that she would grow up beautiful after all.

'Coming home with me now?' he asked quietly.

'In a little while . . . you go on, Carlie.'

She smiled suddenly at his anxious face and leaned over to kiss his cheek. It was a little, fond gesture of dismissal that said she must be left to manage on her own now.

He walked back to the castle, trying to decide whether to seek out Ottavio or Jane. He had just decided that it should be Ottavio when the man himself came out on to the upper terrace in front of him.

'You haven't seen Francesca, I suppose?' Ottavio enquired casually. 'She won't come to any harm here, of course, but Jane's getting a little anxious . . .'

'Yes, I saw her, and now I need to see you.'

Ottavio listened to the brief story with the remote expression of a man listening to events that concerned the lives of strangers. Charlie was irritated by his detachment until he noticed Ottavio's hands clenched at his sides to stop them trembling.

'What in Heaven's name prompted your wife to tell Francesca now,' he finished by asking, 'after all these years?'

'I think I can guess. A little while ago we met for the first time in years someone who used to call herself a friend of Elena's. I don't make any secret of what Jane means to

255

me – couldn't if I tried – but this was the sort of creature who would be happy to let a friend know that her husband was living with another woman. Elena never wanted me herself, but someone else taking *her* place in my heart . . . *that* could provoke her cruelty.' He turned to face Charlie. 'Thank you for trying to help Francesca . . . Jane always wanted me to tell the children – largely for Marco's benefit – but I stupidly refused.'

'Perhaps it wouldn't have been the right time until now,' Charlie suggested diffidently. 'Fran said she'd follow me home – I don't know how much longer she'll be.'

Ottavio nodded, and Charlie walked on into the castle, unable to think of any more comfort to offer.

To a man who waited anxiously it seemed a long time before a slender figure in a pale dress separated itself from the greenness of the lowest level of the gardens. Ottavio flung himself down the nearest flight of steps and met Francesca as she reached the grass path between one terrace and the next.

The expression on his face told her that Charlie had spoken to her father . . . not her *father* at all, she must remember, though how would she ever be able to think of this gentle, loving man as anything else? She closed her eyes to shut out *his* pain, but his voice reached her.

'*Tesoro mio*, I didn't want to tell you until you were old enough to understand why . . . why grown-up people have to do the things they do. Jane wanted me to explain . . . it's my fault you've heard it in this way.'

'It's my mother's fault,' Francesca corrected him coolly. 'She needn't have told me at all.'

'No, but perhaps it was something she felt she owed to . . . to the memory of Nicholas Brereton. She loved him very much, Francesca. If you don't understand that now, you will some day.'

She gave a little shrug that almost defeated him, but he struggled on.

'Perhaps, then, you'll want to go to England . . .'

'*No*,' she cried out. 'I'll *never* go there. Apart from Jane and Carlie, I hate the English. Even if I can't stay here, I *won't* be one of *them*.'

'Then you'll be what you've always been – my beloved daughter, who belongs at Castagnolo.'

His arms reached out to her and, after a terrible moment in which he thought she was about to reject him, she threw herself into them.

'Is my name really Br – Brereton?' she muttered against the tweed of his jacket.

'You are Francesca Maria Buonaventura, my darling; and now may I escort the Signorina Buonaventura home?'

Her trembling mouth suddenly smiled at him, and they turned to climb the steps together.

20

Marco received so thoughtfully his father's explanation of events fifteen years ago that Ottavio found the conversation even more difficult than he'd anticipated. When he reported this to Jane afterwards, she was sympathetic but unsurprised.

'He's growing up now . . . we aren't always going to be allowed to know what he's thinking.'

'But I *did* know,' Ottavio pointed out ruefully, 'and it was very disconcerting. He managed not to say that the failure with his mother had been mine all the time, not his, but my son *pitied* me! I could hear him thinking that he'd manage his own life better when the time came.'

'He's sixteen, my love – confident that life *can* be arranged in any way he wants. Long may such heavenly confidence last!'

She was right about Marco, but not entirely so. He was young and clever and brave – those things he knew for certain. Unlike poor little Francesca, he was a true Buonaventura, and Castagnolo's magical world would be his one day. But when it came to the rest of the world, then confidence broke down. His English friend knew it, but so far he hadn't told the man he most wanted to resemble – his 'happy warrior', Zio Fausto. The phrase came from an English poem Jane had read to them years ago; Marco remembered it because it perfectly described his uncle.

When the time came, he was anxious to be promoted from the Avanguardia to the adult ranks of Il Duce's famous blackshirt militia, even though it meant enduring his father's unspoken disapproval. He kept repeating to himself one of the militia's commandments, as if by repetition his heart as well as his mind would learn to accept it: 'He who is not prepared to give his body and soul to the nation and to serve Il Duce without question is not worthy to wear the Black Shirt.' It was unthinkable not to be worthy of his uncle, but he remembered how incredulously his friend David had smiled when he heard the slogan. For the first time in years they'd parted with relief at the end of the holiday, but the friendship survived – more precious to both of them because they knew without being told that it was now threatened by the world they lived in.

They were scarcely aware of the greatest threat of all when it came at the beginning of 1933. Months before David left St Paul's to go up to Oxford, a man called Adolph Hitler became Chancellor of the German Reich. He greatly admired Italy's leader, it was said, but their first meeting didn't take place until the following summer in Venice; Fausto and Alexandra were part of the Duce's entourage and they broke their journey back to Rome afterwards to pay a rare visit to Castagnolo.

The Marchesa, as usual, ignored the never-healing rift between her sons.

'Darling – we never see you; couldn't you come a *little* more often?'

Fausto looked for once at a loss, Alexandra murmured something about the demands of public life and Jane rescued them both by hurrying into the conversation.

'The trouble is that we lead a quiet life here and keep forgetting how time-consuming it must be to rub shoulders with the high and mighty! Did you catch a glimpse of Herr Hitler, by the way, Alex, or were ladies kept out of sight as being too distracting?'

'Of course I saw him,' Alexandra answered, 'a little man in baggy, striped trousers and a yellow mac; insignificant, poor fellow, beside his host. All the same, it was tactless of the huge crowd in St Mark's Square to ignore him completely and shout "Duce, Duce" all the time!'

It had indeed been tactless, but Alexandra didn't blame the crowd – like them, she was heart and soul a Fascist, because that was what Fausto remained. Jane still had to remind herself of the fact because, after nearly ten years of marriage, Alex *looked* so unchanged from the girl in St Peter's Square who had longed to go everywhere and see everything. A sophisticated life had added a gloss to her fair English beauty, but there was no outward reminder that she and Jane must now struggle to ignore the same pitfalls that bedevilled Ottavio and his brother.

Fausto waited for his nephew to drag him off for a shared walk, as usual, but the suggestion had to come from *him* in the end because Marco seemed content to sit staring into space while everyone else talked.

'Nearly the end of schooldays,' Fausto remarked as they climbed the hillside together. 'What happens next?'

'The University of Bologna. Papa suggested Oxford – David Rushton is already there – but I refused.'

'I'm glad, caro; England is no place for you, and Oxford is filled with the decadent sons of rich men. Remember what its Union voted last year – *not* to fight for King and Country – can you imagine such a shameful attitude *here*, now?'

Marco shook his head reluctantly. It was strange to be querying anything his uncle said, but he must try when it sounded so silly.

'David's not decadent, nor are his friends that I've met. I liked them – liked England when I went there, as a matter of fact.'

He hoped that Zio Fausto, who *hadn't* been to England, would leave the subject alone now, even though for once it seemed difficult to find something else safe to talk about.

'Don't get too fond of the English, caro . . . they are not true friends of Italy.' Fausto saw the expression on his nephew's face and anticipated a protest. 'Alexandra and Jane belong here now – of course, I exclude *them* from the people you shouldn't like!'

'Is Herr Hitler going to be a friend?' Marco asked instead.

'I think so – although at the moment he is only a disciple of the Duce's. He has a great deal to learn about Fascism, but we can teach him how to make his country proud and great again.'

'. . . by persecuting the Jews?' Marco asked coolly. 'I know he is, because a friend at school has Jewish grandparents in Munich.' His shuttered face was turned away, rejecting the smile his uncle would have offered him.

Fausto accepted that the days of hero-worship couldn't last for ever, but it was a shock to discover how fast and questioningly Marco was growing up.

'The Duce does *not* condone the persecuting of Jews,' he said sharply. 'It's a mistaken policy on Hitler's part, but of course he will realize that; we all make mistakes and have to learn from them in time.'

'*Are* we learning? David says we live in a country that becomes more and more regimented by authority – they have free elections in England; newspapers can print what they like; and people who oppose the government are not thrown into prison or exiled to lonely, barren islands.' His voice cracked on the words, revealing the turmoil of unhappiness and doubt he struggled with inside.

Fausto stood still, forcing Marco to stop as well and look at him. 'Listen, caro, please. England has centuries of settled laws and traditions behind her; we have been one country for little more than fifty years. Is it any wonder that we have to be disciplined a little? Too much freedom now to disagree, obstruct, destroy, would be like allowing a child to gorge on food that was too rich for it. We must be patient, that's all.'

It seemed reasonable, even though Marco felt sure it wouldn't convince his friends, but a worse fear than all the rest needed dragging out into the open.

'Is it true that we might find ourselves *fighting* England

one day? Is that why we must all learn to be warriors for the Duce?'

Fausto nodded slowly, refusing the easy option of lying to his nephew. 'For the sake of Italy we may have to accept even *that* necessity. We have a mountainous country and a large population – we need space for our people, markets for our industries. Both in the Mediterranean and in Africa, where we should naturally be allowed to colonize, we are blocked by a small, arrogant, smugly selfish nation accustomed to believing that it can rule the world. If the Duce were to decide that we must fight for the right to take what we needed, then we would fight England.' He saw his nephew's expression and smiled reassuringly at him. 'Don't worry, caro – it won't come to that. England, and France too, have lost their warlike spirit and they know that our demands are just. We shall never need to go to war.' Marco thought it was safe to believe what sounded so confident; a grin of pure relief wiped away the anxiety from his face, and at last he could allow himself to enjoy his uncle's visit.

'I'll show you our new dispensary and meeting-room,' he said cheerfully. 'It was Jane's idea, but we all have to help – even Grandfather teaches the children which stars to look for at night!'

Fausto and Alexandra were back in Rome when news was made public of the Nazis' murder of Chancellor Dollfuss in Vienna. The Duce immediately condemned it on behalf of his neighbours across the Brenner Pass, and the whole German plan to annex Austria which made the murder necessary.

Remembering his recent conversation with Marco, Fausto wrote at once to reassure *him* that the whole thing was a brutal, tragic blunder abhorred by the Duce and the Party. A warmly affectionate letter ended with the plea that his nephew should remember what Fascism was achieving for Italy, and invited Marco to visit Rome and see for himself the visionary work being put in hand under Mussolini's guidance.

Marco replied enthusiastically about the draining of the Pontine Marshes, but made no reference to Austria; nor did he accept his uncle's invitation. They were busy at Castagnolo getting ready for the *vendemmia*, and after that he must leave for his first term at Bologna.

Even in the following spring vacation he didn't go to Rome, but spent Easter with David Rushton on a walking-tour in Scotland. They were back in London, footsore but happy, in time for James Rushton's seventy-fifth birthday celebrations.

Marco had known that Jane would be at Vine House for the occasion, but he was slightly put out to find that a bigger delegation had arrived from Italy. His aunt and cousin were being entertained in St Peter's Square by David's Great-Aunt Alice; even more astonishing, Francesca was there as well.

'You said you'd never come to England,' Marco reminded her when they met at James's party.

'I changed my mind – decided I'd like to come and see where Jane and Carlie grew up.' She almost blushed for what was only a small percentage of the truth. It had seemed necessary to come because she must be absolutely sure that she belonged to Italy. It was the coward's way out to go on disowning her father without proving to herself that she need have nothing to do with England.

'I suppose Lorenza decided that *she* must see where David grew up,' Marco said resentfully. 'Couldn't you at least have left *her* behind? She's such an idiot and she'll stick to David like a limpet.'

'He doesn't seem to mind,' Francesca pointed out with more truth than tact. 'In fact, I'd say he rather enjoys being stuck to by Lorenza.'

Even Marco could see why. At seventeen, Lorenza was bound to attract attention among the Anglo-Saxon girls who eddied around David Rushton. Her body was lithe and already temptingly curved; she had a mane of black hair and a luscious mouth. Most attractive of all, she was strongly inclined for pleasure – given and received. He now realized why she reminded him of David's beautiful mother, Laura Rushton.

'Lorenza's pretty,' he conceded, 'but she smiles too much – you don't!'

'I don't smile enough, you mean, unlike Mr Dickens's Mrs Fezziwig who came in "one vast substantial smile"!'

Marco grinned, remembering not the name but the fact that however vehemently Francesca rejected her English blood, she shared Jane's passion for England's authors and poets.

'You still haven't said what you're all doing here,' he pointed out.

'Lorenza and I are having our minds broadened by foreign travel,' Francesca explained primly. 'She is enjoying the experience more than I am.'

Her brother frowned, inclined to be serious. 'Why *don't* you like it here? I do . . . it isn't Tuscany, but it's beautiful in its own gentle way, and Scotland isn't gentle at all – it's grandly beautiful and harsh.'

Francesca gave a little shrug, unwilling to have her feelings about England analysed.

'They're freer here than we are, Fran,' he said abruptly. 'You could stand in Hyde Park and shout to your heart's content about the wickedness of the rulers of the land . . . provided you didn't do bodily harm to someone else or damage his property, the policemen would smile and walk on! It's different from the state we live in.'

'Zio Fausto says they're decadent . . . too weak and easy-going now for their own good,' she objected.

'I know – I suppose we shall see who's right in the long run.'

For Jane, the evening wore a veil of unreality through which she tried to glimpse the people they had once been. It was ten years ago that at just such a Rushton gathering as this she had found herself engaged to marry William. Now he was man of forty-one, with thinning hair and an air of self-satisfaction she doubted that he deserved. Laura, still just on the right side of forty, seemed unchanged. She'd been sensible enough not to follow fashion by cutting her glorious hair, and the weight of its burnished coil still drew attention to her graceful white neck and shoulders. She was especially charming to Marco, but for once uncertain of her attitude to Jane. Beforehand she had decided that it should be tolerance faintly tinged with family shame. Confronted by Jane herself, sheer irritation got the upper hand – her one-time sister-in-law had no *right* to look so happy and serenely poised.

'I scarcely know how to introduce you now, my dear Jane – what a blessing everyone here is an old friend!' Laura's veiled disapproval was not real; she cared very little how Jane lived, but to have seen her free to marry Ottavio Buonaventura and become a marchesa would have been intolerable.

William caught the end of his wife's comment and smiled determinedly at the woman he had once thought it would be boring but convenient to marry. She still had the trick of laughing with her eyes when her mouth was serious. Disconcerting, he'd always found it, and did now.

'Old friends are the best, Janey,' he said heartily. 'Don't you agree, and miss them a little sometimes?'

'I don't think I distinguish much between old and new,' she answered. 'I should miss *anyone* I reckoned a friend.' It was quite as beautifully ambiguous as Laura's remark had been, and she was still smiling at it when Aunt Alice beckoned her away.

'Expected you to look different,' she said bluntly.

'More like the wretched immoral creature I *am*? I'm afraid that's what Laura expected.' Amusement lit Jane's eyes again, because it had been a pleasure to disappoint William's wife, but Aunt Alice was shaking her head.

'I'm not talking about living with a man you can't

marry. The rest of it's been a struggle, hasn't it, at that place I still can't pronounce? Years of hard work and worry, from what Charles says, even though he can never wait to get back there.'

'Yes, but years of great happiness, too. The hard work continues but the worries are less now, because we know that when it's looked after Castagnolo can pay its way.' She hesitated about what to say next. 'We don't see Alex often, but Anna can tell you that she's very content with her life – apart from losing the babies she and Fausto might have had.'

Alice thought of saying that miscarriages came of living in a country like Italy, where the elementary rules of hygiene were probably not known. She decided against it and nodded in the direction of Francesca instead.

'Takes after her mother, I suppose – not a bit like Ottavio. She's strangely unItalian altogether, but perhaps they don't *all* make a song and dance about everything and talk nineteen to the dozen. David's very taken with her cousin, by the way, but he'll have to find an English wife when the time comes, to keep James happy.'

Jane sifted through this medley of observations and chose a safer one of her own.

'Father *says* he's feeling his age . . . is there anything to worry about?'

'Nothing that I know of, except wounded vanity because his mirror tells him he's getting old, like the rest of us. He can still work George or William to a standstill, and he won't let go of the reins until David's ready to take over.'

Jane smiled at the irritation in her aunt's voice, mingled with reluctant admiration. Alice couldn't help wishing that her own husband had been half as deedy as James. Her children were something of a disappointment, too. George did nothing but beget children, and William was completely under Laura's thumb. Lionel was lightweight like his father, but not so lovable; and Eliza, who had only come to the party under protest, was wearing grubby trousers and sandals for the occasion! For a moment Alice's face looked so defeated and sad that Jane leaned over and kissed her cheek.

'London's very tiring, I find,' she said gently. 'Come and pay us a visit – Ottavio's mother loves company, and our sunshine would do you and Uncle Edward good.'

'Perhaps we will – before it's too late. Edward says it *will* be, one of these days.' In case it had sounded too ominous, Alice suddenly smiled at her niece. 'I'm *glad* you're happy, Jane.'

Among all the other people filling the drawing-room at Vine House, it wasn't until late in the evening that Charlie found Anna Lambertini alone; the curtains hadn't been drawn and she was standing in one of the long window embrasures, staring out at the lamps that made a lighted garland along the riverbank.

'It's beautiful,' she said softly, knowing without looking at him that he was there. 'I shall be able to picture you now, sitting at your window upstairs watching the river. It's much more interesting than the Tiber at home.' She glanced quickly at him, then looked away again because he was watching her. 'Shall you be at Castagnolo this summer?'

'I'm not sure . . . I think perhaps not,' he said slowly. 'Jane and Ottavio would be too kind to say so, but they must get tired of having me come back each year as regularly as the housemartins and swallows. Perhaps I'll cut a dash and do something adventurous for a change – sail down the Nile or up the Ganges!'

'I think it should be the other way round,' Anna said with difficulty. She had no idea which it was, but anything was better than allowing herself to beseech him to come to Tuscany as usual. Sometimes, when she tried to re-create in her mind's eye the darkly handsome, interestingly intense image of the Ernesto Lambertini she had married, it seemed absurd that all she needed *now* for happiness was this quiet man who stood beside her. There was nothing remarkable about Charles Rushton, except his gift for making people love him.

'Nile or Ganges – they both sound adventurous enough,' she murmured. 'Exotic setting and lots of dusky, black-eyed maidens, I dare say!'

'Just what I need,' Charles agreed untruthfully. The faint flower perfume she used just reached him and he was close enough for his arm to be touching hers. It was the most he'd ever allowed himself, but suddenly his hand reached down to grip hers. 'Anna, are you all right . . . in Rome?'

'Yes, quite all right, thank you.' She heard herself say the words and decided that they sounded absurd. His hand pulled her round to face him, and his eyes demanded a truer answer to the question.

'Not quite so all right if *you* don't come this summer, though.' Her pale mouth tried to smile away the confession, in case he should glimpse the desolation she struggled with inside.

'Then I shall forget about the black-eyed maidens,' Charlie said after a moment. 'Let them have their adventures with someone else.'

Tears pricked her eyelids but she didn't look away from him, because they both knew that the time had come to be truthful. 'I'm being selfish . . . you must do what *you* want to do.'

'Then I shall come to Italy – unless I can persuade you to come with me somewhere else . . . "over the hills and far away", as our nursery rhyme says. How does *that* sound, my darling love?'

Anna closed her eyes against the tenderness she couldn't accept, but the tears seeped through – she could feel them hot on her cheeks. 'It sounds like Heaven . . . and just as impossibly out of reach,' she said in a low voice. 'Do you understand about Ernesto, Charlie? There's no joy in our life together, but with us marriages are entered into for a lifetime. He wouldn't leave me and I can't abandon *him*, or the children.'

'I know that – have always known it. I can't imagine a time when I shan't love you, but there's no need to add me to the list of things you worry about. I shall grow into an eccentric old bachelor who has a lovely time being humoured by the rest of the family!' He lifted her hand to his mouth, left a kiss in the palm and folded her fingers over it. Then he smiled and released her; she used her other hand to wipe away her tears, and after a moment or two took refuge with Jane.

It would have been no surprise if Alice Rushton had observed that secluded conversation. For once *she* missed it, but there was someone else who did not. Irritated by the sight of Lorenza still in a state of entrancement with Marco's friend, and bored by Lionel Rushton's attempts to be entertaining, she looked round for Carlie. If he'd crept away to his studio upstairs, he wouldn't mind if she went up there, too. She was edging towards the door when she discovered that he was still in the room after all; but he wasn't alone, and the woman with him, almost hidden by the long curtains, was Zia Anna. It would have been so natural to go and join them that she almost did . . . Carlie would smile as he always smiled at her and she would know that she was welcome. But in one of those stepping-stone moments that cross the flood of experience between adolescence and growing up, she knew with equal pain and certainty that this time she *wouldn't* be welcome.

The rest of the evening had to be endured, and so did the rest of the London visit. She smiled more than usual to pretend that she was enjoying herself, and counted the days until it was time to go home – no doubt about *that*, at least. Castagnolo was where she belonged; once back there, she need have nothing more to do with England. She had no intention of saying so, even to Marco, who seemed to have a strange admiration for the place; but the truth was jerked out of her in a sudden fierce quarrel with David Rushton.

While Lorenza and her mother went shopping with Jane

one morning, James instructed his grandson to entertain their other visitor, who had explained that she didn't find shops fascinating. She *wouldn't*, David thought glumly as they trudged in silence along the Chiswick towpath. Nothing about Francesca Buonaventura corresponded with what he knew of all the other girls he'd ever met.

'You should have told your grandfather you didn't want to get landed with me,' the tiresome creature by his side pointed out suddenly. 'Don't you ever *not* do what he says?'

'Frequently,' said David stiffly. 'Not as a rule, however, when he's relying on me to look after a guest.'

'Well, it's very kind of you both, I'm sure, but quite unnecessary. I can enjoy a walk by myself and I'm not likely to come to any harm – this is peaceful, law-abiding England, not violent Tuscany.'

He shot a glance at her, but even when her mouth was grave he had the feeling that she was laughing at him. It was what he disliked about her most – that, and the way her cool, grey eyes seemed always to be measuring him. Damn it, why couldn't she at least *try* to look and behave as Lorenza did? It would have been a pleasure to leave her to find her own way back, but he must see the walk out now or she would think she had beaten him.

'Marco's happy here, but my impression is that you're not,' he said. '*You* ought to be, I should have thought.'

He had expected to provoke her, but her reaction still startled him. She stopped in her tracks and a sudden flame of anger lit her grey eyes.

'Why *ought* I to be?'

The words were flung at him out of her fear that Marco had unforgivably told this elegant, arrogant, self-satisfied creature about her father.

'Because, you little termagant, I can't think of a nicer advertisement for this country than Aunt Jane, setting aside the fact that you're as thick as thieves with Uncle Char as well.'

Francesca stooped to pick up a stone and fling it in the river. She was still flushed but in control of herself when she spoke again.

'Setting aside both Jane and Carlie, I don't like England, and Marco ought to remember that his home is in Italy . . . we're Italians, both of us,' she insisted with a fierceness David didn't understand.

'And proud to be, I'm sure . . . with Mussolini sending troops to Africa and ranting about the new empire he's going to set up there; it shouldn't be too difficult – a mechanized army against tribesmen armed with spears!'

'What about *your* Empire . . . how was that won? By kind words and gentle persuasion?'

'Whatever happened in the past belongs to the past. We run our colonies with efficiency and justice and stop them slaughtering each other,' David shouted. 'They *need* us there; the Ethiopians don't need Mussolini's blackshirt bullies.'

It was a lamentably childish performance; he cringed at the memory afterwards of something quite out of keeping with a Balliol man almost at the end of his second year. At the time, though, nothing mattered except his longing to overmaster a hostile, argumentative Italian who didn't understand the rightness of the British Empire and the wrongness of the one Mussolini hoped to acquire.

'My uncle wears the black shirt,' Francesca said coldly. 'He's a gentle, civilized man, not a bully.'

'He can be as pure as driven snow, but the régime he upholds is *evil*. Now, if you think we've failed to enjoy this walk for long enough, we can turn round and go home.'

They completed the return journey in silence, with emotions complicated by the fact that they were acutely aware of each other. Francesca walked along wide eyed so as not to weep for the turmoil of feelings that assailed her. David loped beside her, torn between certainty that she was impossible, fear that he hadn't behaved very well and admiration for the free and beautiful way in which she moved. It would be nice to see her run, but on the whole what he mostly longed for was for Aunt Jane to take Francesca Buonaventura back to Tuscany.

Marco escorted them home, careful to look after them on the journey as well as his father would have done. But he was disinclined to talk, or notice that Zia Anna seemed deep in thoughts of her own, while Francesca and Lorenza – having quarrelled as to the pleasure or grief of having said goodbye to David Rushton – could only manage to be stiffly polite to one another.

He stood in the corridor of the train, watching the sleeping towns of France flash by in the darkness, and felt very lonely. Then the door of the sleeping-compartment behind him slid open and Jane crept out.

'I don't sleep in trains,' she whispered. 'It always seems unfair to leave the engine-driver awake on his own!'

He grinned because it sounded just like Jane. The corridor light fell dimly on her face and he noticed with a slight sense of shock that she was no longer young . . . not old, of course, but time was rushing headlong into the future, just as the train was hurtling them across France.

'I'm glad Papa has you,' he mumbled, suddenly aware that he'd never said so before.

'I'm glad we all have each other.' She smiled at him with deep affection, knowing better than to remind him of the hostile, unkind child who hadn't wanted her at Castagnolo. 'Now, what else shall we be glad about? I enjoyed our visit to London, but I'm happy to be going home – you, too?'

'I'm not sure,' he said surprisingly, then appeared to give the conversation an abrupt turn. 'Jane, Eliza Rushton's an odd sort of person, isn't she?'

'Well, yes . . . but sincerely convinced of what she believes, which happens not to be what the rest of the family believe.'

'Difficult for her . . . lonely, too, I should think. She knows a lot about Communism – we had a long talk . . .'

Jane forbore to say that they were bound to since Eliza talked of nothing else; Marco's face looked serious and she realized they were approaching the matter that had been preoccupying him all the way home.

'Eliza even knows about the things that are happening in Italy – all communists do, apparently. Men like Antonio Gramsci, and Pavese and Levi are being imprisoned for life or deported to punishment islands. They're not murderers or violent men – just writers and thinkers who see something wrong with Fascism. How *can* we treat them like that, Jane?'

She thought how easy it would have been to continue Eliza's work and undermine his faith still more; but he had grown up with his allegiance given to what Fausto believed in. She wouldn't help to tear him in two.

'I can only tell you what I think your uncle would say. Self-government is still a luxury for Italy. A country has to grow used to ruling itself before it can allow its people the right to speak and write and act against the system. Fascism isn't sure enough of itself yet to give people that right.'

'What if it never is?'

'Then it will probably fail.'

Marco stared out of the window; there was no need to look at him – she could see his pale face reflected in the glass and feel the turmoil that consumed him.

'David said the Duce was mad to lay claim to Abyssinia and even more mad to teach Adolf Hitler Fascist tricks that will ruin us all one day. We had a row about it – I said he was just the mouthpiece for a Communist history tutor at Oxford, but . . . suppose he's right, Jane?'

The low, agonized question scarcely reached her above the clatter of the wheels; the train dived into a tunnel that threw back the roar of sound they were making, and she had a vision of terror in which Europe, like the train

273

out of control, plunged over an abyss hidden in the darkness.

They emerged in a minute or two into the sleeping countryside, and she made a grab at self-control.

'We can frighten ourselves to death predicting events that may never happen, or we can put our faith in humanity,' she muttered at last, 'and God. Don't let's forget *Him* . . . even though a Communist Oxford don may very well do so!'

She saw Marco's strained face relax in a grin; they both knew that she hadn't answered his question because she was unable to, but they returned to their berths and pretended to sleep.

Jane never forgot that conversation and, although they never referred to it again, she was certain that Marco remembered it too.

He was still at Bologna University when a victorious Italian army entered Addis Ababa on 5 May 1936. One man's dream of a new Roman Empire was in the process of being realized. In a speech from the Piazza Venezia broadcast to people assembled in every square throughout the length of Italy, the Duce announced Victor Emmanuele III's new title – not only King of Italy but Emperor of Ethiopia. The roars of acclamation easily drowned the still, small voice of protest here and there. The King was Emperor, but Benito Mussolini was almost God himself.

Other things happened in that eventful spring and summer, scarcely noticed by people obsessed with the great African adventure.

'They won't see what's happening until it's too late,' Ottavio complained desperately at dinner one evening. 'The Rhineland reoccupied by German troops without a murmur from anyone, and Ethiopia – a member state of the League of Nations – raped by *us*, while they murmur half-heartedly in Geneva about sanctions!'

The Marchese gave a little shrug that disapproved of the

ugly word 'rape' at his wife's dinner-table and wearily accepted its truth at the same time.

'My dear boy, what did you expect? England and France still imagine that we shall help them contain Hitler's vaulting ambitions; it seems to have escaped them that things have changed. Two years ago Hitler had to accept Mussolini's reprimand for the mistake of murdering Dollfuss. Now, he is confident enough to know that we shall agree to a document describing our unfortunate neighbour across the Alps as a *German* state!'

'I'm going down to Rome,' Ottavio decided. 'If the men like Fausto who surround Mussolini can be made to see reason, at least they will give him sound advice.'

'He doesn't want advice,' Don Giuseppe said quietly. 'Our great leader is intoxicated with the Fascist idea – proved successful so far, I must say – that might is right. Whoever fails to take what he wants by force is a fool. Go to Rome if you like, but your time would be better spent spraying the vines at home.'

Rather than do nothing, Ottavio did go but returned more depressed than when he'd set out. He was so disinclined to talk, even to Jane, that she had to resort to irony to provoke him out of despair.

'You're so eager to describe your visit that words fail you,' she suggested helpfully. 'You're about to say that Alex was welcoming and beautiful, Fausto surprised but friendly and that you explained with gentleness and sweet reason *exactly* what you wanted him to do!'

'I roared at him like a demented bull!' Ottavio confessed ruefully. 'Fausto pointed out that he didn't need *my* advice, and the Duce probably didn't need *his*, and we parted on terms that even Alexandra could do nothing to gloss over. I wasted two days, exactly as my father said I would.'

'Dearest, you *tried*,' Jane said, kissing him. 'Apart from praying to their Father in Heaven, it's all poor mortals can do.'

'Then I hope He is listening, my love.' Ottavio saw the

little frown of worry in her eyes and forced himself to smile. 'Take a walk with me, please; I shall feel better with some fresh Tuscan air in my lungs, after Rome.'

'And we also have to edit a trifle the account of your visit for Mamma! Fortunately she's too busy counting the days till Marco comes home, to plague you with questions about Fausto and Alex.' Jane stopped suddenly as they walked out of the room. 'Could you *not* mention to Marco about going to Rome? He seems to have settled down again now, but he was in a torment of conflicting ideas and loyalties for a while.'

'I won't do anything to shake his faith in Fausto, if that's what you mean.'

Jane smiled gratefully. 'You never have, and I suppose it *is* what I mean.' She tucked her hand in his and they walked out into the sunlight.

Gino Scarelli was in the nursery plantation, inspecting the newest olive trees. He smiled at them with the contentment of a man who had seen the necessary spring rain followed by a succession of hot summer days. The harvest prospects were good and the best of Castagnolo's wine now regularly travelled all the way to London to be handled by that great man, the Signorina Jane's father; Gino asked nothing more.

Jane watched him talking to Ottavio and came to the conclusion that they should ask nothing more themselves. After years of hard work and disappointments and fresh starts, Castagnolo was self-supporting again; more than that, it was cherished and beautiful. The world outside must take care of itself – it need have nothing to do with them.

She continued to think so until the end of the summer. By then the cruellest of civil wars was raging in Spain, and it was known that Mussolini had committed Italian troops and aircraft on the side of General Franco's revolt against the Republican government. Even so it need have nothing to do with *them* at Castagnolo, Jane told herself desperately.

They celebrated the *vendemmia* as usual, Charlie came as usual and David – a student no longer – arrived unexpectedly, almost as Marco was due to leave for his last year at Bologna.

The two of them disappeared for a day's walk on the hills and returned an hour after everyone else had got up from the dinner-table. They forgot to apologize, having something more important to say.

'David's going to Spain,' Marco said, addressing his father, 'and I'm not going back to college. He's old enough to fight, and so am I – on the side of the Spanish government.'

'You are both just going to wander into Spain, looking for the Republican Army?' Ottavio enquired, trying to sound lightly amused when his strong inclination was to shout or weep. It was cruel to belittle them, but if he had to expose their youth to stop them going, that was what he must do.

'There's an International Brigade already formed,' David explained quietly. 'That's what we shall join; hundreds of others, all sorts of mixed nationalities, already have. We're young and fit and we can handle guns.'

Ottavio told himself that David Rushton was barely twenty-one, his son a year younger – they couldn't, in the day they'd spent together, have become these resolute young men who might insist on going to a war that had nothing to do with them, however much he ordered them to do nothing of the kind.

'We have to go, Papa,' Marco said with a gentleness that amounted to pity for his father. 'Fascist aircraft are helping to bomb defenceless women and children – *Italians* are doing these things.'

His tragic dark eyes confirmed that at last his choice had been made. Fausto would never again be able to convince him that whatever Il Duce did was right because it was done for the honour and glory of Italy.

He and David left Castagnolo a week later. While Jane

struggled to help the distress of everyone else in the household, Francesca, dry eyed and silent, watched them go. She blamed David Rushton for persuading Marco to go with him – she would hate him for the rest of her life. It wasn't much help, but it was the only comfort she had.

21

Jane read the copies of *The Times* Ottavio brought back from Florence, but it was difficult to feel concerned about the Abdication crisis shaking England. When she confessed this to Ottavio, he looked amused.

'Now I *know* you're a good Italian, my love, when a matter that rocks the English monarchy to its foundations leaves you only mildly interested.'

'I've become a good *Toscana*, at least, when the prospects for gathering a fine crop of olives this December seem more crucial than knowing whether Edward VIII is to reign or marry. He'll make up his mind without *me* agonizing over it.'

As the months went by afterwards and Edward's place on the throne was occupied by his brother, there were other newspaper reports that Jane *had* to agonize over. She saw everywhere the slow, insidious acceptance of the need to rearm, and knew that when countries rearmed they usually ended by fighting – as if the bloody, inhuman slaughter going on in Spain wasn't enough to appease the gods of war. In the middle of all that suffering were the two young men she prayed for – schoolboys only a little while ago and now separated from them by horrors that couldn't be shared. It was dreadful to look at Ottavio's drawn face; almost worse to remember her father in London, probably dying Johnny's death all over again day by day for David.

She took refuge in work, thankful that the demands of Castagnolo and its people were never-ending. Inside the castle, the Marchese exhausted his frail strength in writing learned papers about the universe, and Donna Giulia pored over zodiacs and astrological tables in search of evidence that Marco was protected by Divine Providence or a lucky star. A mixture of Christianity, astrology and wishful thinking were usually enough to keep her cheerful. When these remedies failed Jane mopped her tears and kissed her, and waited for the storm of despair to pass.

Francesca, now well free of the schoolroom and attending classes on viniculture in Florence, had a less tender way of dealing with her grandmother's swings of mood.

'Don't weep for Marco and David, Granny; we're supposed to applaud, not wring our hands.'

'Dearest, you're as brave as they are,' the Marchesa said tearfully, '. . . those brave young men.'

'Not brave – *stupid*! They're in Spain because they can't resist the excitement of playing at being soldiers. Zio Fausto *says* there's no need for them to be there at all.'

Francesca's outburst was intended to relieve her own feelings, but she was taken to task for it because it was overheard by her grandfather.

'Your uncle might also agree that Italian peasant conscripts needn't be there either, fighting on General Franco's side for a dollar and two pesetas a day,' he said sternly. 'God knows there's no need for *any* of our troops and airmen to practise their skills against unarmed Spanish civilians.'

His tone of voice almost silenced her, but she wasn't quite ready to lower her flag, even for an elderly man she loved as much as this one.

'If men didn't fight, there would be no wars. Marco should be *here*, helping us take care of Castagnolo. He *hates* the madness of it . . . the cruelties of his own side as much as the rest. His letters are heartbreaking, but he won't give in and come home as long as his damned, dear, English friend stays there.'

She wasn't reprimanded for her language only because Giuseppe was intent on the argument. 'Men *have* to fight sometimes; they have abstract principles to defend that women find less essential than their own work of carrying on the human race. In this one matter, women are wrong,' he said with steely courtesy. 'If we abandon abstract principles there is nothing to lift us above the beasts in the field, and we don't deserve that humanity should survive.'

Francesca's grey eyes were bright with tears in the pallor of her face. She wanted to say that she understood what her grandfather said . . . wanted him to promise her in return that humanity *wasn't* bent on its own destruction. But she couldn't explain any of it, least of all the painful truth that Castagnolo, at the height of its summer fruitfulness and beauty, was more than she could bear when Marco was crouching in some rat-infested crater in Madrid. She fled out of the room, leaving silence behind her.

'The poor child is only nineteen,' the Marchesa said finally, with reproach. 'You were a little harsh on her, Giuseppe, even given the fact that we are not *expected* to understand the things that men consider important.'

He smiled a little, but grew serious again. 'At nineteen she is not a child, my dear, but old enough to know that emotions aren't enough; even courage isn't enough. She has been taught to use her mind – that is what she and the generation she belongs to *must* do if we are to survive.'

Marco returned to Italy in the spring of 1938, although the fighting in Spain dragged on for another year before the Republican forces were defeated by Franco and his Fascist supporters. By the time he reached Castagnolo a wound in his leg, neglected and allowed to heal badly, had left him with a noticeable limp. The scars that weren't visible were worse, Jane realized, but he didn't talk about them, nor about a certainty branded on his mind by the past eighteen months. He would do no more fighting, because war was an obscene outrage against the intelligence of any reasonable human being.

He walked about the hills alone, or with Francesca if she promised not to chatter when he wanted to think. If there were hard, dull tasks to be done for Gino, he shared them with the labourers more cheerfully than he sat at his grandmother's dinner-table. When she protested, he smiled at her.

'Are you thinking it's not fit work for the *padroncino*, Nonna? I've done worse things than walk up and down the vines with a tank of copper sulphate on my back!'

'It's not fit for someone who needs rest,' she insisted. 'You're as thin as a wand and pale as a ghost, still. Other young men worry their parents because they're *too* pleasure-loving and idle – *tesoro*, couldn't you be just a *little* more like them?'

A grin of pleasure at his grandmother's cautious recommendation made him look twenty-two again, but he shook his head. 'I'm not like other young men,' he said unarguably.

Francesca was the first to hear what his alternative was to be to leading the life of mildly licentious pleasure prescribed by the Marchesa. Tired of always having him locked inside the thoughts in his own head, she asked a blunt question one day.

'You didn't finish your law studies at Bologna – are you going back at the end of the summer?'

'No, I'm not.'

It wasn't encouraging but she tried again. 'Are you thinking there's too much to do here? It's true that Father works harder than he should, and so do all the men who are his age, or older. The young ones still drift away to factories in Milan and Turin, the fools.'

Marco turned his head to look at her, suddenly noticing changes that hadn't been there before he went away. She'd been scarcely more than a schoolgirl then, but she wasn't a schoolgirl now. He saw much more clearly than before the differences contributed by their different fathers – they shared the inheritance of their mother's features, but Fran owed her slender height to the Englishman, and her straight brown hair, and the grey eyes that shone like jewels when she was angry. She hadn't grown any more like Lorenza – the thought made him smile because it reminded him of David, condoling with him years ago on having such a tiresome sister!

'You always *were* an opinionated creature.' He said it out of a long silence, unaware that she supposed him still thinking about her last remark.

'Because I say anyone who chooses to leave Castagnolo is a fool?' she asked quietly. 'You would have said the same thing yourself not so long ago.'

'I know.' They climbed upwards in silence through the woodland that covered the flank of the hill. Above it, a sweet-smelling tangle of gorse and juniper led to a vantage-point offering them the whole of Tuscany spread out to the west. Sunlight caught the domes and towers of Florence far below them in the valley, and the surrounding hills were a deeper, softer blue than the sky they lay against.

'I used to try to remember this view when things were very bad in Spain,' Marco confessed suddenly. 'David could remember it too, just as clearly.'

'No view of his own to think about?'

'*His* precious mental picture was of the feet of the cox in front of him when he was rowing in the Oxford boat!'

'Just what I'd expect,' Francesca observed tartly, irritated to see Marco begin to smile.

'I said much the same thing – poured scorn on him for not being able to think of something more poetic than a boy's large, ungainly feet. He explained seriously that, being a non-rower in the boat, the boy and his feet had to be very small – quite dainty, in fact! We started to laugh and couldn't stop, even amid the horror and violence going on around us.'

Francesca almost said what she'd never admitted before – that she saw why the two of them were friends; but it was hard, even now, to allow David Rushton any virtue. She wondered whether *he'd* described the little scene to Charlie, but didn't say that out loud either.

'You still haven't told me what you're going to do,' she pointed out at last. 'I can't help feeling that you haven't come home to stay . . . you've alighted on us for a little while but don't look fixed here any more.'

'I'm not; I've got a job waiting for me in Milan.'

'Can't it be done here?'

'*Mustn't* be. Father's unpopular enough as it is with the people who rule our lives; having his son helping to run a clandestine press against the régime from Castagnolo would probably get *him* imprisoned.'

'He might be glad to take the risk,' she said sombrely. 'Doing something would lessen his despair of ever getting rid of Fascism.'

'There's nothing for *him* to do – he has Castagnolo to worry about. But there *is* resistance, Fran, and we have to help it grow – organize small underground cells of anti-Fascists and make sure they have something else to read than a diet of government lies.'

Marco's set face, at variance with the boyish dark hair being tumbled by the breeze, confirmed what she already knew. His youth had been left behind in Spain, along with some dead and buried spring of gaiety. From now on life was going to be a struggle, valuable but joyless.

'It sounds a dangerous thing to do, running a forbidden press, but you don't need me to tell you that,' she said sadly. 'Zio Fausto thought your Communist friends at Bologna talked you into joining the International Brigade – he hoped you'd get over that enthusiasm if you saw enough of them.'

'I did! . . . but I can't believe in Fascism again either, even to make him happy. Fran, we had to fight blackshirts in Spain – sent by Mussolini even though he'd signed a pact of non-intervention in the war. His instruction to General Franco was that any Italians like me, who were captured fighting for the Republicans, should be shot. That is the régime Zio Fausto still believes in.'

They sat in silence, content to be together on a peaceful

hillside for a little while . . . both wondering if they would ever have the chance to be there again.

'What about you?' Marco asked suddenly. 'We've done nothing but talk about me.'

'No ambitions to change the world, or even save Italy from the Fascists. I just want to stay here, helping to take care of *this* place. Do you remember what Castagnolo used to be like? Farmhouses falling to pieces . . . an air of neglect lying over everything, even though it still managed to be beautiful . . . and people disheartened who should have been happy?'

'Of course I remember . . . I used to promise Gino that he and I would save Castagnolo together some day! He was kind enough to pretend to believe me.'

'It *is* being saved – with the help of Jane's money. Father eventually told me about that, long after he told you. But we can't stop now that the land looks happy again. If you aren't here by the time he gets old and tired, I shall be able to take over. He and Charlie can sit on the terrace with Jane, tasting the wine I've made, and you can bring us news of the big, mad world outside Castagnolo.'

Marco nodded and smiled, but his thoughts were still on the past Francesca had recalled.

'Do you remember Jane's first morning with us? I was certain that she must go, and that, if she didn't leave quickly enough, I'd be able to frighten her away!'

'It's quite a good thing you were wrong, wouldn't you say?'

The teasing understatement suddenly reminded him with a jolt of pain of his friend, because it was just the sort of thing David might have said. Francesca chose to ignore the fact, but there were times when she didn't sound or behave like an Italian at all.

'You talk too much English with Jane,' he said sharply. 'Come on – let's go home.'

They were almost there before she spoke again. 'You didn't say anything about David. I suppose he's back in London, counting Rushton's wine-barrels underneath London Bridge?'

'No, he's still in Spain. He won't leave until the Republicans win or get beaten, even though he's no more of a Communist than I am.'

'Then whose side *is* he on?'

'The side of the ordinary man who wants to think and choose and vote for himself. It's a simple point of view, but Englishmen are prepared to sacrifice a good deal for it. That's just as well because they all may have to before long.'

Marco left Castagnolo for Milan soon after that walk with Francesca and it seemed to Jane, although she didn't say so to the Marchesa, that this time he'd gone more completely than when he'd set out for Spain. The boy who'd wanted to grow up to be *Ser Padrone* at Castagnolo in his turn was now a man caught up in the perilous business of influencing what other men thought. He would only come back to them as a visitor, when he came at all . . . *if* he was allowed to come at all.

Anxiety nagged at her and finally drove her to quarrel with Ottavio because he seemed so unconcerned.

'Milan is less dangerous for Marco than Madrid,' he pointed out, 'and at least he's accomplishing something *there*.'

'*Is* he? Tell me what, please.' The satisfaction in Ottavio's voice provoked her, raising echoes of the time years ago when a miserable harvest hadn't mattered and only the way it was celebrated *had*. 'Tell me what clandestine little meetings are going to achieve, and forbidden journals passed from hand to hand in dingy boarding-houses. Is *that* what you want for your son – a life lived in the half-light of hopeless, everlasting conspiracy?'

She recognized the expression of shocked anger that settled on Ottavio's face, even though she hadn't seen it for a long time.

'This is Italy,' he reminded her bitterly, 'where people can't help being theatrical. Have you forgotten that we must be allowed to act out our little melodramas of protest as long as we don't imagine they achieve anything! Dear God, Jane, how are we ever to get rid of Fascism if we're not reminded that there *are* alternatives?'

'I don't know,' she shouted. 'I only know that I don't want Marco to break his heart over another hopeless cause. *One* of those has nearly destroyed him already. Listen to the crowds cheering themselves hoarse in Piazza Venezia every time Mussolini opens his mouth . . . look at the pictures of them lining the road wherever he appears . . . what hope have poor young men like Marco got of changing anything?'

'Not much hope at all, maybe; but *you* were the one who used to say that anything was better than doing nothing.'

They glared at each other like enemies, driven by tensions outside themselves and fears that already they couldn't control. This was the feverish Europe of 1938, but she thought that the nightmare was only just beginning.

'I was wrong,' she said with sudden quietness. 'Our only chance is to do nothing and leave each other alone – no-one screaming out loud, or plotting in the dark, about what the rest of us must become . . . fanatical wearers of a label of some kind.'

The anger faded from Ottavio's face, leaving it pale and immeasurably sad.

'Look at the truth, Jane. *We* are not going to be left alone, and nor is this country. Mussolini and his precious son-in-law have yoked us to Nazi Germany, and Hitler's star is rising. Sooner or later he will feel strong enough to provoke a war that even England and France must fight. In the end Italy will have no option but to fight it too.'

'Fausto doesn't say so,' she insisted desperately. 'He's been to Berlin with Mussolini and Ciano . . . knows that

287

the Duce *distrusts* Hitler and has no intention of being dragged into a ruinous war.'

'Thieves always distrust one another – it doesn't stop them robbing together when the opportunity comes.' Ottavio moved across the room and came to stand beside her. 'My dearest love, look what is happening to us already when there is only Marco's work in Milan to agonize about. How shall we ever manage if my country comes to fighting yours? I could bear it more easily if you decided to go home than I could watch you learning to hate Italy and me.'

His hands, familiar and dear, touched her face with infinite gentleness, then caught and held her close. 'You would have to go, my heart, before it was too late.'

She pulled herself away a little so that she could look at him. 'My home is with you,' she said simply. 'I could never hate anything that you loved. As long as we don't allow ourselves to fear things separately we shall be able to manage – little lonely individual terrors are what eat our hearts out and destroy us.'

Ottavio kissed her mouth and then wrapped his arms about her again.

'Then we will be frightened and brave together, my love . . . I promise it!'

In the following months there was much to be fearful about. Hitler's *Anschluss* completed the Nazification of Austria. His next demand – for the Sudetenland, which had been incorporated in Czechoslovakia after the Great War – brought Europe to the verge of another war. Rather than step over the edge, the British Prime Minister, Neville Chamberlain, convinced himself that the German demand was not unreasonable; the French, obliged by treaty to support Czechoslovakia's sovereignty, convinced themselves that they were not obliged to do anything at all.

With any further territorial demands categorically denied by the Wehrmacht after Chamberlain's dramatic flights to Germany, his prediction of 'peace in our time' seemed achievable . . . but not for very long. It didn't survive the following spring when Hitler's armies occupied Prague and what remained of free Czechoslovakia. Even so, still one more territorial 'demand' was needed to stir England and France into the inevitable necessity of another European war, but Hitler provided that as well. Germany invaded Poland on 1 September 1939, and two days later the democracies' ultimatum for her to withdraw expired.

Jane never forgot the broadcast sound of Chamberlain's voice telling Europe that Great Britain was now at war with Germany. She was unaware of the tears running down her cheeks, or of the Marchesa weeping in sympathy, until Don Giuseppe stood in front of them holding glasses in his beautiful, frail hands.

'Come, my dears . . . it's time to drink to England – she and France must win, and the madmen who rule Germany must be defeated.'

Jane looked at Francesca's white face and saw its sudden brave grin.

'Can't you just hear David Rushton assuring Carlie and Mr Rushton that there's nothing to it, really, and that in any case God is always on the side of England?'

22

Charlie's letters described life in wartime London in terms that made it sound frustrating, tedious and unheroic – people falling over obstacles at night in blacked-out streets and losing themselves at unidentified railway stations; middle-aged gentlemen like himself with broom-handles and pitchforks on manoeuvres against an imaginary enemy; and everyone attached permanently to gasmasks smelling evilly of rubber and cardboard. It was all unreal, said Charlie, and some of it was comical; but beneath the daily irritations lay their fear that it wouldn't be unreal or comical for much longer.

Aunt Alice wrote carpingly from St Peter's Square, leaving them in no doubt at Castagnolo that she had little faith in Neville Chamberlain's ability to conduct a war, and no faith in Paul Reynard's ability in Paris to conduct anything at all. Apparently, only one ray of light had been shed on the general darkness – Eliza's faith in Communism had been badly shaken by Russia's pact with Germany just before the start of the war; now it was completely destroyed by the Russian invasion of Finland. She was so disillusioned, her mother said, that she might soon give up politics altogether and become a normal woman instead.

The troubled decade died unlamented in the first winter of the war, but in Tuscany there was little to remind them that a war was in progress in Europe at all. On her visits to the estate farms Jane was sometimes greeted with the news that a son of the house had received his summons to report for conscript duty, but it meant nothing, the farmer's wife always insisted tearfully – they all knew that Il

Duce was far too clever to drag them down the road the Nazis were travelling. Jane agreed, and prayed in Father Francesco's church each Sunday that her friends might be right. She couldn't help putting more faith in what Charlie said. One day the waiting war would suddenly become real, and then it might engulf them all, though Benito Mussolini were blessed with the wisdom of Solomon and the cunning of the Devil himself. She found it possible to stay cheerful during the busy hours of the daytime, but often lay sleepless beside Ottavio at night, staring at the nightmare future her imagination conjured up.

In the cold spring of the New Year the Marchesa, and then Francesca, required nursing through a particularly virulent attack of influenza. Tired from looking after them, Jane overslept one morning and woke to find Ottavio sitting by the bedroom window, with a sheet of paper in his hand. She had the impression that he'd been there for some time because he was reluctant to wake her with bad news. Her mind rushed blindly at half a dozen different possibilities before she realized that he knew she was awake. He got up and came towards her and she was suddenly still more frightened not to be able to read the expression on his face.

'Good morning, my love,' he said quietly. 'I couldn't bear to wake you when you needed sleep so badly.'

'But you've got something to tell me, all the same. Ottavio I don't want it broken gently . . . tell me straight out, please.'

He looked down at the paper in his hand and, even in the midst of sharp anxiety, she could now see that what *he* struggled with was excitement.

'Then straight out it shall be! My darling Jane, I wonder if I could persuade you to marry me?'

She was sure of having heard correctly, and he was too kind a man to play cruel jokes; even so, she couldn't believe him and was angry with herself for the little leap of hope her heart had given.

'You . . . you haven't by any chance forgotten that you're married already?' she muttered crossly.

'No longer, dearest. Read Harrington's letter, but I can tell you the news more quickly – Elena died a fortnight ago after a brief illness.'

Jane read the letter, which was brief enough, and put it down again with a little sigh. 'She was only forty-five – it's young to die when life is still so enjoyable; and he, poor man, sounds very lonely now.'

'I know, and I try to feel sorry,' Ottavio answered, 'but the truth is that, however hard I try, what I'm really feeling is full of joy for *us*.' His expression suddenly changed because Jane's face still looked sad and serious. 'You're going to say it's been too long a wait . . . you don't want to marry me at all because I can't make *you* happy any more than I could Elena . . .'

She held her fingers over his mouth to cut off the torrent of words, caught between laughter and tears.

'My darling one, you *know* how happy I am. I've enjoyed a life of sin, but I'm sure I shall like being married equally well!'

She was kissed and hugged and kissed again, but finally freed herself enough to look at him.

'Ottavio, you'll be careful when you tell the children, won't you – especially Marco. I know they haven't seen Elena for years, but nothing changes the fact that *she* was their mother.'

He nodded, and linked his fingers in Jane's while he chose the words he wanted. 'I did try never to wish her dead, you know, however much I longed to be able to shout to the whole world that *you* were my wife. But during the past few months it's been worse – all my nightmares have been about you being dragged away from me, and me not being able to protect you because you were an Englishwoman and not my wife.' A faint smile lit his face. 'Does it sound dreadful to say that I shall think kindly of Elena from now on, for dying when I most needed her to?'

'It sounds odd, but not dreadful in the circumstances,' Jane agreed, suppressing the fact that her nightmares had been much the same as Ottavio's.

Howard Harrington's news couldn't help but change the colour of that day, but it coincided with something Jane remembered afterwards as the beginning of the real war – the sudden lightning advance of Hitler's troops into Norway. By the time her marriage took place a month later, there was much worse news to hear – the grey river of the Wehrmacht armies was flooding north-westwards into Holland and Belgium as well, and the invasion of France itself was beginning.

In the face of such calamities it was impossible to bewail the fact that the only member of her own family present to see her married to Ottavio was Alexandra.

'Not the wedding-day you would have chosen, Janey,' Alex said mournfully.

'No . . . although nothing can spoil the joy of finally being Ottavio's wife. I should like Charlie to have been here, and my father and your parents, but elderly brides of forty-six don't need supporting like young ones! In any case, what is happening in Europe makes my little disappointment seem trivial.' Jane stared at her cousin's preoccupied face, thinking that although it was beautiful still, it was marked by unmistakable signs of strain and sadness. 'Ottavio is convinced that we shall soon be at war. Does Fausto think so?'

Alex's eyes lingered on her husband, talking to his father across the room. Jane's gaze followed hers, and discovered changes in Fausto, too. He was a year younger than she was herself, still lithe and debonair; but, looked at more closely, lines now scored his handsome face from nostrils to mouth, and even for a brother's wedding his dark eyes had no spark of gaiety.

'Yes, he believes we shall go to war,' Alex answered in a low voice. 'The "pact of steel" commits us to supporting Germany, and besides that . . .'

'. . . the Duce sees the advantages of supporting what seems to be the winning side,' Jane finished for her calmly. She smiled at her cousin, refusing to acknowledge the differences that separated them. 'You and I may discover before we're through that life in the Thames Valley with English husbands would have been easier! . . . or do you feel so completely Italian now that you don't care what happens to England?'

'It's nothing to do with me any more,' Alex said desperately. 'Anyway, Fausto says England has only herself to blame for what happens – she and France between them have driven Italy into Hitler's arms.'

Jane took a deep breath and refrained from forcibly shaking her cousin. A bride didn't quarrel with a guest on her wedding-day, and Alex and Fausto had been kind enough to come all the way from Rome. Even so, it was a relief when the Marchesa beckoned to Alex across the room.

'Apologies for my husband's absence, as usual,' said Anna Lambertini's voice behind her, 'but no doubt you expected that. Dear Jane, you're looking beautiful and radiantly happy, and my brother seems to have become a young man again – I may have to believe in matrimony after all!'

Her smiling mouth insisted that she needn't be taken seriously; life itself mustn't be taken seriously, because beneath the brightly coloured surface on which she now chose to float lay cold, black depths of unhappiness that waited to overwhelm her. Jane's own opinion was that Anna was the saddest *proof* of a belief in matrimony; without that, she would have abandoned Ernesto long ago. He had given her children and a comfortable home and ignored the hunger in her heart for shared warmth and loving kindness. Jane had learned to hate Anna's husband and anticipated that before the end of her connection with him she would probably have to tell him so.

'I didn't bank on you and Lorenza coming, in case some

important official function kept you in Rome with Ernesto.'

'Nothing would have been important enough to stop me seeing you married to Ottavio – even if I weren't the least necessary guest at any official function!' Her eyes lingered on the other people in the room, as Alexandra's had done – apart from Ottavio's family, only a few old friends were there who shared his political opinions; no-one for Jane, except her cousin.

'Damnable, stupid war,' Anna said with sudden fierceness. 'Charlie ought to be here . . . and your father.'

'And Marco and his uncle ought not to have to pretend that they aren't avoiding one another. It's a damnable, stupid world altogether.'

Anna stared at the face of her friend beneath its charming wedding-hat of cream straw and veiling. The years at Castagnolo had been anything but easy, but Jane was just as slender and upright as she'd always been, and her thin, brown face was still lit by a smile that made it beautiful.

'It's hard to believe we first met fifteen years ago – *you* don't look any different,' Anna observed with a touch of envy. 'Do you remember Ottavio bringing you in that day? You were clutching some roses and trying not to look as you *felt* – like a fly being introduced to a couple of malevolent spiders!'

'Not malevolent,' Jane protested, 'although it's true your dear Mamma couldn't quite bring herself to *welcome* a Capricornian!'

'No regrets about staying . . . giving up your own life for Castagnolo and my family?'

'Twinges of longing sometimes for the most trivial English things – the taste of buttered muffins, or the cry of the flower-sellers in London – "Vi'lets, lady . . . luvley vi'lets?" ' She smiled at the sadness in Anna's face. 'Don't feel sorry for me. I didn't give up a richly happy life at home; I've found that *here*, and even been able to share it with Charlie. I couldn't have asked for anything more.'

'Shall we ever see him again?'

The low murmur barely made itself heard above the other voices in the room. They had never talked about her brother before, but Jane had the sudden certainty that Anna needed to talk about him now.

'My dear, I don't know, any more than you do,' she said after a pause. 'At the moment, any reasonable human being has to say that Germany looks easily capable of winning on its own, whether Italy joins in or not. But at the bottom of my heart I simply refuse to believe that England will be beaten, or that I shan't see Charlie again. If Fausto or Ernesto tried to tell me otherwise, I should pity them for being fools.'

'Ernesto *would* tell you so. Fausto, being kinder, would say nothing at all.' Anna stared down at her fingers, tightly laced together. 'Charlie suggested once that we might run away together, like children – "over the hills and far away" – just turning our backs on loneliness and pain. I refused then. If he asked me again, I should go – but now he could be at the other end of the earth for all that I can reach him.'

Jane's hands reached out to hold her friend's trembling fingers. 'At least you knows he adores you – it's more than any other woman can say.'

Anna's dark head, now faintly meshed with silver, lifted in a brave little gesture of pride. 'Yes . . . I can say that to myself.' Then she gave a faint smile. 'It runs in our family, this weakness for the Rushtons! Lorenza is heartbroken over the news of David's engagement to someone in England. At twenty-two she has a better chance of recovering than me, and there are plenty of young men flocking round her in Rome; even so, it's her first taste of unhappiness.'

'Francesca may have a different problem – no young men at all. It worries me that she has no friends apart from the estate people she's grown up with. I don't say that to Ottavio, though, because he's felt guilty for years about the isolated life we lead here.'

'Shall I ask Lorenza to invite her to Rome again? I always have the feeling that a calendar in her bedroom is being ticked off with the days until she can go home, but at least she has to meet young men when she's with us. Who knows; one of them might strike the spark in her that Fausto did in Alex.' Anna stared at the tall, brown-haired girl now talking to Marco. 'The likeness to Elena in both of them makes their differences *more* noticeable. I still expect to find Ottavio's sweet disposition in her and, unreasonably in the circumstances, keep being disappointed!'

'She's not sweet at all,' Jane agreed slowly. 'I think it's cost her something to accept as hers people who are much less controlled and reticent than *she* is. But she made up her mind years ago that they *are* hers; she belongs to Italy and Castagnolo, and she won't change now.'

'So you're left to worry alone about poor England. Alex doesn't – she's blindly obedient to her adopted faith, as all converts are.'

'Has to be . . . has to be *seen* to be, as Fausto's wife,' Jane insisted. 'All I ask is that he doesn't tell *me* Mussolini is not responsible for the dilemma Italy's now in. There are limits to forbearance even on one's longed-for wedding-day!'

'And there ought to be limits to gloom. Janey love, I've done nothing but whimper and whine so far. Perhaps God's in His Heaven, after all, waiting to work miracles . . . perhaps, to begin with, He'll grant our beloved leader the wisdom to keep Italy out of the war.'

That miracle didn't happen, although others did in the next few dreadful weeks – including the evacuation of the British Army from the inferno of the Dunkirk beaches, once the Germans had broken through the French line and overrun northern France. By the early days of June it seemed in Rome that a complete victory for Hitler was not only inevitable but very close – so close that Italy was in danger of being left out of a share of the spoils and the glory. On the morning of 10 June the news was broadcast that German units were within forty miles of Paris . . . the war was as good as over.

At midday Ottavio received a message from the headquarters of the Fascio in Florence. After a little while he went in search of Jane, and found her in the hot glare of the kitchen garden, stripping broad-bean pods with Francesca. She had spent the past weeks in such incessant tasks, so as to have no time in which to think about what was happening in France.

'We have our instructions from the Prefect, my love,' he said quietly.

Her face was shadowed by the linen sun-hat she wore, but he knew that if he could see her eyes they would be dark with pain.

'What does he want *now* . . . our help in turning in more boys who ignore their conscription papers? We'll let him rot in hell first.'

'Certainly, sweetheart, but it isn't that. We're required to collect everyone on the estate together at six o'clock for an announcement from the Duce this evening.'

'To tell us that we're at war?'

'Almost certainly; if he doesn't make the choice now, he's afraid he'll be too late.'

Jane went on stripping beans, but frowned because her hands were trembling and hid them in the pockets of her skirt instead.

'Poor Italy,' she said unsteadily. 'Dragged by madmen into yet another war it doesn't understand or want. How do we collect everyone together to hear this joyful news?'

Ottavio glanced at Francesca, who stood white faced beside Jane. 'Will you ride round, *tesoro*? Gino first, so that he can find some children to help you.'

She nodded and walked away and Ottavio stretched out his arms to Jane. They stood holding one another, not saying anything, until at last she kissed his cheek and freed herself.

'I could weep and weep for two pins, or strangle the first Fascist I meet, but Francesca will expect me to have finished the beans before she gets back.'

'Damn the beans,' Ottavio said fiercely.

'Certainly not! We may need them one of these days.'

They filled the interminable day with other tasks after that, until at last it was time to greet the people filing into the courtyard, the place where they had always come in time of trouble – farmers and their wives, labourers who lived on the estate, even the hired hands who travelled about Tuscany for the harvest work. Ottavio brought out a radio, and the men, women and children gathered round to listen to the brayed command from the loudspeaker . . . *'Attenzione! Attenzione!'* Martial music, the cheering of the crowds crammed into the Piazza Venezia, and then the voice of the Duce, hoarse and over-emphatic.

The Italian declaration of war has already been handed to the Ambassadors of Great Britain and France . . . People of Italy, hasten to arms and show your tenacity, your courage and your valour.

The harangue went on, insisting on the rightness of the war and the wickedness of Italy's enemies. Jane looked round the courtyard at the mass of closed Tuscan faces and sensed the dumb resentment of people who asked only to be left alone. Germany had traditionally been their enemy, England their friend. Even if all that had changed, there would be no hastening to arms from this corner of Italy, at least. They were at war because the Fascists said so; but from now on they would salt away their money and their food from the eyes of the authorities and they would hide their sons from the soldiers who came looking for them.

Marco, hidden in a 'safe' house in Milan, went on with

299

his dangerous work of printing the truth about the war, but news from England was now limited to the broadcasts they managed to hear illicitly from the BBC on a small wireless hidden in the Marchese's tower room. In France events moved quickly towards complete collapse; Paul Reynaud was replaced by Marshal Pétain, who immediately asked for an armistice with the Germans. The invasion of England could only be a week, a day, perhaps a tide, away.

But the dreadful, beautiful summer of 1940 wore on, and still the invasion hung fire while the Luftwaffe fought the RAF over the skies of southern England. They failed to beat them in the end, and the bombing of London began instead. Jane listened to the forbidden broadcasts and thought of elderly people like her father and Edward and Aunt Alice huddled into air-raid shelters. She thought of Charlie, on duty in the battered docks along the river, and knew what mental anguish meant. Sometimes, but not always, she was aware of Francesca coming to sit beside her – saying nothing but silently holding her hand for comfort.

The German armada didn't sail for England but other disasters mounted. Hitler's hold on Western Europe, the Balkans and Greece slowly became complete, and his armies began their invasion of Russia. Mussolini's early successes against the British in North Africa were wiped out by counter-offensives, but even this small success didn't last long. With General Rommel and his Panzer divisions to take control of the desert war, the regained British territory was lost again.

Hope was kept alive by willpower, and by the Japanese attack on Pearl Harbour at the end of the year that brought America into the war. The Duce made one of his carefully orchestrated appearances on the balcony of the Palazzo Venezia to inform the Italian people that *they* were now at war with America as well. Ottavio was finally convinced of Mussolini's insanity but Jane was thankful that he kept this opinion to himself whenever Alexandra made the tedious wartime journey from Rome to Florence. She did this frequently enough for Jane to wonder sometimes whether she'd managed to disown England completely after all.

One morning in the late spring of 1942 she appeared at the castle even more unexpectedly than usual. She was wearing the dark uniform of the Italian Red Cross, and looked so well in it that Donna Giulia was distracted for a moment from everyday anxieties.

'*Tesoro* . . . how lucky that you're fair! That uniform must look dreadful on sallow, black-haired Italian women.'

'My Italian friends put up with it, Mamma, for the sake of being useful.'

The Marchesa blushed faintly, feeling that she had been reproved; dear Alexandra was bound to be serious now, when Fausto was such an important man – a member of the Fascist Grand Council and a close friend of the Duce himself.

'All well in Rome?' Jane asked quickly. 'Fausto . . . Anna and the children?'

'Fausto is desperately busy, of course . . . Galeazzo Ciano is a charming man, but a good deal of the work of his Ministry seems to get left to other people while he plays golf.' It was as close as she would allow herself to get to criticism, or to the fact that Fausto's work now seemed largely concerned with the Government's frequent meetings with Hitler's representatives.

'Lorenza's learning to be a nurse, Anna says,' the Marchesa reported with pride.

'She is determined to be useful, as we all must be,' Alex agreed. 'Emmanuele has already joined his squadron, and dear Vittorio can't grow up fast enough to copy his brother. They are children for Anna and Ernesto to be proud of.'

There was an awkward silence, in which Jane faintly shook her head at Francesca. Alexandra was bound to

301

disapprove of Marco, still running his illicit press in Milan instead of fighting for the Duce; but if she was rash enough to say so, nothing would prevent this uncomfortable visit from turning into an open quarrel.

'We hear reports of food shortages in Rome,' Jane murmured. 'Can you carry something back with you, Alex – a ham and some cheeses?'

'No . . . no, thank you. Other people have to manage without family farms in Tuscany – Fausto would say that we must do the same.'

Jane reflected that if she saw more of Alex she would grow heartily sick of hearing the views of Fausto Buona-ventura. The gulf that separated them now was so wide and deep that even family affection couldn't quite carry them across it.

'Zia Alex . . . Nonna's right about the elegant uniform,' Francesca said suddenly, 'but what do you actually have to do?'

There was a different quality about the silence now – Jane had the sudden certainty that her cousin's visit hadn't been without a reason after all; Francesca's abrupt question had given Alex the opening she both needed and dreaded. Her face had gone pale, and she chose to look at the Marchesa, not at Jane.

'The International Red Cross supervises the running of all prisoner-of-war camps,' she explained in a low voice. 'The Italian organization receives information from Switzerland about our own prisoners abroad and sends out information about prisoners being held in Italy.'

'My dear, such very harrowing work it must be,' Donna Giulia said gently.

'Yes . . . especially when you see names that you recognize – the sons of old friends, even.' Alex glanced at Jane, then looked away again. 'I recognized an English name recently, too. David Rushton's unit was captured in a desert battle earlier this year. He was wounded but he's recovered enough now to be transferred to the fortress of

Vincigliata at Maiano, where a lot of British officers are being held.'

Jane tried numbly not to think of David, but of the incredible wartime chance that had brought him to a prison not very far to the north of Florence . . . she tried not to remember that if Marco hadn't refused to fight for Mussolini, the two of them might have been trying to kill each other in the deserts of North Africa.

'Will they hear in London – my father and David's mother and fiancée – that he's alive?' she asked in a voice that didn't sound like hers.

'Yes . . . eventually; it will take a little time for the news to reach England.' Alex looked round at them, trying to smile. 'It could be worse . . . and at least he's out of the fighting.'

Francesca got up and walked over to the window to stare out at the sunlit terrace. Her mind grappled with an idea that seemed unbearable – men deliberately penned other human beings inside prison walls, depriving them of the right to walk out into the sunlight or feel the breeze of evening after a hot day.

'Nothing could be worse for David Rushton than being taken prisoner and locked up by *Italians*,' she said flatly. 'He'd rather be dead than beaten by people he despises.'

The Marchesa's voice broke a long silence. 'Then, poor boy, we must hope he was captured by the *Germans*, if he would have minded that less.'

Francesca bit off a sound that was half-sob, half-hysterical laugh, and bolted out of the room.

'Dearest . . . if it sounded unkind, she didn't mean to be,' Donna Giulia said gently to Jane. 'We live in such terrible times . . .'

'And there's no reason, even in such times, why she should suddenly change her mind about someone she's never liked.' Jane gave a tired little shrug, but managed to smile at Alex. 'It was good of you to bring the news yourself – a real kindness.'

'Don't thank me – I wanted to escape from Rome. You can't imagine what it's like, with everyone gloating about the way the war is going. They love listening to Bastianini – he was the former Ambassador in London, and he keeps saying that he knows England is finished.' Her huge, troubled eyes stared at Jane. 'You tried to tell me once that we might find ourselves torn in two. I'm bound to be on Fausto's side, but that doesn't stop me wanting to kill Bastianini.'

Jane smiled wholeheartedly – for the first time in months, it seemed. 'That's the spirit, Alex dear. If you don't mind confessing to the Ambassador that we still manage to tune in to the World Service of the BBC, you can tell him that he knows something the English don't – no-one's told *them* they're beaten yet.'

23

Francesca didn't ever refer to David again; nor did she tell anyone of the imaginings that haunted her mind, forcing her to share his captivity. Each time she walked out into the early-morning sweetness of the garden or sat in the summer darkness watching fire-flies dance above the terrace, she remembered the boys who'd run together like wild creatures across the hills. Now, one of them was caught and caged, and the other spent his life in hiding. The pain of it was beyond weeping for, and so she did what they all did – kept despair at bay by working through the hours of daylight, and sleeping the sleep of exhaustion at night. Meals were brief now, and there was always a good reason for escaping the after-dinner conversation – inevitably about the war – that filled the gap until bedtime.

One night she crossed the courtyard late and saw the dark bulk of the tower broken by a tell-tell square of lamplight. Her grandfather had not been up there for so long that he'd forgotten the blackout. She climbed the winding stone stairs, trying to remember, as she occasionally did, that the frail, gentle, old man she went towards wasn't her grandfather at all. She didn't belong to him, or to anyone else except Marco, now that her mother was dead. Her mind, but not her heart, accepted the truth of it, and she knew with absolute certainty that Giuseppe Buonaventura's heart rejected it, too. They were agreed, the two of them, that she *was* his grand-daughter, because love made her so.

He was sitting at his huge work-table when she went in to pull the curtains. It was strewn with books and papers, as she always remembered it, but his precious telescope was covered like a parrot's cage at night-time. He smiled but shook his head when she gestured to it.

'It's not the moment to study distant prospects, *tesoro*. What is happening *here* needs all our attention.'

'Well, if I were prone to star-gazing, this is the time *I'd* choose,' she said frankly. 'Anything rather than look at the world we live in.'

'Then you'd be wrong, Francesca. I used to be wrong in the same way myself – I'd creep up here and dream of discovering some beautiful little planet no-one else had found, when all the time I should have been thinking about Castagnolo instead.'

She brought to the table beside him the little stool she'd always sat on as a child while he recited for her the names of all the constellations. It meant, he thought, that she needed someone to talk to, although she wasn't in any hurry to begin. She sat without fidgeting, because he'd taught her to do that long ago, but the long, thin fingers laced about her knees spoke of the tension inside her. She looked tired and discouraged; even so, the fine-boned purity of her face gave him pleasure, and it occurred to him once again that he wished he'd known the man called Nicholas Brereton.

'You work too hard, cara,' he said gently.

Her little shrug agreed that it was so but said that that wasn't what troubled her. 'We all do – Jane, Papa, poor Gino who works as hard at seventy-one as he did fifty years ago. What else is there to do when all the young men have either been taken away to fight, or else are in hiding so that they *don't* have to fight?'

She was silent for a moment, because two important questions needed to be phrased carefully. 'What shall we do if England is beaten? What shall we do if she isn't, and Italy loses the war instead?'

'In *that* case we shall have to rejoice, because Nazi Germany will have been beaten as well.'

'That would mean the end of Fascism - and Zio Fausto's

dream of a new era for Italy. But unless it *does* end Marco will never be able to lead a normal life again.' Her clear grey eyes were fixed on her grandfather's face, challenging him to solve a problem for her that she knew couldn't be solved. 'I'm not sure that Marco ever *will* settle down here again. Castagnolo isn't enough for him now . . . he's got used to a more dangerous life.'

Her voice lost the struggle to force itself through the tears that suddenly clogged her throat. With the single exception of her grandmother, she despised women who wept, because there was surely *something* more useful they could find to do. But there was nothing to be done between Marco and the uncle he'd adored . . . and nothing she could think of that would change her brother back to the boy who'd wanted to grow up so that he could take care of the Buonaventura inheritance.

'My dear, Fausto has had his dream, and even *he* may see in the end that it doesn't match reality,' Don Giuseppe pointed out quietly. 'Then it will be Marco's turn, but I doubt if *his* dream will last either. Nothing lasts in Italy except the ability of its people to survive every disaster . . . they will survive even the one we're entangled in now.'

A gleam of amusement lit Francesca's face, wiping away strain. 'And the Anglo-Italians among them must learn to do likewise . . . all right, I shall sing as I pick grapes tomorrow – see if I don't! I might even convince myself that we shan't have to struggle through another harvest with only old men and children to bring it in.'

She didn't suggest convincing herself, he noticed, that their friend Charlie would ever be back to share another *vendemmia* with them; but there were limits to what even the bravest heart could manage to pretend. Francesca kissed his cheek and went away without saying that she had faced the likelihood of never seeing her friend again. In that case she would have to make do with memories and the sketches Charlie had sent, and the carved wooden animals for the Christmas crib that now had the place of honour on her bedroom windowsill.

They got the grape harvest in, but only just, before the fine weather broke earlier than usual. The heaving mass of juice and skins and stalks was still in the huge open vats in the *cantina*, being lovingly tended by Gino, when the skyline of the city in the valley was blotted out by gathering clouds. The first rains of the autumn began to fall, persistent and cold, hinting that winter would be early as well.

Darkness fell quickly in such weather, and Jane climbed the hill-path from the village one evening reflecting that from now on her first-aid classes must start earlier to avoid a dark journey home for girls from the outlying farms. She doubted that much practical knowledge would be remembered in an emergency, but the lessons themselves were enjoyed, and the laughter and chatter that went with them were precious nowadays. She fought a constant battle to keep her own anxieties hidden; it was all she could do for England – keep her faith in it outwardly serene and bright. But the battle was tiring, and almost the worst of all was a suffocating sense of isolation – the journals put out by the Government-controlled press were unreadable, and the Italian wireless broadcasts highly suspect; only the distant voice of the BBC announcer, heard through the crackle of atmospherics, gave them some chance of knowing what was really happening in the outside world.

She climbed slowly, too bone-weary to do more than plod as the village women did; this was what it would feel like to be old – one foot put down after the other, deliberately and with a conscious effort. They would *all* be old by the time the war ended . . . if it *ever* ended. The mournfulness of the thought matched the evening so perfectly that she almost smiled, wishing Ottavio were there to share it with her. Then, for a brief second or two, she thought he *was* there – had come down to meet her – because she could see the tall figure of a man making a darker shape in the dimness ahead of her. But it was a taller, slighter figure than Ottavio's . . . a stranger, who waited without coming towards her. She blinked raindrops out of her eyes, angry with herself for the small tingle of apprehension that set her heart racing. This was Castagnolo, and no-one who belonged there would do her any harm . . . but this was wartime and people roamed the countryside for reasons of their own. She ignored the undoubted fact that the stranger had edged into the deeper shadow of a tree, and made herself walk on. He was ten paces away when she saw his tall figure waver and crumple in front of her – she reached him and *knew* him in the same moment.

'Aunt . . . Aunt Jane?' David's voice was a murmur almost lost in the rising noise of the wind and the thudding of her own heartbeats. 'Thought it w – was you.' His head sagged on the sodden material of a jacket that seemed too large for the thin frame it covered. 'D – didn't dare g – go to the castle in c – case . . . got you into t – trouble.'

Her hands touched his bare head, feeling the tremors that shook him and the burning heat of his forehead under the matted wet hair. She was frightened by his condition, but in some strange way not surprised that he should be there – it was as inevitable as every other extraordinary thing about their life that now had to be taken for granted.

'Well, you're coming to the castle now,' she said unsteadily. 'Can you walk, or shall I run and fetch Ottavio?'

'I shall m – manage . . . upsa . . . upsadaisy, m – mustn't be lazy . . . ' The hoarse voice tailed off into a mindless chuckle that was more shocking than all the rest because she thought he didn't know that he was crouched in the rainswept darkness, laughing to himself. Too frightened to leave him alone in case he found the strength to wander away, she linked his arm round her neck and spoke as sharply as she could.

'Get *up*, David – we're going home.'

He repeated the words after her, like a lesson to be

learned, but a gleam of lucidity shone through his fever long enough for him to haul himself up with the help of the tree beside him.

'Now, *walk*, dear boy . . . please, walk if you can.'

'Walk if you can . . . if you can . . . if you can . . .' The feverish instruction to himself accompanied every step they took, but somehow they shuffled slowly upwards through the rain to the courtyard entrance of the castle. The door was open because Enrico had just come out to empty vegetable peelings into the bins that held scraps for the hens. He stared at the sight of them huddled together at the postern door, but turned to run when Jane called out, 'Fetch the Signore, Enrico . . . *subito!*'

Half an hour later she and Ottavio stared down at David's sleeping face – the hectic flush of fever stained his gaunt cheekbones, giving him a spurious impression of health; his hands twitched on the sheet revealing that one of them was heavily scarred, had ugly stumps where two of its fingers should have been. Jane turned her head against Ottavio's shoulder to hide her weeping, and his arms enfolded her.

'At least he's here, my dear one. Now we can take care of him.'

For the next two days and nights David hovered on the edge of delirium, scarcely aware of the women who alternately sponged his sweating body and kept it covered, and patiently mopped up the liquid that he craved and then, more often than not, vomited up again. But by the afternoon of the third day there was a change – his thin body rested quietly and, although the flesh on his face had fallen away leaving the eye-socket, cheek and jaw bones sharply exposed, his skin felt cool for the first time.

That evening when Francesca carried in to him the bowl of soup that Jane decreed, he was awake and his eyes were lucid again. They observed a tall, slender girl whose skin was still brown from the summer sun; her hair hung over her shoulder in a plaited rope and her grey eyes looked

310

unfriendly. In that respect she hadn't changed, in others she had, and the change was startling.

'Luisa's best *minestra*,' she said coolly. 'It would be nice if you accepted *this* without spitting it back at us afterwards.'

He hauled himself up against the pillows, angry that even this small movement exhausted him and ashamed that *she* should be there to know it. God knew how much trouble he'd been, but it didn't worry him that any of the other women in the household had seen his helpless need of them – only *this* one would have despised him for it.

'I'll do my best.' Even his voice was a thread of sound he didn't recognize; he wanted to shout and swear and laugh and weep, and suddenly doubted whether he could do any of those things. It would be a miracle if he even managed to hold the soup bowl without slopping it all over the bedclothes.

Francesca put down the tray then sat on the edge of the bed with the bowl between her own beautiful long fingers.

'You're not required to do anything but swallow.' She held the spoon to his mouth, tipped it up neatly and shook her head when he tried to say something. 'Just swallow, please . . . I can do the talking, if we *must* have conversation as well.'

Her eyes rested on the stubble of beard darker than his tangled mop of auburn hair. 'Enrico is coming to shave you after supper. Being convinced, like all true Italian males, that "*far bella figura*" is a necessity of life, he thinks you will feel better when you look presentable again.'

She went on calmly spooning the *minestra* into his mouth, and he discovered suddenly that he could taste food again and was ravenously hungry besides. Obedient to her instructions, he said nothing at all until she put the empty bowl back on the tray.

'Can't I have some more? I'm still hungry.'

'Tomorrow. Your inside has to be allowed to get used to food gradually again. Today is Friday, and you've been

311

here three days – can you remember how long you were wandering about before that?'

His brows, darker than his hair, pulled together in a frown. She remembered that frown – it was how he'd often looked at her when they were children, because the dislike between them had been mutual.

'It was on Saturday night that we got out. The oldest-serving prisoners threw a party – supposedly to celebrate a year in the bag. They hadn't much to celebrate with, but they managed to make the noise we needed. It seemed the sort of mad thing the English *would* do, so the guards didn't bother to investigate.' After months of imprisonment his face had lost its desert weathering, and the freckles that went with his colouring now stood out lividly against the pallor of his skin. She tried to remember how old he was: a year older than Marco, so twenty-seven now.

'The tunnel took much longer than we'd expected, and it was really too late in the year by the time it was ready. But we had to go then, or never.' He looked at the remote expression on Francesca's face and told himself that his futile story had no interest for her. But having started to talk, he suddenly couldn't stop, and talking was better than thinking about his friends, probably lost by now on some windblown, rainswept mountain. 'The break-out went quite well, but things started to go wrong after that – the weather for one thing.' He leaned back against his pillows, with exhaustion settling on him like a dead weight again.

Francesca glanced at his grey face and suddenly re-arranged the evening programme. 'Enrico can smarten you up tomorrow . . . you won't be receiving guests tonight.'

She nodded, but didn't smile, and went away leaving him to lie and stare at the vaulted, frescoed ceiling above his head. He was a thousand times better off than his friends – warm, dry, safe for the time being, and in his right mind again. Only Francesca made him feel that he was a burden whose duty it was to leave Castagnolo as soon as he could walk as far as the door again.

He remembered their quarrel on the towpath at Chiswick. She didn't like the English now any more than she had then, but he couldn't blame her this time if she resented the risk he was inflicting on the rest of the household at the castle. He didn't believe she was afraid for herself – Francesca Buonaventura had almost no other virtue that he could think of, but he was strangely certain that she had courage.

Enrico's kind attentions the following morning left him feeling tidy enough to smile cheerfully at the Marchesa when she called to see him. She enquired sweetly whether he'd slept well, promised that breakfast was on its way and warned him against any undue exertion. When Jane appeared a moment later with his tray he was uncertain whether to laugh or weep.

'Donna Giulia behaves as if I'm an unexpected guest she's delighted to see,' he pointed out unsteadily. 'Does she realize that I'm someone you could all get into serious trouble for harbouring?'

'Oh yes, she realizes that – but you're still Marco's friend, and she *is* delighted to see you.' Jane calmly checked his pulse and temperature, put more pillows behind his back and offered him a breakfast of milky coffee and rolls.

'You're on the way to recovery again. That fierce attack of dysentery was not something new, I assume?'

'No, it keeps recurring since I had it in the desert, but it was damnably ill-timed. I was beginning to feel rotten even before we left Vincigliata, but it was then or never. A kind farmer and his wife tried to give me some food, but I couldn't keep anything down. They wanted me to stay but I was afraid of endangering them by getting seriously ill – so I've endangered *you* instead. I didn't mean to, Aunt J. My plan was to ask you to lend me some money, and some clothes that wouldn't be quite such a giveaway as the doctored uniform I set out in. Looking less noticeable, I

313

can use the local buses to make my way to Livorno and jump a boat that's going to Marseilles, or Spain. It seems a better bet than trying to cross into Switzerland, which is what the others were going to do.

'You're not up to doing *anything* at the moment, but suppose you managed to get back to England – which would be a minor miracle in itself – would the army take you back?' David saw her eyes resting on his mutilated hand and the livid scar that ran from knuckles to elbow.

'As a working member it's not quite what it was,' he confessed, 'but at least a German surgeon had the goodness not to just hack it off! It seemed to me that they were *less* kind to some of their wounded Italian colleagues than they were to *our* chaps – which makes the whole thing even more insane.'

'It *is* insane,' Jane agreed with a catch in her voice. 'The whole, blood-soaked mess is insane. We still manage to tune in to the news from London, and it's less dreadful than it *has* been. There's a new offensive starting in the desert, led by General Montgomery, and the Russians are fighting magnificently, but I haven't heard from Charlie or my father since Italy entered the war . . . don't even know whether they survived the bombing of London.'

'They *did*, Aunt J. I can tell you that for sure because I've had an occasional letter through the Red Cross.' A fleeting grin touched his mouth, suddenly making him look young again. 'Can you imagine my grandfather *not* surviving, or Aunt Alice, for that matter? Apparently, she used to walk about with a kitchen knife in her handbag in case German parachutists landed in the garden!'

Jane's thin face smiled at the memory of her aunt but grew sad again. 'We don't see Marco, you know. The system we live under doesn't allow for opposition, so he leads an underground existence in Milan. While *he* keeps hope alive in people who pray to outlast Fascism, *we* try to keep Castagnolo going here – without the help of any young men at all.'

314

'How can you possibly manage without them?'

Her shoulders lifted in a foreign shrug learned from her husband. 'Ottavio works like a labourer when the doctor insists that he ought not to work at all, and Francesca toils like a man, when she's a tired, thin, anxious girl of twenty-four. But we don't do it just for Castagnolo – we're bound to grow all the food we can. Already there are people going hungry in the cities, and the war has scarcely touched us yet.'

'What about Fausto and Alex . . . I don't suppose you see them, either?'

'Well, Fausto is an important man. He still comes occasionally because he loves his parents, but he genuinely believes that Mussolini had no choice but to make common cause with Hitler. Since Ottavio sees the war as the final damnation of Italy they can find nothing to say to one another.'

'What do you and Alex find to say?'

'We talk about the past – it seems safer,' Jane said sadly. She straightened her shoulders in a little gesture that put away the difficulties she could do nothing about, and smiled at her nephew.

'We're *very* glad you're here, you know. Life suddenly seems much more bearable – more normal, somehow! Now, another little rest and you'll be ready for some more nourishment . . .' She picked up his tray and walked out of the room – a tired, indomitable, middle-aged lady with too much to do and far too much to worry about.

When the door closed behind her, David swung his legs over the edge of the bed, certain that even if he couldn't quite start his long walk to Livorno and the Gulf of Genoa, there was some task or other that he could do for Jane. Only . . . his legs were not things of flesh and bone at all, but made of cotton wool that crumpled into a heap on the floor the moment he tried to stand on them. The bed loomed above him like a haven he couldn't reach, but he was on his knees, hauling at the bed-post with his good

315

hand when the door opened again. Francesca stood there, silently observing this pitiable performance. Anger suddenly flushed his grey face with colour and gave him a brief but Heaven-sent spurt of strength. He clambered upright and stood there, trembling with wrath and returning weakness.

'This is a bedroom, not a bloody railway station,' he shouted. 'Kindly knock next time or, better still, don't come at all.'

She turned on her heel without saying a word, and went out slamming the door. David fell across the bed and lay there not moving, until the fear that another visitor must soon be due to arrive made him drag himself back under the blankets again.

24

Jane took the problem of hiding David's presence in the castle to Ottavio.

'We're straining Enrico's discretion to breaking-point, and the rest of the servants are bound to find out in the end. I'd rather they were told and given the satisfaction of knowing that we trust them.'

Ottavio agreed that she was right and said that he would undertake the task of explaining the arrival of their guest. He reported afterwards that everyone seemed happy to have '*il Signor Davido*' back again . . . '*è come nei anni buoni*,' Caterina had said for all of them, with a smile of pleasure on her round face.

'But it *isn't* the same as in the good years, 'Tavio,' Jane said anxiously. 'Did they understand that they must never talk about David outside?'

'Dearest, they understand perfectly, and they'll lie like troopers if any Fascist militiaman comes looking for him. They will *enjoy* doing that, as a matter of fact!'

Her worried expression relaxed into a smile then grew serious again. 'I want to let Anna know as well that David's here. There's no other way of explaining how I know that Charlie's survived the bombing of London. She must be given that comfort because *he's* the cruellest anxiety she's had to bear.'

Ottavio blinked at the implications of this side-light on his sister. It made clear things that had puzzled him about her, but he thought that only Jane would have resisted the temptation to share Anna's secret with him until it was necessary.

'Does *she* represent an anxiety for Charlie?' he enquired after a moment.

'I'm afraid she's bound to, because the love and longing are shared.' Jane looked at her husband with a smile of sad regret. 'They haven't had our good fortune. Anna saw her vow to Ernesto as given for a lifetime, and even if *he* could manage without her, she couldn't leave the children to Leonora Lambertini to bring up.'

Ottavio thought for a moment what his own life would have been without Jane. Charlie had to go through the days and years without *his* love, and poor Anna's smile had slowly become more bright and empty. He lifted his hands in a little gesture of futility and abandoned a subject about which there was nothing he could bear to say.

'Of course tell Anna, my dear, but *not* Alex, I hope.'

'No, that would be unfair – she shouldn't be asked to have secrets from Fausto.' Jane stood biting her lip, contemplating the anxiety that now kept her company night and day. 'Tell me what you think of David's chances of getting away,' she said finally. Her husband shared the Italian's wish to always make his listener happy, but she knew he was incapable of lying to her.

'My dearest, I doubt if he has any chance at all,' Ottavio said bluntly. 'His poor friends are already reported in the press as having been recaptured, and what chance does *he* have of hiding in an Italian crowd? His height and colouring would mark him out, even if his accent didn't the moment he opened his mouth. I doubt if any ordinary man or woman would give him away, but they couldn't prevent a Fascist spotting him.'

Jane gave a little grimace of despair. 'The alternative is to walk from here to the coast – spending nights in the open with the weather getting worse all the time, and his health as frail as it is.'

'That's an even starker madness. Forbidding him to leave probably won't have any effect, but instead of trying to fatten him up, I recommend a semi-starvation diet that keeps him in a permanent state of weakness!'

He was rewarded by a gleam of amusement that made her look less strained for a moment. 'It may come to *that* if I can't find any other way of keeping him here.'

David was careful to wait until her back was turned to test each small new physical effort that his body would agree to make, but he was anxious to be gone. The Marchese and Donna Giulia behaved as if to have an escaped prisoner in their home was all they asked of life, and the servants vied with each other to wait on him. Each service offered was a personal victory over the Fascist Prefect of Florence whom they hated with a hatred that was genuine as well as operatic in its intensity. But one member of the household made him feel an unwelcome burden.

The day he got as far as the bathroom by himself was a small triumph of independence over her. He staggered back along the corridor again, determined to resist the siren call of his warm bed. There was planning to be done, and he must get his brain as well as his body working again. The maps he'd borrowed from Ottavio were spread out on the table in his room and he began to study them. He must find a route that would keep him away from the centre of Florence, and – in view of the wintry weather – avoid the exposed hills to the north. If the buses looked too dangerous to use, his route must be round the south of the city, and then westward, following the course of the river.

'Getting tired of our hospitality, my dear David?' Francesca's voice behind him had its usual mocking edge and this time it provoked him to real anger.

'I'm *not* your dear anything – quite the reverse, I'd say; and you make it perfectly clear that I have no right to hospitality which puts everyone else here in danger. Well, about *that* I agree with you.'

'So, like good Captain Oates, you are about to walk out into the night, never to be seen again.'

It was one of the infuriating things about her that, thanks to Jane, she was familiar with things English, whereas he still knew very little about Italy. His only effective tactic was not to rise to the fly she cast over him.

'You're not supposed to jeer at my little attempts to be heroic,' he said gravely, and had the rare pleasure of seeing her disconcerted.

'Your attempts are doomed,' she pointed out after a moment. 'Any blackshirt worth his salt will identify you even before you're questioned and have to open your mouth.'

'Not all Italians have black hair and olive skins, especially if they're northerners.'

'In other words, we're a polyglot lot – how true! But we don't hold ourselves or walk like you do. The English have a way of planting their feet on the ground as if it belonged to them – I suppose quite a lot of it still does.'

'But probably not for much longer, if that makes you feel any happier . . . my dear Francesca!' He took pleasure in repeating the phrase she'd used to him, then was betrayed into smiling because the game they played of scoring points off each other suddenly seemed so childish. It was an unexpectedly charming smile – lifting the corners of his mouth and lingering in his eyes. They were hazel eyes, and she noticed for the first time that they reminded her of Jane's. His face had been fined down by hardship and responsibility, and she could now see why it was that Lorenza had grown up dazzled by him. Thinking *that*, she remembered someone else.

'What is your fiancée's name?'

'Patricia, although she's usually called Pattie.'

'I suppose she's as blonde and beautiful as Zio Fausto's wife?'

'She's not at all like Alex,' he said with a brevity that was unintentionally snubbing. The truth was that it was hard to retrieve the mental image of a girl he hadn't seen for more than two years. She was small and vivid and dark-haired, with the supple body of a trained dancer – he could remember *that* about her; but the shape of her mouth, the expression in her eyes, even the attraction that had made him want to marry her . . . these things had been temporarily mislaid in two years of war.

'Patricia must be very anxious about you,' Francesca said politely.

'I hope she's too busy to be anxious. She chose the naval branch of the women's services to enrol in – on the grounds, I seem to remember, that its uniform was more becoming than the others!'

'Well, there's no need for you to worry about *her*. Charlie would take care of her for you – that's what he's best of all at.'

David heard in her voice the gentle note that only his uncle seemed able to evoke, and the conviction that anyone who had Charles Rushton to look after them needed no-one else.

'You love *him* very much, and you love Jane,' he said suddenly, 'but you won't accept the rest of us at any price. I wonder why?'

For once the sharp reply he expected didn't come, and he was startled to see that she looked vulnerable. Her full bottom lip quivered before it was caught and held between her teeth . . . *almost* she had been about to confess something that now he wasn't to know after all. She shrugged the question aside instead, and her mask of cool indifference was in place again.

'*You* don't accept *us*. It must have been a cruel blow to be captured by the Italians – those excitable, incompetent creatures who had the impertinence to think *they* ought to have an empire too.'

He blunted the edge of her sarcasm by nodding agreement. 'Charlie used to do his best to shed a little light on my darkness, but when I was a child I was ready to believe whatever my grandfather believed. Even when I began to visit Castagnolo my opinion didn't change. I wasn't too blind to see that it was beautiful, but the excitability and the incompetence couldn't be missed either.'

The blandness of the verdict roused her to rage. 'Then I'm very *glad* you were worsted by Italians in the end.'

'So am I!' he said astonishingly. 'I might not have discovered, otherwise, that they are brave and limitlessly kind as well – from the Don Giuseppes of this world to the farmer's wife who found me hiding behind her chicken-house and didn't turn me in.'

His unexpected confession almost routed her, but there was one escape route left. 'So we *should* have been allowed the empire Mussolini dreamed of after all.'

David looked down his long, thin, Rushton nose. 'Certainly not! Whatever gave you such an impossible idea?'

Her mouth twitched, she could feel a spring of laughter stirring inside her; but to share amusement with him was the dangerous first step to relaxing her defences. She had to stay safely behind her little barricade of prejudice and hostility, because on the other side of it lay a world full of uncertainty and danger. There was Castagnolo to take care of, and its people; *they* took all her energy and love, and it was too late now to find out whether she could have learned to like David Rushton.

'Marco is coming to see you,' she said abruptly. 'I told him you were here. I always have an address for him. When it has to change, he sends another one.'

'Isn't it dangerous for him to come?'

Her shoulders lifted in a little shrug. 'What does he do that isn't dangerous? At least now there are other people arriving here, to mingle with and get lost in.'

'I'd have thought you had fewer visitors in wartime.'

Furiously reproachful eyes glared at him again, the weak moment when she might have made friends with him forgotten.

'Our visitors don't come for pleasure. They're hungry enough to *walk* here from Florence in search of food

322

because your navy's Mediterranean blockade is starving Italy.'

'And German U-boats have been blockading England. Don't blame *us* because everyone gets hurt in war.'

'But some get hurt more than others – *we* shall be, I think, because that seems to be the fate of this poor country. Jane prays that you won't try to leave. *My* advice is different – get out as soon as you can.'

He wasn't provoked because she spoke gravely, for once intending no sarcasm. Instead of malice, a desolate sadness haunted her eyes and he found himself wishing he could lessen it.

'You've been trying to read the Marchesa's cards and misunderstanding them.'

She shook her head and a reluctant smile tugged at her mouth. 'My darling Gran won't let me near her precious cards – she says my vibrations are wrong, because I'm an unbeliever!'

He gave a shudden shout of laughter and this she couldn't help joining in. Nothing was less grim than it had seemed a moment before, but for the little time it took to laugh with him they might have been any two people on the verge of discovering that they'd been wrong about each other. He wasn't full of arrogance and pride, and she wasn't a girl whose face was certain to be cold with dislike whenever she looked at him. But the moment didn't last long; remembrance of all the years of mutual dislike was stronger.

'You said Marco might come,' he said abruptly. 'When?'

'I don't know. We aren't given notice of his visits. He'll just appear one day.'

'Does he realize what a struggle it is here for the rest of you?'

'Yes, but he's like Zio Fausto – it's the future of Italy as a whole that matters now, not this small part of it. There's another problem, too – he's ashamed of liking the idea that Castagnolo will belong to him one day.

He still *does* like it, but he believes he ought not to.'

David struggled with himself. It sounded an uncommonly daft point of view, but she would resent the slightest criticism of her brother. 'You seem to understand him rather well,' he commented instead.

'Well enough to know that he's never going to be happy again. He can see too many things wrong with the world that he isn't going to be able to put right.'

'That's futile!' Self-restraint failed in the face of such lunatic despondency on the part of his friend. 'We can all see what needs to be changed, but we're still allowed to enjoy life when we can.'

'You could try telling him so, but it wouldn't make the slightest difference.'

'I feel more inclined to tell him to forget his qualms of conscience about owning Castagnolo one day, and to damned well do something to help it *now*.'

'The practical English point of view!'

'Quite right, and you can spare me the jeers about it. What would have become of Castagnolo by now but for Jane's English practicality?'

She flushed with the sharpness and the truth of what he said, unable to confess that her mockery had only been to revenge his criticism of Marco. There were times when she regretted the sophisticated poise that came so easily to Anna Lambertini, or Fausto's wife. Nothing would have persuaded her to exchange the pinchbeck glamour of Rome for the true gold of Castagnolo, but it was painfully clear that country life left her at a disadvantage in dealing with David Rushton.

'We were talking about *you*, not Jane, but that isn't what I came for,' she said hurriedly. 'I'm supposed to warn you to stay out of sight this afternoon. The Fascio in Florence are sending people to decide how many children we can take in from Genoa and Turin, where they are being heavily bombed now. Everyone has to get hurt, as you say – even defenceless children, apparently.'

Her voice was expressionless but he could sense the anger she struggled to control. She was right to be angry, and he was suddenly too tired to explain that he hated the atrocities of war as much as she did.

'Thanks for the warning,' he said instead. 'Presumably they won't be inspecting your grandfather's tower. If I start soon I ought to be able to make it to the top before they arrive.' Her cool nod stung him into saying something else. 'I'd go altogether if I could, but at the moment I'd probably be recaught so quickly that it would be obvious where I'd been hiding. I don't want that to happen.'

'Explain to my father; it doesn't concern *me* how long you stay.'

'Or whether I get shoved behind bars again – I realize that.'

The sudden colour in her face seemed to confirm what he said. She couldn't explain how vividly her imagination had made her share his captivity. Unable to offer the truth or a lie, she ran out of the room leaving him staring at the maps in front of him but not seeing them. He was trying to visualize the face of the girl he hadn't seen for two years, and seeing instead Francesca's – flushed, tired, and unchangeably hostile.

The journey to the top of the tower required an effort that left him trembling with weakness; he made it with gritted teeth, trying not to remember days past when he'd raced up the winding stairs with Marco, both of them capable of holding a conversation at the same time. The rooftop walk enabled him to watch the arrival of the Fascio officials. Half an hour later he saw them drive away again – now, it was safe to crawl downstairs again. He set off and missed by a few minutes the arrival of another car, not bargained for or warned against.

Two doors led out of the base of the tower, one into the inner courtyard, the other into the main entrance hall of the castle. He opened this one and walked into a scene that he never forgot – Ottavio, in conversation with his brother, and a stranger wearing the uniform of a high-ranking officer of the Fascist militia. The moment of silence lasted, it seemed to him, the eternity that spans all disasters. His mouth felt dry and the thudding of his heart could surely be seen as well as heard. A single thought hammered at his stunned brain – that it would be madness to try to run away; but what else was there to do, or say? Then he saw Fausto coming towards him across the stone flags of the hall – his arms held out in friendly greeting. 'Caro Antonio . . . how frail you *still* look. I hope Ottavio's taking proper care of you.' His arms clasped David's shoulders affectionately while he muttered, 'Smile, but say nothing.' Then he half-turned to glance at his companion. 'My cousin is recuperating here, Colonello . . . medical men are notorious, are they not, for neglecting themselves when there are many wounded to be seen to.'

Finally released, David managed to smile at the stranger. He accepted the clue he'd been given, murmured '*Mi scusi, Colonello*,' and walked languidly out of the hall, like a man who had no inclination or energy for small talk.

'Poor fellow,' Fausto was saying behind him, 'not at all well, still, I'm afraid, and definitely unsociable.'

'We're doing what we can, I assure you,' Ottavio observed faintly, then shrugged like a man beset by family problems that must be put aside for graver issues. 'Now, Colonello, shall we inspect the cellars? There is no doubt that they are dry, but you will want to be assured of that for yourself if we are to take care of national treasures for you.'

The frail and silent cousin didn't appear at lunch afterwards, but by now Colonel Goldoni was more interested in the wife of his host. It was extraordinary that both the Buonaventuras should have married English-women. Fausto himself, of course, was one of the Party's most important hierarchs and his foreign wife was a devoted Fascist; *that* was well known, but so was the fact that Ottavio Buonaventura's reputation was different. The

Colonel felt bound to remember that and not to be over-awed by the setting and company he now found himself in.

'Congratulations, signora,' he said to Jane with a flashing smile. 'You speak our language like a native.'

'But you know, obviously, that I am not,' she replied calmly. 'I *have* lived here for nearly twenty years, though.'

'Long enough, I hope, to have become a good Italian . . . otherwise you might resent sheltering our great works of art from the Anglo-American barbarians who want to destroy them!'

'I shouldn't dream of resenting Botticelli's paintings in the cellars, any more than I shall resent the children from Genoa and Turin who are going to occupy our bedrooms.' She would normally have been tempted to add that London's Wren churches and Coventry's cathedral had also been destroyed by barbarians, but she was still shaking inwardly from David's recent danger, and across the table Ottavio's expression implored her to be careful.

'You must surely feel torn, though, signora,' the Colonel suggested. 'Would your loyalty to Italy enable you, for instance, to turn away an escaped British prisoner if he happened to knock on your door?'

The question stopped her heartbeats for a moment while she searched his face for signs that his question had a deliberate intention. He came from Rome, but it was conceivable that he knew a prisoner from Vincigliata was still missing.

'Your question is academic, fortunately,' she heard the Marchese say gently. 'In this part of the country, at least, it seems that such men make for the nearest safe frontier – Switzerland!'

'We expect that, of course, and take precautions accordingly. But I should be interested in the signora's answer to my question.'

He was damnably persistent but *not*, she thought, suspicious about 'Antonio'. She managed to smile at him

327

and give a careless little shrug. 'I shan't know until I find myself confronted by such a situation, but I'll confess that I would much prefer it not to occur!'

It was the Marchesa's turn to come to her aid by leaning confidentially towards their guest. 'I can see that you have a philosophical interest in analysing other people, Colonello . . . it's a characteristic of those born under the sign of Scorpio. I think you must share a birth month with my husband.'

Goldoni stared at her, bemused by the twist the conversation had taken. 'I was born at the beginning of February, Signora Marchesa.' Courtesy prevented him from adding that he could have nothing in common with the frail old aristocrat who sat at the head of the table. Men like Giuseppe Buonaventura were the worst stumbling-blocks to creating a different Italy – not because they actively fought against change, but because they refused to see that any changes were being made.

The Marchesa was looking disappointed in her guest, but Fausto smilingly took charge again. 'Dear Mamma, before you climb on to your favourite hobby horse I positively *must* drag my friend away; we still have to visit the castle at Montegufoni.'

'Do you *have* to rush off?' Jane enquired bravely as he got up to go. 'Antonio will be rested by now and hoping to see you – it was quite a surprise for him to . . . to bump into you like that.'

'I'm sure it was!' Fausto's voice was expressionless, but his eyes met hers for a moment before looking away. 'Tell him I hope he's soon well enough to leave you – he ought to get back to work again.'

She kissed his cheek in a rare gesture that the Colonel mistakenly supposed was habitual between them. 'Yes, but he must stay until he's strong again.' Then she held out her hand to Goldoni. 'Have no fear for your treasures, Colonello; we shall take the greatest care of them.'

He bowed over her thin fingers and was driven away a

moment later. It was a relief to escape from a situation he was far from at home in, but he was also left with the feeling that something important about the conversation he'd just taken part in had escaped him.

25

The children from Genoa arrived before the paintings did; a dozen bewildered morsels of humanity, clutching all that was familiar to them – the bundles they refused to be parted from. Looking at their numb faces, Jane understood that even weeping was beyond them. The strange and frightening place they were in now was simply one more thing to be endured. They huddled close to each other, sensing that survival depended on staying together, and stared blankly round the castle entrance-hall when Jane explained that this was to be their home for a little while. The idea was incomprehensible: 'Home' was a tenement alongside the docks at Genoa, full of noise and friends and sudden tears and shared living – not this echoing, empty place bigger than the church they'd sometimes been taken to.

They sat in silence, eating the hot supper waiting for them, and accepted unprotestingly the baths and washing of hair that followed. Only the sight of a line of cots covered in brightly coloured blankets brought a flicker of relief to their small, strained faces. Beds were for sleeping in – they were very tired, and they were going to be left to sleep together. Time enough tomorrow to endure whatever came then.

By the end of the second day they were still there and a new pattern was beginning to take hold. The dormitory they slept in, the big kitchen where noisy, cheerful women set out their meals, the other people who seemed to belong there, were all becoming familiar. Coached by Francesca in the game of finding their way about staircases and corridors, they no longer got lost inside the castle, though outside it lay a strange new world they hadn't yet ventured into.

To her surprise, David didn't avoid the children but practised his simple Italian on them instead. They didn't seem curious about *him*, beyond staring at his damaged hand until they got used to it and ignored it. She wondered at his ease in dealing with them until the explanation occurred to her – they were fellow-wanderers. They didn't belong at Castagnolo, and the freedom to be where they did belong had been taken away from them.

David fought every day against the weakness that still dragged at him. It was the beginning of November, and he wanted to be away from Castagnolo before the present spell of mild, damp weather broke – after that the winter would set in in earnest. He forced himself to walk further each day, and concealed from Jane the effort it still cost him to do so.

One morning he roamed through a landscape muffled in a thick mist. It had seeped into the castle courtyard as well, veiling in mysterious whiteness the people who gathered there as usual; they came every day now, in search of the food they couldn't afford to buy on the black market in Florence. David didn't avoid them, any more than he avoided the children; he was simply a shabbily dressed inmate of the castle who answered their greeting and smiled pleasantly at them.

'*Buon giorno, Signore*,' said a voice beside him. '*Cattivo tempo, non è vero?*'

'*Si, si . . . brutto*,' he agreed, walked on and then suddenly turned round again. The man who had spoken to him leaned against the side of a cart, patiently waiting his turn to buy vegetables from Gino. His mouth was almost hidden in a thick, dark beard but his eyes were familiar. David blinked away the beads of moisture clinging to his own eyelashes and stared again.

'Good God in Heaven – it's *you*!'

Marco smiled, but answered still in his own language.

'*Italiano, amico mio – l'altro è troppo pericoloso.*' He jerked his head in the direction of the *frantoio*, and David followed him into its olive-scented dimness. They wrapped each other in a hug that might have seemed strange in England, but seemed only natural here. Marco stared at his friend's drawn face, and then at his mutilated hand.

'No more fighting for you, either, Davido.'

'No, but there'll be something useful I can do if I can only get home.'

'Your chances are much better of being caught again, and sent to Germany this time.'

'I dare say, but I must try all the same. Apart from anything else, I'm a danger to everyone at the castle. They don't need me here, but they need *you*; can't you stay Marco?'

'No, I must go back to Milan soon, the same way as I came, hidden in a potato-lorry . . . shades of the aristos, my dear, in the French Revolution!'

'Forget the bloody charade altogether and come back here. Don't you even *want* to? You used to adore this place.' He saw Marco open his mouth to speak, but gave him no time. 'Even if you *like* the life you lead in Milan, you ought to be here. Your father and Jane and Francesca work twelve hours a day to keep Castagnolo going, with the help of old men like Gino. They'll be worn out before the war ends.'

'I know . . . I *know*, but what I should like or Castagnolo needs scarcely matters any longer. There are much larger issues at stake than that.'

'You can't save Italy from Mussolini single-handed. Your grandfather is certain that he won't survive the war, in any case.'

'It's true, although it might *not* have been without our work in keeping the opposition alive. But the real question, my friend, is whether Italy itself can survive. Once your armies have control of North Africa they are bound to invade this country, and the Germans are bound to oppose them – then our poor people will know what bloody war means, if they don't know already.'

'They *do* know – Jane looks after a dozen children bombed out of the slums of Genoa, and the estate is being run without a single young man – if they're not dying in Russia or the desert, they're in hiding so as *not* to be called up.'

'And if I came back I should be spotted at once – arrested and imprisoned, or got rid of altogether by the thugs who underpin the Fascist system. This isn't England, Davido.' He shrugged the fact aside and gave a sudden grin that made him look young and familiar again. 'Why don't *you* stay and help Francesca until your people arrive? They will, eventually.'

'No thanks. With the exception of Jane and Uncle Char, your sister prays nightly that perdition will take the English . . . that it will take *me* especially! There's no reason why she should like me, but I've never fathomed out why she hates the rest of us.'

'Perhaps you'll understand her better if I *tell* you the reason,' Marco said slowly. 'She's half-English herself. A man called Nicholas Brereton seduced my mother, but died before Francesca was born. I doubt if my father would ever have told her the truth, but Mamma eventually did. Francesca repeated the choice she made when Elena first wanted to take her to America – she belonged heart and body and soul here, and everything else was to be rejected.'

David considered this revelation in silence for a moment or two, wondering why it hadn't occurred to him before. 'Fate has played a cruel trick on her in that case,' he muttered finally. 'Every time she looks in a mirror she must be reminded of the fact that her father was not an Italian.'

Marco nodded, then frowned at his watch. 'Five more minutes and then I must go. I daren't miss my ride back to Milan, and the driver won't wait if I'm not down on the road in time.' He touched David's shoulder affectionately. 'Don't get yourself killed if you can help it – and stay out of sight of militia blackshirts; they wouldn't abide by the Geneva Convention even if they knew what it was.'

'Well, one of them was fooled the other day – I blundered into him making a surprise inspection of the castle. I stood gaping at him like a landed fish but your uncle had the goodness to rescue me. I became his sickly cousin Antonio, temporarily enfeebled by the strain of patching up wounded troops! In the circumstances I couldn't even thank him, though Jane tried to afterwards.'

'F – Fausto did that?' Marco stammered. A smile of pure happiness lit his face, wiping away bitterness. He was the young man who had gone with David to fight in Spain, confident that their side would win because good was bound to triumph over evil. 'Give him my love if you should see him again,' he said softly.

It didn't seem very likely but David nodded, and then gripped Marco's hand. 'Go with God, as they used to say in Spain.'

'So they did . . . I'd forgotten that. *Arrivederci, Davido.*' He lifted his hand in a little gesture of salute and limped out into the misty courtyard. A moment later, although David tried to watch him go, he was simply one of the veiled figures that came and went and were lost even before they'd plunged into the whiteness blotting out the drive.

He crossed the courtyard himself, weighed down by more than the awareness of his own chronic tiredness; however hard he tried to brush it aside the feeling remained, sharp and painful enough even to overshadow Marco's confession about Francesca, that he had just said goodbye to him for the last time. Which of them would never return to Castagnolo he had no way of knowing, but his own chances looked slim. Hundreds of hostile, lonely miles lay between him and England, and he could be tripped up and detected at any one of them.

It was rare nowadays for Francesca to be at the luncheon-table; today, she was there, winding spaghetti round her fork so deftly that she might have been trying to demonstrate how totally Italian she was.

'Davido, did you see our dear boy?' the Marchesa enquired tremulously. 'He couldn't stay long, and we didn't know where to look for you.' Her eyes brimmed with tears because in a world now filled with so much heartbreak it was bound to have happened that two friends had missed the chance of seeing one another. He covered her trembling fingers with his own warm, good hand and smiled at her.

'He was waiting for me, Donna Giulia. In fact, I walked past him – the beard fooled me for a moment!'

'Oh, that horrid beard. It makes him look like a revolutionary, but he says that's exactly what he is.'

'Not for much longer, perhaps. He shares your opinion that Mussolini's days are numbered.' David was looking at Ottavio now, but it was the Marchese who suddenly answered.

'Of course. Years of corruption and violence and incompetence will come home to roost, and the whole rotten system will collapse like a house of cards that a child blows on.'

'Then whoever takes over can make peace with the Allies and Italy can hold up her head again,' said Jane hopefully.

David looked at her husband and saw him give a little shake of the head. What else Marco had said was not to be repeated, at least not in front of his mother and Jane.

'That's what we must pray for,' Ottavio said tiredly. 'Now, dearest, excuse me . . . if I don't go out soon, Gino will have the tractor started again, and he needs a rest very badly.'

'So do you,' Jane said quietly. If she begged him not to go back to work he would only smile and promise to rest once the winter ploughing had been finished. Francesca saw the anxiety in her face and quickly got up from the table.

'Dear Papa, I'm afraid you'll have to leave the ploughing

to me. Apart from the fact that your furrows aren't *nearly* straight enough, you know perfectly well that Gino will only agree to rest if *you* do. I can't manage if both of you get ill, so Lucia must chain Gino to his armchair this afternoon while Jane does the same for you.' She softened the instruction with a little wave and walked out of the room, leaving the Marchese faintly smiling.

'Never argue, 'Tavio,' he recommended. 'When a woman makes up her mind, there is nothing for a sensible man to do except give in gracefully!'

'Especially when she's right,' Jane said pointedly.

Ottavio held up his hands in a gesture of defeat. 'My ploughing is obviously worse than I thought. It must have tried Gino very high not to tell me so! Nevertheless, Francesca can't be left to toil out there on her own . . .'

'She won't be,' David interrupted him. 'I shall give her the pleasure of despising my efforts instead.'

He followed Francesca out of the room and caught up with her at the postern door that led out of the court-yard. He leaned across her to fumble at the catch with his maimed hand and she was aware of the warmth of his body, close and faintly disturbing. Not only that – his eyes were examining her intently, as if seeing her for the first time. The misty world was very quiet and they were alone in it, staring at one another. She was nervous, and angry with herself for feeling so.

'What are you doing out here?' she demanded abruptly. 'You're supposed to spend the afternoon recovering from the walk you take in the morning.'

'Pitiful, isn't it? I thought I'd like a change . . . a little ploughing, perhaps, so that you can have someone else's performance to criticize.' He misread the expression on her face and tried to sound more confident than he felt. 'Tanks and tractors . . . I dare say they're much the same.' She still didn't answer and he was shaken by sudden doubt. 'Oh, God . . . not oxen! You don't still plough with *them*?'

'We do, but only on the steeper slopes, I leave them and

the *chianini* to Gino – he hates machinery. We can use tractors on the lower fields.' Her grey eyes were fixed on him, clear and speculative as he remembered them from his earliest visit to Castagnolo as a schoolboy. An arrogant, insufferably critical lout of a boy he'd been, he also couldn't help remembering. She'd known it, too, as clearly as he knew now that she still held the fact against him.

'If you're serious, you can come and try,' she said finally. 'I'll plough and you can come behind me with the harrow – until you get tired of it.'

He thought she only agreed because she couldn't waste time arguing with him. There was too much work to be got through. All the people on the estate expected it to provide their food, and apart from a dozen extra children in the castle itself there were the daily visitors from the city, seeking whatever could be spared.

The tractor pulling the harrow was a beast of a thing to control; the seat he was perched on was damnably uncomfortable and the whole contraption shook and rattled underneath him like a soul in torment. But for as long as Francesca ploughed, he followed, making a mess of every turn until he learned by the errors he made. He was beyond feeling tired, and only dimly conscious of the pain that throbbed along his damaged arm. The world contained only the smell of mist and wet, newly-turned earth, and those neat brown lines that he must follow until the end of time if need be.

The afternoon was merging into evening by the time she stopped in a corner of the field, switched off engine and lights and climbed down. He steered to a halt behind her with a final flourish that was only necessary for his pride, and clambered to the ground wondering whether she would be kind enough to leave him to crawl up the hill to the castle at his own pace. He stood leaning against the tractor, willing his legs to stop shaking and pretending to look round the darkening landscape. It was a strange moment to feel so oppressed by sadness that he couldn't trust his voice to speak.

'Are you all right?' Francesca asked quietly beside him. 'You shouldn't have gone on so long, but I'm very grateful.'

'I'm tired, but so must you be, and I'm stupidly aware for the first time of feeling homesick. Tuscany doesn't normally remind me of England in the least, but just at this moment it makes my heart break for a damp autumn evening at home – lamps beginning to glow along the river, the cold smell of the water flowing past the garden, and crumpets being toasted by the fire indoors . . .' His voice petered out into the silence that lay all about them.

He wasn't aware of Francesca moving, but suddenly her hand was tucked into his, warm and – for the first time ever – friendly. 'I'm sorry you're not where you belong,' she said simply. 'It's the worst thing of all that I can think of.'

Her voice was as gentle as a hand softly smoothing away pain. He could feel the warmth of her body and smell the faint sweet perfume of her skin. In the dying light her face was a pale blur haloed by the beads of silver moisture that clung to her hair. There was no conscious thought operating in him now; only instinct and need combined to pull her close to him and hold her wrapped in his arms for a moment that was outside time – not measurable, but inevitable. His face rested against the damp softness of her hair, but when she moved her head it was the most natural thing in the world not to let her go but to find her mouth with his own. The first kiss was gentle; her lips were soft, as he'd known they would be, and tasted of the cold, sweet, Tuscan air. The second kiss warmed them into life, and suddenly gentleness was lost. Need had the upper hand, and a rising surge of passion flaming between them that took no account of fatigue and heartache and the memory of old antagonisms. There were only the two of them left

338

in a cool, dark world, clinging together as if two bodies must be made to merge into one.

It was Francesca in the end, breathless and trembling, who struggled to free herself, because in a remaining small sane corner of her brain a voice began repeating the name of his fiancée.

'W – wages for the h – hired hand,' she stammered, putting a hand across her burning mouth that still wanted to offer itself to his. He misread the gesture and exhilaration died like a flame blown out by the wind. Exhaustion took its place, dropping over him a blanket of cold despair.

'The hired hand apologizes if his . . . his demands were rather high,' he said unsteadily. 'He suggests following behind at a respectful distance on the way home in case he forgets himself again.'

Francesca saw in the same moment both the gravity of her error and the impossibility of accounting for it. It was hard to find *anything* to say when her body still clamoured to be close to his, but the best she could do was admit to the weakness that *was* excusable.

'I was hoping for a little help up the hill – it's been an exhausting day altogether,' she murmured desolately.

All of that, he realized, even without the emotional strain of Marco's visit. She was a delicately-built girl of twenty-four who had to do the work of a farm-labourer; she was the daughter of the *padrone*, who had to offer her share of strength and care and affection to all the simple people who looked to the Buonaventuras for the provision of these things in times of trouble. She was beautiful and lonely, and surely sometimes aware that *she* wasn't quite where she belonged. Thwarted passion and hurt pride didn't matter now any more than his own stifling fatigue. All that was left was the longing to help her.

'Provided you don't mind going slowly, we'll crawl up the hill together,' he suggested.

With her hand tucked inside his arm they set off, still conscious of each other but aware that what had happened between them must be an episode complete in itself – having no link with the past and no connection with the future. It would even have no effect on the present, because they couldn't allow it to.

'Marco would have hated missing you,' she said after they'd walked a little way in silence. 'Did you realize that I used to resent you taking him away from me when we were children? How peevish and silly it seems now!'

'I asked him about coming back. He said he *couldn't* at the moment, even if he wanted to, but he's convinced that the Fascists can't last much longer.'

'He's convinced of something else,' Francesca said slowly, 'and it isn't the happy ending for Italy that we pretend to believe in for my grandmother's peace of mind.'

'I know – an invasion by the Allies, and then bloody war fought all the way up the peninsula with Germans who are already establishing themselves in every key position.'

'The prospect isn't very encouraging, is it?' she enquired flatly. The careful restraint of it would have made him smile at any other time; was there one true-born, one hundred percent Italian who could have been capable of saying such a thing?

'The immediate prospect's fairly damnable,' he agreed after a moment's pause, 'but look a bit further than that and take heart. With America in the war, and Hitler's colossal blunder in invading Russia, we are now certain to win in the end. The next few months or years may be terrible, but Italy will survive them because her small, ordinary people are indestructible.'

Francesca turned to look at him, although all she could see was his tall figure moving beside her in the semi-darkness.

'That's not how you used to feel about Italians.'

'True . . . but I now know that what I felt about a lot of things has since proved to be pretty barmy . . . "How much a dunce that has been sent to roam, excels a dunce

340

that has been kept at home"'!' He turned his head towards her and she imagined that she saw him smile.

'Are you still determined to walk to the coast in search of a boat?' she asked after a moment.

'Yes, but it's going to be a different coast from the one I had in mind. The sensible plan now is to go south, not west, and be there to welcome my friends when they come ashore.'

Sensible, dear God, to creep through two thirds of a country his own country was at war with, a country that had Germans placed in all its key positions! She stopped walking, transfixed by the pain that suddenly gripped her heart. It seemed necessary to beg, implore, forbid . . . but she wasn't allowed to do any of those things, because whatever he did was no concern of hers.

'I doubt if Jane will like your new idea any better than the first one,' she muttered unsteadily.

'Well, I shall leave the details vague . . . the details *are* rather vague, as a matter of fact, even to me!'

There was nothing more she need say, because they were climbing the last slope that led to the courtyard postern. He opened the door for her, as he had on the way out, and she must needs brush past him again. His hands fastened on her shoulders, rooting her to the spot.

'The trouble with hired hands is that they're never satisfied,' he said gravely, and bent his head. Her lips opened under his, incapable of not responding, as a flower can't help opening its petals to the sun, but she pulled herself away and flung words at him desperately.

'Leave *soon*. Find whichever coast you please as long as you leave us here in peace, to manage on our own.'

'I thought of going tomorrow,' David answered, and walked away from her across the courtyard.

26

He got up at the first grey hint of dawn, thankful to abandon the pretence of sleeping. Nightmarish fancies had swirled around his tired brain, that wouldn't be overcome by thinking about Pattie; however hard he struggled to recall small, endearing details about the girl he'd undertaken to marry, he could only remember the feel of Francesca in his arms instead. In an hour or two he would be walking out of the castle, taking his life in his hands. The chances were strong that he would never see her again, but he knew that until the day he died he would have no difficulty in remembering *her*.

His note of goodbye was written, his knapsack already stuffed with the necessary things donated by Ottavio – spare socks, pullover, maps and a compass. On his way out he would raid Luisa's pantry for some small items of food that he could carry with him. She would forgive him whatever he took because ever since he'd arrived her cry had been that caro Signor Davido didn't eat enough to keep a bird alive. He felt more guilty about the two books purloined from Jane, but she wouldn't begrudge him Bunyan's pilgrim as a travelling companion. *The Empress of Blandings* was less necessary, but it was going with him as well, as a reminder that simple gaiety had existed once, and might again some day.

The early-morning darkness of November still filled the castle passages, but he groped his way downstairs and along the stone-flagged corridor without crashing into anything. The door leading into Luisa's domain was shut, but when he opened it light sprang at him, shocking in its unexpectedness. Early as it was, someone was up before

342

him – Jane was sitting at the huge table in the middle of the room, her head buried against her arms in a gesture of weariness and despair.

'Janey . . . something's wrong?' His uncle's name for her, which normally he never used, came unthinkingly to his lips. He dropped his knapsack on the floor and knelt beside her at the table. 'Tell me what's happened.'

She lifted her head and looked at him with tired, sad eyes. 'Ottavio's ill, but thank God I was prepared for it and knew what to do. The doctor has been saying for months that he must stop working like a man half his age. 'Tavio just used to smile at him and go on with whatever needed to be done. Last night's heart attack wasn't serious, but another one . . .'

'Shouldn't we fetch the doctor . . . get him to a hospital?'

'There's no need, although I shall call Dr Bertolini presently. 'Tavio's sleeping now, and the doctor would say that rest is all he requires.' Her face suddenly shone with its luminous smile. 'In any case, he'd hate to be taken care of by anyone but me.' She glanced up at the kitchen clock, but the sight of David's knapsack on the floor gave the answer to the question she'd been about to ask.

'You came looking for food before leaving . . . you were going away without saying goodbye.' She could have wept for this final anxiety in a world that seemed entirely filled with grief and worry.

'It seemed the best way . . . to write you a note and just disappear,' he mumbled. 'Now it strikes me as being ridiculously theatrical – you too, probably.'

She pressed thin, trembling fingers over her eyes for a moment, and the sight of them hurt him more than anything else he could remember.

'Janey dear, before I set off on my own travels shall I go and find Marco – bring him back here by the scruff of the neck, if need be?'

She smiled faintly, but shook her head. 'I think that would be certain to get you both arrested! Desperately as we need him, he would be recognized immediately and arrested as an enemy of the State. There's no safe life for him at Castagnolo until Mussolini falls.'

'And Ottavio's will be an invalid's life from now on.' David's mind ran desperately over the burden of her responsibilities – the castle and its household, the children, the acreage farmed directly by the Buonaventuras, and a score of small farms whose tenants relied completely on the family in charge. 'My dear, all that needs to be done here can't be managed by you and Francesca, even if you kill yourselves with trying.'

'It can't *all* be done,' she agreed with a helpless little shrug. 'Gino's heart will break when I say that the vineyards must be left to run wild again, but it's the only choice we have. We *must* grow all the food we can. There are people going hungry already, and things are getting worse all the time.'

She pushed herself up from the table and stood looking at him – a slender, tired, indomitable woman. There were probably others like her scattered over Europe, women that he didn't personally know or love; *their* grace and strength would have to be enough to redeem the whole sorry mess or the human race might as well blow itself off the face of the earth.

'I came down to have a little grizzle to myself and make a cup of tea – being still English to that extent at heart!' Jane confessed. 'I'm glad I did, or I should have missed saying goodbye to you. The only trouble is that I don't seem able to say it without weeping, and that's something you would surely rather be spared!'

The clock gave the little lurch that always spurred it into chiming the hour; outside in the thinning darkness a cock crowed. David listened to these small sounds without knowing that they measured the time it took him to make up his mind.

'Don't say goodbye at all, unless you'd really rather get rid of me. I don't think I'm a danger to you because everyone here has got used to taking me for granted. They know what I am, but accept the fiction of Ottavio's feeble-minded cousin! I can help you through the winter and then, if Marco's guess is right, the Fascist régime will have collapsed and he can come home again.'

His own mouth relaxed into a smile at the half-disbelieving wonder in Jane's face, but she had to force herself to refuse what sounded like a gift from God. 'You *wanted* to go, and you still think you should, however hopeless it seems – that hasn't changed. Our situation has, but we mustn't allow it to influence *you*.'

'Other things have changed as well. By next spring our people will probably be making a landing in the south, from North Africa. *That* will be the time to go and find them – it's a much better bet than trying to get myself half across Europe.'

'*Anything* seems better than that to me,' she confessed, 'whether the Allies arrive here or not.' She blinked away the tears that now threatened to brim over and smiled at him with trembling lips. 'I can't go on pretending that I don't want you to stay – right now I want it more than the greatest treasure I can think of.'

'Then I'll unpack my luggage again and we'll make that cup of tea.'

She rested her head against him for a moment and then straightened up again. 'Put the kettle on while I take another look at 'Tavio upstairs.' David watched her walk to the door, still tired and anxious but no longer weighed down by the need to fight despair. It was hard to relinquish the idea of walking to freedom, because it had occupied his mind and all his energies for months past, but the truth was clear – a *Boy's Own* dash for the coast might do a little for his self-esteem; in practical terms it was likely to achieve nothing but his recapture. At Castagnolo, apart from helping Jane, he could at least try to grow some food and keep a few people from starving. When she reappeared with the news that Ottavio had woken for long enough to smile at her and then drift off to sleep again, he'd given up doubting whether he'd made the right decision.

They sat drinking tea together at the table, companionably silent, but thoughtful. Jane wrestled with the problem of keeping Ottavio so harmlessly busy from now on that he would be unaware of doing nothing arduous. David was facing several facts at once – the most obvious one being that in helping Jane he would have to break his word to Francesca. It put no strain on his imagination to guess what *her* reaction would be to the news that he was there to stay for the winter. The strain on his own self-control would be far greater, but it was something only he need know about. He wouldn't go near her if he could help it and would make sure that he *never* touched her. All he had to do was remember in future that he loved a laughing, dark-haired girl called Pattie Ashwell.

'Marco told me yesterday about Francesca's father,' he said abruptly, having just decided that she was the girl he would *not* think about. 'She's the only one of you who makes me feel I shouldn't be here. It's nothing new – she always did even as a child!' It was a blatant lie to pretend that he hadn't just missed out something shatteringly different about their relationship. But the moment when a dark autumn evening had been lit by a flare of shared passion was scarcely for thinking about, much less describing to anyone else.

Jane considered what he'd said and answered truthfully as usual. 'I can't altogether blame her . . . you *were* a rather starched-up schoolboy! It wasn't your fault – Grandfather Rushton made sure you'd grow up believing that all foreigners waited for the moment when they could take advantage of you. You've changed a lot since then, whether you realize it or not.'

'Francesca hasn't changed,' he pointed out, 'but perhaps you don't think she needed to.'

'No, but I wouldn't expect anyone else but me to find her perfect as she is!' Jane admitted with a smile.

'What's going to become of her? It isn't exactly a normal life she leads here.' He saw his aunt's face cloud over with anxiety again.

'It's *never* been normal . . . she and Marco were always cut off from the children in the neighbourhood, whose parents thought it was too dangerous to mix with us. She's grown up isolated from everyone except the people who belong at Castagnolo. If ever we suggested a visit to Lorenza in Rome she'd go with the stoical resignation of a small saint accepting martyrdom. Marco was her friend – she didn't seem to need any other.'

Jane stared at David's thoughtful face. It was still hollow cheeked and marked by more experience than a man of twenty-seven had usually had time to cram in. She had realized in the past why Francesca condemned him for being arrogant and intolerant, but life had since taught him what to value. Courage was important still, but so were kindness and generosity of heart; he now knew that success and failure weren't always what they seemed and that there were many different kinds of beauty.

'She had the future all worked out,' Jane commented slowly. 'In a land where it was always golden afternoon 'Tavio, Charlie and I would sit on the terrace enjoying the view and the finest wine in Tuscany – made by *her*, of course! Now, the future is too threatening to be thought about – one day at a time is all we can manage.'

The kitchen clock gave its asthmatical whirr and chimed the half-hour. Jane got up from the table but stood looking at David, smiling gratefully. 'This would have been the most dreadful day of my life – 'Tavio's illness, and then finding you gone. I know you'd rather be doing what you'd set your heart on, but having you here means that nothing seems as hopeless as it did an hour ago. I shall be able to tell the others about him without weeping.'

He nodded without smiling. 'Don't expect Francesca to enthuse about the new hired hand, though.'

'Not if I say that you promise to be hard-working and biddable at all times?' Jane teased gently.

'Say it by all means, but she may not believe you.' He kissed his aunt's cheek and picked up the knapsack. 'Time to unpack Ottavio's socks again!'

Jane didn't tell him afterwards that Francesca's reaction to his change of plan had been to say nothing at all. Nor could she tell him, because she didn't know herself, that Fran's recollections of the wartime winter that followed remained etched on her memory afterwards with the precision of patterns etched on glass.

There were some ingredients of daily life that were painfully different from the past – bombers flying overhead to add to the destruction of Turin and Genoa, hungry people in the courtyard patiently waiting to buy food, and the castle echoing to the noise of a dozen children who shouldn't have been there. But even the familiar things were changed: all her life she'd listened to the chatter of the women spreading cloths to catch the olives and smelled the heavy, sweet fragrance when the fruit was crushed; she'd caught her breath at the beauty of the persimmons hanging their scarlet globes from bare winter branches, and felt against her face the stinging cold of the north wind blowing off the mountains. She'd known all these things, but not with the peculiar, aching vividness that came of living through them with David Rushton there too.

She didn't admit to the reason; nor acknowledge even to herself that everyone else inside the castle was happier for having him there. It was inevitable that Lucia Scarelli's heart as well should go out to someone hunted by the militia, but irritating that Gino's Tuscan caution should be abandoned so completely for David Rushton. Francesca did her own work, spent what spare time she had with the children and refused to hear in David's voice an echo of her old friend, Charlie.

*　　*　　*

Italy's third wartime Christmas was approaching when Donna Giulia sat down at the dinner-table one evening looking happy enough for the fact to be commented on.

'My dear, you know some good news that we *don't* know; share it with us,' her husband begged.

'It's not exactly good news, but I think I *have* been a little cleverer than you give me credit for,' she claimed with touching pride.

'You've unearthed an ancient recipe for making jam that doesn't require sugar,' Jane suggested hopefully.

'Nothing so mundane,' was Ottavio's guess. 'She's discovered the philosopher's stone, and we're about to become rich beyond the dreams of avarice.'

'Well, you're both wrong,' the Marchesa said with dignity, then offered their guest a shy smile. 'As a matter of fact it concerns David. I kept thinking of his poor family in London, writing letters to that dreadful prison and never getting a reply because he's no longer there.'

'I've been worrying about it, too, but couldn't think of anything to do,' David admitted.

'But you *did* think of something?' The Marchese stared with fascinated interest at a wife who, to his great delight, sometimes entirely confounded him.

'I remembered that Ernesto knows everybody of the slightest usefulness. As soon as Anna said that he was going to Switzerland again, I asked her to give him a letter for his friend, the British Ambassador in Geneva.' She looked sadly at David. 'My dear boy, I'm afraid you won't get letters *back* via the Diplomatic Bag, but at least your poor fiancée and your grandfather will know that you're alive and well, and that you are here with us.'

David got up and walked round the table to kiss her cheek. 'It's masterly – I'm very grateful to you.'

The Marchesa blushed and offered them her other small triumph. 'I also persuaded Anna to spend Christmas here, with Lorenza and Vittorio, while Ernesto is in Switzerland again.'

Ottavio glanced at his father. 'If the industrialists and bankers are deserting the ship by starting negotiations in Geneva, we can be sure it's sinking. Salvemini was right years ago to predict that foreign wars would be the downfall of Fascism.'

'I think it's despicable,' Francesca said clearly, entering the conversation for the first time. She saw surprise and disapproval in several pairs of eyes fixed on her, and a question in David Rushton's.

'Whatever *we* happen to think of the Fascists, men like Ernesto have grown rich and influential on the strength of this régime,' she insisted fiercely. 'Now, when it all looks like falling apart, they can't scramble away fast enough. It's the same with the crowds that used to cram into every city square chanting "Duce, Duce" . . . adulation one moment, the next they're ready to spit on him.'

'Those same crowds are now being bombed every night,' Ottavio reminded her. 'They are short of food and fuel and clothes, and their sons are dying needlessly in African deserts and Russian snow. Why should *they* be loyal?'

'They accepted Fascism,' Francesca said stubbornly.

'My dear, they were spellbound by a magician,' her grandfather pointed out. 'Such an entertainer's tricks are not supposed to fail. The moment they do, the audience realizes that it's been gulled and demands its money back.'

'You're saying that honour and loyalty don't count, because self-interest excuses everything. I *won't* agree with you.' Francesca's grey eyes had the sparkle of anger, or tears – David wasn't sure which, but he was certain of their beauty; she was lovely altogether in her defence of what she believed in.

'Consider the difference between self-interest and survival,' he suggested quietly. 'It *is* a matter of survival now for the ordinary people of this country; don't blame them for abandoning the charlatans who've dragged them into ruin and suffering.'

'Bankers and industrialists *always* survive, but the rich

are permitted a little self-interest, so I suppose we mustn't blame *them* either!'

He ignored the scorn in her voice and seemed disappointed that she hadn't been able to work out the answer for herself.

'Of course clever men like Ernesto Lambertini *must* survive. How else can a country exhausted by twenty years of corrupt, extravagant government be rebuilt again?'

Francesca couldn't help but see the force of his argument – it could be made to sound right and reasonable; but hers was a principle not an argument, and she wasn't ready to relinquish it. 'We must also remember that Ernesto conveniently knows the British Ambassador!'

'There's that as well,' he acknowledged gently, blunting the edge of her sarcasm, 'and you'll have to allow me to be grateful for it. I've felt painfully separated from England – now, thanks to someone Ernesto knows, I shall be in touch with Pattie and my family again.'

'Nice for you,' Francesca agreed, knowing that he'd neatly outflanked her. She could certainly have reminded him of a time when the recollection of an English fiancée *hadn't* been uppermost in his mind; but perhaps he'd say that soldiers far from home, like influential bankers, were allowed a little self-interest. She could despise him for forgetting Pattie so easily, but she hated herself more for being trapped in a memory that he had probably now forgotten. Her body knew something it hadn't known before, and it ignored her mind's instruction that it must forget those few moments in a darkening field when his hands and mouth and the closeness of his body had left her trembling with passion. He would leave when the spring came. If she remembered that and kept away from him, she could manage; the rest of her besotted family were more than enough to dance attention on him.

Christmas was very near by the time Anna drove up the hill with Lorenza and Vittorio, having hoarded enough petrol for the journey. After months of separation the reunion seemed to bring back joy, and Jane was thankful – for the children's sake as much as theirs. They still missed their own families, but at least the air of expectancy and excitement inside the castle was a distraction from grief and seemed to belong to Christmas.

David heard the late-afternoon bustle of the Lambertinis' arrival, but stayed where he was in the *frantoio*, helping Gino to bottle oil from the huge flagons that held the yield from the olive harvest. It had been a good year, and even when all the households on the estate had taken their share, there would be a surplus for people who trudged hopefully from the city. It was dark when he finally said goodnight to Gino and crossed the courtyard. He could hear more voices than usual inside the castle but, anxious not to intrude on a family gathering, walked quickly across the hall, making for the staircase and his own bedroom.

'Too tired to come and say hello, or too disinclined for us?' enquired a voice behind him.

He turned round on the stairs to look down on the lovely, smiling face of Francesca's cousin. They hadn't met for six years, and an interval that hadn't improved *him* had unquestionably benefited Lorenza. She was a confident, beautiful young woman, instead of the excitable adolescent he remembered.

'Certainly not *disinclined* to come and find you,' he confessed, 'but reeking a little too much of olive oil . . . I'm less skilled at bottling than Gino Scarelli is! A wash is indicated before I crash my way into a family party, but at least from here I can safely say what a pleasure it is to see you again.'

'I don't mind the smell of olive oil at slightly *closer* range,' she pointed out helpfully, but he smiled and shook his head. 'It's your family party as well,' she said next, 'apart from Aunt Jane, Aunt Alex is also here – Mamma persuaded her to come with us at the last minute.'

'Then perhaps I shouldn't appear at all.'

'Because you're an escaped prisoner-of-war and she's the wife of a member of the Fascist Grand Council? My dear David, surely you've learned something about Italy by now – it's *families* that matter, not who's on this side or that.'

'An admirable point of view, even if it doesn't help you to win wars! But what about Vittorio, who isn't part of my family . . . is *he* going to be able to forget that I shouldn't be here, and that his brother's squadron is still fighting my friends over the desert?'

'For a schoolboy of sixteen he's very gentle and sensible – Mamma's influence, I expect! He's changed his mind about fighting the Duce's lost cause; he wants to be a doctor instead.'

'Is that what people think in Rome – that it's now a lost cause?'

'Not for Fascism itself, perhaps, but certainly for Benito Mussolini,' she said thoughtfully. 'I don't say that in front of my aunt, of course – Zio Fausto is still very loyal to the Duce. He's bound to be; all his adult life has been spent in serving him.'

David nodded, but didn't comment on a devotion that *had* split the Buonaventura family into this side or that. Instead, he lifted his hand in a small gesture of salute and went on up the stairs, too busy thinking about what she'd said to realize that she stood watching him. Lorenza sighed and was overheard by her cousin, who had chosen that moment to cross the hall.

'Still dazzled by our dashing prisoner?' Francesca enquired.

'Still regretting his English woman. I made it perfectly plain from the age of ten that I was his, body and soul. It's all the more unfair when I can take my pick of willing victims in Rome!'

'Maddening for you. Still, *you* are here and the English woman is not – it might make this visit a little more exciting for you.'

'True!' Lorenza's enchanting smile reappeared, and

Francesca was surprised to find that it persuaded her to grin as well. She had been very wary of this sophisticated Roman cousin since childhood, aware that much more separated than linked them together. But suddenly it was a relief to pretend it didn't matter why David was there. In a world where men slaughtered one another, where women were sent to concentration camps for being Jews, and children torn from their families in order not to get blown to pieces, a little pretence was needed to keep sanity alive.

'What's life like in Rome?' she asked suddenly.

'Feverish – a new wave of rumours every day; even the wildest speculation is listened to, and everyone has a secret to hide. The poor people are cold and hungry and getting ill, and the hospitals are crammed with our own wounded troops. They're all pathetic, of course, but the men who've been brought back from Russia are in the worst state, and they're almost incapable of describing what they've had to endure. I suppose they're the lucky ones, even so – thousands have been left to die in the snow.'

It wasn't her frivolous, carefree cousin of the past talking now, Francesca realized, but a woman who had seen terrible things and had to try to lessen unbearable suffering.

'Have a rest while you're here . . . you've earned it,' she said gently.

When David reappeared downstairs in time for dinner he was diffident about greeting the visitors he hadn't yet seen, but both Alex and Anna kissed him with warmth and kindness, and the young, serious-looking boy who was Lorenza's brother seemed impressed rather than shocked to be in the same room as an escaped British prisoner.

Afterwards Jane went into her cousin's room to say goodnight, and found Alex standing at the window in the dark, staring at the moonlit hills outside.

'I'd forgotten that there was anywhere peaceful left,' she said, pulling the curtains so that Jane could switch on a lamp. 'Not that it must seem peaceful to you with a dozen children in the house, apart from all your other worries.'

'The children are painfully well-behaved, and all the worries are made bearable by having David here. For a little while longer I needn't think how we shall cope when he leaves. He's confident now that the Allies will eventually invade us from the south.'

'So is almost everyone else. Our forces are trapped – between the British Eighth Army and the Americans who've landed in Morocco and Algeria. The desert war is almost over, and then it will be our turn.'

Jane looked at her cousin's composed face, noting the self-control learned painfully in the dangerous years of marriage to Fausto. Alexandra was still beautiful at the age of thirty-eight, but the girl who had wanted to see and experience everything was now a woman taught by life to conceal her feelings from the world.

'Perhaps there will be no need of an invasion,' Jane suggested. 'The Duce declared war; presumably he can also negotiate an armistice?'

'No, he can't do that,' Alexandra said abruptly. 'Fausto knows that the Germans won't allow him to – *that* is our true situation, you see; come victory or defeat, we're yoked to Hitler's cart-tail.' She shivered as though raked by a deadly wind, and her face was no longer calm, but full of desolation. Jane held out her arms and Alex allowed herself to be enfolded in the comfort of them, while tears poured silently down her cheeks. At last she lifted her head and scrubbed at her wet cheeks. 'Sorry, Janey – Fausto would be ashamed of me!'

'He's in Berlin, not Castagnolo, and we all need a safety-valve from time to time.' She offered a spare handkerchief and looked lovingly at her cousin.

'It's Christmas. For the time it takes to celebrate the birth of Christ with the children here, shall we put away anxiety and the memory of all the pain there is in the world?'

Alexandra nodded and faintly smiled. 'Agreed! What-ever happens, Janey, at least we'll have *this* one more Christmas.'

27

It was a respite all the more precious because it couldn't be made to last very long. For a little while nothing else mattered because they were together again despite the war, but the moment of departure hovered above them, its dark wings throwing a shadow over happiness.

Lorenza's cup had an additional reason for not over-flowing – her quarry was disappointingly elusive. She couldn't even blame the pressure of work outside, because only the livestock were attended to over the time of Christmas. Defeat was accepted with a better grace than Francesca expected.

'His fiancée must be Venus, Cleopatra and Helen of Troy rolled into one,' Lorenza reflected sadly. 'Even so, it's inhuman to be so faithful when he hasn't seen her for years.'

'Blame the cold blood of the English,' her cousin recommended. 'I believe a good horse or dog is more likely to get them excited.'

Lorenza grinned but shook her head. 'Wrong in *this* case, and you can take it from me because I'm infallible in such matters. There's nothing wrong with our friend's blood; it just doesn't happen to run faster for me. He's courteous and *kind* – what could be worse, I ask you?'

Francesca smiled too, because there was more humour in the situation than her cousin realized. But Lorenza's disappointment was real, and the blame was David's. Fran thought it perverse and entirely typical of him to reject what any normal, appreciative male would have been delighted to be offered.

'Don't you remember how supercilious he always was?'

she asked. 'Italy had nothing to offer that he couldn't find better at home, and presumably that still includes women.' It was unfair, and she knew it very well, to pretend that the young David Rushton had much in common with the man he was now; but even if she had had any wish to be fair, it was more important to soothe her cousin's hurt pride.

Again Lorenza shook her head. 'I don't think he *is* supercilious now. In fact, when he smiles at Granny or Jane it's perfectly obvious that he loves them both, and then he reminds me of your friend – Charlie. I said that to my mother and for some reason I didn't understand she almost burst into tears. Still, they *were* glorious summers – with all of you here, and us at Fiesole; I don't suppose we shall ever have so much fun again.'

'We shall have to find happiness differently, that's all.' Francesca's expression changed and she smiled ruefully at her cousin. 'I didn't reckon they *were* all that glorious then – Marco always abandoned me the moment David arrived, and you flirted shamelessly with both of them. You were so damned pretty, and so nice to everybody, that I nearly hated you. I don't now.'

'I'm still pretty and nice, so it's you who must have changed,' Lorenza observed thoughtfully. 'I suppose you haven't changed about wanting to stay here, though?'

'No, and it's just as well. Someone has to take care of Castagnolo, assuming it's still here when the war ends, and it won't be Marco.' Her sombre face warned that the subject of her brother was painful and not to be pursued.

'Well, it won't be the wilds of Tuscany for me either,' Lorenza said instead. 'I've seen enough pain and horror to last me a lifetime, and there's more to endure yet. I shall look around for a rich husband who asks nothing better than to shower his wealth upon me!'

'Then for your sake I hope a few rich men survive the war as well,' Francesca said generously.

Then they tacitly agreed to abandon the subject of the

future, both aware that it was too uncertain and too threatening to be talked about. Only the Marchesa bravely ventured on to the same dangerous ground when she was saying goodbye to her daughter and daughter-in-law.

'Giuseppe and 'Tavio prefer to think that, being women, we don't understand the true state of things, so Jane and I pretend not to, in order to please them. But we understand very well, and you must both promise me to come here if Rome becomes intolerable.'

Alex blinked away tears that had beset her too often during this emotional visit. 'I promise to come the moment Fausto agrees to.' She could think of no situation in which he would desert the man who had ruled Italy for twenty years, even if everyone else did, but it was one fact that Fausto's mother need *not* understand.

Anna kissed Donna Giulia goodbye and tried to smile. 'I expect I should have to come alone – Ernesto would insist that someone had to stay and parley with the enemy, and he'd be very good at that!' It sounded more ambiguous than she'd intended, and she hurriedly obscured the fact with a little teasing. 'Papa's right when he says you have a medieval mentality – in times of trouble cram all your dear ones and dependents inside the castle, barricade the gates and ride out the barbarian storm!'

'Why not?' Jane asked on the Marchesa's behalf. 'It worked pretty well in the past, and I doubt if there's a pin to choose between barbarians then and now.'

'True . . . which makes me wonder whether the human race has learned anything at all during the past thousand years or so.' Anna kissed her sister-in-law goodbye with warm affection. 'Darling Jane, keep David here as long as you can – for Ottavio's peace of mind as well as his own safety. Even a little emotional blackmail would be permissible in the circumstances, so trample on any inconvenient English tendencies still hovering inside you and think Italian!'

Jane agreed that even this she might manage, and smiled

until the car was out of sight. Then, with her arm tucked inside Francesca's for comfort, she walked into the hall again, accompanied by the fear that such a visit might never take place again.

The new year of 1943 started with the rumours that had been flying around Rome hardening into certainties the whole country knew about. Tripolitania, oldest and only surviving remnant of Italy's empire, had been taken by the British Eighth Army; the desert battles were almost over. In Russia the momentum of the German advance had been lost irrecoverably, and Hitler's troops would have to face the same bitter hardship as Napoleon's, in another retreat from Moscow.

Something almost more astonishing, Jane thought, was happening inside Italy. Its people were openly criticizing the man who had governed their lives for twenty years. When Marco paid one of his rare visits to Castagnolo he reported that the days of the Fascists were numbered.

'But you aren't jubilant about it,' his father observed after staring at him. 'Why not, when it's what you've been working towards for years?'

Marco gave a little shrug combining acceptance with despair. 'I suppose nothing *could* be worse than the condition the Fascists have reduced us to, but I'm becoming sickened by the prospect of what's going to happen next. Already the wrangling is starting – monarchists, liberals, democrats and people who just hate Mussolini, all fighting each other as soon as the Fascists look like being beaten.'

'Isn't that the parliamentary process – party wrangling?' Jane enquired. 'It *is* in England.'

'In England you don't have a well-organized Communist party scenting that its moment has come after years of persecution – we do! While all the others squabble among themselves the Communists will take over Italy . . . unless the Germans get here first and succeed in beating the Allies after all. *That's* still a possibility, too – there's a lot of talk about German secret weapons.'

It was an outlook so infinitely depressing that Jane found it a relief to concentrate instead on the daily struggle life had become, to provide food, warmth and shelter for the people who depended on them. During the harsh winter of 1943 they rediscovered ways and means of surviving that had been almost forgotten in easier years. Oil and flour and cured hams were buried, to escape confiscation by the militia during their frequent raids; the farm women began to spin their own wool again from Castagnolo's sheep, and they learned that nothing could be wasted. Olive kernels made useful fuel, and even the remains of kitchen fat combined with potato-peelings and soda produced a soap that was better then none at all. Ottavio spent his days indoors indispensably organizing the resources that the estate could provide, and David's most essential daily task was now to visit the young men existing in isolated farm buildings up in the hills. They now hid from a worse threat than conscription into the army. Their fate was likely to be transportation to work as slave labour in German factories starved of manpower. Many didn't survive the journey; still less survived the conditions under which they were made to work.

Even life in hiding was preferable, but in the bitter weather of that winter they needed to be taken food, clothes and care when they fell sick. Sometimes Francesca had to climb the frozen hills with David to inspect their ailments and decide whether the risk of bringing them down to the castle must be taken. On these perilous journeys, when they might be caught by raiding parties of militia, they said little to each other, but there grew in each of them the certainty that the other could be trusted. There grew, also, between them a kind of happiness – recognized as precious because it belonged only to these strange, dangerous days they were living through together.

On a cold, sullen morning at the end of January they

got back to the Scarellis' farmhouse to tell Lucia, as usual, what must be got ready for the next trip. She looked so relieved to see them that David wasn't surprised to be hustled upstairs. The little secret room below the rafters where Jane had nursed Mario Scarelli the night he was wounded by the Fascists was now David's bolt-hole when militia or carabinieri were seen making their way up to the castle. Half an hour later Gino appeared, to say that the coast was clear – the police had gone, this time without commandeering anything worse than a set of old tyres that the *padrone* didn't much mind losing. There was trouble, though, Gino reported. The trouble concerned two of the children, whose parents had been killed the day before in another bombing raid on the dockside in Genoa. Eight-year-old Lisa, and Caterina, two years younger, were now orphans . . . more helpless casualties of a war that no sane person in Italy had ever been able to understand.

David found Jane and Donna Giulia cutting up old curtains with the desperate concentration required to blot out other thoughts. Such salvaged pieces of material made strange-looking dresses for small girls, but the velour was warm and nothing else now mattered.

'Gino told me the news,' he said briefly. 'What will happen to those children?'

'They'll stay with us, of course,' Jane answered as if the question hadn't really needed asking. 'Relations may feel obliged to claim them eventually – families *do* feel that obligation here – but they're probably poor and painfully overcrowded already. In that case they'll be thankful to let Lisa and Caterina be kept here.' She looked at David out of anguished eyes. 'God forgive me, I was feeling rather smug this morning – no-one here unaccounted for, hardships being shared and everybody helped by the comfort of belonging to their own tightly-knit community. *That* much good, I was thinking, had come out of this dreadful war . . .' She had to stop speaking because tears clogged her throat; then she picked up her scissors again and went on with her work.

David didn't see Francesca again for the rest of the day. He knew that she'd gone down to the village to bring the children home from school as usual, but the explosion of noise that always signalled their return for tea in Luisa's warm kitchen was missing. They came in, white faced and silent, to sit toying with the food in front of them. The security born of several peaceful months had been wiped out in the moment it had taken for the news to be explained to them.

Francesca didn't appear in the dining-room that evening, and, after a miserable meal shared with the rest of them, David chose not to climb the tower staircase for the usual news broadcast from the BBC. The details of still more bombing raids on Italian cities were more than he wanted to hear. He walked out on to the terrace instead, surprised to discover after so wretched a day that the night had become full of a cold, unearthly beauty. The sky was brilliantly star-scattered, and lit by an almost three-quarter moon. Not bombers' weather . . . the people of Genoa and Turin and Milan could breathe a little more easily tonight.

He wasn't aware of sharing the terrace with anyone until she moved out of a patch of shadow and walked towards him. Moonlight showed him the exhaustion on her face, and its uncharacteristic despair. He knew that her day had begun before dawn with a visit to the hidden hill-dwellers and ended trying to comfort frightened, unhappy children – she had enough reason to look exhausted and sad. The instinct to hold out his arms was stronger than his promise to himself not to touch her again, but she stopped short of him, rejecting even the risk of comfort.

'How are the children?' he asked, in a voice that sounded too loud for the quietness of the night around them.

'Sleeping, now . . . having cried themselves to sleep.'

Her hostility was like ice laid against his skin. The closeness born of arduous journeys up and down the hills had shattered as surely as the children's peace of mind. It was a strange moment to realize that, however much she hated him, he would love her until he died.

'You blame me . . . *us* . . . our side, don't you?' he said hoarsely.

She turned away from him and leaned her arms on the stone balustrade. While he waited for her to answer he was aware of things he would remember always even though they didn't matter at all – the sparkle of frost on the stone in front of him, the velvet darkness of the cypresses against a moonlit sky, the ugliness of his own mutilated hand that he'd never quite got used to.

'I hate us all,' she said at last, ' . . . and the whole bloody insensate mess we make of everything. It scarcely matters now *who* began this hideous war, or which side has committed the worst atrocities since then – it's the accumulation of horror we're capable of that matters.'

'You're wrong,' David said quietly. 'Blame us, if you like, for taking so long to make up our minds to go to war and for all the dreadful errors we've probably made since, but don't ever forget that without Nazi evil it would never have begun at all. Your bogus fool of a leader helped Hitler sow the wind, and now Italy must reap the whirlwind.'

'Yes . . . the whirlwind is coming,' she agreed. 'Will it leave anything but destruction behind . . . not only for children like Lisa and Caterina, but for those who come after . . . "unto the third and fourth generation"?' A faint smile touched her mouth making her face beautiful. 'Jane's upbringing, you see – I can quote the Bible as well as you can!'

'Not only Jane's influence,' he said impulsively. 'Marco told me about your father.'

Francesca stared down at her fingers, spread like the white, bone ribs of a fan on the top of the balustrade. 'He had no right to.'

'It was only to help explain your obvious aversion to *me* – like the Allies who in your opinion can be blamed as much as Hitler for the war, I was part of the Englishness you were determined to resent. It wasn't only that, of course; you also disliked me for my own sake, and why not? I doubt if a self-satisfied oaf of a boy ever gave anyone more reason to do so.'

Francesca's cold hands abandoned the balustrade and buried themselves in the pockets of her coat.

'Perhaps it was true then, but I pretended to Lorenza when she was here that *that's* how you still were – arrogant and intolerant. She disagreed, even though you were disobliging enough not to fall in love with her. A very sweet nature has my cousin, Lorenza – not like me at all.'

David smiled at the note of regretful acceptance in her voice, but knew he must resist the temptation to say what loveliness she had instead. 'Lorenza is beautiful and kind, but I hope she remembered that a girl in England is waiting for me to go home and marry her. We would be married already if I hadn't been sent overseas in quite such a desperate rush.'

'I dare say she *did* remember that,' Francesca agreed flatly. She shivered suddenly, and huddled deeper inside her coat. 'I don't know why we're out here, pretending its midsummer. The inside of the castle isn't exactly warm, but at least the temperature isn't below freezing.'

'We shouldn't be able to see the stars from inside,' David murmured. 'If I promise to keep you warm, will you tell me the names the stars travel by? You must have been taught them by your grandfather.' Without waiting for her to answer, or take flight, he moved behind her, imprisoning her inside the circle of his arms. She was held so closely against him that she could feel the beat of his heart, and his mouth brushing her hair. The long, exhausting sadness of the day, and the brilliant beauty of the night were part of the flood of emotion suddenly pouring over her. Above the clamour in her blood she remembered she was supposed to talk of stars.

'Well, there's the P – Pole Star, of course, and C –

Cassiopeia to the r – right, and Andromeda not f – far beyond that . . .' Her voice petered out, unable to compete with the tears that brimmed over her eyelids and trickled down her cold cheeks. All the loveliness and all the sadness of the world seemed combined in this one moment of time to overwhelm her. His hands twisted her round so that he could see her face; its delicate bones and huge, shadowed eyes belonged to a head on some antique coin. She was desolately, unforgettably beautiful.

David traced the outline of her mouth with one trembling finger, and then bent his head to cover her lips with his own. When he freed them at last he tried to smile, but his voice was uneven.

'Shall we agree that the stars are lovely and then leave them to travel across the heavens without us? Shall we redeem this dreadful day by at least making each other happy?'

She pulled herself away from him even before she answered. 'No, we won't. I wouldn't in any case, because of that girl who's waiting for you in England; but you wouldn't forget about her for Lorenza – I won't have her forgotten now just because you feel sorry for me. It's . . . it's humiliating!'

She brought the word out fiercely, but feared that it made no sense – it had nothing to do with the welter of fear and excitement and longing that shook her like a fever. But if she surrendered now she would have to admit the truth at last, to herself as well as him.

'My dearest darling, it's nothing of the kind,' she heard David say gently. Her eyes skimmed his face and found no trace of pity there – only the longing that she felt in her own blood, and the sort of tenderness that she'd sometimes glimpsed in Ottavio's face when he looked at Jane. 'I'm afraid I could have forgotten Pattie easily enough if I'd wanted to make love to Lorenza. The truth is that I couldn't think about *either* of them when heart and mind and body were entirely concerned with you!'

'Truly?' she asked with a shyness he found touching and unexpected. Her eyes were fixed on him gravely, but when he nodded she smiled, and the dreadful day was already somehow redeemed.

They went inside together and climbed the stairs to the room she slept in at the far end of the children's corridor. With the door closed behind them and a lamp lit, Francesca stared at him, suddenly overcome by the strangeness of having him there. It seemed impossible that all the years of resentment and dislike should have led up to *this* capitulation. She said so, and saw him smile.

'Whose capitulation? I rather fear it's mine!'

There was something else to be said, and after a moment she managed it, with an effort of lightness that only just misfired. 'David – I've been very strictly reared . . . I shan't know what to do.'

His gentle hands began to undo the buttons of her jacket. 'I'm very glad, because I've always thought that I should make an excellent teacher!'

It seemed that he was right. Tenderness led inevitably to passion, shared and leaping between them so naturally that teacher and pupil exchanged rôles, changed back again, and learned together what joy there still was to set against the miseries of the world.

They slept at last, held in each other's arms, but when David woke in the dimness of the winter dawn he was alone. For a split second he felt cold with the disappointment of happiness only dreamed after all; but the room he was in was not his, and now in the half-light his eyes focused on Francesca's slender body curled up in an armchair by the empty fireplace. She didn't move when he walked towards her, didn't smile . . . he knelt down but managed not to touch her.

'Was I wrong . . . teacher hopeless, lesson no good after all?'

'The lesson was . . . was very enjoyable,' she said primly. 'Do you suppose we could repeat it – quite soon?'

366

'Now, I should think!' His arms encircled her and she was carried back to bed. Afterwards, with desire needing no coaching this time, she lay staring at his face, committing it to memory while she had this one chance. It would be terrible beyond bearing if she couldn't recall exactly in all the lonely years ahead the shape of his long mouth, and the little lines that fanned the corners of his eyes when something happened to amuse him.

David smoothed back her long, brown hair, gently traced the curve of eyebrows and mouth, and kissed the hollow beneath her cheekbones. 'Am I allowed to come again . . . or not? It's for you to say, my darling.'

She took time to answer, knowing that she was being asked more than the question he'd put into words.

'You mean, do I understand that there's nothing permanent about such visits? Yes, I do. When the time comes for you to go south, I shan't have the right to try and stop you.'

The temptation was fierce to accept what she said – to blame the war for making puppets of them, dancing helplessly whenever Fate pulled strings; but even at the risk of burying their precious new seam of happiness, she had to understand the whole of the truth. He propped himself on one arm, so as to be able to look at her.

'I must go, Fran dearest, and not come back. Even if I can scarcely remember what Pattie looks like and my heart breaks with love for you, I still made *her* a promise. Even if she were to release me from it, there's still my grandfather – living through all the years since my father was killed with the dream that Rushton's would be carried on by me. I belong *there*, as much as you belong here, and even with you at stake, I can't convince myself otherwise.'

He saw a faint smile touch her mouth and knew that the whole truth was something she had understood all the time.

'We shan't have time to quarrel – fortunate lovers, you

might say!' Then she turned her face so that it was hidden against him. He gathered her close without answering and lay staring at a future that contained every possibility but that of ever being happy again.

28

As if to make amends for the severity of the winter, spring came early; and as if to soften the ugliness of what else was happening in the world, it seemed to Francesca that it came more beautifully than she could remember before. Never had the vines put out tendrils of quite such vivid green, or the plum and cherry trees launched *these* white fountains of blossom into the spring sky. The pain and the dangerous joy of being alive almost balanced each other, but in the end joy won.

She was unaware of being watched, or of having given herself away. Jane recognized *that* symptom of blindness too, and wasn't sure whether to laugh or weep at being reminded so precisely of herself twenty years ago. The girl she had been then wouldn't have welcomed advice or interference, any more than Francesca would welcome these offerings now, but in the and anxiety outweighed caution.

'It took me a little while to work out why you were getting more beautiful every time I looked at you – then I knew,' she said one morning. They were alone together, cutting up strips of felt to make new slippers for the children, and for once they were unlikely to be disturbed.

'Is it so obvious that *everybody* must know?' A faint colour touched Francesca's cheekbones, but she asked the question serenely, not minding whether they knew or not.

'Not everybody. Your grandmother does, I think, but we almost bust our stay-laces in our determination *not* to discuss you.' She smiled faintly at the thought, then grew sober again. 'It doesn't mean that we're not both worried about you.'

Francesca got up and walked round to Jane's side of the table. Having deposited a kiss on the cheek nearest to her, she perched herself on the edge of the table.

'You wouldn't have done *that* once upon a time,' Jane observed. 'I never knew a child more miserly with her smiles or her affection. Now it's like watching a frozen stream melting and sparkling in the sunlight.'

'Isn't the stream better that way?'

'Certainly more beautiful as long as the sunlight and warmth last,' Jane agreed.

Francesca stroked a wisp of silver-brown hair out of her friend's eyes, and smiled because it was a service David often performed for her when they were lying in bed together.

'I'm glad you're not shocked . . . angry, even,' she said gently.

'My dear, how could we *or* your grandparents be?' A twinkle of amusement lit Jane's eyes for a moment. 'They were even broadminded enough to *urge* Ottavio and me to a life of sin! But the cases are different, Fran. It was possible that your mother would come back to Castagnolo, but very unlikely; for you there's no doubt, is there, that David will leave, sooner or later?'

'No doubt at all, which is why we have to seize our happiness while we can; no, not seize it – "kiss the joy as it flies" . . . isn't that what William Blake advised, if we are to live in eternity's sunrise?' She looked at Jane gravely, intent on making her understand. 'We don't talk about the future, because there isn't one for us. But we have the present; that will have to do, for me at least. David has someone to go home to.'

Jane nodded; there was nothing more to say and she went back to her work with a little sigh.

Sooner or later, they had agreed, David would leave Castagnolo. Francesca counted the weeks of springtime as they went by, like shining beads strung on her necklace of memories. Every day brought nearer the one that would be his last, because it would be time for him to set off in search of his invading army. Actuality limped far behind rumour as always, but no-one seemed to doubt any longer that history would repeat itself with its usual sickening monotony. Italy would be fought over yet again unless its ineffectual king, or its inept government, positively chose to negotiate an armistice with the Allies. Nothing, now, was expected in the way of leadership from the Duce – rumour said that he was plotted against, sick, dying. After twenty-one years the *Era Fascista*, inaugurated by the famous march on Rome, was ending with a whimper rather than a bang.

Jane thought that no-one could regret it, but she was saddened by the change in Fausto when he arrived unexpectedly one day, on his way back to Rome. The ardent idealist convinced of the rightness of the Fascist cause had become *this* tired, despairing man who watched from far too close at hand the disintegration of all he had believed in. She saw the pity in Ottavio's face as well, and knew that years of bitter disagreement seemed unimportant now. Fausto was his brother, and he needed a friend. When dinner was over, Jane nodded at the Marchesa's questioning look, privately amused by her mother-in-law's instinctive resurrection of the habits of the past. Tonight the old order reigned again for an hour or two, life was civilized and the ladies were going to leave the men to talk and sip wine in peace.

'I've been in Milan,' Fausto said when they were left alone, '. . . in fact, I happened to see Marco there – by accident, not design.'

Ottavio stared at the glowing wine in his glass – ironically, it had been made the year his son came back from fighting against Franco in Spain; it was the best the estate had ever produced, and now the vineyards were having to be neglected again. 'Is it true what Marco claims – that the Communists are getting the upper hand?'

Fausto gave a tired little shrug. 'You could say it's why

I was in Milan. They'd organized massive strikes there and in Turin, in the very factories that are crucial to the war effort. There's one thing to remember about such people – they're Communists first, Italians a long way afterwards. The Duce has been right all along to hate them.'

'He hasn't been right to drag us into this fruitless war,' the Marchese said gently. 'Can't he get us out of it, my dear boy, before it's too late?'

Fausto sipped his wine and took his time about answering. 'I don't think so,' he said at last. 'We have an alliance with Germany, solemnly entered into when things were going well. It would be an act of betrayal to renege on it now that things are going badly; the honour of Italy demands that we stand or fall with our partners.'

It was, David reflected, the kind of argument he might have expected from Fausto Buonaventura – in his mouth the word 'honour' meant something, and he would die defending it if necessary. If there had been more men like him among the bullies and sycophants and time-servers who had grown fat on Mussolini, the history of Fascism might have ended differently – might not have ended at all.

'Marco speaks of conspiracies against the Duce,' he said abruptly. 'Is that true, too?'

'Yes, even though he trusts his friends enough to disbelieve it,' Fausto agreed. 'There are men stupid enough to think that they can survive themselves if they get rid of *him*. Victor Emmanuele III himself thinks this, encouraged by the generals who have hated Benito, but he and they are equally mistaken.' He gave another characteristic little shrug, and suddenly smiled at David.

'Something to tell your grandchildren about, my friend – this strange time when you were at large in Italy, watching history being made?'

David nodded and agreed, even though there were things that his grandchildren, if he lived to beget them, would *not* be told. Nothing was stranger than that he should be in the castle at all, sipping wine with a member of the Fascist Grand Council; but the link that held Rushtons and Buonaventuras together transcended not only ordinary life but even the strains of wartime. He couldn't imagine a time now when their lives would *not* be intertwined.

They said goodbye to Fausto the following morning, and Donna Giulia repeated slightly differently the instruction she had given Alexandra.

'Think of *her, tesoro*,' she pleaded, 'even if you refuse to think of yourself. She won't leave without you.'

'I know, Mamma.' His rueful smile agreed, but refused what she asked at the same time. 'The difficulty is that *I* can't abandon duty, either. As awkward creatures there isn't much to choose between us!'

'But neither of you would have the other any different,' his mother said slowly. 'You were made for each other. I've always seen that, of course, but never so clearly as now.'

Fausto smiled with an echo of his old tenderness. 'I've always known it – more clearly than anything else. 'Tavio and I both got wives we didn't deserve, and they've even managed not to hate us or Italy during the last couple of years – God knows how. It's the sort of tolerance only women are capable of.'

'In the same way that *we* don't hate David, of course,' the Marchesa said calmly. 'We know and love people, not ideologies and stupid theories, and groups with labels stuck on them. You'd do better to let us run things, you know . . . not old ladies like me, of course, but women like Francesca.'

'She's changed – those clear, grey eyes always used to look me up and down even in childhood and say that she was disappointed! This time she even smiled kindly at me.'

'It sounds a strange thing to say, now of all times, but she's happy, and for years I've so wanted her to be and feared she never would be . . . only . . .'

'You're afraid it won't last when David Rushton goes?' Fausto suggested when her voice died away.

His mother nodded, unable to say how threatening and hopeless life would seem altogether when David was no longer there – to do two men's work, and make the children's toys, and wrap them all in his male strength and gentleness. Fausto stared at her worn face, framed by a halo of silver hair; she'd grown old and frail while his back was turned, and he hadn't always realized how much he loved her.

'The war will end . . . it *has* to, my dear . . . and we must all live to be happy again. Shall we make each other a promise about that?' he asked her.

She nodded again, kissed him on both cheeks and let him go, not saying that it was a promise they could easily be made to break.

After his visit it seemed to Francesca that the slow-motion crawl of events began to gather speed, as if whoever was responsible for winding the projector of their lives was getting impatient for the end of the reel to come. The Duce went to Salzburg to confer again with his master, and returned briefly reinvigorated enough by Hitler's promises of eventual victory to try to regain control of a country that was slipping steadily out of his grasp. But no amount of public invective against Churchill and no new 'bludgeon squads' to remind Italians forcibly of their loyalty to the Party could conceal the miseries of everyday life – the constant Allied bombing, the shortages of food and fuel, and the growing, sickening knowledge that they were fighting on the wrong side – had always been, even when it seemed to be winning.

In the middle of May Italian troops in Tunisia finally laid down their arms, and on that same day the Mediterranean island of Pantelleria surrendered almost without firing a shot.

Ottavio listened with a wry smile to Mussolini's

statement that their enemies were knocking at the gate. 'Perhaps the suggestion that the Allies are making a polite request for admittance is meant to reassure us. Or has the Duce finally learned the art of understatement?'

'Like anything else he may have learned, the lesson has come too late,' the Marchese said sombrely. 'Now, the British and American armies will invade Sicily. After that it will be the turn of the mainland. Please God, whoever is in charge of this unfortunate country by *then* will immediately ask for an armistice.'

He was right about the course of events, but his prayer wasn't granted. The first Allied parachutists were dropped over Sicily on 10 July, and their landing-craft swarmed on to the beaches a few hours later. Another urgent consultation with the Führer seemed to offer one last chance of salvation, but the delegation returned from its meeting-place in Feltre with nothing changed – the war was to go on. The only change was in what it found at home – the unthinkable had happened; the Holy City itself had been heavily bombed for the first time.

'We went only to be humiliated,' an ashen-faced Fausto confessed to Alexandra. 'Instead of help, we got a whipping for the inadequacy of the Italian army and the "unwarlike spirit" of its people.'

'The Führer didn't suggest how people can be expected to be warlike when they're bombed, starving and don't know what they are suffering for?'

'He understands nothing; I suspect him of being insane.' In Fausto's calm, despairing voice and haunted eyes Alexandra recognized the horror of what he now knew – the vision of a reborn Italy, confident and proud under the Duce's masterful leadership, had faded like a desert mirage; the reality was what it had always been – suffering, ruin and defeat. She went to sit beside him and wrapped her arms about him in a silent, desperate longing to give comfort. They remained like that for a little while, until

Fausto loosed her hands and took them in his own. Then he kissed her mouth and tried to smile.

'Beloved one, I'm sorry – I meant to offer you Heaven on earth . . . all the joy and brilliant success and perfect happiness that life seemed capable of when we were young, not *this* disaster.'

'You've *given* me joy and perfect happiness – more than any woman could ask,' Alexandra said softly. 'There's even been a good deal of success as well. We were proud of what had been achieved in the past twenty years; why forget that now?'

'Men who should know better are ready to forget. Benito is caught, my darling, because *two* traps have been sprung – one by the King, plotting with the generals, the other by the Duce's own men, even his son-in-law, plotting among themselves. He might have survived one conspiracy, but he can't outwit them both – in his great days, yes, but not now that he is disheartened and sick.'

Alexandra determined never to say that plots were only a symptom, like the poison that oozed out of festering wounds. Fausto must be left to believe that the Duce had been betrayed, not that Fascism itself was being condemned and rejected.

'Promise me something,' she said instead.

'To cut our losses and run with the pack that bays at his heels?' Fausto asked, then caught her hand and kissed it in a mute gesture of apology. 'As if you would suggest such a thing. Dear heart, forgive me.'

She nodded and faintly smiled. 'Promise me *this*: not to regret any of the last twenty years, or allow yourself to be destroyed by the bitterness of thinking them wasted. No time is wasted if we've lived it fully – and we *have*, my love.' It was like a trumpet-blast, defying despair.

He remembered telling his mother of the tolerance that women were capable of; he realized now that he might have mentioned their courage as well.

'We'll regret nothing,' he promised her unsteadily, '. . .

why should we when we have each other? Has there been time to tell you recently that I love you very much?'

In the joy of being together again, and in the tenderness of making love, they could forget for a little while what else was happening. While people still toiled among the bombed ruins of the workers' quarters of San Lorenzo and Tiburtino, the conspirators rehearsed their parts for what was to be the final scene of the Duce's melodrama.

A meeting of the Fascist Grand Council – especially called for the first time in years – began on a blisteringly hot Saturday afternoon in July, ended in the small hours of the following morning with a vote of nineteen to seven in favour of stripping Mussolini of his powers. The control of the war was to be given back to the King, and the constitution overset by Fascist laws was to be reinstated. By the following afternoon the man who had ruled Italy for twenty-one years was not only replaced but under arrest. Rumours ran like wildfire through the city, soon confirmed in a proclamation from the King. Marshal Badoglio was the new head of a military government.

People poured out into the streets rejoicing . . . the *Era Fascista* was over, which meant that the Fascist war must be over, too. If they had stopped to listen to the Marshal's own proclamation – that Italy must 'remain loyal to her pledged word' – they would have understood that the war, Fascist or not, was continuing after all.

David pondered the news broadcasts heard with Ottavio and Don Giuseppe, aware that his time at Castagnolo was running out. The moment when he must abandon a desperately vulnerable and precious household was coming so near that he must stop thinking in terms of which cornfields would soon be ready to cut, which parts of the olive orchard he could next get dug and mulched . . . all these things would have to be left to Francesca and Gino. Francesca . . . his heart seemed to turn over at the thought of leaving her. He'd left Pattie with regret unmodified by any young man's normal excitement about going to war

377

– the bloody years in Spain had seen to that. The mild sadness of leaving his fiancée was something he could scarcely remember now, but walking away from Francesca when the time came would be like leaving his heart behind. He worked among the vines for long hours, tying in the forest of new shoots, knowing that, however frantically he toiled, he could accomplish only a fraction of what needed to be done. Francesca didn't come near him to say so, and he thought she guessed why he hid himself away.

He left her early one morning while she was still sleeping, so as not to have to say what was on his mind. The sun hadn't climbed above the rim of the hills but there was light enough to recognize the thin figure huddled in a corner of the courtyard.

'*Giorno, amico mio* . . . I was hoping you'd come out before hunger drove me over to see Lucia Scarelli!' Marco said softly.

'What's wrong with the kitchen here?'

'I wanted to avoid seeing Jane or Francesca. David, I don't want them or Father to know – especially Father – but I shan't be in Milan after this. After Spain I swore I'd never fight again, but it's the only thing left to do now.'

'You're going to come out of hiding . . . join the army to fight the invasion when it comes?' David asked the question even without believing that it was possible, and saw Marco shake his head.

'Surely you know better than that. We're going into the mountains to organize a resistance movement to *help* the invasion. I'm not sure that we can achieve a great deal, but it can't be left entirely to the Communists – they'd claim afterwards that only *they* had fought for Italy.'

'Who are you going to fight *against* – I thought the militia were being merged with the army.'

'We shall fight the Nazis – who arrive by the thousand in troop-train after troop-train. Make no mistake about it, David, this is an occupied country already. The German 'advisers' control every key point – airfields, railways, power stations, broadcasting – now their battalions are pouring in as well, because neither the King nor his brave Marshal had the courage or the sense to begin by blocking the Brenner Pass.'

'Would it have made any difference?' David asked quietly. 'Hitler would have found some other way of sending them.'

'I know – but it's indecently easy this way – like a woman holding up her skirts and asking to be raped.'

There was a little silence broken only by the early-morning sounds of the countryside stirring into life. David listened to one of Gino's prize cocks heralding another day, and thought that his own people had something to be thankful for – they had suffered much during this never-ending war, but not the bitter self-disgust that was tearing Italians like Marco apart.

'Where will you go?' he asked at last.

'Up into the hills between Bologna and Florence – we'll be well placed there to watch some crucial roads and railway lines.'

'If you're short of volunteers, I think I can find you some. They've been hiding in the woods above the castle for months; I know because we've been feeding them. I'd be thankful to have them go somewhere else – I don't want Francesca making that trip alone when I'm not here to go with her.'

'You haven't got a dog's chance of getting through to the south, old friend. Why not stay here? At least until our lords and masters catch up with you you're doing something useful!'

'That's been my reason for staying here up till now. If you'd come here and look after them I could go with a quieter heart.' The strengthening light showed him his friend's thin face. It was taut and fine drawn to the point of haggardness, and the fire of a martyr glowed in his deep-set eyes. The normal life of a young man of twenty-seven had been so entirely abandoned for the cause of Italy that David doubted if it could be rediscovered now. But he made one last attempt.

'Come and take care of Francesca for me – I can scarcely bear to leave her otherwise.'

Marco's sombre face was suddenly illumined by a grin. '*Madonna mia*, is *that* how it is after all these years of circling round one another with your fists raised?'

His friend nodded without smiling. 'Yes – that's how it is.'

'I'm sorry, Davido, but I *can't* come yet . . . not until Italy's free again; then I'll be back, and I'll never leave Castagnolo again. All I can do now is to relieve you of those volunteers – tell me where I can find them; we're short of men.'

'You can come with me this evening; until then you'd better get Lucia to feed you and find you somewhere to sleep.'

Marco nodded. 'That's something else I shall do one of these fine days – sleep and sleep and sleep!'

They climbed the hills in the cool afterglow of sunset; for the time the journey took the illusion could be made to last that the world was as beautiful and peaceful as it looked. There was no need to talk; they were both content to be together, reliving memories of past escapades and pleasures. Almost, they were boys again – no danger more fearsome than their imaginations could conjure up lurked in the trees around them, and there was nothing to find at the end of their climb except an owl's sleeping-place.

Obedient to Marco's hug of goodbye when they reached the hut, David left the consignment of food he'd brought and walked away. He didn't look back, and made the return journey forcing his mind to concentrate on the future, not the past. The future *had* to be thought about; there might, or perhaps might never, come a time when it was safe to remember the past.

Two days later he went back to the hut alone, to confirm what he already knew. The young men had left and, with them, every trace that they had ever been there. There was nothing to connect their stay with the inmates of the castle down below. David looked round the deserted place and smiled – his friend would have insisted on *this* attention to important detail. It was a comforting idea to keep him company on the long trudge home again.

29

Gino accepted with relief David's careful explanation of why there need be no more visits to the hut. Jane and Francesca looked surprised by the suddenness of the young men's departure; but then everything that happened now seemed unpredictable and largely inexplicable. Against all sanity or common sense the war was going on after all, and German troops were pouring southwards through the country to oppose the Allied invasion when it came. Like everyone else, they knew it was the signal that many restless young men had been waiting for. The time for passive acceptance was done; aided and armed by soldiers deserting from the army, they were forming themselves into resistance groups.

The people who came from Florence, desperately begging for vegetables, fruit or a small jar of olive oil, spoke in low voices of the numbers of German troops billeted in the city. Ottavio knew that it was only a matter of time before the first of their scouting parties reached Castagnolo, commandeering food for themselves. When it happened one early-summer morning, Jane had to leave him to deal with them while David was hidden in the tower and the household made to look as blameless as possible.

'Well, what happened?' she asked fearfully afterwards.

'They took what they came for, more or *less* politely! The Prefect in Florence had obviously warned them that, with known anti-Fascist views, we were unlikely to be helpful.'

'He's right about that,' Jane agreed fairly.

'I know, but it makes us a target for their attentions. I insisted that, with extra children here, we have very little food to spare, and also pointed out that the militia have long since relieved us of anything *they* might find useful. All the same, they will undoubtedly be back. We shall have to be much more careful in future about keeping a watch for them, for David's sake.'

The same idea had already occurred to Francesca, and she felt certain that it was monopolizing David's mind, too. He behaved as he always did – worked, played with the children, shared in the dinner-table conversation at night, and even calmly discussed with Ottavio and Don Giuseppe the progress of the fighting in Sicily. But she watched his face and felt cold despair begin to settle on her heart.

During the long hours they spent working outside she left him alone, aware that she could neither change the decision he was coming to nor persuade herself that she even had the right to try. Hadn't they agreed at the beginning to be thankful for a love affair that couldn't grow stale? That night when he came to her as usual, he stood for a long time staring out at a summer sky studded with the Marchese's precious constellations. She lay watching him, then slipped out of bed and went to stand beside him. Perhaps with her hand tucked into his she would feel brave enough to put into words the knowledge that a terrible pain was coming upon her.

'You're going away, aren't you?'

She felt him nod, long before the answer came. 'Yes . . . I should have gone ages ago, but the truth is that I couldn't bear to leave you.'

'Why go now, then, just because the Nazis are here? What difference does it make, and what hope have you got of getting away? They're everywhere, multiplying like ants, infesting every inch of Italy.' She heard the climbing note of anguish in her voice and jammed a hand against her mouth to stifle the rest of what she'd been about to say.

David turned round to look at her . . . it was the last

time he would see her with starlight on her face. She was lovely, and dear beyond forgetting, and he must go and leave her unguarded in the very midst of their enemies.

'I must go just *because* the Germans are here,' he said quietly.

'Why? You've been safe for months; no-one at Castagnolo would ever give you away.'

'Not knowingly, perhaps, but what about a small child not even aware that she was being questioned? What about one wretched informer, desperate for something to barter with? That could happen even here, and if I were caught, you'd all be punished.' She opened her mouth to protest but he laid a finger across her lips. 'It's happening already, Fran. The partisans ambushed two German soldiers in Pontarno the day before yesterday – Gino told me. As a little lesson that such rebellion mustn't happen again, six of the villagers were taken out and shot.'

She found nothing to say; they lived in a world now where these things happened. In the dark night of the spirit they all stumbled through it was hard to believe in a resurrection of light and gentleness and sweet normality. The only way to survive present horror was to cling to the belief that there might be a different kind of future, but it would be a future without him, whether they both lived or died. She struggled against the hysterical longing to weep and laugh at the same time – she could hear her past self boldly insisting that loyalties weren't for jettisoning the moment the cost of clinging to them became high. She still knew it to be true but, dear God, how very high the cost was.

'When will you leave?' she asked finally. 'No, don't tell me, and don't say goodbye . . . just go. I'll pray to God in Heaven that you're walking safely towards England and Pattie.'

'And I shall think of you every day of my life – picture you here, and grow old lonely for you. Fran . . . I know the ifs are enormous, but if I should get to England and find that Pattie had forgotten me, would you come?'

He had to wait a long time for her answer, but finally it came.

'There's one more if, David. If Marco comes home to take care of Nonno and Nonna, and Ottavio and Jane, and Castagnolo . . . then I'll come to England.'

He lifted her in his arms for the last time and carried her to bed, but he didn't make love to her and she knew why. That part of their loving was over, for the time being and perhaps for ever. Passion, leaping like a flame between them, belonged already to the past. What remained, for as long as he was there to hold her cradled in his arms, was simply tenderness, ineffable and heartbreaking.

He left the next day, having said goodbye to the others but not to her. When she returned late in the afternoon from visiting a sick woman at one of the outlying farms, Gino was waiting to stable the mare, a task she normally expected to do for herself, however tired she was. It didn't need that small kindness, nor Luisa's tearful face when she walked through the kitchens, to tell her what she already knew – the castle felt empty without him.

Marco's new adventure didn't remain a secret very long; he was seen and recognized when an army depôt was broken into and raided for weapons. The Commandant of the local carabinieri, who respected Ottavio as much as he despised the Prefect of Florence, came in person to the Castle to deliver a warning. He accepted the glass of wine Ottavio offered him, but sat frowning at it instead of drinking.

'They do no *good*, you know. What is a futile gesture of defiance here, perhaps a goods train derailed there . . . ? It achieves nothing, and innocent people who weren't even there are savagely punished. Why can't they see that, these brave young men?'

'They see only that doing *something* is better than doing

nothing,' Ottavio answered slowly. '*That* is what breaks the heart and spirit of young men – doing nothing. I have to say that I agree with them.'

The Commandant gave a little sigh and sipped his wine. 'I dare say I might too, if I didn't have to look at what follows – the result of the bloody reprisals. But I waste my time and yours; you cannot change young men, and I cannot change the Germans.' He picked up his cap and offered an afterthought on his way to the door. 'You will hear the news soon enough – Sicily has surrendered to the Allies.'

Perhaps it was another stage passed in their long purgatory; but, as always, there was worse to come. Francesca seemed hidden behind a frozen composure so complete that she was scarcely aware of events outside the places she had shared with David, but Jane watched Ottavio and his father retreat further day by day into shocked abhorrence of what was happening to Italy – Fascists now being cruelly witch-hunted by the government that had replaced them, while troops fired on unarmed Fiat workers who went on strike. Everywhere rumour, confusion and deceit spread like weeds in an atmosphere of fearful anticipation about the future, and over every city now hung the ever-present threat of bombing by an enemy no further away than Sicily.

There seemed to Jane no reason why this terrible state of affairs should ever change – they were locked into everlasting misery. Then, on a day at the beginning of September, another unexpected jerk by the mad projectionist in charge sent events lurching on again. The King agreed to accept unconditional surrender, rather than see Italy totally destroyed.

'It's late and long overdue, but at least it's come,' Jane murmured, inclined to think that her husband might have abandoned his usual caution for once and cried, 'Thank God . . . Thank God,' as she wanted to do. Instead, Ottavio's face was a mask of despair.

'I think we have just *ensured* the total destruction of Italy, not avoided it,' he said bitterly. 'That announcement should have been made in the very moment that Mussolini was deposed. Failing that, it should have coincided with an Allied invasion. As usual, we shall suffer for the utter stupidity and cowardice of the people who rule us – if that is what their lamentable performance may be called.'

Jane was halted on the brink of a protest by the expression on her father-in-law's face. It was clear that he agreed with Ottavio, and over all the years of her life at Castagnolo she had learned to rely on the Marchese's detached and gentle wisdom.

' 'Tavio's right, my dear Jane,' he said now. 'The confusion is complete – the army is told not to fight those who were its enemy a week ago; they are *not* told what to do about the men who now *become* their enemy.'

It became painfully clear that he was right, and that the confusion wasn't shared by the Germans. Whole units of a disorientated Italian army were easily disarmed then herded into cattle-trucks and shipped to prison camps or forced labour. The King and his Marshal abandoned a capital controlled by German troops and fled to the comparative safety of Brindisi; national disintegration seemed complete.

But haphazardly and heroically resistance began – among isolated groups of soldiers where there were still resolute officers to lead them, and among workers in factories. The partisans like Marco, originally driven out of society to fight against Fascism, were joined by thousands of volunteers. Overnight a new source of recruits appeared: at the announcement of the armistice, for lack of any other instructions, the Italian guards at prisoner-of-war camps simply unlocked the gates. Now, ex-prisoners roamed the countryside, trying to avoid the Germans, looking for a partisan group to join or making their way southwards. All of them needed food, clothes and information.

The first time Francesca walked into the *cantina* and heard an English voice trying to make itself understood to Gino her heart stopped beating. In another moment she knew it wasn't David's – but the man had come from the same camp at Vincigliata. When they had fed him in Lucia's kitchen and sent him on his way, Francesca earned her first and only rebuke from Gino.

'There will be more of these men coming now . . . our people must never turn them away, or give them up to the Germans.' He stared at her without saying anything, and she suddenly shouted at him, 'I know there's a risk, but *promise* me, Gino.'

'Our people will never turn them away, for Signor Davido's sake – you should know that without promises.' He walked out of the kitchen, leaving her standing there, feeling shamed and sick. The tears that she hadn't wept since David's departure chose this moment to overflow, and she was gathered into Lucia's arms and held like a broken-hearted child.

At last she scrubbed at her cheeks and tried to smile. 'I *should* have known better, Lucia . . . I'll apologize to Gino later.'

She was calm again, but the storm of weeping had released her from the numbness that had been a barrier shutting out everyone else. Now that she could do what hadn't been possible before, she went in search of Jane. For once her friend was idle; a mound of haricot beans lay heaped on the table in front of her, but instead of shelling them Jane sat still, exhausted by the effort of always having to look cheerful. She kept them going, Francesca realized all over again; *her* love and courage and common sense were what they all drew on, as they had for all the years that she could remember.

'I've just been ticked off by Gino,' she said without preamble.

'For working too hard, I hope.'

'No, for suggesting that anyone here might not

understand about helping . . . helping anyone who comes *needing* help.'

'Like prisoners on the loose?' Jane suggested carefully. She saw Francesca nod, and registered the recent signs of weeping. 'Dear girl, of course they understand – not about why last week's enemies are now friends; they never understood why they were enemies anyway. It's a matter of simple humanity and self-respect – the treatment that one human being in need is bound to receive from another.'

Francesca started snapping pods for something to do with her hands. 'I couldn't talk about David before,' she said after a while. 'Now I can. It's just as well, because it's time to tell you that I'm pregnant.'

'Did . . . did *he* know?'

'I didn't know myself. Now it's certain. Old Dr Bertolini's confirmed it for me.'

'We never dare talk about the future as a rule,' Jane murmured, 'but just suppose *one* blessed day when the war is over we hear that David is alive – will you tell him then?'

'I doubt if I shall ever tell him, Janey . . . I knew all along that he belonged in England, and he knew that I belong here. A child doesn't change that; it might only make him feel it *ought* to change things, if he knew.'

Jane stared at her pale face and saw in it no trace of fear or regret. 'You're glad, aren't you? It's something salvaged from the wicked waste of war.'

Francesca's smile was sweet and sure. 'Something salvaged for all of us,' she said.

From then on their visitors – sometimes hungry partisans, sometimes lost prisoners – played a dangerous game of hide and seek with German patrols. Precious supplies of food had to be hidden from sudden raiding-parties, and somehow the welfare of dozens of people who depended on the Buonaventuras had to be seen to. Life was so precarious and difficult that one anxiety lost its power to disturb because another was always waiting to push it aside.

There was scarcely time to stop and give thanks when the long-awaited invasion finally began on 9 September – with the Americans trying to break out of a beach-head at Salerno, and General Montgomery's desert army arriving from Sicily to begin its slow, bitter struggle up the eastern side of Italy. More astonishing, because more unlooked-for, was the Germans' audacious rescue of Mussolini a few days later from his confinement on the Gran Sasso high in the Abruzzi mountains.

They were still considering the implications of this when Fausto arrived with Alexandra in a car driven by a German soldier. Jane left her brother-in-law with Ottavio and Don Giuseppe, and carried Alex off to the little room the Marchesa liked to refer to grandly as her boudoir.

'Darling . . . look who's here – your fellow-Libran!'

Donna Giulia blinked and looked uncertain whether to smile or weep. 'Dearest, we've been so worried about you . . . heard such terrible things. Is Fausto all right?'

'Perfectly, Mamma. There were enough *hated* Fascists to be thrown to the lions! Fausto has never got rich, never been cruel to anyone; no-one hates him.'

'But what happens now?' asked Jane.

Alexandra's eyes looked troubled but she answered calmly. 'Now that the Duce is free again he is resuming leadership of the new Fascist Republican Party. Fausto will serve, of course.'

'Back in Rome?'

'No, that has been declared an open city to save more needless destruction. The new Republic will have its headquarters in the north – at Salò, on Lake Garda.'

'And be the tool of the Germans?'

'Be *supported* by the Germans,' Alexandra corrected mechanically. She saw Jane's expression and made a sudden fierce protest. 'All right – you disapprove. But someone has to remain loyal – someone has to help the

Duce apart from the Germans; you might have known that it was bound to be my darling Fausto.'

'Of course,' Jane agreed quietly. 'But, Alex, this puppet government can't last. In the end the Germans are going to be defeated. What happens to you and Fausto then?'

Alexandra gave a tired little shrug. 'Who knows? Who knows *anything* now except what each day brings?'

The Marchesa broke the silence in the room. 'What about Anna and Ernesto – is *he* going to be part of this new republic, too?'

A sardonic smile touched Alexandra's mouth, spoiling its beauty. 'My worthy brother-in-law is being the honest broker, as usual . . . busy *behind* the scenes, conducting negotiations with everyone at once. He doesn't have to worry about who comes out on top – it's bound to be *one* of his friends!' She gave a little grimace of disgust at her own bitterness and smiled more sweetly. 'Anna is her precious self – thin and tired, and saving her immortal soul by staying out of everything except the orphanage she works for. I don't think she sees much of Ernesto, but that doesn't worry her.' Alexandra hesitated, then risked a question of her own.

'No news of David, I suppose?'

'None, but we didn't expect any,' Jane said steadily. 'We *are* visited by some of his ex-fellow-inmates quite often – I hope they spot Fausto's driver before they give themselves away.'

'And before they give *you* away. It's frowned upon, Janey – aiding and abetting, didn't *our* lovely policemen used to call it at home?' Her laugh turned into a sob, but the conversation ended because Francesca appeared to say that Fausto was getting anxious to leave again. They all went out into the courtyard to wave goodbye, but no-one felt inclined to speak when the car disappeared round the first curve of the drive on its way down towards the valley.

* * *

That winter of 1943–4, above all others, seemed to Jane to be the very abomination of desolation foretold in the Old Testament by Daniel. If the armies struggling through mud and rain and bitter opposition to inch their way up the peninsula wondered why they were there at all – hadn't these bloody, hopeless fools *chosen* Hitler? – she feared that the Italians themselves now scarcely distinguished between being occupied and liberated. They only knew that the cure was more painful than the disease. Even when the countryside wasn't being destroyed by battles, partisans and their Fascist/German enemies practised reciprocal cruelties that led them further and further down a descending spiral of evil.

It was a horrifying world to bring a child into, and Jane watched with a sense of awe Francesca's calm concentration on the baby growing inside her. *This*, she seemed to insist, was where hope and sanity lay, and her priceless gift to them was that it became a truth they all recognized. Her son – Niccolò David – was born in the late spring of 1944, and, as if to mark the fact that something momentous had happened, in the same week the deadlock that had trapped the Allied armies was suddenly broken. Monte Cassino surrendered and the German line fell back northwards.

Rome was liberated two days before the first landings in Normandy, and by August the fighting was raging round Florence. Faithful to a pattern followed time and time again in the past, Castagnolo gathered-in its people for shelter, but while they were made comfortable in the cellars, Ottavio stood on the terrace hour after hour, looking at the pall of smoke and the flash of gunfire over the city.

'You can't change anything by watching,' Jane pointed out gently. 'If Marco *is* there among thousands of other partisans, taking no rest yourself won't keep him safe. My love, be sensible, please, because I can bear *anything* but having you ill again.'

Ottavio allowed himself to be led back indoors, but stopped for one more brooding glance at the valley. 'It's a new Dark Age, Janey, when men slaughter each other like this and grind the priceless treasures of civilization into dust. The hopeless, heartbreaking pity of it is that it's nothing new – we never learn!'

'No, but somehow we stagger on. We shall again this time, because there's nothing *else* to do.'

He couldn't help smiling at such English pragmatism. She had lived in Italy for nearly twenty years and still not been fundamentally changed by it; he prayed that she never would change, because they needed her just as she was.

But when total defeat was accepted in the following year, and the Germans abandoned the Duce and his few remaining followers to the vengeance of the men his régime had persecuted for twenty years, there was no leniency for a sick man, no pity, not even a fair trial. He and his mistress, Claretta Petacci, tried to escape to Switzerland, but they were shot out of hand by partisans. Their bodies were strung up in the Piazzale Lorelo in Milan for the people to spit on. Jane acknowledged to herself that Ottavio was right – it was another Dark Age they were living through.

There were others reported as caught and killed with Mussolini, but the names of Fausto and Alexandra were not among them. It seemed an agonizingly long time before the news reached Castagnolo of what *had* happened to them.

30

David Rushton arrived home via a German prison camp liberated by the Americans. It was still difficult to realize that he was a free man, and even harder to remember that five years of his life had been swallowed up since he sailed from England for North Africa.

He was almost home, but suddenly so reluctant to arrive that he stopped his taxi cab and began to walk instead. This grey, shabby city, with aching gaps where houses had once been, was *his* – the place he'd proudly claimed to belong to. It was disconcerting now to feel like a ghost, invisible to the grey, shabby people who passed him by. Everything here had changed, but he had changed most of all.

When he turned into Chiswick Mall, remembered habit sent him to watch the river flowing past the bottom of the garden. The wooden bench, childhood's look-out post, had gone, and the lawn had disappeared under blotches of yellowing potato plants and sprawling mounds of marrows. He looked up at the house and saw an old man's face watching him from one of the drawing-room windows – it was time to go inside.

His grandfather had negotiated the stairs and waited in the hall – still upright at eighty-five, but held so by willpower and a silver-topped cane. David hugged his frailness, shocked by the bird-like feel of old bones.

'You weren't in a hurry,' muttered James.

David understood what was meant – not the long years of being away, but the minutes spent outside just now, staring at the water.

'You're looking well, Grandfather,' he said gently.

'Kept my hair! That's something *you'll* be grateful for – Rushtons always do.' He blinked away telltale moisture from his eyes and tried to smile. 'Thought I'd never see you again, although I pretended to your mother that you were certain to come home again.'

'Where is she?'

'Upstairs . . . told her I wanted to see you first. The rest of them had it in mind to be here too, but I said you'd need time to get used to being home again.'

A gleam shone in his eyes, and David's thin face broke into a grin. Whatever else had changed, James was still in charge!

'Quite right, Gramps – I don't know that I'm up to Aunt Alice and Eliza yet, if they're as I remember them.'

'Alice has mellowed with age,' James conceded with a certain regret. 'Eliza's just as frightful, though – worse, in fact, now that your fellow-servicemen have been fools enough to vote a Labour government into power. They'll regret it soon enough, but meanwhile we all have to suffer.'

The sudden querulousness of old age had overtaken him, but David knew it was due to tiredness and the strain of waiting. This stubborn old man, who certainly wouldn't admit to any kind of weakness, had figured in his life from the earliest moment he could remember; it would have been unthinkable to come home and not find him there.

'I'd better go and find my mother, before we start catching up,' he suggested casually. 'No hurry now, though; we've got time for talking again.'

James stared at him from under thick, white brows, summoning courage to ask the only question that mattered. 'Have we? It depends what you're going to do, boy.'

'I thought of staying here – at least, until you decide that Rushton's are better off without me!'

James told himself that he *wouldn't* break down and weep, but relief made him tremble, and he didn't protest when David eased him gently into an armchair. 'Better go and see your mother.' He could be generous now . . . might even have smiled kindly at Alice if she'd walked through the door. Another question occurred to him as David began to climb the stairs.

'How was Jane when you left the castle? Extraordinary that you should have landed up at Castagnolo of all places.'

'It's a long time ago that I was there,' David said evenly. 'They were managing well enough when I left, but the invasion was just about to start – the fighting must have raged all round them in the end.'

'We still don't get any letters, but I suppose the postal service went to pot, along with everything else. Unfortunate country,' James remarked with unusual restraint, '. . . genius for backing the wrong horses!'

David nodded but didn't answer, and went on up the stairs to find Laura Rushton waiting for him in the wide alcove made by a bend in the staircase. Perhaps she'd chosen to be there because its circular window and padded seat had been his favourite vantage-point as a child. From its curtained seclusion he'd watched the life of the river. Every barge could only be making its way to his grandfather's warehouses at London Bridge, every tide was part of London's 'liquid 'istory'.

'Darling, I was forbidden to come a step further!' His mother's rich voice hadn't changed, and that, also, was remembered from childhood. 'It's marvellous to have you home.'

She allowed herself to be hugged, then stood smiling at him – no longer young, but still elegant, still carefully made up and still offering the same captivating warmth to everyone she met.

'You look just the same,' he said quickly, '. . . wonderfully the same.'

It was hard to say as much for him. She noticed that his hair, several shades darker than her own, was already streaked with grey, and the lines that scored his face from nostril to mouth belonged to a man ten years older than his actual age. She knew she looked so much younger than hers that it seemed to make their relationship ridiculous.

'*You're* over-thin, my sweet,' she said with careful tact. 'I'm not sure what we can do about it because we're still on these damnably monotonous wartime rations – a treat in store for you will be one of Mrs Todd's omelettes made with dried, reconstituted eggs! You'll be wishing you still had Red Cross parcels.'

She saw a shadow cross his face and sighed inwardly. It was wonderful to have him back, but how still *more* boring would life be if every word they uttered had to avoid all reference to the past four years. Life had been hard for all of them, not just for prisoners-of-war.

'Tell me about Pattie,' David suggested, aware that it was more than time to enquire. 'I know she was serving out in Malta, but surely *she's* demobbed by now?'

'Of course – in fact already rehearsing for a show, lucky girl, but she'll be here this evening.' Laura examined her son's face and found it unrevealing. 'She had a very adventurous war, darling, but she was *wonderfully* faithful . . . no-one could have had a more loyal fiancée.'

He nodded, wishing he felt more grateful to a girl whose face he could scarcely recall. Laura tucked her hand affectionately inside his arm, aware for a moment of his struggle to appear excited about returning to a life that now seemed to have belonged to someone else.

'Don't worry, my sweet . . . you just need a little time to get used to being David Rushton, civilian, again. Being captured *once* must have been bad enough . . . having it happen a second time . . .'

'. . . was, Lady Bracknell would have said, suspiciously like carelessness!' he suggested with a sudden grin. 'It *was* – I'd got as far as the outskirts of Naples and success made me over-bold. I made the return journey in a cattle-truck, in rather less time than it had taken me to walk the other way.' He omitted to say that he'd been lucky not to be shot, since he'd been caught not wearing military uniform. The war was over – it was time to stop reliving its excitement and horror, joy and pain. Forget it, David Rushton, civilian, forget it all and smile at Pattie this evening. Then, thankfully, he remembered someone else not yet mentioned.

'I know the rest of the family have been told not to come rushing round, but what about Uncle Char? Surely *he* must be here?'

Laura looked puzzled for a moment, then smiled. 'Of course, you don't know – he got himself into the army.'

'*What?* At the age of fifty-something?'

'He was forty-eight at the time.' She made the correction carefully, having been born in exactly the same year herself. 'There wasn't any question of fighting, of course. He was enrolled as some kind of adviser – telling them where there were works of art that had to be avoided; more often, probably, telling them how to patch up things that *had* got damaged. It was a job after his own heart.'

'I can believe it,' David agreed slowly. 'Where is he now?' Even as he asked the question, he knew the answer. Where else would Charles Rushton be if not watching over the treasures of Italy?

'Naples seems to have an attraction for the Rushtons,' Laura commented. 'That's where *he* was when last heard from, but he's due home any time now.' She twisted the bracelet on her wrist and then looked at David. 'Darling, I hope you won't mind that you're not in your old room – we switched you and Tom so that he wasn't at the top of the house during air raids. Everything's up there for you to arrange as you want it.'

It was a reminder of the other people he hadn't asked about – her husband, William, and his half-brother and -sister. He had to fumble in his memory for the name of a girl who hadn't been born until he was fifteen.

'How are they all – William, and Tom and Meg?'

'Looking forward to seeing you this evening. Tom will

pester you with questions. At seventeen he's a shining light in the OTC at St Pauls, and determined to go to Sandhurst if he can.'

'Not to the firm? What does Grandfather think about that?'

Laura gave a little shrug. 'I don't think he cares. There are all George's children if Rushton's needs recruits, but you're the only one that matters. Waiting for you has kept James alive.'

David remembered the tremulous old man downstairs and knew that what she said was true. James and Rushton's had survived for *him* and it wouldn't have been humanly possible to reject either of them. In time he would feel at home with them again, perhaps even recapture the excitement of the small boy who'd been taken to see the cellars at London Bridge. He could still see in his mind's eye the serried ranks of bottles shining in the dimness, and smell the old, dank, river air that seeped in from the outside.

'Did the cellars survive the air raids?' he asked.

'Surprisingly well, although the offices above ground didn't. Poor William and George still run things from a patched-up warehouse at the moment. They'll tell you about it when you're ready to start work, but first you must get strong again – forget about Rushton's for the time being.'

She meant to be kind, and he had no right to feel irritated. How could he expect any of them to understand the churning mess of emotions that he scarcely understood himself? After eighteen months' captivity in a German camp much harsher than the one at Vincigliata, he expected to crave normality – the freedom to work and play and laugh with friends and relearn to love his fiancée . . . all this would surely be enough to make life seem worthwhile. But he'd learned to survive hardship and unhappiness since then by retreating far inside himself – there'd been moments of unexpected peace in observing minutely whatever tiny fragments of the natural world were visible to a prisoner, and moments of satisfaction in working out for himself the things that he believed in. He wasn't the same man who'd gone away to war – he'd travelled in far, strange countries of the spirit, and he'd been allowed to love Francesca.

'I'll go and settle in, shall I?' he suggested.

'Do, my sweet,' she agreed quickly. 'Plenty of time to talk afterwards.'

It began to sound like a promise they would all keep making to each other, but he smiled and climbed the next flight of stairs.

His new room was next door to his uncle's attic bedroom-cum-studio. The sloping ceiling required care, but he liked the bird's-eye view of the river. His clothes were already neatly put away in cupboards and drawers, but books and pictures and gramophone records were piled in heaps on the floor. There was no reason not to start sorting them out immediately, except that even *these* treasured things seemed to have belonged to someone he no longer knew.

He almost fled from the room and went on impulse into Charlie's studio next door. The smell of paint and turpentine still lingered in the stale air, and sketches and pictures covered every available space on the walls. He stared, transfixed by memories, at a child's drawing of a pair of white oxen, with majestically spreading horns and tasselled noses. A large sketchbook, entitled simply 'Tuscany', lay on Charlie's table under the window. He sat down without knowing that he did so, and began to look at his uncle's sketches – Giotto's lovely Lily Tower, the perfect curve of the Duomo's dome glimpsed between the uprights formed by narrow streets, an elderly horse and driver caught snoozing in the shade while they waited for a customer . . . Florence, as it was before opposing armies did their best to reduce it to a heap of rubble.

Not only Florence; Castagnolo was there as well –

battlemented tower, terraced gardens, a laughing boy astride a dolphin in a lily pond, and a small girl with vine-leaves dangling from the brim of her straw hat . . . Francesca, aged seven, bringing in the grape harvest.

David closed the book, and got up to stare out of the window, seeing nothing but the images that flashed across his mind's eye. So carefully and deeply had he buried them, and now so completely were they found again, that he hugged his body against the pain that was tearing him apart . . . 'by the waters of Babylon we sat down and wept, when we remembered thee . . .' – that long-ago psalmist's anguish meant something to him now. After a long while he went back to his own unfamiliar room. When a tall lad of seventeen knocked at the half-open door he was methodically sorting books.

'Tea's ready,' Tom said shyly. 'I don't suppose you even remember me.'

He found Aunt Alice downstairs as well, a little shrunk with age, like his grandfather, but still well able to slaughter embarrassment out of hand. Thanks to her, Vine House was feeling less strange when William arrived home – florid and more thickset now, but determined to be heartily amiable to his stepson. By the time fifteen-year-old Meg, with long, thin legs and a wondering stare for her elder brother, returned from a tennis match, they only waited for Pattie.

She came just as James got impatient and instructed William to open the champagne hoarded for this occasion. David watched her walk towards him with the springy step of a dancer. He'd worked out her age – twenty-five now – but she looked younger. A mass of dark curls framed her face; her skin was very white and her mouth very red. She looked exotic among the fair Rushtons, and David tried to remember whether that was what he'd found attractive about her. Her smile wavered, reminding him that this reunion was an ordeal for her as well as him, especially watched by the rest of the family.

He kissed her lightly, then held her at arms' length.

'My dear girl, can you believe this is happening? I can't!'

Her smile reappeared, enticing but not remembered. 'I rehearsed what I'd say, over and over again, and now I can't remember a word of it. What a confession for someone who hopes to become an actress!'

His answering grin helped, because it made him look less old and unfamiliar. Her imagination *had* painted this scene a hundred times, but always in colours excitingly bright. In the hectic days of service life on wartime Malta she hadn't regretted her engagement at all – being sought after but loyal to her prisoner-of-war fiancé had seemed the best of all possible worlds; but the reality was *this* tired-faced man with an ugly hand she couldn't bear to look at.

David saw her eyes skim over it and wondered whether she would manage not to shudder when he touched her. What was there to say next? He had no idea, but James saved him by calling out that the champagne was getting flat. The wine helped, too – Rushton's best to celebrate a moment that was supposed to be full of joy. He smiled at Pattie, promising himself that somehow their life together would work out. It had to because, if not, five years of her life would have been wasted on his behalf.

Over Laura's festive dinner of pheasant provided by a landowning client of the firm, he talked a little about the desert and his time in Germany, but not about Italy. It wasn't mentioned until William spoke about the chances of being able to import its wine again. David clamped shut the door of memory in his mind and dragged the conversation away from Tuscany to his uncle, inspecting damaged treasures in Naples.

By then, Charlie was no longer there. He had been in Rome for a month by the time David's home-coming dinner took place. Now, on the point of leaving for London, he had finally given in to the temptation to call on Anna

Lambertini. To lessen the disappointment of not finding her, he'd told himself all the way to the Piazza Navona that she almost certainly wouldn't be there. The house would be shuttered, empty, inhabited by strangers by now . . . he rehearsed every possibility except the actuality of lifting the ornate iron knocker and staring at Anna herself when the door opened.

He had nothing ready to say, couldn't have remembered it in any case; he could ony look at her and think that she was ill. Her dark hair had now turned to silver, and it was drawn back from a face so thin that its framework of bones was clearly visible. She wore a black dress, and its collar of white lace made her skin look sallow. For a moment of time that lasted as long as eternity she stared at him without saying anything, supporting herself with hands that clutched the door and the doorpost.

'I expect the uniform's confusing,' said Charlie unevenly. 'It *is* me.'

Then Anna smiled, and she was more beautiful than he remembered.

'I know,' she murmured. 'For a moment, though, I thought I was dreaming . . . going mad, maybe.'

'I pretended you wouldn't be here – even made myself believe it, which is why I can't think of anything intelligent to say now.'

She gestured him inside and closed the door, then led him upstairs to the huge room that overlooked the square. Its formal elegance had survived the war, but he thought its height and size had defeated her – long-dead Andrianis were still in charge, and *she* was the ghost, not they.

As if the same thought was in her mind, she made a sudden confession. 'I've never belonged here, and I've come to the conclusion finally that I hate Rome!'

'At least it's yours again,' Charlie said.

'Is it?' Her wry smile reminded him of the streets choked with American jeeps and of the troops lounging on every corner – well intentioned perhaps, but an occupying army nevertheless.

'Things are better than in Naples,' he muttered. 'I've been working there for months on damaged pictures, but the *human* misery is indescribable. If we've achieved a victory for you, it isn't very noticeable.'

'The Germans have gone, and so have the Fascists,' Anna said gently. 'That *is* a victory, my friend.'

Charlie lifted his hands in a little gesture of despair. 'There's so much to say that we need to spend the rest of our lives talking – except that there's so much that needs *doing* as well. Will you stay here . . . even though you hate it?'

'No . . . quite soon now I'm going back to Fiesole for good. Ernesto will go on living here, of course, and since Lorenza and her husband make their home here, he won't be lonely.' Her mouth twisted in a wry smile again. 'I'm not sure that he is ever lonely – not while there's a financial deal to be put through, or some business negotiation to be steered in the way he thinks it should go!'

'And in Fiesole what will you do?'

'Pass the days *quietly* . . . grow flowers, watch the sunsets and let old wounds heal. We all have some healing to do, I think.'

'David should be home by now,' Charlie remarked, as if that were part of the process she spoke of. 'I suppose you never knew that he was caught again about a month after he left Castagnolo. He was sent to Germany after that.'

'They missed him at the castle – begged him to stay, but he was afraid they'd be punished if he was caught *there*. We've lived through terrible times, Charlie . . . you don't know how terrible.'

'I kept trying to get in touch with Jane, but the telephones still don't seem to be working, and if my letters have reached *her*, no reply has come back yet. Are they all right . . . ?' He saw the expression on her face and cried, 'Anna, tell me, please.'

'We didn't hear anything, either, during the final stages of the fighting, or for weeks after the armistice, but Ernesto managed to get to Castagnolo on his way back from Geneva one day.' She stopped talking and Charlie had to prompt her.

'Go on, my dear.'

'Some of the farms had been damaged, but the castle itself was all right.' Anna linked thin fingers together and seemed to be reciting the facts of a lesson learned by heart. 'My parents are very frail, but still alive; Ottavio had a second heart attack, but my darling, valiant Jane watches over him; and she and Francesca between them struggle to get the estate back into some kind of working order again.'

'Can't Marco help? Surely he could put aside politics *now*?'

Anna got up and walked over to one of the long windows so that her back was to Charlie. 'Marco is dead. He fought with the partisans here, you know.'

'My dear, I'm so sorry . . . as everywhere else, I suppose their losses were appalling.' Charlie's shocked answer made her swing round to stare at him.

'I doubt if what happened here was *quite* like anywhere else – this is Italy, remember,' she said bitterly. 'When the Germans surrendered they left their friend Mussolini to fend for himself. He hesitated until it was too late, and then tried to escape to Switzerland. Fausto and Alexandra were among the handful of people who hadn't abandoned him by then to save their own skins. They were part of a German convoy making for the frontier, but got caught by partisans on the shores of Lake Como. You must know already what happened to Mussolini and his mistress.'

'And Fausto . . . and Alexandra?' Charlie forced the words past the obstruction in his throat, but didn't recognize his own voice.

'Marco was in the partisan group and saw them. He'd known for years all sorts of ways of smuggling people into Switzerland, and made Fausto see that this was his only

405

chance of saving Alexandra. They got to Switzerland safely – Ernesto sometimes sees them there.'

'*One* happy ending, thank God,' Charlie muttered.

'Yes, except that Marco was shot by his own men for letting them "escape". The leader of the group was an avowed Communist who saw a convenient way of getting rid of someone who was going to challenge him when the war was over. I reminded you that this is Italy, did I not?'

Charles closed his eyes against the sadness in her face. 'How did Ottavio and Jane hear about it?'

'One of the others – Marco's friend – went afterwards to tell them; that's when Ottavio had his second heart attack. Eventually they were able to bring Marco's body back and bury it at Castagnolo.'

Anna's white face was wet with tears now and she was scarcely aware that Charlie had moved until she felt his arms enfold her. It was the moment to be swept by a storm of weeping that seemed to be washing away the loneliness and heartbreak of years. She was spent when it was over, but somehow finally at peace. When he fumbled in his pocket for a handkerchief and mopped her face, he wasn't a stranger in uniform any longer, with greying fair hair and heavy spectacles. The kindest, gentlest man she had ever known was smiling at her, as he'd smiled one evening years ago at Vine House.

'I have to leave for London tomorrow, but may I come and visit you at Fiesole?' he asked softly.

Anna nodded, not smiling, but her face was filled with the radiance of returning joy. 'You remember what the Arabs say – "my house is *your* house," come when you can, Charlie.'

He bent and kissed her mouth, then picked up his cap and walked out into the crowded life of the square.

31

James Rushton died in the spring of the following year and Jane paid her first visit to England in eleven years to attend his funeral.

David was waiting at Victoria Station for the boat-train to arrive. She recognized his tall figure behind the barrier and saw him wave. It was nearly three years since that morning when he'd walked away from Castagnolo – they had been the longest and most terrible she'd ever lived through but, by some strange and compensating grace offered by Heaven, wonderful as well. She couldn't tell whether he had found them that same contradictory mixture because his welcome for her was warm, but unrevealing; her first, quick impression was of a man who had taken to hiding himself behind a façade of charming courtesy. He looked older, which was reasonable enough when she herself felt as old as Methuselah, and James's death was certain to have saddened him; even so, his disciplined smile suggested none of the happiness she'd seen shining in his face once upon a much more precarious time at Castagnolo.

'Dear Davido . . .' The Italian version of his name came unthinkingly to mind despite his shabby jacket of Harris tweed and college tie. '. . . I can't think why I call you so when you look as English as can be – I suppose because the dozens of messages I'm meant to pass on to you all begin like that!'

She thought his smile changed, as if the mere reference to Tuscany had some power to relax his guard.

'Call me what you like, Janey, but I'll have the messages when you've recovered from the journey. According to

William, it's still no fun travelling about the Continent. He was in France when Grandfather died, but he got back yesterday.'

He signalled to a taxi and handed Jane inside. 'You miss my father, I expect,' she remarked quietly as they drove out of the station forecourt.

'Yes; he was a friend, and friends leave gaps – as Marco still does. It was hard to believe when Charlie first brought *that* news back from Anna . . . what a sadness for Ottavio, especially.'

'And for Francesca – Marco was the only blood relative she knew. But she's convinced that he was ready to die – because he'd given up searching for happiness, not believing it to exist any more. It sounds a terrible theory to me.'

David sat still under a stab of pain, then forced his mind to grapple with the last thing Jane had said. 'Still nailing *your* colours to the mast of optimism and hope? How do you manage it in *this* year of gracelessness, I wonder?'

'By remembering that there are still more *good* people in the world than evil – I don't see why we can't between us do the Devil down.'

It made him smile wholeheartedly at last. 'When you put it like that, nor do I. My money is on you, Aunt J, against the legions of the damned!'

She felt less strange with him now, able to touch on something personal. 'We've kept expecting to hear that you were married – did your grandfather's illness hold things up?'

'No, although he and Pattie didn't hit it off very well together. She has been busy re-establishing her stage career, and I've been busy re-establishing I'm not quite sure what,' David said vaguely. 'Between us, we don't seem to have had time to get married.'

He pulled down the window to tell the driver that they'd overshot Vine House, and Jane was left with the impression that he was glad the conversation was over.

She went inside a house that she had once loved very

much, wondering what could be more important for two people separated for five years than finally marrying. But the speculation had to be put aside – Laura Rushton was waiting for her in the hall, with a smile that perfectly combined a welcome for someone she had never liked, with the sadness of the occasion, and the pleasure of knowing that mourning-black became her very well.

James's will, read after the funeral, began with the usual legacies to servants and old colleagues at Rushton's. Anticipating nothing for herself since her share of her father's estate had been advanced to her years ago, Jane scarcely listened to the lawyer's voice . . . a controlling share in Rushton's for David – well, that had been expected, even if a remainder split equally between George and William might seem poor reward to them for years of effort. Vine House became David's too, with the proviso that Laura and her family must be allowed to share it with him for as long as they wanted to – that was expected too, and surely right, though perhaps a little hard eventually on David's wife, who might prefer their home *not* shared. The real surprise came last – the remainder of James's entire estate left to Charlie, free of any restriction at all. Jane smiled at him across the table, knowing what the inheritance would mean – no more pointless attendances at Rushton's in a soul-destroying attempt to turn himself into something he was not: a businessman. Astonished gratitude to a father who, more often than not, had seemed to disapprove of him struggled in his face with pure joy at the prospect opening up in front of him. Jane saw him beginning to visualize a future in which he could paint all day and every day, if he felt like it. Remembering Anna and Fiesole, he was visualizing even *more* happiness besides, but this she didn't know. The blankness of David's expression worried her until she saw him smile at his uncle – nothing but happiness there for Charlie, although something about his own inheritance troubled him.

She didn't expect to discover what it was, but the day

after the funeral, when she was packing to leave for Italy, David suddenly appeared in the doorway of her room. Glad as she was to be going home, his drawn face made her wish that she'd agreed to stay longer at Vine House.

'Dear boy, how tired you look,' she said gently. 'It's no wonder, of course; funerals are barbarous things, even if your grandfather *would* have enjoyed the high and mighty who troubled themselves to come and say goodbye to him.'

David grinned slightly, then eased his long body into a chair with a little sigh of relief. He seemed content to sit there without talking and she was painfully aware of subjects that *couldn't* be talked about. While she still searched for something safe to say, David broke the silence.

'It won't be long before Charlie follows you out to Italy, you know.'

'Do you mind about the will? I suppose I mean about his freedom to choose what he'll do?'

'How could I mind? My inheritance was far too generous as it was, but George and William are kind enough not to say so.' He lifted his head suddenly to stare across the room at Jane. 'We didn't often tempt Providence, Francesca and I, by talking about the future, but she did once nearly agree that, with some rather large ifs permitting, she would come here to live with me.'

'The largest if, apart from surviving at all, was Pattie, I suppose.'

'No; I should have told *her* the truth. The catastrophe we *couldn't* get round was Marco's death. I wrote several times, asking her to let me find some way of helping Castagnolo that didn't entail *her* devoting her life to it. The letters were sent back, marked "return to sender" to make sure I knew that she'd received but not opened them. In the end even I could understand – the past was over and done with . . . what had happened in the stress of war had no relevance to her life in peacetime.'

Jane bit her lip so sharply that the taste of blood was in her mouth. How could the past be over and done when its legacy was a small enchanting boy of two? Never in her life had she come as close to breaking a promise wrung from her as she was now, but the promise held and she didn't mention Nicco.

'So now you don't intend to tell Pattie anything?' she murmured instead.

'What would be the point? I shall behave like a true gent after all, marry the girl who has been faithful enough to consider herself bound to me and live more or less happily ever after!'

His mouth sketched a bright, mocking smile that lasted while he walked to the door. Jane thought it wouldn't have lasted beyond that. She buried her face in the pile of clothes in front of her, defeated for a moment by an unbearable weight of sadness, then dragged herself upright and went on with the task of packing.

She and David didn't talk of personal things again, even on the way to Victoria Station the following morning. But once the boat-train had pulled out, taking her away from him, he could have wept with the pain of loneliness, of precious things lost and memories that wouldn't die. Without thought for the direction in which he headed, he walked the streets of London trying not to trace in his mind's eye Jane's journey back to Castagnolo. She had agreed with him: the past was over and done with. If his future wasn't the one he'd have chosen, at least he *had* one. In time he would make a better job of pretending to enjoy a home that seemed to belong to everyone but him; he'd learn to convince himself that Rushton's needed him, that Pattie loved him enough to find time soon to become his wife.

In the days following his grandfather's funeral she was more elusive than usual and, when he did succeed in seeing her between theatre rehearsals, cool to the point of hostility. Instead of retaliating when she snapped at him, he tried to find an excuse, but didn't phrase it very tactfully.

'These wretched people work you too hard – you're tired of lumbering about that damned stage all day.'

She overlooked the insult, aware that a vital moment in their affairs had suddenly been reached.

'Wrong, David . . . I'm only tired of smiling at your entire family, and pretending that we're delighted with the way things have turned out.'

He stared at her, for a moment at a loss to understand what she meant.

'If you're referring to my grandfather's will, I *am* delighted. Instead of condemning Charlie to another dozen years on the treadmill, James had the merciful kindness to see that for his soul's sake he needed to be free *now*.'

It was Pattie's turn to stare. Five years ago he wouldn't have dreamed of talking in such terms; mixed with the resentment smouldering inside her was the knowledge that she no longer knew or understood him.

'It was a fairly stinking will, if you ask me,' she said finally, stung to frankness. 'Not a penny of money to *you*, and this barn of a house to live in, that you can't even sell for as long as Laura is alive.'

'I wouldn't dream of selling it – it belongs to the Rushtons.'

His certainty provoked her to open hostility. 'Yes, and to *prove* the point, all the Rushtons haunt the place – God knows why; it must be the coldest, dampest, most inconvenient house in London.'

David immediately forgot how often he'd wondered himself why it was always full of his relatives and their friends. 'I was under the impression that you liked my family and my home.'

'It's *not* your home – your mother goes on behaving as if it's hers, and she always will.'

That was true too, but he was suddenly angry with her for pointing it out, not with James for landing him in an intolerable situation, nor with Laura who still assumed that everything she wanted was hers.

'I thought the arrangement suited you very well,' he said coldly. 'No household cares, even when you decide that you can finally spare the time from cavorting about a stage to become my wife.'

'Cavorting' – the intolerable word roused her to fury.

'How *dare* you talk to me in those terms. Other people think my career is important, even if you don't.' To prove it, her voice now quivered with outraged passion and he was distracted for a moment by the knowledge that she'd never shown that amount of passion for *him*. He'd done his best; even allowed loneliness and sheer male longing for a woman to persuade him that he still wanted her for his wife. Her body was seductive and her mouth invited kissing, but he'd felt no answering stir in *her*. She'd accepted but not contributed to his love-making, leaving him faintly ashamed of it.

'I think what I am offering you is important as well,' he insisted quietly. 'Pattie, be sensible. Vine House is too big not to share. There's room for my mother *and* for us – to have a life of our own and bring up our children.'

She heard the appeal in his voice, but the warning as well. Their engagement *had* suited her because the stage was a notoriously precarious business, and a useful buffer against hard times was what every player needed. Besides, she'd felt sorry for him; but she wasn't sorry enough to settle down and live in the shadow of Laura Rushton with a man she scarcely recognized as the young David of their engagement. What was more, she attributed James's will to malice, not kindness.

'We shan't be bringing up children just yet,' she pointed out. 'I'm not madly keen on motherhood at all if you want the truth, but if your idea of marriage is to make me pregnant straight away, it isn't mine. I've had to waste five years, thanks to that bloody war . . . I can't afford to waste any more.' She saw the expression on his face and knew that she had gone too far to retract now. Still, she hadn't meant to hurt him, and it was a pity to lose the buffer unless she had to. She walked across the room and twined her arms round his neck – her body just brushed his, reminding him of its possibilities, and confident of its effect.

'Darling David . . . I didn't mean to sound quite such a bitch, but you *did* make me see red – "cavorting" indeed!' The corners of her mouth tilted up in an entrancing smile, inviting him to agree that if she'd been unreasonable, so had he.

'That was frustration talking,' he agreed. 'I admit that you move very beautifully, and don't cavort or lumber at all.'

Pattie kissed him as a reward for the concession, and offered one of her own. 'I admit I was feeling peeved with James, but it was mostly on *your* account, darling. He needn't have given *all* that money to Charlie, and left *us* the problem of Laura and her family. Still, I suppose we can fix that, and I didn't mean to drive you mad with frustration! We'll get married next week if you want to.'

She was certain enough of his need of her to feel confident. David smelled the fragrance of her skin, and felt the warmth of her body promising that it could dispel his own cold loneliness. He was tired, discouraged and aware of having made mistakes that had permanently cost him happiness. What did it matter now if he made one more and married this girl who had once attracted him? He thought the words, 'All right, next week', were on his lips, but heard himself say instead, 'We'll marry whenever you like, provided we get some things clear first. This will remain our home, Pattie. Aside from the fact that it's beautiful, we are damned lucky to have it when thousands of people exist in prefabs and old army camps. We shan't "fix" my mother now, or in the future. This is her home too, and it's where Tom and Meg belong. I accept your longing to be a success on the stage, but it can't be at the expense of our life together. I don't just want a woman to sleep with when she happens to be appearing in London.

My old-fashioned idea of a wife is someone who *wants* to be with me . . . wants the children I would try to give her.'

He had no idea whether she would rage at him in true theatrical style, or collapse in sweet feminine surrender. She took him by surprise by doing neither.

'Now I'll have *my* say, and then we shall understand each other,' she suggested calmly. 'Five years ago you were a laughing, carefree, normal young man, like the dozens I met out in Malta and could have had at any time. *Now* . . .' her eyes strayed to his mutilated hand but quickly looked away again, '. . . the war has changed you in a way it hasn't changed me, and we don't fit any more. I still want bright lights and laughter – not a slow death here, washing disgusting nappies and listening to you and William trying to pretend that you like one another. But more than anything else I *have* to be in the theatre. I'm a good dancer already, and I'm going to become an even better actress – see if I don't, David.'

'I hope with all my heart that you do.' He suddenly smiled at her with great sweetness because the worst of his mistakes wasn't going to be made after all. 'My dear, when Pattie Ashwell is the toast of Shaftesbury Avenue and I'm a crabby, old, unknown wine-merchant, I shall boast of having known her quite well . . . see if I don't!'

'I think you'll be less crabby for not marrying *me*,' she said honestly. 'Successful or not, I shall be happy doing what I want to do. I don't think you've been happy since you came back to England, so perhaps you weren't cut out to be any old wine-merchant after all.'

She kissed him goodbye and he might have confessed that he liked her more now than he had done for months if he hadn't been staring at the bright, blazing truth she'd just uncovered for him. James was dead, Rushton's was safe in the hands of his family . . . he didn't *have* to go on pretending any more.

32

Jane arrived back at Florence Station to find that she was met there as well. Anna Lambertini anticipated her first anxious question.

'Nothing's wrong, I swear it. Ottavio is fine, and Nicco has just discovered the art of conversation – he's now talking the front leg off a donkey.'

'Hind leg,' Jane amended, 'though why it should be one rather than the other, I have no idea. Anna dear, it's blissful to find people waiting for me wherever I go, but why are you here instead of in Rome?'

'I'm here for good. Ernesto and I have agreed, with the utmost cordiality, that we can now part company. I almost left months ago – would have done but for wanting to see Vittorio happily settled in medical school. Now there's nothing left to wait for.'

She led the way out to the car, settled her passenger inside and paid off the porter.

'I was going to say that, however great the cordiality, it's a sad ending to your married life,' Jane observed, 'but it seems daft to say anything of the kind when you're so serene and sure of yourself at last.'

It could only have been Jane talking. Anna smiled at a mixture of kindness and honest common sense that was typical of her sister-in-law.

'Daft indeed when I've been the opposite of those things for years,' she agreed. 'I used to blame Ernesto for the muddle I was in – having to act one thing, believing another – but it wasn't his fault any more than it was mine; like a lot of other people, we were just trampled on by events!' She saw Jane's compassionate glance and shook her head. 'No need to feel sorry for me; the years weren't wasted – I have the children.'

'All right, no pity; and if you tell me that I must, I'll even try to think kindly of Ernesto. What are you going to do now?'

'Live at Fiesole, because he's given me the villa. I shall spend peaceful months and years putting it in order again – it's almost a ruin at the moment.'

'Nice . . . to have you so near, I mean,' Jane said contentedly.

Anna smiled again at the satisfaction in her sister-in-law's voice and finally started the car. They were stationary in a queue waiting to cross the city's only usable bridge when she referred to Jane's London journey.

'I'm refraining from asking about your visit out of true kindness, not lack of interest! You'll have to go through it all again when we get home.'

'Well, I'll whet your appetite with one surprising piece of news. Instead of heaping everything on David, my father left Charlie enough money to release him from the Rushton treadmill. Picture a man transformed!'

'I can – easily,' Anna murmured. 'What will *he* do now?'

'Come out here, I expect. We used to dream about it together years ago . . . a tumbledown palazzo, and for him the freedom to do nothing but paint. Heaven knows his ruin won't be hard to find; there are enough of them to choose from. But it would break his heart to see Florence as it is now.'

'He's had to look at enough ruins in London,' Anna said unanswerably. She glimpsed and then hid away inside her heart the lovely certainty that he *would* choose Italy. The time to look joy full in the face would only be when he was actually there. Until then she was afraid of jealous gods who preferred not to see humans happy.

Jane was slightly disappointed by her sister-in-law's lack of reaction. 'Francesca will *rejoice* at the news,' she said pointedly, 'and at the prospect of seeing her friend Charlie again.'

'What about her other . . . friend? How was he?' Anna asked, still refusing to be drawn.

'David was as kind and dear as usual, and outwardly cheerful enough to pass for a contented man. Inwardly, I have no idea, because he made sure that I didn't. All I discovered is that he wrote to Francesca and got his letters returned.'

'Did you meet his fiancée?'

'Yes – she's very attractive . . . alluring in the theatrical way that Laura Rushton has always been . . . but too busy being an actress at the moment to become David's wife. To be truthful I suppose I hope she *never* marries him, but with James dead I'm afraid he's desperately lonely.'

She relapsed into silence to watch for the landmarks that had survived the fighting and, when Anna turned on to Buonaventura land, was reminded of her very first arrival at Castagnolo – the overgrown hillsides and neglected vines looked just as they had then. The years of work that had yielded such lovely results would now have to be done again, supposing they could ever find the means to do it, and the faith that defied the chance of yet another Armageddon – this time for Francesca's son to get caught up in.

Nicco was outside in the courtyard when they arrived – an entrancing roly-poly child of two with a shy, sweet smile and confiding manner that could vanquish any opposition.

'All waitin' for you, Gran,' he announced happily as Jane got out of the car.

All indeed – Ottavio was there to see his beloved safely home, and Francesca stood smiling, with the breeze lifting her brown hair. Donna Giulia was flanked by Lisa and Caterina who, instead of returning to Genoa at the end of the war, had simply come to belong to them at the castle. Then, one by one, servants and old friends like Gino and Lucia began to appear as well . . . the *signora padrona* was home, God be thanked, and they must be there to welcome her.

'Some reception committee!' Jane said tremulously to Ottavio. 'I might have been away on a perilous mission instead of a sedate train journey to London.'

'Life *feels* perilous when you're not here,' he confessed simply. 'Dearest, welcome home!'

When everyone had been greeted she was led indoors and the questions began. She wasn't too busy answering them to be unaware that only one person showed no curiosity about the Rushtons at Vine House. But it was Francesca who later knocked at her bedroom door, bringing tea as an excuse for her visit.

'A gift from fortunate, peace-loving Switzerland, generously provided by Ernesto,' she explained. 'It's to make you feel that you wouldn't still rather be in England!'

'I wouldn't, as it happens,' Jane said smilingly, 'although I was very glad I went. They're as short of luxuries there as we are, dearest, so I've brought *you* nothing. I could only raid the cellar for some old brandy for Grandfather and Ottavio, and the nursery cupboards for long-abandoned toys for Nicco. I don't suppose he'll mind that they're a trifle out-of-date!' She saw the expression on Francesca's face and shook her head. 'It's all right – I didn't say who they were intended for.' Then, in the silence of the room, she heard herself say something else. 'No, Fran, it *isn't* all right. I was certain of it even before I went to London. Now that I've seen David again I know that you *must* tell him about Nicco.'

Francesca frowned at the wooden train in her hands, as if she couldn't remember how it had got there. 'Nothing's changed,' she said finally. 'Our life is here, his is in London with another woman. Do you suppose *she'd* like to know that he fathered a child while he was at a loose end during the war?'

She didn't look at Jane's face, but the disapproval she

419

knew she would find there was suddenly in the air between them, sharp as frost.

'Cruelly unfair . . . David wasn't just passing the time in a thoughtless affair; he loved you, and if you don't know that better than I do I'm ashamed of your stupidity.'

Colour tinged Francesca's thin face but she conceded only a little ground, and that with fierce reluctance. 'All *right*, he loved me for a little while. But nothing's changed; it's over and done with now.'

'*I've* changed, at least, and if you don't let David know that he has a son, I *shall*. I should never have agreed to hide Nicco's existence from him; I won't agree to it any longer.'

Francesca went away without replying and Jane didn't reopen the subject again. But two days later she saw among the letters on the hall table awaiting posting one addressed to David at Vine House.

The train journey took longer than he remembered because, in the late spring of 1946, the Continent's roads and railways were only slowly recovering from the devastation of the war. Florence when he reached it appalled him. With every bridge except the Ponte Vecchio blown up by the retreating Germans, and rubble piled high where it had been left to block the Allied advance, there was surely work for years in restoring beauty and order to the city of the Medicis.

He crossed the river, wondering what his chances were of being offered a lift. Almost immediately a van drew up beside him and the driver leaned out.

'I'm going to Arezzo; what about you, my friend?'

'Castagnolo,' David shouted, and accepted an invitation to jump in.

It was a struggle to delve in his memory for Italian words forgotten for nearly three years, but he and his new friend managed to hold a conversation and parted on the best of terms outside Father Francesco's church. David wasn't sorry to have been left there instead of at the entrance to the castle itself, because a combination of excitement and dread was making him feel sick. Apart from that, Charlie had said that Marco was buried in the churchyard, and this was the obvious moment to find his grave.

He searched among the more recent gravestones, only vaguely aware of a woman walking towards him, until she let out a piercing cry.

'*Madonna mia . . . Signor Davido! Caro Signore . . . che piacere, che meraviglia!*' She closed the distance between them at a run and he was clasped against the bosom of Gino's wife, to be kissed and wept over. At last he was able to explain why he was there.

'*Si, Signore . . . ecco dov'è il povero . . .*' Still exclaiming and now weeping with a mixture of joy and grief, Lucia led him to a plot in the corner of the churchyard. Instead of the elaborate statuary marking most of the graves, a simple stone cross carried the details of Marco's brief life; instead of the stiff, artificial wreaths favoured by Italian mourners, someone – Jane or Francesca – had planted the wild rose of Tuscany and it now smothered the grave in a foam of pink blossom, delicate but brave enough to bloom everlastingly.

David stood up after a while, to find Lucia still patiently waiting until he should be ready to leave.

'Who's was that?' he asked, pointing to the blank wooden cross next to Marco's. 'An unknown soldier buried here by mistake?'

Unmistakably and shockingly, Lucia sniffed. 'You could say so, signore, but animal is more like if you ask me. It was the Signora Jane who said he must have a Christian burial.'

She had nothing more to say, a fact unusual enough in itself to prevent David asking further questions. He walked with her up the hill path, saw her to the door of the *fattoria* despite her protest that she'd had time enough in fifty years to learn the way, and then retraced his steps in order to approach the castle by the garden terraces.

Everywhere there was evidence of neglect and deliberate damage that no-one had yet had the heart or time to repair – broken steps, smashed tubs and trampled plants littered the gardens that Jane and Ottavio had once made beautiful. But the May morning washed everything in its golden light, and some at least of the ruin was hidden by bright curtains of blossom.

He saw Francesca before she saw him, because her attention was on someone else – a small child who chuckled as he trotted towards her pulling a wooden animal on wheels on the end of a piece of string. There was time to stare at her and recover from the pounding of his heart. She was so painfully thin that even belted tightly around her the dress she wore seemed much too large. Her beautiful long hair had been cropped as short as a boy's, but after the first moment of disappointment he realized that, instead of looking unfeminine, it even accentuated the delicate bones of her face.

It was the child who saw him first. 'Man!' he announced in Italian, in a surprised clear voice.

'Certainly a man,' Francesca agreed, half-turning to get a glimpse of the visitor. When he stepped out of shadow and she could see him clearly he watched her face go very white. Then she bent down to lift the small boy in her arms, as if danger threatened that she must protect him from. She was trembling with shock, but it was she who found something to say.

'This is . . . is a friend of Gran's, darling . . . you must say hello.'

The child's face wore an expression of frowning concentration while he considered a stranger who wasn't smiling at him as people usually did. '*Sono Niccolò,*' he said, getting down to the exchange of important information. '*Come ti chiami?*'

'*Sono Davido . . . buon giorno, Niccolò.*'

422

It was a beginning from which an enjoyable conversation could be launched, but before Nicco could get properly into his stride, Francesca put him down and whispered something in his ear. After another stare at the visitor that turned into an engaging grin, he picked up the string of his wooden horse and trundled it across the terrace to the open door.

'Niccolò what?' David asked hoarsely.

'Buonaventura . . . what else?' Francesca's lips felt stiff and her heart seemed by turns to stop and then go racing on, making breathing difficult. She had tried to imagine this conversation, told herself that he might come and that she must be prepared for what she would say to him – but he'd arrived too quickly and she wasn't ready yet.

'I'm sorry about your grandfather,' she remembered to murmur, but David wasn't even listening.

'He reminds me of someone. It's . . . it's . . . dear God in Heaven, it's *me*, smiling like that in old photograph albums at home. Francesca, he's *mine* . . . isn't he?'

'He's ours,' she corrected him coldly, 'but you already know that.'

The expression on his face told her that he hadn't known, and she realized what might have occurred to her earlier – he couldn't possibly be there in answer to a letter sent a mere three days ago.

'I *did* write, but only after Jane got back from London. I suppose you must have left before it arrived,' she muttered.

'I've been in London for nine months . . . did it take that long to compose a letter?' He had imagined a thousand times what it would be like to see her again; hadn't in his worst dream visualized shouting at her as if they were enemies.

'It took that long to make up my mind to write at all. I only did because Jane refused to be bound by her promise any longer. I accepted finally that you had a right to know, but that's as far as it goes. You don't have to feel

423

responsible for us; in fact I won't have you involved at all – your life is in London with a woman who probably wants children of her own.'

The irony of that almost made him smile, but there were still too many questions to be asked.

'Did you know about the child the day I walked away from Castagnolo?'

'I suspected I was pregnant – wasn't sure until Dr Bertolini confirmed it afterwards.' She allowed herself a glance at him and saw that dawning joy was taking the place of anger and shock. Jane had been right, and *she* had been wrong – he should have been told sooner about his son. The years in Germany and England had aged him; she would need time to rediscover in this tired-faced man the lover who had once been able to make her complete and entirely happy.

'Burn my letter unopened when you get home,' she said suddenly. 'I wrote it with a very bad grace, and all it *should* have said was simply thank you. The only joy we've known recently has come from Nicco – he's given us all something to go on living for.'

Her directness, at least, was unchanged, and it would deal unsparingly with him if she refused to allow him back into her life again. He must give her time to get used to him, and even push aside for the moment the sheer wonder of knowing that between them they had created a child. Castagnolo itself seemed the safest subject to concentrate on.

'I can see the mess all around here – but what about Castagnolo generally?' he asked after a long pause.

She gave a tired little shrug. 'It's not quite the devastation that it was. At least we've got the farms that are occupied, weatherproof and habitable again. Some are still empty, but that's because old people have died and their children have chosen an easier life away from the land. Perhaps they'll tire of cities and noise and the stench of too many motorcars in the end. Until they do, we have to concentrate on growing food and let the vineyards run wild. It's a grief to Ottavio and Gino – in the years just before the war Castagnolo wine had become something for connoisseurs to reckon with.'

'It can be again.'

'Perhaps.' She didn't bother to say that it was a possibility that seemed remoter than the moon but asked a question of her own instead.

'What made you come now, not knowing about Nicco?' She didn't sound hostile any longer, only immeasurably remote. It was much too soon to offer her the truth – that, released from commitments at last, he'd simply obeyed the prompting of his heart.

'I wanted to make a pilgrimage,' he said instead, '. . . to find Marco's grave and the people who helped me on my way south. They were brave and generous to many more of us than just me. I hope we never forget it.'

However brave they'd been, the Germans had caught him in the end, and Francesca was aware that his second captivity had left its mark on him. But the war had marked and changed them all and she must remember it or fall into the trap of thinking that life had relented after all and said that she might be loved and happy.

'I got a lift to the village,' David said. 'Lucia happened to be in the churchyard and showed me what I was looking for. Do you remember how Fausto once saved me when I was hiding here? Then Marco saved Fausto and Alex. It seems to leave *me* owing a debt to someone.'

Francesca considered this, then shook her head. 'I think you might be said to have paid your debts already.'

He thought of something else about the churchyard. 'There's an unmarked grave next to Marco's. For some extraordinary reason Lucia almost spat on it.'

'The reason wasn't extraordinary in the times we were living through,' she said gravely. 'We were "liberated" by Moroccan troops of the French army – animals, Lucia calls them, and it's true they did almost as much damage as the

Germans. The soldier in that grave was shot by Gino. That's why he lies there – we didn't know what else to do with him.'

'You mean it was an *accident* . . . Gino shot him by mistake?'

'Not at all – it was the only way he could stop the Moroccan raping me.'

The words dropped so unemphatically into the space between them that he nearly missed the horror of what she'd said. But her hands were trembling and he felt in his own body the same sick revulsion that suddenly made her shiver.

'I'm sorry,' he muttered unevenly. 'God alone knows what you all had to live through.'

'We survived . . . at least, enough of us survived; but we miss Marco sorely.'

'Was he the only reason you returned my letters so brutally?' The moment the words left his mouth he knew it was too soon to have asked the question.

She turned away from him and he waited for her to say that the war had taught them all a little brutality. But she was saved from answering because another voice suddenly called from the doorway behind them.

'*Davido . . . caro Davido . . .*' He turned to see the Marchesa standing there with arms held wide. It was time to go inside.

For dinner there was one of Lucia's capons, hastily despatched by Gino; there was wine from a pre-war vintage that had been buried for safe-keeping; there was much talk and gentle laughter, and the thanksgiving that comes from knowing that somehow they had lived through desperate times. David looked round the table at the faces of his friends and lifted his glass in a private toast to Italy. Afterwards, when only he and Ottavio were left alone to pace up and down the terrace, he asked about Fausto and Alexandra.

'I know what happened,' he said gently. 'Anna told Charlie in Rome. But what are they doing?'

'Still living in Geneva. Fausto wanted to come back but Ernesto managed to persuade him that Marco would have died for nothing if they'd returned to be caught up in a Communist vendetta.' Ottavio smiled sadly at his guest. 'Don't sentimentalize us Italians, my dear David; our kindness to each other is only equalled by our cruelty!'

'But vendettas don't last for ever; law and order *are* returning, aren't they?'

'Yes, thank God, but time is needed. For the moment Fausto is occupied in writing a truthful history of the Fascist era – he says that much is owed to Mussolini – but one day I pray he'll be able to return here. We need *his* help, and Alexandra's, desperately.'

David stared up at the starlit sky, and then lobbed a quiet question towards it. 'Do you by any chance need mine?'

Ottavio wheeled round to try to examine his face. 'Are you . . . are you serious? Yes, I can see that you are. I suppose it's because of the boy?'

'Yes, though not entirely. I came here not knowing about him but still wanting to help Castagnolo. Anything we can salvage from the ruins of war seems to represent a kind of victory. Will you let me stay if Francesca agrees that there's room for me?'

'But you have commitments in London . . .'

'None that matter now. For the first time in my life I'm a completely free man.'

Ottavio said nothing for a moment or two. With arms folded across his chest he began his slow perambulation of the terrace again and David walked beside him wondering what insuperable objection even this kind and loving friend was going to raise to the rest of his life's happiness. Then he saw the ghost of a smile that lit Ottavio's worn face.

'Between us, my dear Davido, we might just be able to

convince Gino. There's a new grape that the clever viniculturalists are beginning to plant . . . added to the traditional varieties, it's . . .'

'Ottavio, what about *Francesca?*' David almost shouted. 'She *also* is stubborn, I grant you, but I must leave her to *you!*' He smiled at his guest with deep affection, then went inside to share with Jane the possibility that Castagnolo's days of tragedy might soon be over.

It was understood in the household that David's visit was to be brief – he was leaving to retrace the journey he'd made before his recapture. The Marchesa wept whenever he talked of going, Don Giuseppe looked sad and Nicco took to keeping him always in view, so that his new friend couldn't suddenly disappear. Francesca observed his liking for David's company, and tried to whip up anger in her heart against a man who found it too easy to ingratiate himself with all and sundry. She managed never to be alone with him as a rule, but one morning when she thought the three of them were on the terrace she suddenly realized that Nicco had disappeared.

'It's all right – I haven't abducted him,' David said quietly, seeing her anxious glance round. 'He's in my bedroom, hunting for a farewell present I've hidden there.'

'Farewell?' Her eyes searched his face for confirmation of what she thought she knew – he was leaving, of course. The novelty of owning a son had worn off and it was time to return to his sophisticated life in London. 'Oh yes, your little pilgrimage,' she observed with all the indifference she could manage. 'I suppose you'll go straight home from Rome, or Naples.'

'Ottavio knows that I should prefer to come back here. I haven't told *you* so far because you've avoided me like the plague, and I was too terrified of being turned down to *make* you listen to me.'

She managed a shrug that was almost careless. 'It isn't up to me, my dear David. You must know that my grandparents and Jane and Ottavio would be delighted if you stayed for ever.'

'That was my intention, more or less.'

She opened her lips but no sound came; only her eyes, huge and sombre in the pallor of her face, questioned what he'd said.

'Listen, Francesca. A long time ago we talked about belonging in different places – me to a life in London, you here. Even then only my mind recognized its commitments, not my heart. That knew it belonged here. Now, James is dead, and Rushton's is safely in the hands of men who know more about running it than I shall ever know. The girl I was committed to has had the honesty to admit she would rather be an actress than my wife, and my mother lives in the house James left me and runs it perfectly. I can't think of a single human being who actually needs me in London. *That's* why I came here – in the hope of being needed, and being allowed to help put this lovely, damaged place together again.'

She stared at him, with a flame of indignation now lighting her grey eyes. 'I don't believe you. You came and found Nicco – a shock, but flattering because he liked you – and the rest of us as war-scarred and pitiable as Castagnolo itself. Well, I won't *have* you feel sorry for us, and obliged to stay and help these poor benighted Italian fools sort out the m – mess they always m – manage to make of their lives.'

The shout of defiance frightened a lizard on the wall beside her into disappearing in a flash of green. She tried to watch its route and failed. Anger suddenly died and an immense sadness took its place. 'Go soon, please,' she added more quietly, 'before Nicco discovers that it's easy to love you, and everyone else gets used to depending on you again.'

David closed the gap between them in three fierce strides and took hold of her in a grip that bruised her shoulders.

'Dear God, you haven't understood a single bloody

thing. I don't pity you, girl, I *love* you!' The sudden frozen whiteness of her face frightened him into remembering the Moroccan Gino had had to kill. Violence was the very last thing he should have offered her. He dropped his hands as if what they touched burned him.

'Fran, forgive me . . . I meant never to touch you until you said I might. I didn't come imagining that you'd let me love you again because that miracle happened once before. I'm asking you to marry me because I love you more than life itself, not because I can work for Castagnolo, or because I want a hand in raising Nicco. If you say no, and I'm never allowed to touch you again, I still want to be here, taking care of you all.'

Her eyes suddenly brimmed with tears, shining like jewels; but she managed one last protest. '*Now* you tell me, *stupido*, when you're going away. David, I could . . . could box your ears!'

His mouth was beginning to relax because, faint as the horns of elfland, he thought he could hear joy chiming on the wind. Francesca saw the change in him and heard the same enticing music, but it was far off and might still be carried away from her. 'Do you have to leave?' she asked hoarsely. 'I'm not sure I can bear to see you walk away again . . . not after last time.'

He pulled her trembling body within the shelter of his arms, thinking that he would probably never know the full extent of the damage and hurt of the past three years.

'Listen to me, dear heart. This time it's different; there's no longer anything to dread, and the rest of our lives belong to us, together.' He tilted her face up to look at him. 'Shall I put off going? Sooner or later I must settle things in London, but it doesn't have to be done now, and one day we can seek out together the people who helped me.'

The temptation to say, 'stay, please' was almost overwhelming, but she knew it was as good as admitting that she was always going to be afraid of life. She shook her head and managed to smile at him. 'Go and do these necessary things while I explain to Nicco that the visitor he likes so much actually belongs to him! But travel safely this time, and come back as soon as you can.'

He held her wrapped close in his arms, passion held in check because the moment for it to burst into flame again between them still hadn't come. It didn't matter now . . . the moment *would* come, and then glory would be shining all around. They stood there together for a long while; might have stood longer still if a small triumphant voice hadn't finally insisted on making itself heard.

'Davido . . . *Davido*, listen, please . . . I found the present. Is it to keep, or can I open it now?'

Nicco's face beamed up at them – confirmation, if they needed it, that confidence in the future was possible after all, and so were hope, and joy, and all lovely things.

'Open it now,' said David.

THE END